Booky
A TRILOGY

That Scatterbrain Booky

With Love from Booky

As Ever, Booky

Booky
A TRILOGY

That Scatterbrain Booky

With Love from Booky

As Ever, Booky

BERNICE THURMAN HUNTER

Cover by
Tony Meers

Scholastic Canada Ltd.

Scholastic Canada Ltd.
175 Hillmount Road, Markham, Ontario L6C 1Z7

Scholastic Inc.
555 Broadway, New York, NY 10012, USA

Scholastic Australia Pty Limited
PO Box 579, Gosford, NSW 2250, Australia

Scholastic New Zealand Limited
Private Bag 94407, Greenmount,
Auckland, New Zealand

Scholastic Ltd.
Villiers House, Clarendon Avenue, Leamington Spa,
Warwickshire CV32 5PR, UK

Grateful acknowledgment is made to the author for the photographs on pages 4, 40,174, 188, 313, 317, 338, 369, 436, 468, and 483; to the Eaton's Archives for the photographs on pages 38, 46-47, 63, 67, 95, 200 and 244; to the James Collection, City of Toronto Archives, for the photographs on pages 75, 118-119 and 150-151; to the Canadian National Exhibition Archives for the photograph on page 142; and to the *Globe and Mail* for permission to reprint the article from the July 15, 1936 *Globe* on page 302. Photo on page 334 by Gordon Wyatt. The author acknowledges the use of "Be Good, Sweet Maid," from "A Farewell" by Charles Kingsley.

8 7 6 5 4 3 2 1   Printed in Canada   8 9/9 0 1 2 3 4 /0

Contents

That Scatterbrain

Booky

To Mum and Dad
who loved me

That Scatterbrain Booky

1
A note from school

Skinny legs flying, I ran straight home from school. My mum was in the kitchen starting supper.

I asked the same old question. "Where's Dad?"

She gave the same old answer. "Out looking for work."

It was September, 1932, the heart of the Depression.

I handed her the note the school nurse had given me and ran lickety-split up the stairs to the bathroom.

When I came back down (with my dress caught in my bloomers), I knew something was wrong because Mum wasn't paying much attention to the note. I already knew what was in it. I had sneaked a look on the way home from school. *Beatrice is twenty-two pounds underweight,* said Miss Malloy's sterile handwriting. *We recommend that you contact your relief authorities. Any Canadian child exceeding the twenty-pound underweight limit is eligible for free government milk.*

Ordinarily this information would have upset my mum to no end. But today she just plucked my dress out of my bloomers and remarked absently, "You'll have to eat up, Booky."

I already ate up everything in sight, so that didn't mean much. But her calling me Booky did. It meant she wasn't mad at me and I wasn't going to get heck for anything. And it meant she loved me. That funny little nickname told me so.

My mum was a pretty woman. She had dark wavy hair, high olive cheekbones, and big brown eyes that flashed when she was mad and sparkled when she was glad. Today they were circled with blue and tired looking.

Her stocky five-foot frame was too well rounded for her liking. "I only weighed ninety pounds on my wedding day," she'd regularly sigh. But in spite of that she was a very good looking woman.

In her flat little size-three house shoes she was barely two inches taller than me. Standing on tiptoe, I kissed her ruddy cheek. She gave me a fierce hug that cracked my skinny bones.

That was my mum.

"Change your dress, Booky," she said, slivers of potato peelings flying from her paring knife.

"Okay, Mum."

I wasn't always so obedient, but when my mother called me Booky (she pronounced the first part Boo, like Boo-hoo) I'd jump off the roof for her. I ran back upstairs two at a time.

My sister Willa wasn't home yet. She was the oldest and in high school. She had a long walk home. My brother Arthur was next. And then me. His school bag was on the table, so I knew he had been in and gone out again. He was lucky. He never had to stay in for arithmetic. That's what had kept me late, arithmetic.

In my old play dress and holey running shoes I made a beeline for the back door. Rummaging under the rickety porch steps I found my hoop and stick, and controlling it expertly, I flew like the wind up the street to Audrey's. Not once did my hoop wobble or fall over and have to be started again.

Audrey Westover was my best friend. She was adopted. That meant her parents could afford her. They picked her out on purpose. When I first found that out I ran all the way home to ask my mum if I was adopted too. I hoped I was because that would mean Arthur wasn't really my brother. Mum greeted the question with a big hoot of laughter. "Go on with you, Bea," she chided good-naturedly. "It's easy enough for me to get children without going out looking for them."

Now that was my chance to ask something I'd always wanted to know—how people go about getting children—but just then the lady from next door came over to borrow an onion and the thought went clean out of my head.

I could hardly believe the difference between the Westovers' house and ours. Ours, the one we were living in now, was a skinny, stuck-together row house. The uneven floors, upstairs and down, were covered with cracked linoleum, splotched brown where the pattern had worn off. Naked light bulbs dangled on frayed black wires from tattered, papered ceilings, and we didn't own such a thing as a house lamp. All our furniture was old second-hand stuff.

Outside, the house hadn't seen a lick of paint in years. Both front and back porches were made of peeling, rotted wood with broken steps and unsafe, worm-eaten railings.

Behind the house stretched a narrow weed-patch yard, enclosed by a high dilapidated board fence. We never managed to stay in one place long enough to have a flower bed or to grow grass from seed. Mum said that was her heart's desire, to stay put long enough to have a perennial bed across the front and a vegetable garden in the back.

7

But one thing redeemed our house. Inside, it was the cleanest house in the world. Our old furniture gleamed with lemon oil. Hawe's floor wax shone on the patternless linoleum, and the air fairly tingled with vinegar and Lysol. I'll bet anything you could have eaten your supper right off our kitchen floor without getting so much as one germ in your mouth.

By comparison, the Westovers' house was a miniature mansion: a fashionable bungalow situated at the far end of Lilac Street. It had a cement front porch with a wrought-iron railing, and it was all hemmed in with grass and shrubs and flowers.

Inside, it was so filled with carpets and furniture and lamps and things that it gave me a peculiar, crowded feeling. But the biggest difference, the one I noticed the most, was on their supper table. (Except that at Audrey's, supper was called dinner and dinner was called lunch. To me, lunch was brown-sugar sandwiches in a paper bag.) The Westovers' supper table was always loaded down with more food than they could possibly eat at one sitting. I couldn't get over that. Most of the time they had food left over. At our house there were never any leftovers and we often went away still hungry. Of course I knew the reason for the difference. Audrey's father had a job. In a bank.

They usually ate early because Mr. Westover finished work at four o'clock. He'd drive all the way from downtown Toronto to east-end Birchcliff in his 1929 Model A Ford. It was the only car on Lilac Street, and when it came rattling round the corner blaring *AhhOOgaa!* kids would run like stink from all directions and jump on the running board for a free ride.

Sometimes Mrs. Westover let me sit on the back kitchen steps and pat the dog while Audrey ate her supper. Spot was a friendly Boston Bull. Mrs. Westover said he had a pedigree, but I looked him over from his pushed-in nose to his twisty tail and I couldn't find a thing wrong with him. Spot ate the very same food as the rest of the family. Just smelling his lovely, meaty dish was enough to make me drool.

Often, after supper, Mrs. Westover would offer me the leftovers. "So it won't go to waste," she'd say offhandedly. But I knew it was her way of being charitable without making me feel my neck. She was nice, Mrs. Westover. Audrey's father was nice too. He never seemed to mind how much food his wife gave away. Not even once did I see that "What's going on here?" look cross his face. Sometimes he even joked with me. I think he liked me.

On this particular night I came galloping back down the street with my hoop and stick under my arm, half a store-bought apple pie in one hand and a loaf of yesterday's bread in the other. Mum was pleased as punch.

Dad came in the back door right behind me. He always came home about the same time as the working men. He looked tired and thin. Under his wispy fair hair his square-jawed face was pale and drawn.

"Hi, Dad!" I gave him a toothy grin to cheer him up.

"Hello, Bea," he answered without a trace of a smile.

Everybody was home now, so we all sat down around the oilcloth-covered table. All except little Jakey who still used a high chair.

There was no butter on the table, so we dipped our bread in the stew Mum had made. Boy, she made good stew! Even without meat. We sopped up every drop until the last crust of bread was gone and our plates were shiny clean. Then Mum divided the pie into six skinny pieces. Dad said he was full and didn't want any. Even I didn't believe that. He just wanted us kids to have his share. So Arthur and I obliged by fighting over it. Willa left the table in disgust. Mum settled the argument by giving the extra piece to me. Arthur got mad and stomped out of the room.

"The school nurse says Bea is a bit underweight," explained Mum, trying to sound casual. "She can do with something extra."

"I've *got* to get a job!" declared Dad for the umpteenth time.

I finished the sliver of pie in no time flat. Then, seeing Mum and Dad looking depressed over their tea, I said, "Don't worry, Mum. You neither, Dad. I'm strong as a horse—watch!"

Willa was at the sink with her back to me, doing the dishes. I crept up behind her and lifted her bodily off the floor. She must have outweighed me by fifty pounds at least. It felt more like a ton. But I had to prove how strong I was so I hung on, staggering backwards.

"Bea! You put me down!" screeched Willa.

I could hardly wait to oblige. I thought I was going to faint, and I must have turned white because Mum looked scared and made me sit right down and have a sip of tea.

"Tea revives you," she said.

"Don't you do that again!" Dad said with a show of anger. "You might have broken your back, you foolish girl."

But I think it made them feel a bit more cheerful, just the same, because they didn't have their usual fight after supper.

2
My big confession

Willa finished up the dishes and wiped around the sink and stove. Then she folded the dish towel neatly and hung it on the drying rack. Getting her books from her school bag, she settled herself at the dining room table to do her homework. Arthur followed her example. They were both good students, but Willa was the extra-clever one.

Two years before, in Senior Fourth, she had won the gold medal for achieving highest honours in Scarborough's high school entrance examinations. Hundreds of kids had competed—and our Willa had won.

Mum and Dad were proud as punch and couldn't stop bragging about her. On and on they went until all our friends and relations were sick and tired of listening. Poor Willa. She was absolutely mortified. Finally, she hid the gold medal in a secret place, and when Mum asked her where it was so she could show it one more time, Willa wouldn't tell. She could be stubborn when she felt like it.

I was proud of Willa too, but it was awfully hard on me, having such a clever sister. Her picture, with the medal pinned to her blouse, hung in the hallway of Birchcliff Public School and my teacher would never let me forget it. Every time I got a bad mark in arithmetic, which was nearly every day, Miss Birchall would raise her shaggy eyebrows and exclaim for everyone to hear, "Surely *you* can't be Willa Thomson's sister?"

She knew darn well I was. Her sarcasm shrivelled my soul.

It was hard on Arthur, too, having a gold medallist for a sister, but in a different way. Arthur was smart enough and he always got good marks, but his teacher and the principal were never satisfied. They kept at him to work harder and do better so he, too, would win a medal and bring honour to the school. At least I was spared that kind of torture. If I had liked him better I would have felt downright sorry for him.

Everybody knew from my daily zeros in arithmetic that I was a hopeless scholar. Miss Birchall even said that if I didn't soon improve I might lose the whole year. That threat scared the daylights out of me so I begged Willa to help me.

She tried, she really did. But the minute I saw all those numbers on the page my brain went numb. In desperation I'd count on my fingers under the table. Then Willa would catch me and bawl me out and I'd start to cry and leave the table in disgrace.

Once I got up the nerve to ask Miss Birchall, "Why can't I just pass in spelling and reading and composition? Why is arithmetic so important?"

"Because it takes *brains* to do arithmetic!" she snorted, withering me with that look. "Any ninny can get good marks in spelling and composition."

After that I knew I was sunk. I couldn't make head nor tail out of arithmetic, especially problems. Who but a wallpaper man needed to know how many rolls it took to paper a room nine by twelve anyway?

That night I sat with Arthur and Willa and tried to learn my nine times-table. They took no notice of me, except from time to time Arthur gave me a dirty look for sniffling my nose. So I'd stare him down and he'd stick out his tongue; then we'd both go back to our books.

Just looking at Arthur made me sick. He was such a handsome, well-behaved twelve-year-old. The kind grown-ups, especially ladies, really take to.

Actually we looked a lot alike, since we both favoured Dad's side, but Arthur was prettier than I was. He had blond curly hair (mine was blonde too, but dead straight), big blue eyes (mine were the same colour, but not so big), a neat nose and white even teeth (my nose was too big and my front teeth were saw-edged—Mum said they would wear smooth in time but it hadn't happened yet).

Willa was nice looking too. She had Mum's dark wavy hair and Dad's blue eyes and fair skin. Everybody said it was a lovely combination and she'd start to "turn heads" any day now.

There was only one thing I liked about myself. It was my flat chest. Poor Willa had breasts and she had to wear a tight undershirt to hide them. Every night I thanked God for my flat chest and begged Him not to give me breasts.

Pretty soon I got tired of the nine times-table and Arthur's dirty looks, so I asked Mum if I could get Jakey ready for bed. She let out a big sigh and said yes. Then Dad went down the cellar and put a boilerful of water on the gas plate.

Jakey was the baby of our family. He was the only one who favoured Mum's side. He had big brown eyes, dark curly hair and dimples, just like her. And there was a special tie between

Mum and Jakey—I mean over and above the fact that he looked like her.

When he was a tiny baby he took sick and nearly died. The sickness was called "summer complaint" and when little babies get it they have diarrhea and their milk won't stay down. Then they lose all their body water and they die. Most of them. But our baby was lucky. Mum and Dad rushed him down to Sick Children's Hospital as fast as the streetcars would go and Mum gave him a blood transfusion that saved his life.

Dad was mad because they wouldn't use his blood. The doctors said it was the wrong type. "How can that be when I'm the father?" Dad demanded angrily. So the doctors explained, as best they could, that children don't always inherit their father's blood. They said a transfusion from Dad might even kill Jakey (who was nearly dead already) so Dad had to give in, but he never really got over it.

Mum told us all about it when they got home. "I laid on a stretcher and they put Jakey on a table right beside me. Then they put a needle in my arm and a needle in Jakey's little ankle and a glass tube joined us together. I could see my blood flowing into his tiny, white foot. He was so weak he didn't even cry. Poor little gaffer—they 'bused him."

"What does 'boozed' mean, Mum?" I asked, all agog.

"It means abused, hurt. My mother used to say that when she heard a baby cry."

Poor Mum. She always blamed herself for Jakey's illness because the doctors at Sick Kids' said it was caused from unboiled milk. Of course Mum didn't know that milk needed to be boiled to be purified, but she said ignorance was no excuse. So she went to the library and got all the newest medical books and wrote down as many of the latest remedies as she could find.

All that attention made me terribly jealous of Jakey. In fact, I had been jealous of him right from the start. And no wonder. The very day he was born, upstairs in the middle bedroom, Dad dropped me like a hot potato. It was the shock of my life. For six years I had been the youngest and had been treated kind of special. Particularly by Dad. He used to dandle me on his knee and piggyback me around the yard and dance with me standing on his shoes. Then along came Jakey.

He was a beautiful baby. And he was a boy! That's when it first dawned on me how all-fired special it was to be a boy. Dad kept saying, "It's a boy! A boy! I've got another son!" You'd have thought it was a god from heaven instead of just an ordinary, everyday baby.

Everybody congratulated Dad and told him how lucky he was. And Uncle Charlie, Dad's brother, who was going to be a father soon himself, said that if his baby was a girl he'd send it back where it came from.

He laughed when he said it, as if it was a joke, but Willa and I were standing right there and we didn't think it was funny.

We looked each other up and down to see what was wrong with us. I already knew I wasn't the kind of child grown-ups were dying to have, but why on earth wouldn't anybody want Willa? She was just about perfect as children go.

I was awfully disappointed in Uncle Charlie. He had been my favourite uncle up till then. I never dreamed he didn't like Willa and me because we were girls. And what a dumb reason! God made us, didn't He? He must have known what He was doing. And as for my dad, well, I just couldn't get over it. So I took all my hurt feelings out on poor little Jakey.

I'd pinch him when no one was looking, just to hear him cry. I'd bump his cot when he was sound asleep. And I'd grab the bottle out of his mouth in the middle of a suck. Then, when he got older, I discovered that sad songs made him cry. So I'd sing to him by the hour. Songs like "The Letter Edged In Black" and "Hello Central, Give Me Heaven" and "Climb Upon My Knee Sonny Boy."

Mum thought I was being a nice big sister, singing to my baby brother, but I wasn't. I was being awful. Finally my guilty conscience got the better of me. I couldn't sleep for thinking about how terrible I was. So I decided to snitch on myself.

The opportunity came one day when Miss Birchall had a gumboil and had to go to the dentist. For once I got out of school early, so I ran all the way home to catch my mum alone.

It was Tuesday, so she was ironing. She was just folding up Arthur's Sunday shirt as I came in the door. It was stiff with starch and gleaming white. Except for the frayed collar, it looked brand-new out of the store.

Scuffling nervously, I made my confession.

"I'm glad you told me, Bea," she said thoughtfully, tipping the iron on end. "It shows you're not mean at heart. You just leave it with me. I'll speak to your father. And I'll give that Charlie a piece of my mind, you can bet your boots on that."

She tested the iron with a wet finger. It hissed and she cried "Ouch!" and pulled the plug out of the wall. Sucking the burnt finger, she smoothed a threadbare flannelette sheet over the board and continued, "Now, don't be mean to Jakey any more,

Bea. It's not his fault, you know. He can't help being a boy any more than you can help being a girl."

"Oh, don't worry, Mum, I won't." I felt good all over now that the weight was off my chest. "I'll make it up to him, you'll see. But Mum, are boys better than girls?"

Sparks flew from her big brown eyes and the iron moved in quick, angry strokes. "No, they're not. And don't you think it. Some of them aren't half as good. Why, I wouldn't trade you or Willa for all the boys in China!"

"Are we even better than Arthur and Jakey?" If she said yes, I could hardly wait to tell Arthur.

"Not on your tintype!" she said emphatically. "Nobody is better than my boys. But you're every bit as good, and don't you forget it." Setting the iron on end, she gave me an unexpected bone-cracker.

"And another thing you should bear in mind, Bea: this old world is changing, especially since the war. When I was a girl women didn't even have the vote, and only boys were encouraged to get an education. See how different things are now? Just look at your own sister—a gold medallist, halfway through high school and her not even fifteen years old. Girls can be anything they want to be nowadays, Bea. Why, only last spring—May, I think it was—a girl named Amelia Earhart flew across the Atlantic Ocean all by herself. Now doesn't that beat all? And another thing, Booky, these hard times aren't going to last forever, you know. There'll be jobs galore just begging for qualified people some day. Mark my words. So you just work hard and get an education and grow up to be somebody!"

The part about working hard and getting an education worried me a bit. But the part about the lady flyer made my imagination soar. I decided then and there to be an aeroplane pilot when I grew up.

That little talk cured me forever of my jealousy. From that minute on I was nice to Jakey, and soon he loved me best of all.

But one thing I forgot to ask, something I was dying to know and I missed my chance again. If Uncle Charlie's baby was a girl, where would he send her back to?

3
An awful fight

It was that same night, very late, when I woke from a cosy sleep to the sound of my parents' angry voices. Cold shivers crept over me. I couldn't get used to their fighting, even though it happened nearly every day.

I buried my head under the pillow, trying not to hear. But it was stuffy under there and I had to come up for air. They were shouting now—terrible, ugly, fighting words. The kind that lead to blows. I didn't know what to do.

I looked at Willa. She was dead to the world on her back. Her mouth was open and she was snoring. She had a loud snore.

I got up and tiptoed down the hall. Feeling around for the string, I pulled the hall light on. The pale glow lit the staircase and spilled into the boys' room. Arthur was sound asleep, one foot hanging over the edge of the thin, felt mattress. Jakey was curled up beside him, his rump sticking up, his thumb loosely in his mouth. He looked so sweet and clean, the damp, dark ringlets clinging to his little round head. No one would ever dream he'd wet up Arthur's back every single night.

Suddenly a piercing shriek came ringing up the stairs. Then a loud thump, like a fist hitting the table.

I streaked down the stairs and stopped short at the bottom, grabbing the banister post for support. Under my thin cotton nightdress I shook like an autumn leaf. My heart skipped in my chest and gooseflesh crept all over my body.

The front rooms were in darkness. I could just make out the school books piled neatly on the round table. Only the kitchen light was on, a single forty-watt bulb dangling on a black wire from the high ceiling.

My parents hadn't seen me yet. Mum sat at the table, head thrown back, glaring defiantly up into Dad's ashen face. Her cheeks were beet red. His were sidewalk grey.

"No!" he roared at her. "I won't agree to give it up, no matter what you say."

"All you're thinking about is yourself," Mum retorted bitterly. "You're just concerned about what people will say. Well, I don't care what anybody says just so long as it has a good home, proper food, a chance for an education. We're lucky such a fine family wants it."

"What kind of a woman are you anyway?" Dad hissed, spraying Mum's face with spit. "No *real* woman would give up her own flesh and blood."

I saw Mum wince at the cruel words.

"It's not what I want, you fool!" Her voice shook with rage. "We can barely feed the four we've got. This one is unborn— unnamed. If we give it up right away . . ." Her hand touched her stomach, gently, protectively, the way she sometimes touched my face. It was only then that I noticed how huge her stomach was.

Her head jerked up and she looked Dad straight in the eye. "Isn't it bad enough that the ones we've got are underweight and undernourished?" she said coldly.

"I'll get work! I'll get money! I'll get them what they need!"

"Talk's cheap!"

"Shut up, if you know what's good for you!" Dad's fist jabbed the air just inches from Mum's nose.

My feet took wings. Flying through the darkened rooms, I landed with a thud at Mum's side. If it came to a showdown, which it often did, I was my mother's girl.

Shaking from head to foot, I began to shriek between them. "Mum! Dad! Is it a baby? Are we going to get a baby?" I didn't wait for an answer. "Please, Mum, don't give it away. I won't eat so much any more. It can have half my food. I like being underweight. Honest! You can run way faster when you're skinny."

They stared dumbfounded for a minute; then Mum reached out and put an arm around me. Dad's fist seemed to come down in slow motion. Moaning softly, he slumped to a chair and buried his head on the table.

"Don't cry, Dad." I touched his bony shoulder gingerly. "Willa and Arthur and me, we'll help, you'll see."

I had no idea what I meant by help. All I knew was that I had to prevent the awful fight from starting up again.

The colour had drained from Mum's cheeks, leaving them a pale yellow. One arm was still around me. The other was draped over her swollen middle.

I dared to poke it with my index finger. To my surprise, it was as hard as a baseball.

"Is it really in there, Mum?"

She nodded with a wry smile.

"Don't give it away!"

"Don't you worry your head, Booky."

But she didn't promise. Rising awkwardly, she went to put the latch on the door. Dad stood on the chair and unscrewed the light bulb to take upstairs. The one in their bedroom had burned out weeks ago.

Silently we climbed the stairs, Mum pulling herself, breathlessly, hand over hand on the banister.

I crept into bed beside Willa. She was still on her back but she wasn't snoring. Her eyes were wide open, glistening in the darkness.

"Do you know where babies come from, Willa?" I whispered.

"Yes."

I could barely hear her.

"So do I," I said importantly. But there was one more thing I needed to know. "How will it get out?"

"Go to sleep," ordered Willa.

So I did.

4
Thank goodness for Hallowe'en

By the time Hallowe'en came, I was really down in the dumps. Mum and Dad fought nearly every day and every time Dad went slamming out the door he left behind him a cloud of gloom. It was nearly as bad as when there's a death in the family and the body is laid out in the parlour, which is what the front room is called when someone is laid out in it.

Ordinarily my spirits would bounce right back no matter what, but this time they had hit rock bottom. So thank goodness for Hallowe'en.

Mum warned me not to get too excited about it this year. She said 1932 would be a bad year for shelling out. Our front room blinds were already pulled down, so the neighbourhood kids would know we couldn't afford to shell out this year. The darkened windows would keep the kids away just as surely as if a red *Scarlet Fever* sign were tacked to the front door.

But still I could hardly wait to dress up, as I always did on All Hallow's Eve, in my brother's old clothes. It was my favourite costume, my special daydream, my once-a-year chance to be a boy.

When Mum saw me getting ready she said, "Bea, wouldn't

you like to be a ghost for a change? There's an old sheet down in the laundry basket you could use."

"Oh, no, Mum!" I protested. "Don't you see? If I be a ghost this year I'll have to wait another whole year to be a boy!"

"I see," she said, giving my nose a little pinch that made it stick together.

When I was all ready I surveyed myself in Mum's bureau mirror. In his jacket and breeches, with my short, fair hair tucked up under his peaked cap, I was the dead-spit of Arthur. I even felt like him. I guess I wished I *was* him, but I would have yanked my tongue out by the roots rather than admit it.

Pulling on my black linen eye mask and grabbing my Eaton's shopping bag, I ran up the street to Audrey's. A few lighted pumpkins glimmered in the windows of Lilac Street. They stood out like friendly beacons in the dark, chilly night.

Audrey's jack-o'-lantern grinned invitingly from their front porch window. Her mother gave us our first shellout: a rosy McIntosh apple and three candy kisses. "Now, don't you girls go anywhere near the Morris house," she warned at the door. "That mean Mr. Morris threw out red-hot pennies last year and some of the neighbourhood boys were badly burned."

I knew this was true because Arthur was one of the boys. Mum had been mad as hops about it and had even gone down to the police station. But nothing came of it. "That's because old Morris is a monied man," Dad complained bitterly. "The rich, they think they're above the law."

Now the streets were milling with strange, exciting creatures: ghosts and goblins, witches and scarecrows, all drawn to the lighted houses like moths to a flame.

"Do you like my costume, Bea?" asked Audrey, twirling

around so her bride's veil and long sausage curls floated out behind her on the autumn breeze.

"It's gorgeous!" I replied obligingly. "Do you like mine?" I touched the peak of my cap like a gentleman.

"Oh, Bea!" Audrey screwed her nose up scornfully. "It's not a costume. It's only your brother's old suit."

"All right for you, Audrey!" I cried threateningly. But I let it go at that. I didn't want anything to spoil Hallowe'en.

Our first stop was Mrs. Cook's house. Mrs. Cook was known far and wide as the best shell-outer in Birchcliff. But there was a catch to it: you had to pass a test. Everyone was marched into her brightly lit kitchen and ordered to unmask. This yearly ritual scared the daylights out of me because I always had such a darned old guilty conscience!

"Ah, it's you, Beatrice," said Mrs. Cook, towering over me, her flabby arms folded over her big bosom. "For a minute there I thought you were Arthur. Well now, I don't recall you doing any mischief around my property this past summer, so you may put your mask back on and help yourself."

Miraculously, I had passed again. I knew perfectly well I had taken shortcuts across her green-carpet lawn and flying leaps over her flowerbeds during the summer, but I vowed then and there never to do it again.

Audrey passed too, so we both went to the treat-laden table. We ate a mouth-watering piece of chocolate cake on the spot. Then into our bags went a Dad's oatmeal cookie (I took two and Audrey looked disgusted—sometimes she reminded me of Willa), a big piece of vanilla fudge wrapped in waxed paper, a caramel popcorn ball and a taffy apple.

On our way out we remembered to say thank you. Mrs. Cook

looked up from the new bunch she was testing. "Oh, you're welcome, dears. See you next year."

"Shell out! Shell out! The witches are out!" cried a tramp and a clown on the doorstep. "Did you pass?" they whispered anxiously.

"Sure, it was easy!" we boasted.

I don't think any kid was ever turned away from Mrs. Cook's table, but all of us quaked at the possibility.

Off we went, Audrey and me, to scour the neighbourhood for lighted houses. Little by little our bags grew heavy. Mum had been wrong about 1932.

On Warden Avenue we stopped to catch our breath and eat a minty humbug. It had begun to rain, a fine Hallowe'en drizzle. Across the street we saw a bunch of boys who looked as if they were up to mischief. One of them crept over to our side and up onto a dark verandah.

"That's old man Morris's house," whispered Audrey.

Cold shivers ran up my spine. Noiselessly the boy fastened something to the door; then he quickly backtracked, playing out a ball of twine. When I saw his face under the streetlight I recognized, of all people, my own brother Arthur.

"Arthur! Arthur! What are you doing?" I screeched.

"Shut your trap, Bea!"

One of the other boys came over and shook his fist in my face. "Beat it if you don't want a bloody nose," he growled.

"You leave her alone, Tommy," hissed Arthur. "She's my sister." I could hardly believe my ears!

The boys hid in a clump of spirea and began to jerk the string. *Tap, tap, tap,* went the door knocker. No answer. "Pull harder!" *Bang! Bang! Bang!* Suddenly the door flew open and out leapt old man Morris, yelling his head off.

Audrey and I turned tail and ran. The last thing I saw, over my shoulder, was the old man tumbling head-over-heels down his verandah steps and the gang of boys scattering in all directions.

We didn't stop running until we got in sight of Audrey's house. By this time her bride's costume was a bedraggled mess, but the rain hadn't hurt Arthur's old suit one bit.

Her mother was peering anxiously out the window. The candle in their pumpkin had gone out. The minute she saw us she came to the door and said, "For mercy's sake, Audrey, don't you know enough to come in out of the rain?" Then to me, "You get right home, Beatrice." So I did.

Mum was sitting in the middle of the kitchen under the light bulb mending a ladder in her stocking. They were her only pair of real silk so she had to make them last. With threads picked from an old pair, and using a fine needle, she'd weave her way up the long ladder. When she was finished the run would have disappeared like magic.

Willa was making corrugated insoles on the table. She pressed her shoe on the cardboard and traced the outline with a pencil. Then she cut it out and fitted it over the hole inside her shoe.

I dumped my whole bag of treats beside her insoles on the table and told them both to help themselves. Mum chose the piece of fudge. Willa picked a licorice stick. Then Mum said I should keep the rest for myself, but I gave her all my apples, except the taffy apple.

"Glory be," she declared. "I'll make a lovely Brown-Betty tomorrow."

Bone weary but happy, I dragged my soggy bag up the stairs and hid it under the bed for safekeeping. Then I climbed out of Arthur's damp suit and into my nice dry nightdress. It felt good to be a girl again.

After a while I heard Willa come up. She splashed in the bathroom for ages. She was always washing herself, even when she wasn't dirty.

"Did you like your licorice stick?" I asked when she finally slipped into bed beside me.

"You smell, Bea!" she said, ignoring my bid for praise. "Why can't you wash your feet at least?"

Boy, did that make me mad! But I couldn't help feeling sorry for her. It must be awful to be too big to go out on Hallowe'en.

The next day the school was buzzing with rumours about a bunch of boys who had done a pile of mischief around the neighbourhood. Baby buggies were found dangling from telephone poles, backhouses were knocked over (old Mr. Peebles was sitting in his at the time!), and bad words were scribbled with soap all over the store windows on Kingston Road. But worst of all, old man Morris had broken his collarbone when he fell down his verandah steps while chasing some mischief-makers.

By the time we got home from school Mum knew all about it. Then, at the supper table, she told the whole story to Dad. Of course she never dreamed that her darling Arthur had anything to do with it.

While she talked Arthur kept darting pleading looks across the table. Boy, was I tempted. It was the chance of a lifetime to get back at him for all the mean things he had done to me in the past. For sure he'd get the razor-strop if Dad found out.

Dad was very strict about some things, like respecting other people's property and not saucing back your elders and things like that. He had some funny notions about discipline too. For instance, if we got the strap in school, he'd strap us when we got home, for getting the strap in school. Mum said that was a barbaric practice and she wouldn't have any part of it. So if we got the strap (better known as the slugs) Mum would hush it up and Dad would never find out. Of course Willa never got the slugs, and Arthur very seldom, but I got them regularly for my zeros in arithmetic.

When Dad first heard about Mr. Morris's broken collarbone his lips twitched and he said, "Serves him right, the old demon." Then he thought better of it and added, "Still, I don't hold with wilful mischief. Do you know anything about this, Arthur?"

Arthur started to choke on a crust of bread and Mum jumped up and thumped him on the back. "No, Dad!" he lied, his face going blotchy red.

Dad turned to me. "Beatrice?"

Temptation reared its ugly head again. Then I remembered my last razor-stropping. I had followed a parade down to the city limits and I hadn't got home until after dark. Willa sent me straight to bed and told me to pretend I was asleep. I did, but it didn't do any good. Dad roared up the stairs, yanked down the covers, threw up my nightdress and stropped my bare behind. I couldn't sit down for a week.

I decided I didn't want revenge that bad. And besides, hadn't Arthur saved me from a punch in the nose and admitted right out loud in front of all his friends that I was his sister? "No, Dad, I didn't see anything. Audrey and I were too busy shelly-outing. See the swell Brown-Betty Mum made from my apples?"

"It looks good, Bea," he said, smacking his lips.

After the Hallowe'en night, when Arthur stuck up for me and I didn't tell on him, we liked each other better. Not much, but some.

5
Commotion in the night

I was a terrible trial to Willa, I really was. The only thing we had in common was the old iron bed we shared. We didn't talk to each other much. There wasn't anything to say. She was five years older than I was, but that wasn't the worst of it. She was neat and clean and smart and sensible. I was messy and scatterbrained—and dumb in arithmetic.

The thing I did that bothered her most was going to bed with dirty stockings on. The smell nearly drove her crazy. And my running shoes were twice as bad as my stockings. I could hardly stand them myself. Almost every night, in the summertime, Willa would pitch them out the window. Then in the morning I'd have to go out in the brambles, barefoot, to find them.

Of course, I wasn't *allowed* to go to bed dirty. Far from it. I guess my mother was the cleanest woman in the world, but when she sent me up to take a bath, and after Dad had lugged a boilerful of scalding water up two flights of stairs, I'd just sit on the toilet seat daydreaming and yanking on the chain of the water closet overhead, listening to "Niagara Falls."

Then, when the water in the tub had turned stone cold, I'd

pull the plug, give my face and hands a "lick and a promise," put on my clean nightdress and hop happily into bed. Poor Willa. How she wished I had been born a boy so I would have to sleep with Arthur.

The night the new baby was born it was November and too cold to throw my running shoes out the window, so she scolded me unmercifully instead.

I cried myself to sleep and woke up to a strange commotion going on in the hallway. There was a muffled cry that trailed off in a long shuddering moan. It sounded like my mother's voice. Then, straining my ears, I heard an unfamiliar male voice saying terrible things. "Strap her down! Hold on to her legs! Give her another whiff. Cover her nose and mouth."

The awful words made no sense to me at all, but they struck cold terror into my heart. Leaping out of bed, I streaked down the hall screaming at the top of my lungs, "Mum! Mum! Mum!"

Dad caught me by my nightdress and smacked my skinny behind.

"Get back to bed and shut the door!" His voice was a rasping whisper.

Shaking like a bowlful of jelly, I dove back in beside Willa, and crept as close to her as I dared.

"What's the matter, Willa?" I whispered fearfully. "What's happening to Mum?"

"It's the baby," she said quietly.

"The baby? In Mum's stomach? Is it trying to get out? Is it hurting Mum? Why are they strapping her?"

"Shut up!" she snapped, and I couldn't get another word out of her. She just lay there, perfectly still, staring up at the ceiling.

I gave up and buried my head under the pillow, plugging my ears with my fingers. It was pitch dark under there, but I saw lights, orange and blue and red, sailing in all directions like fireworks on the 24th of May.

I must have gone to sleep finally, because the next thing I knew it was morning and I was all alone in the bed. The house was as quiet as a church on Monday. Dressing in a flash, my heart in my mouth, I crept down the hall past the closed door of my parents' room.

The kitchen light was on. I could tell the stove was lit by the lovely warmth wafting through the dining room. I heard spoons clinking and whispered conversation. Then I saw Aunt Myrtle, Uncle Charlie's wife, her bulging apron pressed against the stove, stirring something in the grey graniteware saucepan. (She was in the family way, too. I knew all about that at last!)

"Good morning, Bea," she greeted me pleasantly. "How would you like another baby brother?"

For a second there I thought I had a choice. "I'd rather have a sister this time," I answered innocently.

"Well, like it or not, you've got another brother."

"Dumb-bell!" hissed Arthur.

Aunt Myrtle filled my bowl with thick, grey porridge. "You can go up to see him before you go to school," she said.

She was nice, Aunt Myrtle; we all liked her. But she sure was a terrible cook. Her porridge was as lumpy and tasteless as wallpaper paste (which I had sampled once when Dad papered our bedroom). Mum's porridge was always creamy white with brown sugar sprinkled on it.

"What's wrong with the porridge, Willa?" I whispered.

"She forgot the salt. Be quiet and eat."

Arthur sat, hunched over, spooning in the lumps. Instead of porridge, Jakey was greedily devouring a bowl of bready milk. He'd rather have bready milk than porridge any day. And if there wasn't any milk he'd cheerfully settle for bready water, just as long as there was brown sugar sprinkled on it.

I noticed a dish of butter in the middle of the table. Aunt Myrtle must have brought it for a treat. So I made myself a white sugar sandwich. Mmm, it was good, the way the sugar mixed with the salty yellow butter. Satisfied at last, I jumped up and headed for the stairs.

I could hardly wait to see the baby and my mother. I needed to see for myself if she was all right. Easing open the bedroom door, I peeked in. Mum's eyes were like dark coals in white snow. Her hair was like a black cloud on the pillow. She gave me a weak smile and held out her hand.

I crept on tiptoe to the laundry basket perched on a chair beside her bed. The baby was asleep, wrapped in a napkin and lying on a pillow. He was the worst looking baby I'd ever laid eyes on. He was as skinny as a plucked chicken and he had a lump on the side of his head the size of a teacup. I didn't know what to say, so I blurted out, "Has he got a name, Mum?"

"No, Bea. Can you think of one?" Her voice was low and gravelly.

I thought for a minute. I liked double names myself. Hyphenated. Like Anna-Belle or Betty-Ann. My doll's name was Margaret-Mae (after Grampa Thomson's two milk cows). Once I had asked Mum if she would mind calling me both my names, Beatrice-Myrtle (after Aunt Myrtle). I hated them both, but I thought the hyphen improved them quite a bit. "Oh, Bea, that's too much of a mouthful!" Mum had said, even though I'd explained that the hyphen made it all one word.

"Could we give him a double name, Mum?" I decided to try again. "How about William Robert? And we could call him Billy-Bob for short."

"William is a nice name, after Puppa. I like Robert too. I think Billy will suit him just fine."

I guess she didn't like double names.

Just then Dad came into the room. He was wearing the same pleased expression as the day Jakey was born. But this time it didn't bother me. He rested his hand on my head and we looked in the basket together. I told him the names I had picked and he said he liked them.

Just then the baby opened his big blue eyes and stared straight up at me. I think he knew me! My heart swelled with love and pride. Then I remembered the awful night when Mum and Dad were fighting about giving him away.

"Mum, Dad, you won't give him away, will you?" Before Dad had a chance to open his mouth, Mum said, "Don't you worry your head about that anymore, Booky. The minute I saw him I knew I could never part with him."

I knew I could believe her. I leaned over the bed and she held me tight. Her lips were hot and dry on my forehead. Dad kissed me too, and I tasted butter on his mouth.

Reaching inside the basket with my little finger, I touched the baby's velvet cheek. Then I ran off to school.

6
A special birthday present

I could hardly wait to tell Audrey. Boy, would she be surprised!

Hurrying up the street, my head ducked against the cold east wind, I thought of something funny. It was my birthday and nobody had remembered. Not much wonder with all the goings-on at our house that night. Then I thought of something else. Mum had said Billy arrived right after midnight. That meant he had been born on my birthday. He was my birthday present—a real live baby doll. I felt a tug at my heart at the thought of him, my funny looking, skinny little, bumpy-headed, brand new brother. Then and there I knew he would always be special to me.

The weather had turned raw and ice was on the puddles. But it hadn't snowed yet, if you didn't count a little flurry.

Mrs. Westover let me wait in the back kitchen out of the cold. I didn't say a word while Audrey got her snowsuit on. It was a matching snowsuit, three pieces, the first I'd ever seen. Audrey always had the latest fashions. I was wearing my blue coat that Mum had made over for me from cousin Lottie's. My legs were all covered in duck-bumps where my brown ribbed stockings and navy blue bloomers didn't quite meet.

"Hey, Mrs. Westover," I couldn't hold it in any longer, "guess how many kids there are in my family."

She knitted her brows thoughtfully. "Why, there are four, aren't there? Two boys and two girls."

"No," I squealed gleefully, "there's five! Last night my mother borned a new baby boy. His name is Billy, short for William, after Grampa Cole. I named him and he's mine because he was born on my birthday."

"Oh, your poor dear mother," cried Mrs. Westover, her fat pudgy hand with the big diamond ring fluttering to her bosom.

At first I thought she meant Mum was poor because she didn't have a diamond ring (Mum didn't even have a wedding band right now because she had pawned it to buy coal). But then I realized she was feeling sorry for Mum because she had a new baby. I was never so taken aback. I expected her to be all in a twitter and offer me congratulations. After all, how many kids get a new baby brother for their birthday?

But instead she acted as if I had brought her bad news. I couldn't understand it. And then it struck me. She was jealous—and no wonder. She had only Audrey, and Mum had all of us. Just the same I was disappointed in Mrs. Westover. So I decided if we ever got another new baby she wouldn't be the first to know.

Audrey wasn't a whole lot better. I thought she'd be all ears to hear about the strange goings-on at our house in the middle of the night. I started to tell her all about it as we crossed the windy field leading out onto Kingston Road, but she didn't seem the least bit interested. She just kept changing the subject to the lamb's wool coat her father was having made for her mother for Christmas. She was all excited about it because he said there would be enough fur left over to trim a coat for her. And maybe a muff too!

That sure knocked the wind out of my sails. But not for long. After all, my new coat had a fur collar too. Rabbit. When Cousin Lottie heard I didn't have a winter coat she came right over with her old one and said it was just the excuse she was looking for to buy herself a new one.

Lottie was a spinster and she had a steady job at Simpson's. Everybody made fun of her for not being married, and teased her about not being able to catch a man (which surprised me because Lottie was a good runner. I had seen her win lots of races at our Sunday School picnics). But she didn't care. She said no man was going to sweet-talk her into being a slave to a bunch of kids and a washboard. Mum said Cousin Lottie had a good head on her shoulders.

The coat was huge, like Lottie herself, and Mum had a hard job cutting it up and making it down to fit skinny little me. And all the while she worked, her right foot flying on the treadle, she kept saying over and over that she hoped she had enough time to get done. I didn't know what she meant at the time, but now I understood that the baby was due soon.

© Eaton's Archives

And to make matters

worse, the trial period for the sewing machine had already run out. Not only was Mum expecting a baby any minute, but she was also expecting the horse-drawn Eaton's wagon to pull up to the door and repossess the precious sewing machine.

But she finished my coat in the nick of time, and it was beautiful. Lottie said it was a work of art, and she went right out and bought me a blue toque and mittens to match. I was proud as punch of myself, all decked out in my favourite colour. If it hadn't been for my stockings and bloomers not quite meeting, I would have been as warm as toast.

So Audrey and her mother didn't dampen my spirits for long. After all, I had a new winter outfit and a new baby brother. And I was ten years old and Audrey was still only nine.

* * *

Billy fast caught up to Jakey in the cute department, but without a word of a lie he was the crabbiest kid in creation. If there had been a contest for the world's most crotchety baby, I'll bet our Billy would have won first prize, easy.

Mum made up all kinds of excuses for his crankiness. "They 'bused him," she'd say, or, "He's got a touch of gripes," or, "He's hungry, poor little gaffer. He never seems to get enough to eat."

Well, he wasn't the only one. We were all famished most of the time. Dad said the "pogey" would hardly keep body and soul together. I guess that's why those years were called the hungry thirties.

By this time I was convinced that our baby wouldn't be given away ("He cries so much, who'd want him?" as Willa pointed out), but the fear of losing him still dogged me in my dreams. Morning after morning I'd wake to find myself squeezed into

his little iron cot with my arms wrapped protectively around him. I never knew how I got there and it soon became a family joke.

Dad would say, "Bea went for a jaunt last night and guess where she ended up?" Then they'd all laugh and tease me. But I didn't mind. It was all in fun.

My spare time was so taken up with Billy, helping Mum bath him and taking him for rides and jiggling his cot to make him sleep, that I almost forgot Christmas was just around the corner. I had never been that carried away with anything in my life before.

7
"Hello, Bluebird"

If I live to be a hundred, I'll always bless Eaton's for the Santa Claus Parade. In my opinion, Santa Claus Parade Day was second only to Christmas Day and third to Hallowe'en. And best of all, it was absolutely free.

But Dad said in a pig's eye it was free. He said it was nothing but a big conspiracy by the rich capitalist Eaton Company against the downtrodden poor of Toronto. He always managed to put a damper on the great event by ranting and raving like that.

"What's a conspiracy, Dad?" Arthur was interested in things like that. "And what's a capitalist?"

"Conspiracy is when Eaton's makes poor children hanker after things their parents can't afford," was Dad's gloomy explanation. "And capitalism means that the rich get richer and the poor get poorer."

But he hadn't forgotten altogether what it meant to be a child at Christmas time. He never failed to take us to the parade.

We were up before daylight on that wonderful day, excitedly eating our porridge by the dim glow of the light bulb.

"Eat up," Mum urged us, "so you'll be well fortified against the cold."

And cold it was. Bitter winds swept across Kingston Road from the golf links, chilling us to the bone. The "radio" car went rattling by, its lucky passengers peering out through round peepholes made by warm fingers on frosty windows. But it cost an extra nickel to ride, so we couldn't afford it.

Miraculously, a streetcar was waiting at the city limits. We clambered up the wooden steps and hurried past the driver to the middle of the car where a little square stove nestled up to the conductor's box.

The conductor was out of his box tending the stove. With a miniature shovel, he cleared the ashes from the bottom. Then he flipped open the little top door and added a shovelful of coal to the smouldering fire within. The coal dust ignited instantly in a shower of cheery red sparks. That chore done, he hopped back up on his perch to collect the fares and holler out the stops.

Dad had only one grown-up ticket and three children's. That meant Willa would have to scrunch down and pass for a kid. "If I'd known that I would have stayed at home," she grumbled under her breath.

"When the centre doors open," Dad whispered his instructions as we huddled around the stove, "you three skedaddle past the conductor and down the steps. I'll carry Jakey and put the tickets in all at once. That way he won't notice how big you are, Willa."

Poor Willa. She must have been six inches taller than the line on the pole that marked the difference between adults and children. But Dad's plan worked like a charm and he got transfers for all of us. Ten minutes later we boarded the Danforth car without a worry in the world.

It joggled and lurched along the tracks at a snail's pace (Arthur was sure he could run faster), and we finally arrived at Bathurst and Bloor. We always went that far along because it wasn't so crowded there. We hopped off not a minute too soon. Jakey's face had started to turn green.

Arthur and I squeezed onto the curb between two big boys who gave us dirty looks. Willa stood right behind us. Dad had no sooner hoisted Jakey onto his shoulders than he said, "I have to pee-pee, Daddy," so Dad told Willa to mind his place and he took Jakey down an alleyway. When they came back Jakey was all smiles, and the fresh air had brought the roses back to his cheeks.

The Mounties went prancing by, close enough to touch. Shivering with delight, we drew in our toes and stared up at the underside of their horses' big, round bellies.

At last came the faraway sound of music—beating drums and tooting horns and jingling tambourines. It was a wonderful parade. We saw Cinderella and the March Hare and Peter, Peter Pumpkin Eater. And in between came the upside-down clowns who patted our toques, and the swaying Humpty Dumpties who shook our mittens, and the glorious marching bands.

But the best was saved for last.

He stood high on a float in his make-believe sleigh, as high as the telephone poles. Santa Claus! The real one—not a helper or pretender. (Mum said only the real Santa was allowed to come to Toronto in Eaton's Santa Claus Parade.)

I held my breath as the mock reindeer drew nearer. (Mum

44

said Santa couldn't bring his live reindeer because Eaton's had nowhere to put them up.) Suddenly he was right beside us, "ho, ho, ho-ing" through his snowy beard, patting his round red stomach and throwing kisses to the four winds.

For a split second, the twinkling eyes met mine.

"Hello there, little Bluebird," he shouted down at me.

I gaped after him, my mouth hanging open, my eyes glued to his red velvet back.

"That was you Santa called Bluebird, Bea!" cried my astonished sister. "He noticed your new blue coat."

And then it was over. Only wisps of band music, like threads of smoke from a chimney, hung in the cold, damp air.

Already the crowds were surging towards the streetcars. Eager children were begging shivering parents to take them downtown to Eaton's department store to visit Santa in his Crystal Palace. Jakey was still grinning and waving from his perch on Dad's shoulders. Dad was wearing a big smile as if he had enjoyed the parade in spite of himself. The smile took me off guard.

"Can we go downtown to visit Santa, Dad?" I asked.

The smile dropped, like a mask, from his face. "No!" he barked, setting Jakey down with a thump. "We're going straight home. Write him a letter."

A lump rose painfully in my throat and my eyes swam with tears. But I knew better than to argue. I knew why Dad wouldn't take us to Eaton's. It wasn't because he was mean. Just the opposite. He was afraid we'd see some wonderful, expensive toy and ask Santa for it and be broken-hearted on Christmas morning when we didn't get it. But he needn't have worried, poor Dad. We understood that bicycles and doll sulkies, hobby

© Eaton's Archives

horses and Eaton Beauty dolls were not for the likes of us.

Willa noticed my face all crumpled up. "Maybe we could drop in on Aunt Maggie," she suggested. "She lives only a few blocks from here so it won't cost anything."

Dad's face brightened right up. "Good idea," he agreed. "Let's go." And he offered Jakey and me each a finger to hang on to.

My tears dried instantly at the mention of Aunt Mag. She was one of Mum's many sisters and a favourite of ours. She and Uncle Alistair lived in the heart of the city in a row house just like ours. Except they owned theirs and the bailiff could never put them out.

Uncle Alistair was an electrician. He belonged to the Electricians' Union and the Liberal Party. Mum said Uncle Alistair hadn't lost a single day's work on account of the Depression. That's what it was to have a good trade, she said. She often threw this up to Dad in the middle of a fight, so it's a wonder he was willing to go and visit them. But everybody liked Uncle Al, even Dad. There was a special bond between them. They had been comrades-in-arms in France from 1914 to 1918.

Aunt Maggie was well known in the family for always having the welcome mat out, and today was no exception. The door flew open at our knock.

"Come in, you're out!" she cried delightedly. "I was only half expecting you."

Her greetings were always little jokes like that. Willa said she had a quaint sense of humour.

"Well, Jim"—she turned her sunny smile on Dad—"and how's your old straw hat?"

Dad surprised us by returning her joke as he hung up his coat. "Pretty cold for it this time of year, Mag."

We followed her down the hall to the kitchen where Uncle Al sat with a tiny boy on his knee and a shy girl peeking round his elbow.

"Dear doctor," exclaimed Aunt Mag, ambling over to the stove in no particular hurry, "I've gone and burnt up the whole breakfast." Flipping the lid off the smoking saucepan with a long-handled spoon, she remarked matter-of-factly, "Burnt to a crisp. Oh well, once burnt, twice shy, I always say. We'll just have to make do with hen-fruit."

Tucking her hands under her armpits, she flapped her elbows and ran around the kitchen crowing "Cock-a-doodle-dooo!" like a chicken in a barnyard. We kids nearly split our sides laughing, and even Dad and Uncle Al had to smile.

Swooping down on the icebox, she took out a dozen eggs and cracked the whole works into a mixing bowl. Then she turned the gas jet high under the skillet and plopped in a big blob of real butter. Into the sizzling pan she poured the whole bowlful of eggs.

"Here, Willa." She handed my sister a long loaf of white bread. "You make the toasty-woasty for your Auntsy-Pantsy."

Arthur and I let out a whoop and even Willa smiled a bit as she began to slice the bread.

"You two straighten up," Dad warned us. Then to Aunt Mag, "You shouldn't be using your good food up on us, Mag. A cup of tea would have done just fine."

"Now you mind your beeswax, Jim Thomson," scolded our cheery aunt. "You just leave the 'brecky' to us chickens."

Arthur got the job of toastmaker and I was the official butterer.

We didn't have an electric toaster at our house so "toasty-woasty" was a special treat for us. The toaster fascinated Arthur. Its shiny sides lay open on the table. He put a slice of bread on each side and closed it up. At the exact right second, he flopped down the sides and the bread turned itself over automatically! When both sides were a lovely golden brown, he juggled them in the air and dropped them on a plate in front of me. The butter gave off a mouthwatering aroma as I spread it on the hot toast. It was all I could do not to take a bite.

What a swell breakfast that was: toast and jam and milk and tea and all the frizzled eggs we could eat. (And it wasn't even Easter!) We mopped our eggy plates with our crispy crusts until they shone. Then, without being asked, we helped Aunt Mag with the cleaning up. (Even Arthur asked for a dish towel!) While we worked she kept us laughing with her homey jokes and sunny disposition.

"It's time we were making tracks," Dad said when the dishes were done. "It wouldn't do to wear our welcome out."

"Fat chance!" retorted Aunt Mag. "You know you're as welcome as the flowers in May."

"Next time you come, Jim," said Uncle Alistair, "be sure you bring along that picture of you and me on leave in Paris."

"Will do," promised Dad. "Been nice talking to you."

It sure did Dad good to reminisce about the war.

"What do you say for all that good grub?" he reminded us in the pleasantest voice we'd heard in weeks.

"Thanks for all the good grub, Aunt Mag," we chorused.

As we went down the front walk she called after us, "Tell

Fran not to wait until a blue moon comes over the mountain—don't be strangers now. Orry-vor!"

We waved back and hollered, "Orry-vor!"

"What does orry-vor mean, Willa?" I asked, skippety-hopping beside her.

"She thinks she's saying *Au revoir*," explained my educated sister. "That's French for goodbye. But Aunt Mag never went to high school so she doesn't know how to pronounce it right."

Then and there I decided to go to high school and learn French. The way Willa said "*Au revoir*" was downright beautiful.

That night I took Dad's advice and wrote Santa a letter. I asked him for my heart's desire, a toy telephone. I had never used a real telephone, so I was dying to have one to practice on.

"Are you going to write to Santa this year?" I asked Willa.

"No, I haven't got time," she said, not looking up from her books. "You can put a p.s. on your letter and tell him I'd like a string of beads if he has any."

Importantly, I added her p.s.

"How about you, Arthur?" I was feeling very generous. "Want me to add a p.s. for you too?"

Arthur looked up from the map he was drawing. "Aw, I don't believe—oww!" He grabbed his leg under the table. Willa was staring at him fiercely. "I want a box of paints," he finished sullenly.

I had a good mind not to add his p.s., since he was so crabby about it, but I didn't want anything to spoil Christmas. I added some for Jakey and Billy too.

When I was finished I took another piece of paper and folded it into the shape of an envelope. Then I pasted it together with flour and water. Tucking my letter inside, I sealed it with a gooey white blob of paste.

"Can I have a stamp, Mum?" I asked.

"I haven't got one, Bea," she said, looking up from her mending. "If you put your letter on the hall table I'll remember to drop it in Santa's mailbox next time I'm down at Eaton's."

"Okay, Mum," I agreed happily. "No use wasting a stamp."

8
A gloomy Christmas Eve

There was nothing to show it was the day before Christmas. No last minute preparations, no whispered secrets, no delicious smell of bread and sage and onions coming from the big mixing bowl.

The red and green crepe-paper streamers were still in the box in the attic. The Christmas tree ornaments, little glass bells and tiny red balls, were still packed in the shoe box in last year's tissue paper.

Gloom hung like fog in the air. Mum and Dad had been fighting steadily for weeks, and now they weren't even speaking to each other. I didn't know which was worse, the yelling or the silence.

Usually on Christmas Eve Dad would go straight out after supper to get our tree. He always left it that late on purpose so he'd be sure to get a bargain. Then he generally got a tree for a nickel.

I sat in the kitchen close to the stove remembering those other years. How we'd all cluster around the front room window waiting with bated breath, watching for Dad to come along with his peculiar, lopsided gait (caused by an improperly set broken leg in childhood), dragging the tree behind him. It was nearly always a misshapen, scraggly old thing, but when Santa got finished trimming it, it was the most beautiful tree in the world. This year Dad didn't bother to go out because he didn't have two cents to rub together.

Willa was sitting on the opposite side of the stove mending her middy blouse. She sewed neat little stitches and when she was finished you could hardly see the patch. Mum had taught her to sew like that. I asked her to teach me too, but she said I was too much of a scatterbrain.

Arthur had his art pad out, drawing a reindeer drinking from a forest stream. I didn't know what to do with myself. I had no storybook to read and I was too down at the mouth to write a composition.

It was more like a funeral day than the day before Christmas. And to make matters worse the house was as cold as a barn, and we'd had to wear our coats all day.

The chair beside the kitchen stove was the warmest spot in the house, so I sat there and Mum gave me the baby to hold. He had colic and was crying. I sang "Rock-a-bye, baby," but instead of soothing him it made him cry even louder; so I swung him back and forth, faster and faster, in my arms. All of a sudden his head hit the stove with a wallop. Screwing up his skinny little face, he let out a bloodcurdling scream. Mum and Dad came running from opposite directions and Jakey squealed and dove under the table.

"Clumsy fool!" Dad bellowed, snatching the baby out of my arms.

I started to cry and couldn't stop even when Mum said it wasn't my fault and not to worry because Billy wasn't hurt.

At least the accident livened things up a bit. Dad and Mum started in fighting again. Willa and Arthur hightailed it up the stairs, and Jakey and I scurried down the cellar to play "Bill and Bob."

Bill and Bob was a rainy day game I had made up for Jakey. He'd ride his wobbly old kiddie car round and round the furnace and I'd be the friendly policeman. "Red light!" I'd say, holding up my hand. He'd come to a skidding stop, his dimples dancing. "Hi, Bill," I'd say. "How's everything at your house?" "Fine," he'd say, brown eyes sparkling. "How's your house?" "Fine," I'd say, bringing my hand down smartly. Then I'd say, "Green light!" and away he'd go, *brrmm, brrmm, brrmm* around the furnace. That's all there was to it. It wasn't much of a game but Jakey liked it better than London Bridge and Ring-Around-the-Rosy put together.

All we had for supper that night was potatoes and mashed turnips. Willa said. "Eww!" and left the table holding her nose. Dad gave her a baleful look. Arthur and I gobbled up her share. Jakey said he wanted bready milk instead, but there wasn't any milk so Dad made him up a bowl of bready water with brown sugar on it.

For the first time, that Christmas Eve, Willa and Arthur didn't hang up their stockings. When I went upstairs to hang Jakey's and mine on the bedposts, Willa followed me up. In a queer voice she said, "Bea, I don't think Santa is coming this year."

Then Arthur hollered from the bathroom, "There is no Santa Claus!" and ran into his bedroom slamming the door behind him.

"Liar! Liar! Ten feet higher!" I shrieked after him, tears

gushing down my face. "And you're mean, Willa, mean, mean, mean! Serves you right if Santa doesn't bring you anything!"

Then I changed my mind about where to hang our stockings. I decided to hang them on the knobs of a kitchen chair and put the chair right by the front door so Santa couldn't miss it when he came in.

"Don't forget to leave Santa a cup of hot cocoa," I reminded Mum as Jakey and I went to bed early. Jakey always slept with me on Christmas Eve because I had the spirit. Willa didn't care. She said it was a nice change to sleep by herself on the davenport. And Arthur was pleased as punch because for once he could be sure that no one would wet up his back.

Jakey cuddled up beside me, eyes snapping with excitement. "Bea-Bea, tell me stories," he said between thumb sucks.

So I recited "'Twas the night before Christmas" and I told him about old Ebenezer Scrooge, and about the baby Jesus being born in the manger in Bethlehem.

My eyes grew heavy and I nearly dropped off, but Jakey wouldn't let me. Lifting up one of my droopy eyelids, he whispered mysteriously, "BeaBea, are you still in there?"

I laughed so hard I was wide awake again, so I told him some more stories I made up out of my head. Then I ran him to the bathroom one more time and made him promise not to wet the bed or Willa would be mad.

9

Arthur was right

Jakey was up like a shot at the crack of dawn. "Bea-Bea!" He shook me urgently. "I need to wee-wee!" For the first time in his life he hadn't wet the bed. So I ran him lickety-split to the bathroom.

Voices floated up the stairway. The teakettle was whistling, and I could hear Billy's hungry cry. Then I remembered what day it was and a sudden thrill went through me. Forgetting all about our dreary Christmas Eve, I yanked Jakey off the toilet and raced with him down the stairs.

Now there were two kitchen chairs sitting side by side at the front door. And four stockings with lumpy feet hung from the round wooden knobs.

Jakey let go of my hand and ran squealing to his stocking. Gleefully, he shook it upside down. Out onto the cracked linoleum rolled an apple, an orange and a little bag of candy. I dumped mine out beside his, and that's all there was in mine too—an apple, an orange and a little bag of candy.

There were no presents under the Christmas tree. There was no Christmas tree. No paintbox . . . no string of beads . . . no toy telephone. Just an apple, an orange and a handful of hard candies in a twist of waxed paper.

"Mum," I said, looking up from the cold floor into her troubled eyes, "did you mail my letter?"

"Yes, Booky," she said.

So Arthur was right. There was no Santa Claus. My eyes were so full of tears I could hardly see the belly button on my orange.

Willa sat on the edge of the davenport wrapped in a quilt. Her brown freckles stood out like black pepper spilled on a white tablecloth. She didn't make a move, so Mum handed her her stocking.

"Here, Willa," she said. "Have your orange for breakfast." Willa took the stocking but she didn't dump it out.

By ten o'clock our treats were all gone, even though we tried to drag them out.

"Let's play Bill and Bob, Bea-Bea," said Jakey. But I didn't feel like it. There was a big lump in my chest.

Willa went upstairs to make the beds. Arthur was putting the finishing touches on his picture. Jakey was under the table sucking his thumb and Billy had dropped off to sleep. I could hear Dad in the cellar furiously sifting ashes. Mum was banging pots and pans in the kitchen. I couldn't remember ever feeling so sad before. My chest ached and I couldn't breathe right.

A sudden knock on the front door made us all jump out of our skins.

"Land sakes!" Mum exclaimed. "Who could that be?"

The knock brought Dad up from the cellar. Jakey came out from his hiding place, Willa came halfway down the stairs, and Arthur and I followed Mum to the door.

A strange man stood on the rickety porch with four long boxes on his arm. "Merry Christmas from the Star Santa Claus Fund," he cried in a put-on merry voice. Then he tipped his hat and left.

On top of each box was a Santa Claus sticker with a message printed on it. *Boy, 10–12, Girl, 8–10, Boy, 3–5,* and one that just said *Baby boy.*

The weight on my chest shifted a little. "Can we open them, Mum?" I said.

"Sure, Bea. It's Christmas."

Each Star box contained clothing, a toy and a candy cane. Out of the *Girl, 8–10* box I pulled a long black sweater-coat and matching toque. Both were trimmed with a double orange stripe. My toy was a Betty-Boop doll with huge painted eyes looking over to one side, black-painted hair and fat stuck-together legs.

Arthur got the same toque and sweater, but his buttoned on the other side. His toy was a Snakes and Ladders game. Jakey got a blue sweater and toque and a picture book. Billy got a blue layette and a rattle. Willa didn't get a box because she was too big. She said she was glad because she hated the black toque and sweater. Dad told her to hold her tongue, so she didn't say boo for hours.

The first thing I did was change Betty-Boop's name to Lucy after "Lucy in the Lighthouse." That was one of my favourite stories in the Junior Third Reader. Whenever I couldn't sleep at night for Billy crying or Mum and Dad fighting or Willa snoring, I'd imagine I was Lucy struggling up the spiral staircase with the heavy lantern. Breathlessly I'd hang it in the narrow lighthouse window so its wavering light could be seen far out to sea. It was thrilling to be a heroine and save all those sailor boys from certain death on the rocky reefs below.

Willa did a real nice thing for me that day. She made Lucy a cute little dress out of a blue-checkered scrap from Mum's rag bag. She said she would have made bloomers too if Lucy's legs hadn't been stuck together.

Usually our Aunt Aggie in Muskoka sent us a chicken for Christmas, but this year there wasn't one. Instead Mum made a big pot of potato soup for our noonday meal. It wasn't much, but it was delicious: thick and hot with onions swimming in it and parsley floating on the top. I could have eaten a whole barrelful, easy. But there was only enough for one bowl each.

As she stacked the bowls, Mum started in grumbling. Then Dad said a swear word and stomped off down the cellar. I was just about to follow him when another knock came at the door.

"Land sakes!" Mum declared again, and I followed her instead.

Mr. Westover stood on the porch. He looked embarrassed. Gawking past him I could see Audrey in her fur-trimmed coat sitting on her mother's lap in the Model A Ford. I waved and she waved back with her fur muff.

Mr. Westover handed Mum a brown parcel. "Merry Christmas, Mrs. Thomson," he said and quickly walked away before Mum had a chance to say, "Same to you."

Curiosity had brought Dad back up the stairs. We all gathered round the dining room table to watch Mum open the parcel. In it was a roast of pork, two tins of ungraded peas, a red jelly powder and a storebought Christmas cake.

Dad scowled at the little pile of groceries. "We don't need their charity!" he snarled.

"Oh, yes, we do!" Mum barked back.

Then she started to scold in earnest. I guess she just couldn't help herself, even on Christmas. All her worries and heartaches came tumbling out together: the rent was overdue and the bailiff was after us again; there was no food in the cabinet; we all had holes in our shoes; the baby needed a doctor, and Willa needed books to study from. On and on she went, all afternoon.

Dad sat as still as a statue. His face was the colour of dry cement. Long before he exploded, my legs had begun to shake.

His anger burst out in a torrent of rage and the swear words he used were something wicked. Mum just hurled them back in his face. Dreadful, hateful, evil words flew back and forth across the room like lightning bolts in a thunderstorm.

I don't know what she said to make him hit her. All I remember was the terrible sound, like a clap of thunder. A piercing scream pealed from her throat, scaring the wits out of us kids. Willa ran coatless out the door, Arthur bolted up the stairs, Billy howled, and Jakey darted out from under the table, bit Dad on the leg and dove for cover again. I clung to the table's edge, my legs wobbling like jelly, and screamed for them to stop. But they didn't even hear me.

At last Dad grabbed his greatcoat from the cellar door and went slamming out of the house. I slid down on the chair beside Mum. My stomach was churning, my head was paining, and my eyes had gone all blurry. I could hear Mum's breath coming in quick little gasps. Her face was beet-red and streaked with tears.

Willa came back, blue from the cold, and went upstairs without speaking. Arthur didn't come down. Jakey crept out from under the table and laid his curly head on Mum's lap. His eyes were big as saucers.

"C'mon, Jakey," I whispered. "Let's go down to the cellar and play Bill and Bob."

By the time Mum called us up for supper, my stomach was cleaving to my backbone. The table was set in the kitchen, which was strange for Christmas Day. We always ate in the dining room on special occasions.

The roast pork looked delicious, all crisp and brown, with a bowl of golden gravy right beside it. Dad walked in in the middle of the meal. He looked neither to left nor to right. He hung up his greatcoat on the cellar door and sat down at his place. His face wasn't grey anymore. Now it was red from the cold. Mum's cheeks had changed from bright red to a pale yellow. There were purple bruises on one side.

We ate in silence, passing the food around. I loaded up my plate with thick, juicy pork, sweet green peas and fluffy mashed potatoes swimming in rich brown gravy. It was so good, my headache went away.

For dessert, Mum served up the store-bought fruitcake with a cup of weak tea for each of us. There was no milk. We cleaned up every crumb of cake. Mum had a thick slice herself, but Dad wouldn't touch it.

I felt so much better after eating that I jumped up to help Willa with the dishes. She gave me a queer look but didn't say anything. Then, while Mum was bathing the baby and Dad was putting Jakey to bed, Arthur said to Willa, "Do you want a game of Snakes and Ladders?" I said, "Can three play?" and

Arthur said, "Sure," just as nice as you please.

We played for a couple of hours on the kitchen table and Arthur and I didn't even fight once. I guess we had had enough of fighting for one day. Especially Christmas Day.

I was glad when it was time for bed. I went up early to be alone for a while. Snuggling under the thin covers with Lucy hard against my cheek, I thought the day over. I understood now why Willa and Arthur had said what they did about Santa. They weren't being mean. They were just trying to save me from being disappointed.

All of a sudden I stopped feeling sorry for myself and started feeling sorry for my parents. I realized the heart-aches they suffered and the shame they felt in front of people like the Westovers and the Star Santa Claus man.

I thought about Audrey and what her Christmas had been like. I knew she had got her fur-trimmed coat because I had caught a glimpse of it that morning. Last year Santa had brought

20 ins.
Tall

Just a Great Big Armful of Value! 1 00

618-607 She's one of Santa's favorites—Miss "EATON Beauty." Mother knows she is such good value and little daughter is fascinated by her long curls, her sweet smile, sleeping eyes, real lashes and moving bisque head. Composition body, fully jointed at head, shoulders, elbows, wrists, legs and knees. Removable shoes, socks and lace-trimmed slip. All ready to be dressed! Size 20 ins. high.. **1.00**
618-625. Head only to fit above doll........ **39c**
618-626. Wig only...... **50c**

© Eaton's Archives

her an Eaton Beauty doll. Then they had gone to her grand-mother's for turkey dinner.

I thought of something else too, something that had lain heavy on my heart for many weeks now. I wondered if it was the Westovers who had wanted to adopt our Billy. That's how they got Audrey, and they still had an empty bedroom. No, it couldn't have been them because I remembered how surprised Mrs. Westover had been when I told her about Billy being born. But it was probably somebody like them, somebody rich and kind and good, who could have given Billy wonderful Christmases so he wouldn't have to find out about Santa Claus too soon.

Deep down in my heart I had never forgiven my mother for wanting to give Billy away. I had been on my father's side of that argument. But now I understood how Mum, who loved her children as fiercely as a tiger, could actually consider giving one of us up. If Billy had lots of milk and a warm cot and parents who didn't fight all the time, he probably wouldn't cry at all. Poor baby.

And poor Mum too.

Just before I fell asleep I remembered something else. There had been no empty cocoa cup on the kitchen table that morning.

"For sure there is no Santa Claus, Lucy," I whispered, choking back a sob, my tears spilling on her black celluloid hair. "And I don't care! But oh, how I missed our Christmas tree!"

10
Hiding from the bailiff

1933 got off to a noisy start at midnight with everyone in the neighbourhood standing knee-deep in the snow, blowing horns and whistles, banging pots and pans together and hollering "Happy New Year!" to one another. 1932 had been such a bad year we were all glad to see the last of it.

The celebrating was fun while it lasted, but it was over in no time and there was nothing left to do but go back to bed again.

On New Year's Day two lovely things happened that almost made up for Christmas. First, the postman brought Aunt Aggie's chicken. (*Merry Xmas! Better late than never*, read the soggy note tied to the chicken's leg.) And then Dave and Mary Atlas arrived all the way from Saskatoon, Saskatchewan. They were staying downtown at the "King Eddie" and they took a taxicab right to our door. Imagine!

They had "neither chick nor child" themselves, so they made a big fuss over us kids. Mary especially loved our Arthur. She would!

Dave was a barrel of fun. He had been Mum's beau when they were young. So he liked to tease us by saying that if Mum had married him he'd be our father instead of Dad.

As soon as they left that night, with lots of kissing and hugging at the door, Dad went straight down to the cellar. So I followed him. There was something I wanted to know.

"Dad . . ."

He glanced up and I noticed that his eyes were as blue as Billy's.

"Is that true what Dave said?"

"Is what true?"

"That if Mum had married him he'd be our father?"

"No," he answered shortly. "He was only joshing. If you weren't my children you wouldn't be here at all."

Standing on tiptoe, I planted a peck on his sharp-boned cheek. "I'm glad, Dad," I said.

He looked at me sort of surprised. "Get away with you," he said gently. Then he started sifting ashes.

A few days later it was washday, which meant it was Monday. Mum never washed any other day. Sometimes, if she wasn't feeling well, I'd say, "Why don't you wash tomorrow, Mum?" But she'd say no, the wash had to be done on Monday—and the ironing had to be done on Tuesday. It was the same with all her work. The floors had to be scrubbed on Friday and she had to bake on Saturday, just as religiously as we had to go to church on Sunday. That's the way she was.

Mum was tired right out from scrubbing on the washboard all morning long, then lugging the heavy basket up the cellar stairs to hang the clothes on the backyard line. She wasn't a strong woman, my mum. She'd had rheumatic fever when she was a little girl and it left her with a weak heart. So scrubbing on the board for seven people nearly wore her to a frazzle.

About twice a year she managed to get the use of an electric

washing machine. She'd order it "on trial" from Eaton's for thirty days and two dollars deposit. Then when the thirty days were up she'd write Eaton's a letter saying she didn't like the machine and would they please send their horse and wagon out to pick it up. The driver and his helper would lug the heavy appliance up from the cellar, load it on the delivery wagon, and then politely give Mum her money back. Everybody on "pogey" did that. They'd wash everything in sight for a whole month and then swear by all that's good and holy that they weren't satisfied with the washing machine. Of course Eaton's knew what they were up to. But what could they do? Timothy Eaton had promised "Goods satisfactory or money refunded."

On this particular washday Mum didn't have a machine, so she was tired and crabby. I was the only one home for dinner that day. Willa took her lunch to high school, so she was gone all day, and Arthur didn't come home because he got a free meal in the school basement. Every day it was served up to all the poor kids. Except me. I had been expelled from the free meal program.

Right after my last free meal I had been sitting on the school steps telling Audrey all about it—how the chicken soup had no chicken in it, and the sandwiches had no butter on them, and the blancmange tasted like wallpaper paste. (Actually I was just being a smart aleck. I had really enjoyed the whole dinner.) Suddenly a big hand reached down and grabbed me by the shoulder. Unbeknownst to me, Mrs. Rice, the school principal, had been standing behind us on the top step and had heard every word I said. She was a big, strong, strict woman (one of the few women principals in York County) and she dragged me down the hall to her office just like a rag doll. The vice-principal leaped to attention as we entered. For a minute I thought he was going to salute.

"Mr. Lord," boomed Old-Lady-Rice-Pudding in a voice that sounded like thunder, "what do you think of an ungrateful girl who was distinctly heard to criticize the free meal program for the poor?"

I could feel both pairs of righteous eyes boring down on me. My legs had begun to wobble, so I grabbed the desk for support.

"I think said girl should be expelled from said program," said Mr. Lord.

"I wholeheartedly agree. I shall write a letter at once to her parents."

When the stone-faced principal handed me a long white envelope, licked and sealed and addressed to both my parents, I knew for sure I was "said girl."

"Beatrice"—now her voice was like a preacher's at a funeral—"deliver this envelope to your mother and father with the seal unbroken and return it to me tomorrow morning bearing both their signatures."

The plan being born in my mind died with her last words. I had pictured myself happily ripping the letter into shreds and letting it flutter like confetti out onto Kingston Road. Then all I would have to do was go without dinner for the rest of the year and nobody would be the wiser.

Mum's dark-winged eyebrows knitted together as she read it, and her forehead creased in a frown. "Oh, pshaw, Bea," she said worriedly, "you need that good meal to put some meat on your bones."

"No, I don't, Mum. Honest. And anyway I still get the free

milk at recess. The school nurse says I have to have it until I'm only nineteen pounds underweight instead of twenty."

"Well, just the same, you could really do with that dinner. What did Mrs. Rice hear you say?"

"I was just telling Audrey that the blancmange tasted like wallpaper paste. And it did, Mum. It wasn't nice and creamy like yours."

I knew she hated to do it, but after supper she showed the letter to Dad. The colour drained from his face as he read. Without a word he took me by the scruff of my neck and dragged me up the stairs. Reaching for the razor-strop off the bathroom door, he ordered me to pull my bloomers down. I screamed bloody murder before even one blow had landed on my bare behind.

Up the stairs, her cheeks flaming, raced my little mother. Grabbing the strop out of Dad's hand in midair, she shrieked at him, "Leave her alone! It's a free country, you know! Bea's got a right to her opinion!"

I never knew that before! It was my first lesson in democracy. And it must have made some sense to Dad too, because he hung the strop back up and never so much as mentioned the incident again.

As it turned out, Mrs. Rice had done me a big favour. My mother's never-to-be-forgotten words were to ring in my heart for the rest of my life. And ever after that, when I had a fight with Willa or Arthur, I always got the last word by screaming at the top of my lungs, "It's a free country, you know! I've got a right to my opinion!" I nearly drove them crazy.

So that's how come I was the only one home at noon that day. The second I set foot on the back porch, the door flew open and Mum's hand shot out and yanked me inside.

"What's the matter, Mum?" I asked anxiously as she locked the door behind me.

"It's Ratman. He's across the road."

The bailiff's dreaded name made cold duck-bumps pop out all over my skinny body. He had been hounding us unmercifully ever since we'd come to Birchcliff. Three times in the past year he had tried to serve us with eviction papers, and three times we had foiled him by pretending we were out.

Oh, how I hated that man! I used to pray he would drop dead on the sidewalk so we wouldn't have to worry any more about being put out on the street with our furniture. Of course, it never occurred to me that he was only doing his job, and that if he didn't do it somebody else would.

Running to the front window, I peered fearfully through the frayed, starched curtains. He was crossing the street and was near enough for me to see his beady little eyes and rat-like nose.

"Here he comes, Mum!"

Quick as a wink she herded Jakey and me, with Billy in her arms, up the stairs to her bedroom. "Let's pretend we're playing hide-and-seek and Mr. Ratman is 'it,'" she said, trying to make a game of it for Jakey's sake.

But even the little three-year-old wasn't fooled. He wriggled under the bed with me, his eyes as big and black as agates. I held him tight and felt his heart pounding wildly like my own. Billy started to fuss. Then he gave a loud suck as Mum stuffed the dummy in. She jiggled him on the edge of the bed. I could see the curve of her calves under the skimpy counterpane. She had nice legs, my Mum.

The first loud bang on the door scared the daylights out of us. Jakey's little body jerked convulsively and his eyes nearly popped out of his head. I squeezed him tighter, my heart flopping painfully. Billy tried to cry and Mum jiggled faster, making the bedsprings squeak overhead.

The hammering went on and on. *Bang! Bang! Bang! Thump! Thump! Thump!* Then a loud crack that sounded like a kick. Boy, he was stubborn, that Ratman. I thought he'd never give up. But at long last we heard his footsteps creaking down the wooden steps.

"Be still a while longer," Mum said quietly. "He might be back."

We stayed stock-still. Jakey was as good as gold and didn't make a peep.

At last Mum stood up and the bedsprings rose above us. "He's gone," she said, loosening her hold on the dummy. The second the plug was out Billy let loose with a howl that could probably be heard all the way up to Audrey's.

As soon as Dad came in the door she started in on him. "I'm sick and tired of hiding from the bailiff and scaring the living daylights out of these children," she fumed bitterly. "And for two cents I'd go out and get a job myself."

That made Dad boil, because in those days a man would have to be a cripple in a wheelchair before he'd let his wife go out to work. So what followed was their biggest fight ever.

Talk about scared! Jakey dove under the table, Arthur made a beeline down the cellar, and Willa high-tailed it out the back door without her coat again. I just clung to the back of a chair and shook.

11
Our brand new house

Two weeks later the bailiff caught us red-handed. Another big fight was in full swing when there came a loud banging on the door. With all that racket going on, there was no use pretending we were out.

Dad flung the door open angrily, and there stood Ratman on the porch. His face was long and sad like a hound dog's. Close up he didn't look like a rat at all.

"I'm sorry, sir," he said, tipping his hat, "but you have two weeks to get out." He handed Dad an official looking paper, tipped his hat again, and left. Hearing him say he was sorry took me by surprise.

The next day Mum and Dad started house-hunting again. One good thing, there were lots of empty houses to choose from. People were always on the move for one reason or another. The few that owned their own homes lost them because they couldn't pay the mortgage. And the rest of us got put out on the street because we couldn't pay the rent.

My biggest worry was that we might have to move to the wrong side of the tracks. Or even worse, downtown to Cabbagetown. Mum said that's where the real down-andouters ended up. The ones who had lost their pride.

Dad always house-hunted in those grubby old districts. But he might just as well have saved his energy because Mum wouldn't even look at the places he found. She said children had to be raised in a good neighbourhood. She said environment was important. Dad said environment was hogwash. He said if parents were strict enough and set a good example their kids would turn out right as rain no matter where they were brought up.

Sure enough, home he came with a latchkey from a house on the wrong side of the tracks. I nearly had a fit. What would Audrey say? But before I had time to get upset about it Mum came home with a latchkey from a house on the right side. The only trouble was the rent for Mum's house was six dollars a month. The rent for Dad's was only four.

"Two dollars a month will buy a lot of bread," Dad said glumly.

I had to admit he was right. There was a store on Kingston Road that sold leftover Saturday bread on Monday mornings for five cents a loaf. Even I could figure out how much bread two dollars would buy, if I put my mind to it.

But Mum wouldn't budge. She said her house was in a respectable neighbourhood, far from the railroad tracks and sooty trains and hobos. She said it would be well worth the extra money, and she quoted the Bible to back her up. "Man cannot live by bread alone," she said.

Dad never argued with the Bible.

But right or wrong side of town, the houses we moved to always seemed to have one thing in common. They were full of dirt and bedbugs. People were terrible in those days for

74

leaving their dirt behind them. Dad said it was their way of getting back at the all-powerful landlord. But Mum said it showed a lack of pride and breeding. "No one will ever say that Frances Cole Thomson was brought up in a pigsty," she'd breathlessly declare as she wore her fingers to the bone scouring the house we were leaving. Then she'd turn around and do the same thing to the one we were moving into.

Bedbugs were by far the worst problem. The pesky little devils with their nut-brown shells were almost impossible to kill. Poor Mum would drive herself nearly crazy until the last one was squashed. I remember one time when the filthy vermin (as Mum called them) got into the baby's cot and bit his bottom to pieces. Dad had to take his cot out in the backyard and burn the mattress and pour boiling water down the hollow iron posts before he finally got rid of them. But it was a losing battle just the same. No sooner had you got rid of yours than you caught a new batch from your neighbour. Most people just learned to live with them, like flies in summertime.

But on this particular move we had a marvellous stroke of luck. Right in the middle of the battle of the latchkeys, Willa came home and casually mentioned that there was a brand new house for rent on Cornflower Street. Cornflower Street was just a block south of Lilac, so Mum dragged Dad down to see it, with him complaining all the way. And they got it. For six dollars a month. A brand new house!

There wasn't a speck of dirt or a bedbug to be seen. All Mum had to do was sweep up some nice-smelling wood shavings and scrape up a blob of snow-white plaster off the hardwood floor. Our old furniture never looked so beautiful and never gleamed so lemon-oil bright as it did in its own reflection on those oaken hardwood floors.

Mum was practically beside herself with joy. She went about whistling like a robin in a loaded cherry tree. That's what she did when she was happy. She whistled while she worked, and it was music to our ears.

In our wildest dreams we'd never hoped to live in such a house. It had a big bay window and a wide hardwood staircase with a smooth oak banister that was just perfect for sliding down when nobody was looking.

And it had storm windows to keep out the cold, and a fenced-in yard for Jakey and Billy. And it even had an upstairs verandah, right on top of the downstairs one. We could hardly wait for summertime to take the kitchen chairs out to sit on it.

The cellar had closed-in steps you couldn't fall through, and a shiny new furnace and a real cement floor. Just perfect for playing Bill and Bob in. The cellar floor in the old house had been dank, dark, hard-packed clay.

And the bathroom! The fixtures were all gleaming white and the water closet was right behind the toilet, instead of overhead with a chain hanging down. You could flush it with just a flick of your finger. And best of all, hot water came right out of the tap. So Dad wouldn't have to lug boilerfuls of scalding water up two flights of stairs any more

It would take years, I thought, to get used to all the luxuries in the new house. But I didn't need to worry my head about that. Not even one year went by before the bailiff was back at our door.

12
A visit with Grampa

"'Tis cauld agine!" cried Mum, as she jumped back inside the door after shaking out her cedar mop.

"Who used to say that, Mum?" asked Willa. We were always curious about those funny old sayings from long ago.

"Old Mr. Levis," laughed Mum. "He used to come to our back door twice a week with the groceries, and all winter long he'd greet my mother with the exact same words. 'Tis cauld agine, Mrs. Cole!"

"What does it mean, Mum?" asked Arthur.

"It just means it's cold again," explained Mum.

The cold weather showed no sign of letting up. It was the coldest March we could remember.

On Saturday we kids stayed in all day. Jakey and I spent most of the time in the cellar playing Bill and Bob. After supper he wanted to play some more, but I was tired of it so I got the photograph album out to distract him.

"Who's that, Bea-Bea?" He pointed with a chubby finger at a faded snapshot of two young women, one small and neat and pretty, the other fat and sloppy and homely as a hedge fence.

Pointing to the pretty one, I said, "That's Mum when she was young. Who's that with you, Mum?"

She leaned on the broom handle and glanced over my shoulder. "Oh, that's my old chum, Beulah Haggett. She was a barrel of fun and a sight for sore eyes. She came to a bad end, Beulah did. But it wasn't her fault, poor thing, it was the way she was brought up. Puppa said old man Haggett was as crooked as a dog's hind leg, and Mumma said he was so mean he'd steal the pennies off a dead man's eyes. Their house was as filthy as a pigsty too, and they had so many children they had to eat in relays. I remember one time I stayed for supper and Beulah and I had to wait for the second sitting. Well, dashed if her mother didn't dish up the stew on the same plates the others had just eaten off. I tell you, it nearly made me gag."

Jakey and I squealed with laughter at the story and Willa wiggled her nose and said "Eww!"

Mum continued reminiscing. "They had the most cunning baby in their family. His name was Herbie and that little urchin wouldn't drink anything but tea. Well, one day Beulah put milk in his bottle by mistake and the young whelp took one gulp and threw the bottle across the floor, bellyragging at the top of his lungs, 'Who put milk in my tea-baw?' Tea! Imagine! No wonder the little imp's milk teeth all came in the colour of mud."

"What's that thing on your arm, Mum?" Jakey was pointing to a black band on her coat sleeve in the picture.

"That's a mourning band," she answered quietly, "for my mother when she died. I wore it for a whole year. People don't do that so much any more."

She took the album in her hands and turned the page. Softly her chapped red fingers caressed the photo of a woman with sunken cheeks and sad eyes and dark hair drawn back in a bun. "There's Mumma," she murmured. Then she went back to her work.

The next morning, Sunday, at the breakfast table Mum said, "I have to see Puppa today."

"You picked a fine day for it," grumbled Dad. "It must be ten below out there." He had just come back in from scraping off the porch steps with the coal shovel.

But Mum's mind was made up, so off we set right after our noonday meal, Mum and Dad, Jakey, Billy and me. Arthur and Willa had to stay home because they weren't all better yet from having their tonsils out on the kitchen table.

That had happened the week before. Jakey and I had been making a snowman in the yard and I had to go to the bathroom. When I started in the back door Mum blocked my way and said in a nervous voice, "You can't come in until I call you." I said, "But I have to go bad, Mum," and she said, "Well, you'll just have to hold it," and shut the door in my face.

By the time she called us in I could hardly walk and I had a terrible pain in my stomach.

Coming inside from the fresh air, I noticed a funny mediciney smell in the kitchen. There were red drops on the linoleum around the table legs.

I ran upstairs to the bathroom and when I came out, my stomach easing with relief, I saw Willa and Arthur in their beds—and it wasn't even suppertime. They were both white as ghosts. Willa was asleep with her mouth open. Brown stuff dribbled from the corners. Arthur was crying pitifully.

He had a stained bib around his neck.

Hurrying downstairs, I asked anxiously, "What's the matter with Willa and Arthur, Mum?"

"Dr. Hopkins took their tonsils out," she said, scrubbing the red spots off the linoleum. "Take Jakey down the cellar to play so there won't be any noise. They need their rest."

"Will I have to have my tonsils out too, Mum?"

"Not right now anyway, Booky. Away you go like a good girl while I get the supper on."

So that's how come there were only five of us struggling down Kingston Road against the cold west wind on that Sunday afternoon.

At the city limits we clambered up the high steps of the red, wooden streetcar and hurried down to the stove beside the conductor's box. Huddling around it, we held out frost-bitten fingers to catch its rosy glow.

Two and a half hours later we disembarked in Swansea. Then came the long, cold walk down Windermere Avenue to the cement-block house that Grampa had built.

"Well, this is a surprise!" he beamed, opening the door wide. "I didn't expect anybody on a day like this."

You could tell he was happy to see us, but Evie and Joey, his two youngest children, gave us dark, baleful looks. Not much wonder, because the minute Mum set eyes on them she ordered them upstairs to wash themselves. She acted more like their mother than their sister, which wasn't surprising because they weren't much older than Willa and Arthur.

Grampa always got a big kick out of Jakey. (I guess that's because Jakey was a Cole. The rest of us kids were dyed-in-the-wool Thomson.) He ruffled Jakey's curls and laughed out loud when the little fellow cried, "Have a drink, Grampa, so the drips will fall off your moustache."

Obligingly Grampa took a swig from a murky glass and waggled his head to make the water fly. Squealing with delight, Jakey danced around catching the silver droplets in midair.

This attention to my little brother never made me jealous because Grampa and I, ever since I could remember, had had an understanding. He said we were kindred spirits.

Mum set about the work she had come to do, sweeping and baking and putting up a nice hot supper. Dad walked the baby around the big old house. Billy knew he was in a strange place and his wide blue eyes stared curiously over Dad's shoulder, taking everything in.

Evie was mad because Willa hadn't come. She couldn't be bothered with me. She was a pretty girl with large violet eyes and naturally curly chestnut hair.

"You look more like Mumma every day, Evie," Mum said. "You're pretty as a picture."

The compliment cheered Evie right up and she began to play the Victrola. Lifting the square walnut lid, she searched in the steel cup for a sharp needle. Then she put a record on and cranked the handle on the side of the big box, and out of the horn-shaped speaker came a man's voice singing through his nose. Inside the lid was a picture of a little dog cocking its head as if the singing hurt its ears. When the music slowed down, Evie cranked it up again. She did that all afternoon.

Joey had put on his cap and windbreaker and gone out the minute we arrived. He usually played with Arthur.

Jakey had settled himself on the davenport with the stereoscope. The eyepiece fit snugly around the eyes, blocking out the light like blinders on a horse. A double picture fitted into a slot at the end of a long stick. You slid the picture up and down the stick until it came into focus. Then Niagara Falls and the Rocky Mountains and the animals at Riverdale Zoo stood out large as life in three dimensions.

While everybody was busy doing all these things, I just followed Grampa around. When he was finished with his chores, he sat down beside the kitchen stove and lit his corncob pipe.

"Can I comb your hair, Grampa?" I asked, patting the thick grey bristles.

"If you like, Be-*a*-trice." He was the only person who pronounced my name that way. I liked it from him, but if anybody else had said it I would have had a conniption fit.

The minute I started fussing with his hair he closed his eyes and sucked on his pipe, making a soft, contented *putt-putt* sound. While I combed, I talked a blue streak, telling him everything that came into my head. He answered with a quiet murmur to let me know he was listening.

"It's time you had a trim, Grampa," I said.

"Mmm," he said without opening his eyes.

The scissors hung on a nail on the side of the cupboard. Mum handed them to me without a word.

I chattered and clipped, the steel-grey hair crunching between the blades and falling, like bits of silver wire, onto his stooped plaid shoulders.

"Hold still now, Grampa," I ordered, "while I trim the tea off your moustache." He pursed his lips, trying not to smile, the pipe clenched between his teeth.

It was then I noticed the deep-cut lines on either side of his mouth. I stopped trimming and looked closer at his weather-beaten face. His forehead was heavily furrowed, like a fresh-ploughed field, and fine lines zig-zagged all over his high olive cheekbones.

The faded brown eyes flickered open. He took the corncob from his mouth. "Are you done already, Be-*a*-trice?"

"No, Grampa, but I'm worried about something."

"What might that be?"

"Are you old, Grampa?"

"Old beside you, I reckon."

"Was Grandma old when she died?"

"No. She never lived to be old."

"Don't die Grampa!" The words burst out in a tortured sob and I flung my arms around his neck.

I heard Mum gasp, then I felt my grandfather's strong arms around me. "Don't you worry none about that, Be-*a*-trice," he said, patting my back. "When I go, I won't go far. I'll just set myself down and light my pipe and wait outside the gates. I won't go in without you."

"Really, Grampa? You're not just saying that."

"Cross my heart and spit," he said.

And he did. He crossed his heart, then lifted the iron stove lid and spat a long sizzling stream into the crackling fire. That made me laugh like anything. He only lived three more years after that, but his love for me has lasted all my life.

We left for home right after supper. The temperature had dropped another five degrees.

"It's not a fit night for man nor beast," grumbled Dad.

It was pure torture leaving the cosy streetcar at the city limits. Poor little Jakey had gone fast asleep beside the stove.

What a shock he got to find himself plunked on his feet on the sidewalk in the freezing cold.

Chill winds gusted across the golf links. Dad strode ahead, acting as a windbreak, with Billy tucked deep inside his greatcoat. I staggered after him, clinging to his coattails. Mum brought up the rear, half dragging and half carrying my tearful little brother.

The low-burning fire in the shiny furnace of the new house never felt so good and never welcomed us so warmly as it did on that below zero night when we came home from Grampa's.

13
The Annex

April came at last, but spring didn't come with it. There was still lots of snow on the ground. My galoshes were all worn out so I had stopped wearing them. My shoes were holey and leaked like sieves. Dad had half-soled them twice already but there was no use doing it again because the toes were scuffed out and my brown ribbed stockings showed through.

One morning I came home from Sunday School and went in the back way so as not to make tracks on the hardwood. A big snowdrift leaned against the porch. Mum had a bowl of red jelly setting in it. It looked pretty nested in the white snow. I tested it with my finger. Mmm, raspberry. It wasn't quite set. I licked my finger and went in.

Mum was leaning over the kitchen table, her chin cupped in her hands, reading Saturday's newspaper. Every day the Armstrongs, who lived next door to the new house, gave us yesterday's copy of the *Evening Telegram*. Then on Sundays they gave us the Saturday *Star Weekly*.

Mum read the paper from front to back. Dad didn't bother with it except to read "Uncle Wiggley" to Jakey. He said the news made him sick. Arthur and I always fought over the comics, especially the coloured ones in the *Star Weekly*. His favourite was "The Katzenjammer Kids." Mine was "Bringing Up Father" (I loved how Maggie bounced that rolling pin off old Jiggs's head). Willa liked "Ella Cinders" and "Tillie the Toiler," but she wouldn't fight over it. She'd just wait her turn.

I showed Mum my shoes and she exclaimed, "My stars, Bea, where are your galoshes?"

"They're all wore out, Mum," I said.

"Well, you can't go to school like that. You'd better stay home tomorrow and we'll take a run downtown. Monday is Opportunity Day at Eaton's."

My heart skipped at the prospect. There was nothing in the world I'd rather do than go downtown with my mother. And on a school day too!

Dad stayed home to mind the little ones. It made a nice change for him, not having to go out looking for work.

We walked to the city limits as usual, but this time we didn't mind because spring was in the air.

"We'll go the long way round and drop in on Susan," Mum said, a lilt in her voice. It did her a world of good to get out of the house.

My Aunt Susan was a real live store lady. The name of her store was The Uptown Nuthouse. We kids just loved making jokes about visiting the nuthouse.

When Aunt Susan first opened her store, right in the middle of the Depression, everybody said she'd never make a go of it. "What does a woman know about running a business anyway?" they said, and, "Who's going to waste money on confections in these hard times?" But Aunt Susan just ignored them, and her nut and candy business flourished.

She roasted the nuts herself in a big pot of boiling oil right in the little shop window for everyone to see. And smell! Winter and summer the shop door stood wide open and the tantalizing aroma of roasting cashews drifted deliciously all over the four corners of Toronto's main intersection. Practically everybody who stepped off the streetcars at Yonge and Bloor, no matter what direction they were going, automatically followed their noses into my Aunt Susan's store.

Sometimes Aunt Milly worked there too. She was Mum's fourth-to-the-youngest sister. We could see her now, handing out free samples on the sidewalk. "Step right up, folks. Get 'em while they're hot," she called out gaily. "Fresh roasted cashews, ready or not!"

People who had no money accepted the little treat gratefully and hurried on by. But those who had a nickel to their name headed straight into Aunt Susan's store.

Aunt Milly saw us coming. "Well, it's my Bea!" she said, and I basked in the warmth of her smile. She always spoke of people that she loved as if they were her private property. It was wonderful belonging to Aunt Milly.

She looked so cute and girlish, with her bright auburn ringlets peeking out under the edges of her jaunty red toque, that no one would ever guess she was the mother of three children. And to hear her carefree laughter, no one would ever know that her husband was out of work too, just like Dad.

"What brings you downtown, Franny?" she asked, holding out the steaming scoop for me to help myself.

"Bea needs new shoes in the worst way," Mum said.

"Well, and who could deserve them more?" beamed my loving aunt.

"How have you been, Milly? You look kind of peaked."

"Why, I'm in the pink, Fran, just in the pink."

"Oh, pshaw, Milly," Mum clucked. "You always say that no matter what."

That's the way she was, Aunt Milly, always looking on the bright side.

"C'mon, Bea." She dug in her pocket and came up with a rusty old serving spoon. "You can help me dish out the samples while your mother visits Susan."

Oh, what fun it was! I felt like Lady Bountiful, spooning out the scrumptious cashew nuts and popping them into my mouth any time I liked. Then and there I decided to be a store lady when I grew up, just like Aunt Susan.

I could see Mum talking to her in the shop window. She kept right on working while she chatted, heaving a big batch of shiny redskins out of the boiling oil and resting the wire basket on a peg at the back of the cooker. She shook the basket once or twice and the golden oil streamed back into the black iron pot ready for the next batch. With her free hand she waved at me through the steamy window.

About ten minutes later Mum came scurrying out the open door with a box of hot nuts in one hand and our overdue transfers in the other. "Hurry, Bea," she called on the run, "or our transfers won't be worth a wooden nickel." I dropped the spoon clattering into the scoop and scampered after her to the streetcar stop at the corner.

"Love you!" Aunt Milly called after us. She was one of those rare people who could holler that right out loud and not care who heard it. I threw her back a kiss.

According to the time punched on our transfers we were fifteen minutes late, and stopovers were strictly forbidden by the Toronto Transit Commission.

My Uncle William worked for the T.T.C. Sometimes he was the conductor on the Yonge Street line and if we were lucky enough to get on his car we didn't have a thing to worry about. But if the conductor was a stranger we could be in trouble. Once we got caught red-handed with late transfers and got put right off the streetcar in disgrace. But this time we boarded with a crowd and the conductor was too busy to notice so we got away scot-free.

We settled ourselves on the circular seat at the back and Mum handed me the box of nuts. All the way down Yonge Street we munched and chattered and gazed out the mud-streaked windows. And whenever the streetcar jerked to a stop I went for a free slide around the shiny crescent seat.

Yonge Street hummed and sparkled in the early spring sunshine. Cars honked and horses whinnied. Dogs barked, bicycle bells jangled and the popcorn man's whistle blew a long thin note.

I read all the signboards as we passed. "Smoke Sweet Caporal," "Buy British Consul" and "Drink Coca-Cola." Boy, how I'd love to drink Coca-Cola. I had no idea what it tasted like, but the beautiful girl on the billboard said, "It's delicious!"

"I love Yonge Street, don't you, Mum?"

"Yes," she said, chewing a Brazil nut with her front teeth because the back ones had been bothering her lately. "And did you know, Bea, that it's the longest street in the world?"

"I didn't know that, Mum!"

"Well, you learn something every day."

Helen Hayes and Clark Gable were in a talkie at Loew's Theatre. I hadn't seen a talking picture yet, but Mum said when she had enough money she'd take me.

"Ka-ween Street!" bellowed the conductor. "Eaton's! Simpson's! Have your fares ready. This way out!" He pulled a lever by the fare box and the double doors clunked open. We jostled our way to the sidewalk.

Woolworth's Five-And-Ten-Cent Store stood on the corner of Queen and Yonge. And huddled in the swinging doorway was Old Blind Bill (that's what the sign said that hung around his neck).

"I'm sorry, Bill," Mum murmured as we passed.

"I didn't know you knew Blind Bill, Mum," I said.

"Shush, Bea," she said. "I only know him to see."

Toronto's two biggest department stores faced each other across Queen Street: the T. Eaton Company on the north and the Robert Simpson Company on the south. A steady stream of shoppers dodged each other to get to the opposite side. But Mum and I never went to Simpson's because Mum was a dyed-in-the-wool Eatonian.

We squeezed into the revolving doors together and let ourselves be swept inside. Then we stopped at the foot of Timothy Eaton's statue to wait for Aunt Hester, Uncle William's wife.

It was sort of a custom to meet at the store-founder's monument. And while you waited you gave his big bronze toe a rub for good luck. Mum said that was silly superstition, but she gave the shiny spot a quick little pat just in case.

"I remember the day he was buried," she mused, looking up into the bearded bronze face. "I was just a little bit of a thing and Puppa put me up on his shoulders so I could see. I can still feel the hush that fell over the crowd as the hearse went by. And following it came hundreds of carriages, all draped in black."

I loved to hear stories of the olden days. But before Mum had a chance to say any more we saw Aunt Hester bouncing towards us between the counters, her curls bobbing like little gold springs around her face.

Mum was a bit jealous of Aunt Hester. "She's got neither chick nor child and more money than she knows what to do with," she sighed enviously.

I knew this was true because I heard Mum tell Dad once that Uncle William brought home sixteen dollars every single week.

"Hello there, Tinker!" cried Aunt Hester breathlessly. She always called me Tinker.

The two of them had a little chat, then we made our way down the stairs and through the underground tunnel to the Annex. The tunnel ran under Albert Street. It always smelled of paint and turpentine. It was kind of a nice smell.

We stopped to watch a man demonstrate some cleaning fluid. First he smeared black grease on a patch of carpet. Then he removed it, clean as a whistle, with his magic cleaner. Aunt Hester got carried away and bought a large bottle for fifty cents.

The Annex was Eaton's bargain store. Its basement was a dank, smelly place with low-hanging pipes and uneven, littered wood floors. Mum hated the Annex. She said if Dad ever got working steady again it wouldn't see her for dust.

The basement was crowded, as usual, with crabby, frazzled mothers and whiny, dirty-nosed kids. Mountains of dry goods were piled up on big square tables. Mum stopped at every table to pick things over. Aunt Hester bought Uncle William a set of long drawers for ninety-nine cents and two pairs of socks for a quarter.

"If I had your money, Hester," Mum said, watching her sister-in-law peel off a two-dollar bill from a fat wad, "I wouldn't come near this place. I'd stick to the Main Store where everything is first class. Just look at this stuff, all soiled and messy." She flicked at the second-class goods disdainfully.

"There's not a thing wrong with these socks," replied Aunt Hester indignantly. "And my Thor will take out the spots in these drawers in the very first wash."

Mum winced at the mention of the Thor. I thought how dumb it was that Aunt Hester, with neither chick nor child, should own a washing machine while Mum, with all us kids, had to scrub on the washboard.

Mum was holding up a corselet, eyeing it critically. The flesh-coloured garment had two huge scoops in the front. I looked down at my flat chest and couldn't even imagine ever fitting into such a thing.

By this time my legs were killing me, so I hung onto the table edge and let them go all limp. It felt good. At last they got sick of underwear and we headed for the shoe department.

The minute I laid eyes on them I knew I had to have them. They were black patent leather with white patent bows and they were absolutely gorgeous. I could see myself in Sunday School swinging my feet out for Mr. Henderson, the Superintendent, to see.

Mum was paying a lot of attention to a pair of sturdy brown oxfords, so I grabbed the patents and shoved them under her nose.

"Please, Mum, can I have these?" I begged. "I promise I won't run in them, and I'll take them off after four every day."

"Oh, pshaw, Bea." She was smiling so I knew I had a chance. "You're too much of a scatterbrain to remember not to run. You'd have those flimsy slippers scuffed out in no time."

"No, Mum, I wouldn't! I'm not a scatterbrain!" For the first time I really resented the silly nickname. "I won't run— honest—I'll walk slow and careful all the time."

"Perhaps the young lady would like to try them on," came a man's silky voice from behind. The shoe salesman looked for all the world like the picture of Warner Baxter stuck up on our bedroom wall.

Mum didn't speak quickly enough, and before she knew it, he was down on his knees slipping them on my feet.

In spite of my brown ribbed stockings wrinkling around my ankles, the shoes looked beautiful. I got up and began to strut to show them off. I guess I looked unusually pleased with myself because Mum gave in sooner than I dared to hope.

"How much are they?" she asked Warner Baxter.

"They're a terrific buy at fifty cents," he assured her. "Only last week they were selling for ninety-nine cents and going like hotcakes. This is my last pair, an Opportunity Day special."

"Are you sure they fit, Bea?" Mum said. "They're final clearance so we can't bring them back, you know."

"I'm sure, Mum," I said.

"All right then." She couldn't resist a genuine bargain. And the price tickled her pink. Seeing she was in such a good mood, I begged to wear them home. She said that I could if I

MOTHERS! YOU SHOULD BUY
You'll Find These Values Outstanding

Black Patent

662-633. Black Patent Boudoir Slippers. They have padded soles, low wood heels and dainty poms. Sizes 11, 12, 13, 1, 2 (no half sizes). Per pair..... **79c**

Sport Oxfords

Sturdy Suntan and Brown Leather Sport Oxfords with husky "No Trax" soles and heels. Just the thing for runabout wear because they'll stand lots of hard usage. No half sizes.
662-636. Misses' sizes 11, 12, 13, 1, 2. Per pair..... **1.35**
662-637. Child's sizes 6, 7, 8, 9, 10. Per pair........ **1.10**

Snappy Oxfords

662-582. Just the thing for the modern miss with a flair for style. These Gunmetal Leather Oxfords with the new strap and buckle sport effect are bound to be popular. Have low heels with rubber top lifts. Sizes 11 to 2 (including half sizes).

1.98 Pair

"Jingle Bells"

662-673. Sure to please the kiddies, these Blue Felt, padded-sole Slippers with Red tops and jingling bells. A decided novelty. Sizes 5, 6, 7, 8, 9, 10. Per pair.. **69c**

The "Cavalier"

662-632. Child's Blue Felt "Cavalier" model Slippers, with Red collars and neat pompoms; padded soles. Sizes 5, 6, 7, 8, 9, 10 only. Per pair..... **65c**

Blue Felt

Pretty little Blue Felt Ribbon-Drawn Slippers, with Fawn-colored vamps and padded soles and heels. So cosy! No half sizes.
662-655. Misses' sizes 11, 12, 13, 1, 2. Pair..... **53c**
662-656. Child's sizes 8, 9, 10. Pair........... **49c**

© Eaton's Archives

promised not to scuff them. Warner Baxter wrapped up my old shoes and handed me the package.

From the shoe department we went straight to the Annex lunch counter. It was a stand-up counter with no stools. Aunt Hester treated herself and Mum to a red-hot and a Vernor's and they both shared them with me. First I had a bite of Mum's red-hot, then a bite of Aunt Hester's. I watched a bit worriedly as the level of the sparkling drink crept lower in their glasses. They were chatting and sipping and seeming to pay no attention to me. But they both remembered to save me the last long slurp at the end.

After that we went to the Main Store, just looking. Instead of the elevators, we rode the moving stairs because Mum knew I liked them best. I always got an excited, scary feeling as we curved over the top and the moving stairs disappeared beneath our feet. Arthur told me once about a boy who got sucked in by his shoelaces and ended up a pile of mincemeat. But that couldn't happen to me today because my new shoes were slip-ons.

By the time we were on our way home, my feet were killing me. I knew five minutes after I put them on that my beautiful patent-leather slippers were at least two sizes too small.

"How do your new shoes feel, Bea?" Mum asked as we stepped off the streetcar. She must have read my mind!

"Just fine, Mum." My face turned beet-red with the big fat lie, but she didn't seem to notice.

14
A fair exchange

Willa had the supper on when we got home. Mum had left a note pinned to the kitchen curtain telling her what to do, but Willa didn't really need instructions. Quite often she just ignored the note and did what she liked. Mum didn't mind. She loved surprises.

Dad came in behind us, with Billy on his arm and Jakey trailing after. Arthur wasn't home yet because he had a job with Andy, the baker, after school and on Saturdays. Mum said he could keep the job as long as he didn't fall behind in his school work. She always put education first. She said some people, especially those from the old countries, were more interested in the "almighty dollar" than in their children's futures. "Shove them out to work and rake in the money. That's all they care about!" she said disdainfully. I hoped and prayed Arthur wouldn't fall behind in his school work, because sometimes Andy gave him stale doughnuts as well as his twenty-five cents a week"

"How do you like Bea's new shoes?" Mum asked Willa.

"They're nice," Willa said.

Then I had to prance around and show them off to Dad while Mum went on about what a bargain they were.

At last I escaped to the bathroom. Off came my beautiful patents, and my swollen feet almost yelled out loud. I washed them in cold water even though they didn't need it because Mum had made me take a bath before we went downtown. The pain eased off a little. I dried them gingerly, then slipped into my soft old bedroom slippers and tried not to hobble down the stairs.

Mum noticed instantly. "Where are your new shoes, Bea?"

"I'm trying to keep them nice," I answered piously.

"That's a good girl," she said, obviously pleased.

The rest of the week I suffered the tortures of the damned. True to my promise, I didn't run or scuff. In fact I could hardly walk at all. Back and forth to school I went with tiny, painful steps, just like the poor little Chinese girls with bound-up feet that the missionaries were always telling us about in Sunday School.

On Friday I limped home and crawled up the stairs on all fours. Luckily, Mum was in the cellar. Tears running down my cheeks, I lowered my raw, blistered, swollen feet into the blessed cold water of the bathtub.

But I forgot to lock the door. And there stood Mum.

"For mercy sakes, what's wrong with your feet?" She dropped the clean towels and grabbed my feet in both hands. "Bea!" her voice rose in anger. "Did your new shoes do this?"

Sobbing with pain and shame, I blubbered out the truth.

Both Mum and Dad were mad as hornets. Dad ranted and raved about all the things fifty cents would buy. Mum even listed them: twenty pounds of cane sugar; ten loaves of stale bread; four pounds of creamery butter; oceans of milk and miles of toilet paper.

Willa and Arthur jumped on the bandwagon. "I needed new shoes worse than you!" snapped my long-suffering sister. And she did, too. Only that morning I had seen her cutting out another pair of corrugated insoles.

"Stupid, selfish pig!" hissed Arthur. His boots needed half-soling too.

"You deserve a good thrashing," Dad threatened balefully, and I shuddered at the thought of the strop on the bathroom door.

Tears rolling down my face, I edged my way out of the kitchen. Jakey's big, reproachful eyes followed me from under the table. Even Billy howled at me. I guess he was just hollering from hunger or colic or both, but I felt so guilty I took it personally.

The next day, Saturday, Mum marched me straight back to Eaton's. She was mad all the way and didn't speak once. I hated that worse than a licking. We took the short route and didn't go near Aunt Susan's.

We found Warner Baxter in the shoe department and Mum told him the whole awful story. Dangling my patents at arm's length, his moustache curled up in a sneer, he said coldly, "I'll have to speak to the manager. There's no exchange on 'clearance' you know," and walked away in a huff.

Two red spots appeared on Mum's cheeks. She rubbed her hands together in that nervous way she had and began pacing in circles on her dainty high heels. (She always managed to get beautiful sample shoes for next to nothing because her feet were so tiny.) I couldn't help but notice how pretty she looked with her cheeks all rosy and her eyes flashing like lights on water.

Warner Baxter came back with Rudolph Valentino, of all people! At least that's who the manager looked like to me. He had the same dark eyes and black patent leather hair.

"May I be of service, Miss?"

Miss! Could he mean Mum, the mother of all us kids?

She told the sad tale again in a voice that would melt an iceberg.

"Now, don't you worry your pretty little head." He gave Mum's arm a little squeeze and the red spots on her cheeks grew brighter. "You just leave everything to me." Looking Mum up and down from her dark wavy head to her small dainty feet, he whisked away my shoes.

The mad expression had left her face and she seemed to be holding back a smile.

"I think he likes you, Mum," I ventured.

"Shush, Booky," she said. I knew she wasn't mad any more.

Warner Baxter went by balancing a pyramid of shoe boxes and shot me a withering look. It was all I could do to stop my tongue from sticking out.

Then Rudolph came back carrying a sturdy pair of brown oxfords. "Now, let's see if these fit the young lady," he said, sitting me down and lacing the oxfords on to my injured feet. Oh, how good they felt! Roomy at the toe and absolutely perfect at the heel.

"Up you get and show them off to your charming mother," said oily old Rudolph. Then he added to Mum, "I can scarcely believe you're the mother of this big girl."

"How do they feel, Bea?" asked Mum, ignoring him as best she could.

"Terrific!" It was the latest word in school. Everything was terrific. "Really terrific!"

"Then we'll call it a fair exchange," said Rudolph, leering openly at Mum now. "And if I may be of any further service, you may come to me directly."

Nudging me nervously ahead of her, Mum hurried out of the basement.

"Wasn't he a nice man, Mum?" I chirped happily in my new shoes, knowing she wasn't mad any more. "Let's buy all our shoes from him, Mum, so we won't have to worry if they fit or not. Do you think he looked like Rudolph Valentino, or more like Ramon Navarro?" Ramon Navarro was the latest movie hero Willa had stuck up on our bedroom wall.

"He couldn't hold a candle to either one of them," she answered huffily. "And he's got shifty eyes and B.O. and I don't want to hear another word about it. Now, let's go and have ourselves a treat."

At the far end of the tunnel we stopped in front of a refreshment stand. Mum bought a five-cent paper cupful of "The Drink You Eat With A Spoon" and she asked for two wooden spoons so we could share it. It was a delicious chocolatey-malty concoction, as smooth and cool as ice cream.

After that we did the most amazing thing. We went to Shea's Hippodrome on Bay Street across from the City Hall. There we saw John Boles on the stage singing, "K–K–K–Katie!" and a young red-headed comedian named Red Skelton who put on the funniest act I had ever seen. He pantomimed a lady getting dressed in the morning, wiggling into an imaginary girdle and struggling to hook up a brassiere behind his back. Without uttering a word he had the whole theatre in stitches.

It was a wonderful show and I clapped until my hands hurt. But what followed was more wonderful by far. I saw my first talking picture. It was called "Pack Up Your Troubles," starring Stan Laurel and Oliver Hardy. It was so funny I nearly wet my bloomers. I had seen Laurel and Hardy once before in a silent picture, but oh, they were a million times funnier in the talkies. I became a movie fan for life.

I couldn't get over the talkies. Twice Willa had taken me to the Kingswood in Birchcliff to see silents. But they didn't compare to the talkies. What joy it was just to sit there and listen and not have to read the lines. I could never read them fast enough and Willa said I spoiled the whole show by begging her to read out loud.

On our way home that day everything went right. The sun was shining, my feet were purring, and we got on Uncle William's streetcar. We sat opposite him on the wooden slat seat and he smiled and winked at me. I glanced around to see if anybody had noticed. I was awfully proud of him sitting up there importantly in the conductor's box.

"How are you and Jim getting along, Franny?" he asked between stops.

"Oh, I can't complain, William."

She was in a good mood!

When we got up to leave Uncle William put his hand over the glass fare box to let Mum know she didn't have to pay. Then he gave us each a transfer, and since we walked from the city limits, we got all the way home for free.

Strolling up Kingston Road in the balmy spring air, we talked a blue streak. I asked Mum a million questions about the movie and she answered every one. That's the way she was, my mum. She never held a grudge.

15
My dad, the hero

The first Sunday in May was as warm as summer. We were still living in the new house. Mr. Ratman had been by a few times but he hadn't put us out yet. He just gave Dad fair warning that the rent was overdue.

Mum was doing a lot of nagging lately, and Dad had gone all quiet, like the air before a storm. And then he had a stroke of luck. He got two weeks work painting fences. It was the first wage he had earned in a dog's age, but not the first work he had done. He had put in lots of back-breaking hours doing pogey jobs to earn our relief voucher, hard jobs like breaking up sidewalks and shovelling snow off roofs and cleaning streets and sewers. He always felt better about taking the relief voucher when he had worked for it.

When he got paid for painting the fences he gave Willa and Arthur and me two big copper pennies. We liked the big coins best because they looked like more than the little one-cent pieces.

We knew, without being told, that one was for Sunday School and one was for anything we liked. I could hardly wait to drop mine in the collection plate. I hoped Mr. Henderson would notice the noise it made as much as he noticed the silence that fell when my hand was empty.

I really enjoyed Sunday School that day. We sang some nice hymns. My favourite was "Black and yellow, red and white, they are precious in his sight . . ."

Sometimes I wished I had a black or yellow or red friend. I didn't know anybody from another country. I had seldom even seen a person of a different colour. But I met a Catholic girl once. Her name was Ursula. She went to a strange school called "Separate." Only she was white just like me.

After the hymn singing Mrs. Wardell acted out the story where Jesus tells his disciples to let the children come unto him and forbid them not. She played the part of Jesus and all us kids were the children. Then we finished with the prayer Jesus made up himself, the one that started out "Our father, witchart in heaven, hollow be thy name" and ended up "forever and ever alllmen."

When we got home we changed into our old clothes and Dad suggested we go for a walk while Billy was sleeping so Mum could make the supper in peace. So off we went up Warden Avenue towards Prob's Bush. Jakey rode on Dad's shoulders and Willa walked beside them. Arthur and I ran on ahead.

The sun was as warm as toast so we took off our Star Box sweaters that Mum had made us wear so we wouldn't catch a spring cold. Arthur tied his around his neck by the arms, and I followed suit.

Arthur hated that sweater. He wore it twice to school and then flatly refused to put it on again. When Mum asked why, he explained that the kids who didn't have one (those whose fathers were working and didn't get a Star Box) made fun of the kids who did. They hollered "Tiger! Tiger!" at us because of the orange and black stripes. Even Arthur's best friend, Lloyd Armstrong, poked fun at the sweater. When Lloyd saw it on Christmas Day, he was green with envy. But when he found out it was a charity sweater he joined in jeering with the rest.

Being called "Tiger" didn't bother me much because there were more of us tigers than anybody else in the schoolyard. But when I overheard Old-Lady-Rice-Pudding refer to our sweaters as the "uniform of the poor," it really made me squirm.

We were nearly to the railroad underpass when we heard the train coming. Breaking into a run, we called over our shoulders for Willa to hurry up. Putting her dignity aside, she ran like the wind to catch us. We made it just in time, as the Canadian Pacific thundered overhead. We closed our eyes and made our secret wishes. You had to finish wishing before the last boxcar trundled over or it didn't have a chance of coming true.

"I wish I pass into Senior Third in June," I said out loud, since nobody could hear me. Then I added, "In Jesus name, alllmen!" for good measure—and because it was Sunday. And because I needed all the help I could get. The barbed-wire fence surrounding Prob's Bush had the same scary sign hanging on it that had been there last year. *Private Property! Keep Out! Trespassers Will Be Prosecuted!*

Then Dad did the same brave thing he'd done before. Without batting an eye he lifted Jakey over the forbidden fence, jumped over it himself, and held it down with his foot for Willa and Arthur and me to step across. I couldn't get over how fearless he was.

"Doesn't Dad know that trespassers will be executed?" I whispered to Willa.

"Not executed, silly, prosecuted," she explained.

I didn't know what the difference was, so I decided to ask Arthur. "What's prosecuted, Arthur?"

"Prosecuted means executed. It's the same thing, stupid!"

He sounded very sure of himself and I couldn't help but wonder if Willa was wrong for once. Anyway, I was sure proud of my dad because if Arthur was right and we got caught I knew it would be Dad who got hung by the neck until he was dead, and not us kids. Imagine being that brave, just to take your children for a nice spring walk.

The bush was budding out but it wasn't leafy yet. Thousands of pussy willows climbed up slender brown stalks. "Listen said the pussy willow, I can hear a brook. Spring is coming, spring is coming. Let's go out and look." I sang the words softly.

A fat brown cow was drinking from the creek. At the sight of her Jakey let out an excited squeal and she went crashing into the underbrush.

Dad stretched out on a grassy knoll and rested his head on a smooth rock. I folded my Star Box sweater and offered it to him for a pillow. "Thank you, Bea," he said, tucking it under his head and closing his eyes.

His wispy hair looked like spun gold in the sunlight. His pale skin was stretched tightly over his raw-boned face. "He looks hungry," I thought. And he likely was. He ate little at meal-times, always helping himself last. If there was meat, he ate the fat and gristle. If there weren't enough vegetables to go around, he did without. He drank his tea black, wetted his cereal with water and always took the heel of the bread. It was his way of doing his best for his family.

Arthur had step-stoned out to the middle of the creek. He had one of Mum's quart jars half full of pollywogs already. Jakey was darting every which way after snakes and frogs and butterflies. I was uneasy that he might fall into the deep end of the creek, but a glance at Dad relieved my mind. His eyes were only half closed.

Willa and I wandered off into the bush for wildflowers. Mum liked it when we brought her home a nosegay for the table. In no time at all I had a fistful of violets. I was just about to pick some white lilies, growing thick about my feet, when Willa stopped me.

"Don't pick those!" she cried. "It's against the law." Quickly I drew back my hand, not wanting to risk any more executions. "Trilliums are Ontario's provincial flower and if you pick them it kills the plant. That's why they are protected by law," Willa explained.

"How about these?" I asked, pointing to a patch of pink.

"It's okay to pick those. They're hepaticas. Oh, and here's some adder's-tongue. Mum likes these."

When we had a nice variety we headed back to the clearing. Dad was sitting up, his head tilted back, one hand shading his eyes from the westerly sun.

"Look there." He pointed with a scarred finger to the top of a tall pine tree. Perched on the tip, singing its heart out, was a brilliant bluebird. The sky paled behind it. Just then another, lighter bluebird joined it on the tip. They trilled prettily for a moment, then flew away together.

"Into the wild blue yonder," Dad said.

I'd never heard him say anything poetic before. And there was a dreamy look in his eyes. "That big old pine tree puts me in mind of the one I felled in France," he said. "Only it was bigger still."

"Tell us, Dad, tell us!" begged Arthur. He loved war stories. Especially the one about the pine tree, because our Dad was the hero of it.

"Well," began Dad, picturing in his mind's eye that faraway forest in France, "it was the spring of '17, a terrible, wet, cold spring. It was raining cats and dogs that day and an old French farmer had come out to see what us 'Forresters' were up to. He pointed to the grey sky and kept repeating, '*Le guerre. . .le guerre.*' He was blaming the cannon's roar for the bad weather in his sunny homeland. We were so close to the front that day, we had to holler to be heard over the gunfire. But we didn't complain about the wet and cold and noise because we knew our comrades were wounded and dying up there."

Here he paused in his story, as he always did, to reverently remember his fallen comrades. We waited respectfully. "Me and me mates were on lumberjack duty making a road for the troops," he continued, "and the Sergeant Major had given me a direct order to fell a certain giant pine. He cut a notch in the bark to show me where to begin. Well now, being raised as I was in the bush in Muskoka, I knew that if I was to carry out his orders that giant pine would be bound to fall right across our front lines. I wasn't one to question authority, mind, but I realized that if I didn't speak up some of our brave boys would be killed, and not by enemy gunfire either. Begging his pardon at the top of my lungs, I predicted where the tree would fall. He scratched his head and looked mighty skeptical, so I took a stick and drew a picture on the wet ground. Finally he motioned me to carry on, so I swung my axe and made my wedge, on the opposite side to his, and began to chop. And that big French pine tree fell just as neat as you please, exactly where I said it would. The pine needles were still flying when the Sergeant Major clapped me on the back. He was a fine officer. I never served under any better."

"Tell us more stories, Dad," I pleaded. "Tell us about being on leave in London. Are there lions and tigers in Piccadilly Circus, Dad?"

"No, Bea," he laughed, "It's not that kind of circus. Piccadilly is the centre of London where the streets all come together like the hub of a wagon wheel."

"Tell us about when you and Uncle Charlie went to visit Beatrice Baillie in London, Dad," put in Willa unexpectedly.

Dad grinned at the memory. "Well, as you know, Bea Baillie is a famous comedian of stage and screen—and she's also Lady Bolton, since she married the old Lord. She's cousin to me on my faither's side (that's how Dad said "father") so Charlie and I decided to pay her a call. The first person we asked directed us to her house. Everybody in London knew where Bea Baillie lived. It was a big old mansion off Russell Square and the butler answered our knock. 'Tell Miss Baillie her cousins are here from Canada,' says Charlie, bold as brass. 'One moment, gentlemen,' says the butler suspiciously, and shuts the door in our face. Back he comes and opens the door a crack. 'Lady Bolton thinks she has no relatives in Canada,' says he. Well, that got Charlie's dander up so he hollers through the crack, 'You tell her to think again and maybe she'll remember picking blueberries with us on our father's farm in Muskoka.' Then I put in my two cents worth. 'Tell her ladyship for me, just to jog her memory, that her grandma and my grandma are the same grandma!' Then Charlie yells, 'And if that don't make us kissing cousins I'll eat my khaki shirt!'

"That did it. The door swung open and there she was, the funniest woman in the world. That's how she was billed at the London Palladium. 'Hello, Jim,' she says as nice as pie. 'How are you, Charlie? Sorry for keeping you waiting, but I can't be too careful. I'm in a dreadful hurry to get to the theatre. Would you like some passes to my show? Can I offer you a spot of tea?' We said no thanks to the tea and thank you very much to the passes. It was a wonderful show. We were mighty proud of Bea that night, even if her head was too big for her hat. That's where your name comes from, Bea."

I never knew that before! Imagine skinny little scatter-brained me being named after the funniest woman in the world. Right then and there I decided to be an actress when I grew up.

"Tell us more, Dad," begged Arthur. "Tell us about the time you nearly got your ear shot off."

Dad rubbed the jagged scar with blunt fingers. "Later maybe. Right now we've got to be making tracks. Your mother will have the supper ready."

"Wait a minute," Willa said. "I want to take a picture."

She had brought along her Brownie camera. She had got it free from the Kodak company for being born in 1918. Every Canadian baby born the year of the Armistice got a free Brownie. The only trouble was, Willa could hardly ever afford a film. But she had some that day because Uncle Charlie had given her a shinplaster for her birthday and she'd gone right out and bought a film.

She told us to sit close together on the grass and keep perfectly still. *Click!* went the Brownie, and that lovely, springy day was captured forever on celluloid.

We could hear Mum singing through the open door as we came up the walk. "Mother, may I go out to swim? Yes, my darling daughter. Hang your clothes on the hickory limb; and don't go near the water."

The new house was awash with delicious smells. We were all just about starving and for once there was enough for everybody: golden meatloaf swimming in caramel-coloured gravy, clouds of mashed potatoes overflowing the mixing bowl and green peas peeking in and out of bright orange carrot rings.

The nosegay looked pretty on the white, threadbare tablecloth. Mum said it was prettier than roses.

"There's dessert," Mum said when the last crumb was gone. She went to the back porch and brought in a covered bowl. She lifted the lid and out came the beautiful aroma of oranges and bananas all sliced up together.

When I grew up, that tangy blend of flavours always brought saliva rushing to my mouth and memories rushing to my mind of that sweet spring day in 1933.

16
Dead-end Veeny Street

We had to leave the new house after only five months. Mr. Ratman caught us at the supper table when Mum had the kitchen door open airing out the house. His eyes were sad as he handed Dad the eviction notice, and there was a drip on the end of his nose. He sniffed and made it disappear. I didn't hate him any more.

The house-hunting started again, and so did the fighting. Mum was mad and upset about leaving the new house. She loved its hardwood floors and dry cement cellar and the breezy balcony that we had only just begun to use.

Sometimes Mum had fits of rage that changed suddenly into wild, hysterical laughter. Then the laughter would give way unexpectedly to wretched, heart-rending sobs. It was awful, seeing her like that.

Dad was just the opposite, cold and silent and sullen, his thin face turning grey as ashes. He wasn't the same Dad at all that had risked his neck to take us kids to the forbidden bush for a nice spring walk.

Once again they came home with fistfuls of latchkeys. And once again they fought over where we would move to. As before, there was no shortage of houses. *For Rent* signs sprouted like toadstools all over the city of Toronto. People were always on the move in an effort to keep one jump ahead of the bailiff. Sometimes families were actually put out on the street. You'd see them standing forlornly on the sidewalk amid their furniture. "Like lost souls," Mum would sigh, "with no place to go."

The day before this was about to happen to us, Mum came home with red patches tingeing her high cheekbones and a skeleton key in her hand.

"It's the key to Billy and Maude Sundy's house in Swansea," she announced breathlessly. "Puppa persuaded them to let me have it. He told them we'd make good tenants, Jim. He said you were a willing handyman and I was a spotless house-keeper."

"How much rent do they want?" was all Dad said.

"Eight dollars a month." Mum's voice held a defiant ring.

"That's a lot of money."

"Billy and Maude are good Christians and they're Puppa's friends. They won't put us out."

"Is Billy and Maude's house near Grampa's, Mum?" I asked hopefully.

"Just a hop, skip and jump through the lane, Booky."

Since we were due to be thrown out the very next day, there was no time for argument. So it was settled.

Uncle Charlie moved us in his beat-up old truck. There wasn't room for everybody in the cab, and Mum wouldn't hear of Wins and Arthur and me riding in the back with the furniture, so we had to take the streetcar to Swansea.

The streetcar we got on had reversible wicker seats. Arthur

took hold of the metal handgrip and flipped the backrest over so we could ride facing each other. Then I got sick from going backwards. Willa got up and asked the conductor for transfers so we could get off and get some fresh air. But he just ignored her and kept us standing on the door treadle stop after stop, with me barely holding back the sick. At last a grown-up wanted off so he had to ring the driver to stop. Then Willa had to beg for transfers because we didn't have any more carfare. It mortified her to beg like that, but she knew I couldn't help being sick so she didn't get mad.

All three of us kids were sorry to leave Birchcliff. Between the old house and the new house we had lived there a record two and a half years. We were all leaving friends behind. By the time we got to Swansea, I was already pining away for Audrey.

Billy and Maude's house wasn't much to write home about. It was one of four tall skinny stuck-together houses on dead-end Veeny Street. White scrolly woodwork decorated the four peaked roofs. Inside, narrow rooms were piled, like shoe-boxes, one on top of the other. The cellar was just a hole dug in the soft sand underneath the kitchen. Narrow slat stairs, like a homemade ladder, led down into its earthy depths.

"It'll be a good place to store vegetables," Mum said.

There was no furnace in the dugout, so our coal stove would have to heat the kitchen and the tiny bedroom above it. There was a Quebec heater in the dining room with a pipe going through the middle bedroom on its way to the roof.

"That'll give the girls a nice warm pipe to dress by in wintertime," Mum said.

Joey was sitting on a three-legged stool in the corner by the cold stove eating dried beans out of a honey pail. He kept giving me the evil eye. I knew he wasn't glad to see me, and I think he was jealous of me too. When I told this to Mum she said, "Poor little gaffer. He's stuck like glue to Puppa since Mumma went 'home.'"

Grampa sat down by the table and lit his sawed-off corncob. He tamped it down with a tobacco stained thumb and drew in the flame from a thick wooden match while I told him all about our trip out on the streetcar. He had on a grey flannel undershirt with fireman's braces on top and I noticed how stooped his shoulders were. Mum said that was from shovelling coal into the blast furnace at the Bolt Works for forty-odd years. The Bolt Works was a terrible sweatshop in those days, she said. Six days a week and ten hours a day with never a holiday.

But Grampa was luckier than most, she said—at least he still had all his fingers and thumbs. Not like poor old Andy McCrae who lost half his hand in a Bolt Works accident and then was forever thankful because they didn't fire him. After all, he reasoned, who'd want to hire a cripple with only one good hand?

I didn't stay very long that first day. Joey made me nervous, cracking beans and giving me the evil eye, so I kissed Grampa under his overgrown, tea-stained moustache and promised to come back the very next day to trim it for him.

Flying back the way I'd come, through the lane, in the back door and out the front, I made a beeline across the road to Gladie's.

Gladie was my cousin once-removed. There were seven children in her family and when they saw me coming they all ran out to meet me. Then some twice-removed cousins spilled out of the stuck-together houses, and Arthur came leaping down our front porch steps to join the pack. There must have been twenty of us kids, all laughing and joking and kicking up the dust in the middle of the road on unpaved, dead-end Veeny Street.

Buster, Gladie's big red-headed brother, pulled a nickel from his overall pocket and cried, "C'mon, gang, treats on me!"

So up the street we followed him, like the pied piper, to Hunter's corner grocery store.

Mr. Hunter was behind the counter weighing some white sugar in a brown paper bag. "Will there be anything else, Mrs. Medd?" he asked pleasantly while scrunching the sugar bag closed.

"I'll have six pieces of bologna, sliced thin, and add it to my bill please, Mr. Hunter," said Mrs. Medd, glaring at us noisy kids over her glasses.

The grocer ripped a square of shiny paper off a wide roll that was bolted to the counter top and placed it under the slicing machine. Pressing a long tube of pink bologna firmly against the circular blade, he turned the handle rhythmically. The meat, sliced thin as she said, piled up in the centre of the paper. Then he folded it into a neat, flat package. A ball of string was held prisoner in a wire cage behind the counter. The string ran up to the ceiling, through a series of wire loops, and dangled down over the grocer's bald head. Reaching up without looking, he grabbed it, tied the parcel, snapped the string and let it go. It retracted towards the ceiling automatically.

The bell jangled over the door as Mrs. Medd left the store.

Now Mr. Hunter patted his aproned potbelly, scratched his shiny bare head and winked at Arthur and me.

"I see you folks got here," he said. "Remember me to your mother. Now, what can I do you for?" He chuckled at his own joke.

"I want five cents worth of penny candy, Mr. Hunter," said Buster, importantly showing his nickel.

"Well, help yourself, Buster," said Mr. Hunter. Then he handed me the heel of the bologna.

I was just about to hide it in my pinny-pocket when Arthur said, "Bits on you!" and grabbed my hand and took a great big bite. Darn that Arthur!

Buster went behind the counter and studied the candy display in the store window. There was a wonderful assortment: blackballs with caraway-seed centres, licorice pipes, sherbets, chocolate brooms, miniature ice cream cones stuffed with stale marshmallow, and little round discs with messages written in red dye: *Be Mine, Kiss Me, Ouch!, Hi Toots!* and stuff like that.

The grab bags were piled in the corner. They cost one cent each and if you were lucky there might be three cents worth of stale candy inside. Buster bought five grab bags and dumped them all out on the cement stoop. The he divvied it up. I got a pink disc that said *Good Luck*, which seemed like a good omen to me.

That night Mum said she was too busy to cook supper and we could help ourselves. So I made myself a bologna sandwich on the counter of the kitchen cabinet. Then I had a cup of water and a white-sugar sandwich. I was still hungry when I went to bed.

Dad had all the beds set up. Billy's cot was in the boys' room

The boys' bedroom at the front of the house had no heat at all.

The kitchen was painted an ugly grey from the cracked linoleum floor to the tin-tiled ceiling.

"We'll change it to cream and green," Mum said.

"Where'll the money come from?" grumbled Dad.

Mum ignored him. "At least the house is clean."

The tiny, cramped front room was joined to the narrow dining room by a scrolly wooden archway. Both rooms were covered from their foot-high baseboards to their ten-foot ceilings in peeling, brown-stained paper.

"We'll get some nice flowered paper from Eaton's," Mum said. "They sell off bundle lots for next to nothing in the tunnel."

I'd never seen my mother so cheerful about a move before. I guess that's because she was back home in Swansea where she was born and raised. Her grandparents, all four thcm, had been among the first settlers in the little village. They'd named it after Swansea in Wales.

The minute Arthur and Willa and I arrived that day I ran lickety-split in the front and out the back and through the lane to Grampa's.

"I'm here, Grampa!" I called in his back kitchen door.

He poked his wiry head around from the dining room. "Hello there, Be-*a*-trice. How's my girl?" he said.

Oh, how I loved being his girl. It made me feel special and important, like being a boy, or being adopted, or being the only girl in a family of boys. Ruthie Armstrong, who lived next door to the new house, was the youngest of seven children, all boys but her, and her father called her his little miracle.

121

because Mum and Dad's room was barely big enough to hold their brown metal bed and bureau. The reason their room was so small was because the end had been chopped off to make a bathroom. It was the smallest bathroom I'd ever seen. The sink and bathtub were just about right for a midget family. Only the toilet was the regular size.

Our dresser wasn't set up yet, so Willa wouldn't be able to give me heck for throwing my clothes in the corner. The wooden floors were rough with chipped grey paint. I had a momentary twinge of regret, remembering the shiny golden hardwood of the new house.

I was just drifting off to sleep when I thought of something that woke me with a yelp. Catapulting out of the middle of our sagging mattress, I raced down the strange dark staircase.

Mum and Dad were still working. The flour bin was tilted on its hinges out of the kitchen cabinet and Mum was filling it from a Monarch bag. Dad was wiring a broken chair rung.

"Dad! Dad!" I bounded like a frightened deer through the cluttered dining room. They looked up in alarm, their faces drawn and tired.

"Good gracious! What's the matter?" cried Mum.

"My hoop and stick! I left it under the porch of the new house. Can we go back and get it in the morning, Dad? Before somebody steals it?"

"Don't be foolish," snapped Dad. "It's too far a piece to go for a homemade hoop and stick."

My face dropped a mile and I burst out crying.

"Don't cry, Bea." Dad's voice was suddenly gentle. "I'll make you a new one."

"Tomorrow, Dad? First thing? Promise?"

"Oh, all right. Now stop blubbering and get to bed."

He was as good as his word, my dad. Right after breakfast the next day he went out and found an old sulky wheel and a wooden slat. He did his best, I know, but the wheel wobbled and the crossbar was too short to steer it by. Try as I might I couldn't keep it up for more than half a block. So I put it away under the clothesline stoop, and never again did I have a hoop and stick to match the one that got left behind at the new house.

17
A free ride on the Bug

Swansea was the best place in the world to live in summertime. Not only did we have all of Lake Ontario for our swimming hole, but Sunnyside Amusement Park was just a hop, skip and jump along the boardwalk. Twice that summer Willa took me there. The first time was best because it didn't rain.

Right after supper (Mum told us to run along, she'd do the dishes) we headed through the bush, up and down the hills and valleys of the "Camel's Back," and out onto opulent Ellis Avenue.

It was a hot, humid July night, as all July nights seemed to be in those days, and our dresses stuck to our legs as we walked.

"Whew," said Willa, mopping her brow, "I wish the free streetcars were still running."

"Free streetcars? Down Ellis Avenue?"

"No, silly, on Bloor Street. When I was your age the T.T.C. ran free streetcars along Bloor and down Roncesvalles. Then all Evie and I had to do was walk down the wooden steps into Sunnyside."

"Was it Depression then?"

"No. Dad had a steady job at Gutta Percha then."

"Well, why don't they run them now, when it's Depression and nobody's got any money?"

"I don't know. *C'est la vie*, I guess."

"What does 'say lah vee' mean?"

"It's French. It means that's life."

Boy, Willa was smart!

As we passed the dark, shiny waters of Grenadier Pond, I pictured the slimey green bones of the Grenadier Guards and their horses, all mingled together down there in the bottomless deep. Long years ago, in wintertime, the whole regiment had crashed through the ice and drowned. That's how the pond got its name. Or so the story goes. I sure felt sorry for those horses.

Under the railroad bridge we went, and across Lakeshore Road to the boardwalk.

The wide, weather-beaten boards rumbled pleasantly under the pounding of so many strolling feet. A cool breeze blew in off the lapping lake, ruffling our hair and soothing our sweaty brows.

Swansea's Point, the little peninsula we laid claim to, was almost deserted now. But a few intrepid bathers still romped in the blue-green water. And some girls in beach-pyjamas played catch on the soft white sand.

"There goes the Belly-Wart ice-wagon!" I cried, as the familiar horse-drawn van clip-clopped along Lakeshore, its backboard dribbling a steady stream of water.

"Not 'Belly-Wart,' dummy," sighed my long-suffering sister. "Bell-*U*-Art!"

Wafting on the wind from the Seabreeze Bandshell came the

sweet strains of "In the Good Old Summertime." Our hearts and running shoes hurried to the beat. I had to skippety-hop really fast to keep up with Willa.

"I see the roller coaster!" I squealed excitedly.

"Well naturally. It hasn't moved, you know." Sometimes the five years between us was hard for Willa to bear.

It looked like a giant Meccano toy etched against the deep blue sky. "The Flyer" was its name, and no wonder. The way it zipped around those hairpin turns and plummeted down those mountainous hills, it's a miracle it didn't take right off and go flying into space.

"The next time I get some money I'll take you on it," promised Willa. I think she was feeling bad about being sarcastic.

The minute we entered the concrete park my nose caught the tantalizing aroma of vinegar and chips. "I wish I had a nickel for a cone of chips," I moaned.

"You knew we didn't have any money when we left home," Willa reminded me sternly. So I put on my biggest pout and then she said, "Oh, never mind. We'll go and watch the water chute."

A rowboat had just emerged from the Tunnel of Love with a couple of spooners in it.

"What do they do in there, Willa?" I was pretty sure she'd know. She was fifteen.

"What makes you so dumb, Bea?"

I hated that. A question instead of an answer. And I couldn't even think of a smart reply.

We held our breath as the boat climbed the perpendicular hill and teetered, for a thrilling moment, at the brink of the

126

rushing chute. Then the spooners screamed and I screamed as they plunged headlong into the sloshing water trough below. A giant wave flopped over the side, soaking our running shoes.

Oh, what I'd give to be terrified like that!

"C'mon, Bea, we haven't got all night," said Willa, stamping the water out of her sopping shoes.

We squished along, stopping for a minute to watch the cracking, whirling Whip and to stare up, wide-eyed, at the swooping Ferris wheel.

The Caterpillar stood idle, its green canvas skin folded back. I knew first-hand the thrill of being swallowed up in its billowing, wrinkly hide because my Aunt Hester had taken me on it once.

A fat weight-guesser in a sweaty undershirt eyed Willa up and down. He held out a gaudy doll with stuck-together legs and said in a wheedling voice, "Guess your weight, Miss? Only a nickel and I won't touch a thing."

"C'mon, Bea, we'll be late!" Blushing furiously, Willa yanked me by the arm.

"Ouch! Late for what?" I screeched.

"Oh, don't be so dopey!" she said, disgusted.

Well, at least it wasn't a question.

We passed the games of chance and stopped to watch the one we liked best. A man sat on a swing over a barrel of water. Then the player threw a baseball and if it hit the bull's-eye over the man's head he got dumped in the drink. We hung around until this happened (he came up gasping and snorting and yelling bad words) and then we continued on.

"I wish I had a nickel for the Fishpond," I lamented loudly.

You never knew when a rich stranger might be listening and take pity on you and hand you a nickel.

"You promised if I'd bring you, you wouldn't whine, Bea," Willa warned me with a frown.

What earthly good were all these wonders to a couple of Depression children without two cents to rub together? No good at all, unless they happened to have a relative who worked at Sunnyside. And we did! Our Auntie Gwen, Mum's third-to-the-youngest sister, was the ticket seller on the Custard Cars. Now the Custard Cars, cunning little automobiles that you drove all by yourself, were my very favourite ride in all the world.

"I hope Auntie Gwen is working tonight," I said anxiously.

"She is. I asked Mum," said my wonderful, practical sister.

And there she was, sitting in her little booth, looking a lot like Mum only younger. She was busy putting a roll of pink tickets on the spindle. When she was all set for business, she glanced up.

"Well, look who's here!" she said good-naturedly. "And how's every little thing?"

Willa said every little thing was fine. And we waited. Mum told us not to ask. Just wait and see, she said.

"Would you like a ride before we get too busy, Bea?"

"Yes please, Auntie Gwen!" I chirped, remembering my manners for a change.

Opening the little back door of the booth, she called out the magic words. "George, this is my niece. Give her a ride, will you?" Then she turned back to Willa. "You're too big for the Custard Cars, Willa, so you'll just have to be satisfied to chinwag with your auntie."

Poor Willa! Imagine having to be satisfied with a chinwag!

George told me to hop right into Number 22. Then he kicked something underneath and hollered, "Okay, girlie, step on the gas!"

I did, and away I went at breathtaking speed, alone on the open road. Oh, it was glorious! I could have spent the rest of my life in Car Number 22.

The "road" was a wide wooden track made in the shape of a figure eight. The top circle of the figure eight jutted out into a weedy, empty lot. It was so far away from Auntie Gwen's ticket booth, it was downright scary.

As I steered back to the starting point I pressed down hard on the gas and gave George a wide berth. But at the end of the second circuit, no amount of pressure would prevent Number 22 from coming to a stop.

"Didja run outta gas, girlie?" grinned George.

"Yep! Fill 'er up, George!" I answered cockily.

He laughed out loud and gave the underside of my car another magic kick and away I went again. Four times he gave my car a kick, and then the paying customers began to arrive.

"That's all for now, girlie," said George kindly, as he steered me over to the side.

I used my latest saying. "Thanks a bunch, George!"

"Hurry up, Bea!" Willa sounded impatient. I guess she was tired of all that chinwagging.

I remembered to thank Auntie Gwen, the way Mum said.

She looked at her watch and said, "It's early yet. Why don't you run down to the Bug and ask John for a ride?"

John was Auntie Gwen's new husband. He didn't know us from a hill of beans.

"He won't recognize us," said Willa doubtfully.

"Well, tell him who you are. Say I sent you."

It seemed too good to be true. We made a beeline through the thickening crowd.

Sure enough there he was, a tall, handsome, almost total stranger, standing high up on a wooden platform.

"That's him, Willa! That's him! Ask! Ask!"

"I'm not asking." Willa was shy about things like that. Mum said she was backward about coming forward.

So up the wooden steps I ran. "Are you John?"

"That's right." He looked puzzled.

"Auntie Gwen said to tell you who we are. I'm Bea and that's my sister Willa down there."

Willa was embarrassed to be pointed out, so she hung her head. John still looked puzzled, but before I had to explain any more his face lit up with a smile. (Boy, was he handsome when he smiled. I got my first big crush right then and there.)

"Oh, sure, you're Fran's children. Would you like a ride on the Bug before it gets busy?"

"Yes, please," I answered quickly.

"Okay, Willa," he called to her. "Up you come!"

The Bug was a grown-up ride, so Willa wasn't too big. Thank goodness, because in spite of the iron bar Uncle John snapped across our laps she had to hang on to me for dear life.

Round and round and up and down and over the twisty hills we flew, my sedate big sister screaming her head off just as loud as me. Three times our new uncle told us to "stay put" as he went about snapping people into the ladybug-shaped cars. When he finally unsnapped us we thanked him a bunch and staggered down the steps to solid ground.

We sat down on a green, wooden bench to get our land legs back. "We'd better be getting home," Willa said.

"Can we walk past the merry-go-round on our way?" I said.

She waited patiently as I gazed at the lovely prancing horses and thrilled to the loud music of the calliope. I picked out a horse that reminded me of Major, my grampa's horse in Muskoka. How I wished I could jump on his back and go galloping off in circles. But we had no money, and no more relatives who worked at Sunnyside.

"I'm starved," I said, sniffing the air as we neared a red-hot stand. "Let's look on the ground for money."

"Okay," Willa agreed. She seemed in a much better mood since our ride on the Bug. "But we won't find any."

She was right of course.

Tree-lined Ellis Avenue was very dark at night. Fireflies sparkled eerily all over the pitch-black pond. Bullfrogs croaked hoarsely in the rushes. Willa took my hand and we began to hurry. It was a long walk home.

Going in the back way through the yard, we could see Mum through the faded green mosquito netting on the kitchen window. She was sitting in the middle of the room under the dangling light bulb so she could see to mend a ladder in her stocking. The house was quiet with the little ones in bed.

"Did you girls have a good time?" She sounded tired.

"Uncle John gave us three free rides on the Bug," Willa burst out before I had a chance. "And is he ever handsome! And Bea had—oh, I don't know how many free rides on the Custard Cars."

"I wish I could go to Sunnyside every night all summer," I said. "Can we go back tomorrow night, Mum?"

"For mercy sakes, no," Mum said, clucking her tongue. "That would be too much of a good thing."

I already knew that, but there was no harm in asking.

"I'm hungry," I said for the umpteenth time. "My stomach's stuck to my backbone."

"Have a peanut-butter sandwich," Mum said, "but don't forget to clean up your mess."

"Oh, boy! Have we got peanut butter?"

"Yas." That's how Mum said yes when she was tickled about something. "I sold a bag of rags to the 'Addy-bone' man and I got enough money for a jar of peanut butter and a loaf of Dutch brown bread."

I stirred up the oil in the peanut-butter jar and slathered it on the bread. Mmmm, it smelled good. I had another slice and washed it all down with two cups of water. Then I forgot my mess and went to bed contented.

I fell asleep instantly and dreamed I owned a Custard Car. I drove it everywhere: to the store and to church and to Muskoka to show Aunt Aggie. I even let all the kids in the neighbourhood have a turn. All except Lorraine LaSquare, that is. Lorraine was the only kid on the street who owned a tricycle (her father had a job) and one day she said if all us poor kids would line up on the sidewalk she'd give us each a ride. Well, I was the last in line and when it came my turn she picked up her tricycle and went in to supper. I never got over that. So when it came her turn, in my dream, I picked up my Custard Car with superhuman strength and carried it into the house.

What a perfect dream to end a perfect day!

18
S.W.A.K.

Dad and Arthur had gone up north at the beginning of the summer to help Grampa Thomson with the farm work. At first I was mad because I couldn't go. Uncle Charlie had taken them in his rumble seat and he said there wasn't room enough for me. But when I found out they wouldn't be back until school started again, I was glad I hadn't gone. The holidays seemed to last a lot longer when you stayed at home.

We had a nice time that summer. With Dad gone Mum had nobody to fight with, and with Arthur gone I had nobody to fight with. So the days stretched out in a long, peaceful, lazy-hazy string.

But before many weeks went by I began to miss Dad a lot, and one day I sat down and wrote him a big long letter. Willa made me an envelope and Mum gave me a two-cent stamp. I sealed the letter *S.W.A.K* and posted it on the way down Ellis Avenue.

Ellis Avenue was a long, gradual hill with Lake Ontario spread out at its foot like a huge blue swimming pool. I had never been in a real swimming pool myself, but I had seen two of them at a distance. One was the Mineral Baths on Bloor

Street, and the other was Sunnyside Bathing Pavilion.

The Mineral Baths were right opposite High Park. Willa said the twin pools used to be part of a hospital. At the Sunday School picnic all the kids lined up along the grassy banks and stared across Bloor Street at the lucky people diving from the tower and swishing down the slide into the gleaming mineral waters.

Sunnyside Bathing Pavilion was on the lakefront. We often strolled down the hot, treeless beach while our lunch was digesting and peered through the wire fence at the paying customers. I could never figure out why anybody would pay to swim in there when only a stone's throw away was glorious— free—Lake Ontario. Dad said they must have more money than brains. But Mum said she thought it would be lovely to bathe in that pretty turquoise-blue water.

The lake did have its drawbacks. Some days it was as cold and grey as a witch's heart (as Arthur would say) and other times the waves would come crashing, six feet high, over the breakwall.

But the worst thing that could possibly happen at the lake happened the day that I posted my letter to Dad. So I wrote him another one the very next day and told him all about it.

"Dear Dad." My neat writing that always amazed Willa was spoiled because my hand was shaking.

You will be surprised to hear from me again so soon. And you'll be surprised that Mum gave me another two-cent stamp, won't you? But when I tell you what happened yesterday, then you won't be surprised any more. Remember I told you Willa was taking me swimming? Well, she did but we didn't go in the water. I'll tell you why. Because there was an undertow and seven people got drowned, that's why. And one of the drowned people was someone we know. It was Lorraine LaSquare who lives next door to Hunter's grocery store. Do you know who I mean? She is that stingy girl who never gives me a ride on her bike. And now she can't ride it any more so ha! ha! (Mum just looked over my shoulder and said don't speak ill of the dead, so I won't.)

Do you want to know how come Willa and I got saved from drowning? I'll tell you how. It was all on account of the knots in my shoestrings. Lorraine LaSquare ran into the water hollering, 'Last one in's a rotten egg!' Then she disappeared. Well, by the time I got the knots undone and my shoes off everyone on the beach was yelling, 'Undertow! Undertow!' Willa and I just stood there staring at the spot where Lorraine went under, expecting her to pop up again. But she never did. Willa said that's one time it paid me to be sloppy, because Lorraine's shoes had been tied in nice neat bows. So I guess my sloppiness paid Willa too, because she had to wait for me.

Now I will tell you the best part. Do you know who is a hero and is going to get his picture in the paper and everything? Our cousin Buster, that's who. As you probably know, Buster is a strong swimmer, so he swam around on top of the water, grabbing people from underneath him and hauling them in to shore. He saved six people single-handed. Isn't that wonderful? But seven people got drowned, including my friend Lorraine LaSquare. Isn't that awful? I think I am going to be invited to her funeral. But Mum says the casket will probably be

135

closed because Lorraine won't be fit to look at. Also Mum says since I haven't got a black dress she'll have to dye my old cotton playdress navy blue. Which, come to think of it, might be an improvement.

All us kids have to stay in for three days and not play any noisy games because Veeny Street is in mourning. All the front-room blinds are pulled down. Even little kids like Jakey can't go out and play tag because it is too noisy and disrespectful. Willa said she'll get me a library book to keep me occupied. She thinks I might like Girl of the Limberlost. Ask Arthur has he ever read that book. Willa looked over my shoulder and said don't be silly, it's a girls' book. But I like lots of boys' books, so why wouldn't he like a girls' book, I wonder.

Mum just came in from looking up the street and said the wreath is on LaSquares' front door, so that means Lorraine is home now. She said it is a pearl-grey wreath with a pink bow on the bottom (because pink is for girls). I'm going out to look.

> I hope you found this letter interesting,
> Your loving daughter,
> Bea.

P.S. Are you proud of me for saving Willa's life because of the knots in my shoestrings? Mum says it had nothing to do with shoestrings. It was God's will, she said. But I don't know. What do you think, Dad?

> XXX OOO B.M.T.

After the lake tragedy Mum wouldn't let us go swimming any more. So I spent the rest of the summer playing street games and baseball, and visiting people like Grampa and Maude and Billy Sundy.

Willa was too big to play street games, so when she wasn't busy helping Mum she went window shopping with her friends on Bloor Street. Once she and Evie walked all the way to Yonge and Bloor and Aunt Susan gave them each a box of nuts and a car ticket.

Street games were my favourite pastime. And there were lots of them to choose from—Oyster Sails and Red Light, Green Light and You Can't Cross The River. I liked Oyster Sails the best myself. ("Hoist Your Sails, not Oyster Sails," corrected Willa disdainfully. "Honestly, Bea, sometimes you're as dumb as a doornail.")

Oyster Sails was a twilight game. It never got underway until just before the streetlights came on and our mothers called us in. We'd choose sides, pick a leader and make up secret signals. Then off we'd go, hightailing it around the neighbourhood, the haunting cry of "Oyster Sails!" echoing eerily down darkening lanes and dusky streets and whispering alleyways.

We had a good Sunday School picnic that summer. It was held in High Park. I was hoping it would be at Centre Island because it's lots more fun going across the bay in a ferryboat than just walking along Bloor Street. But Mum said the Baptist church couldn't afford to go to the Island. Gladie said the Presbyterian picnic was going to be held there, so I decided next year I'd be a Presbyterian.

Right at the entrance to the park was a huge canvas sign stretched between two trees. On it in big black letters were the words *Gentiles Only*.

"What does it mean, Mum?" I was curious.

"It means no Jews allowed."

"What are we?" I asked anxiously.

"We're Gentiles," she said.

I was glad because if we were Jews we couldn't have our picnic in High Park.

I won an India-rubber ball in the races and ate fourteen salmon sandwiches for supper. So all in all I had a real good time.

I enjoyed my grown-up friends almost as much as friends my own age. I had lots of fun with Maude and Billy Sundy. Billy was very religious and every time he saw me he'd ask me if I was saved. I didn't have the least idea if I was or not but I always said yes anyway, just to hear him holler "Hallelujah."

Mrs. Sundy had nicknamed me Scallywag. One Saturday morning when I went over to their house she said to me, "Hello there, Scallywag. How would you like to help me with my cedar-mopping?" Of course I jumped at the chance and gave her back kitchen a real good cedar-mopping. Usually Mrs. Sundy just paid me with an apple or a cookie, but this time she handed me a nickel and said, "Away you go to the picture show." So I ran home as fast as my skinny legs would carry me to ask my mum if it was okay.

She was standing on tiptoe in front of the cracked kitchen mirror, plucking out white hairs from among the black ones.

"I earned a nickel from Mrs. Sundy, Mum," I burst out excitedly, "and she said I could go to the picture show. Can I, Mum, if I'm careful crossing Bloor Street?"

"Oh, I guess so, just so long as you don't talk to strangers," Mum said, plucking out a curly white strand. "And while you're up there go to the fifteen-cent store and get me some

Lovalon to cover up these unsightly white hairs. It looks as if I'm going to go prematurely grey, just like Puppa."

Lovalon Black Rinse was a packet of blue-black crystals that turned into hair dye when you dissolved it in hot water.

Mum went to the sideboard to get her purse, tut-tutting all the way about her grey hairs. But she couldn't find it. "My purse! My purse! I've lost my purse!" she cried, and raced upstairs in a panic.

Willa and I ran after her, searching in all the same places. "I don't know why she gets so upset about it," muttered my disgruntled sister, the dust rag still in her hand. "There's never anything in it anyway."

But that's the way Mum was. About twice a week she flew into a frenzy looking for her purse. And it always turned up in the most likely place. This time it was on top of the kitchen cabinet.

"I don't know who could have put it there," she remarked, rummaging breathlessly for the money.

"Will there be any change, Mum?" I asked hopefully, tying her nickel with mine in my hanky and shoving it down to the bottom of my pinny-pocket.

"No, Lovalon costs a nickel. And don't lose it. Money doesn't grow on trees, you know."

All the way to Bloor Street I daydreamed about a money tree in our backyard, just dripping with nickels and dimes. By the time I got to Kresge's, I had picked enough to buy myself a two-wheeler.

I got to the Lyndhurst just in time to buy my ticket and find a seat in the front row. Then the lights dimmed and the curtains parted and the audience erupted in a wild, deafening roar. I held my ears and stamped my feet and hollered with the rest. It's a wonder the roof didn't come tumbling down.

Unlike those of the Kingswood Theatre in Birchcliff, all the picture shows at the Lyndhurst were talkies. This one was about a police dog called Rin Tin Tin. He was a terrific dog, that Rinny. He understood English like a person. And brave. He went through fires and floods and snowstorms, catching all the bad guys and saving all the good guys. Then after that came a cowboy serial starring Ken Maynard and his horse. It was the most exciting thing I had ever seen. But just as the horse and my cowboy hero jumped off the cliff into the cloudless sky the screen went black and a sign flashed on saying *Continued next week*. Try as I might, I couldn't get another nickel, so I never did find out what happened.

Dad and Arthur came home at the end of August. I was sprawled on Grampa Cole's front lawn chewing grass roots when I saw them trudging up Windermere Avenue, bent over double with sacks on their backs. I ran to meet them hollering, "Addybones!" That started a fight with Arthur right away so we got back to normal in no time.

The second they set foot in the kitchen, Mum said, "You two will need a bath before you sit down to the table."

"Ya, Arthur, you smell like panure!" I taunted.

"Ba-nure, dumb-bell! " he retorted.

"Ma-nure, dopey," corrected Willa, keeping her distance.

The stewing meat had been simmering all day long and by suppertime it was as tender as fresh bread. Mum cooked some new potatoes (from the sacks on Dad's and Arthur's backs) with some baby carrots from our own back garden. When they were done, crisp tender, she drained them both into a pint sealer so as not to throw the goodness down the sink. Then she used the vegetable water to make the rich brown gravy, and dumped the whole works into the big mixing bowl. Ahhh, heavenly stew! And to top it off she had made a rhubarb custard pie (rhuberb, Mum called it) from Gladie's mother's garden. Dad said the way his kids ate he'd swear we all had hollow legs. And for once he patted his own lean stomach and declared he was full to the brim.

After supper he gave Jakey and me a big brown copper and Willa a whole nickel. Then he went straight over to Billy and Maude Sundy's. When he came back he announced proudly that the rent was all caught up.

Just before I fell asleep that night I heard my parents' voices sifting up through the dining room stovepipe hole. (The stove had been taken down for the summer and the hole was covered by a tin plate with a pretty mountain picture on it.)

I couldn't hear what they were saying, but I could tell by the soft tone of their voices that there wasn't going to be a fight that night.

POWER

FAITH

COURAGE

CANADIAN NATIONAL
EXHIBITION
TORONTO
1933

·AUG·
25
INCLUSIVE

·SEPT·
9
INCLUSIVE

19
Kids' day at the Ex

Mum was busy as a beaver getting our clothes ready for school. Every stitch we wore had to be turned up or let down, and washed and ironed and mended. Mum could darn a hole or sew a patch that absolutely could not be seen by the naked eye.

It was her way of making up for the things we lacked. She believed, almost religiously, that if we looked "clean and paid for" our teachers would know that we came from a good home and would treat us accordingly. She was only partly right. We did get more respect than the poor shabby kids whose clothes were held together with safety pins, but we ranked well below the ones who looked as if they had just stepped out from the pages of Eaton's Spring and Summer Catalogue.

I dreaded the first day of school. To me it was like the start of a ten month jail sentence. The only thing that made it bearable was that it coincided with the coming of the 'Ex.' The Canadian National Exhibition was the biggest annual exposition in the world. And it was ours!

On the last day of the school year every Ontario youngster

got a free pass for kids' day at the Ex. All summer long I worried that my free pass might somehow disappear out of the sideboard drawer and I'd be the only kid in Toronto who didn't get to go. Mum had to show it to me at least a hundred times over the summer to reassure me.

Then the day before kids' day I was overcome with another big worry. I was petrified I'd sleep in the next morning and miss our free ride. So I decided to run over to Gladie's house and make her promise not to go without me.

I waited at the curb for the Canada Bread wagon to pass by. "Hi, Bessie!" I called out gaily to the familiar old brown mare. Bessie snorted and Andy, the baker, waved a greeting with his whip. From underneath the wagon I could see two feet dangling down. As it passed by, I saw that the feet belonged to Arthur. He was sitting on the step where the baker rests his basket, enjoying a free ride.

"Hookey on behind!" I squealed triumphantly.

Andy yanked on the reins and poor old Bessie stumbled to a stop. Off tumbled Arthur and away I ran, with him in hot pursuit. Gladie saw me coming and flung open the door. I streaked inside like greased lightning and just managed to slam the door in my brother's furious face.

Laughing hysterically, Gladie and I watched through the door curtains as the baker collared Arthur. Waving the whip threateningly, he gave Arthur a good tongue-lashing for hookeying on behind.

Gladie thought up a swell plan so I wouldn't sleep in the next day. "We'll make a long string," she said, and you can tie it to your toe and throw it out your bedroom window. Then I'll come over and yank it in the morning." So we knotted a hundred

144

bits of string together and she promised, cross her heart, not to forget to yank it.

I was scared to go home for supper because I knew Arthur would be out to get me. Of course, he would have done the same thing in my place. Hollering "hookey on behind" was a neighbourhood tradition. But lucky for me I saw Willa coming down the street so I followed her in and Arthur didn't dare touch me because she was still bigger than he was.

Next morning, bright and early, Gladie ran over and pulled the string. And so did all the other kids on the street. By seven-thirty we were all bouncing merrily along Lakeshore Road in the back of Sandy Beasley's rattly old slat-sided truck. The lake rippled like a pan of gold in the sunrise. A cool wind blew across it, standing our hair on end. We looked like a bunch of dandelions gone to seed.

"*One, two, three, four, who are we for?*" sang out Buster lustily.

"*Swansea! Swansea! Rah! Rah! Rah!*" we answered.

Swansea was a separate village in those days and most of us kids were proud descendants of its earliest settlers. (Veeny Street was named after my great-aunt Veeny who was Grampa Cole's dead sister.)

We arrived at the Dufferin Gates a whole hour before they opened, so we had to sit on the curb and wait.

"I hope I don't get turned away," worried big tall Minnie Beasley. "I got no carfare home. I got to wait for Uncle Sandy."

Poor Minnie. Her parents had died suddenly of galloping consumption and she had to live with her aunt and uncle and help take care of their ten children. Mum said it was a shame the way they 'bused her.

145

Someone had given her a kid's ticket, but she wasn't a kid any more. She was eighteen and hadn't been to school for years.

"Let your hair down, Minnie. That'll make you look younger," suggested Willa.

Minnie unfastened her old-fashioned bun and shook a cascade of red ringlets down her back.

"Take your shoes off so you'll be shorter," I said.

"Stoop down and we'll all go through in a bunch, with you in the middle," was Buster's helpful suggestion.

It was exciting, thinking of ways to make sure Minnie didn't get turned away. It made the time go faster. Not one of us had a watch so we had no idea when the hour was up.

Our plan worked like a charm. We all surged in together and nobody questioned Minnie's ticket.

At the fountain, after deciding what time to meet to go home, we broke up into families. Grampa had given each of us a quarter. It was the most money I'd ever had in my life and I couldn't wait to spend it. The first thing I wanted to buy was a gas balloon. But Willa wouldn't let me. She pried open my fingers, took the quarter and snapped it into her change purse. "If you spend it now you won't have anything to look forward to all day long," she reminded me sternly. I knew she was right, but I could hardly bear to part with it.

Arthur and I always buried the hatchet on Kids' Day, no matter what. He was still mad at me for snitching to the baker, but he held my hand when Willa told him to. "We don't want to get separated and have to waste the whole day looking for each other," she said wisely.

We did the rounds of the buildings in the morning. Willa's

favourite was the Flower Building, so we went there first. Arthur's was the Manufacturer's Building so we went there next. Mine was the Horse Palace and we went there last. Willa said, "Pewww!" and held her nose the whole time we were in there.

Then we headed for the Pure Food Building to line up for free samples. At least, Arthur and I lined up. Willa spent her time entering contests. She must have filled out a hundred entry blanks. *Win a bicycle! Win a car! Win a year's supply of groceries!* Who could believe it? It seemed like a terrible waste of time to me, and she hardly got any free samples.

Arthur and I kept running back to the end of the line to get more. By the time noonhour came we were absolutely stuffed with pork and beans, soup, bologna, pickles, cheese and crackers, and I can't remember what all. We were so full we could hardly eat our cucumber sandwiches, so we saved the leftovers for supper.

The Grandstand Show took up most of the afternoon. We got in free with our Kids' Day ticket. We went in early and got wonderful seats right in the middle of the huge curved stand.

It was such a long wait in the boiling sun that Arthur finally said, "Let's go. I'm sick of waiting." And I said "Yeah, and gimme my quarter. I wanna buy some pop and a red-hot."

"Shut up, both of you," barked Willa. "It'll be starting any minute now and it'll be worth the wait. You'll see. And I'm not missing a free show just because you two have ants in your pants."

Arthur and I nearly died laughing at our prim sister saying such a thing. And she was right, as usual. It was the most glorious show in the whole world. There were acrobats and trapeze artists, animal acts and magicians, and a man was even shot out of a cannon before our very eyes and lived to tell the tale. Then, at the end of the whole wonderful performance, came the musical ride of the Royal Canadian Mounted Police in their beautiful scarlet uniforms.

The sun was leaning far to the west by the time we got to the midway. We had no money to spend on rides, so we pressed right on through the crowd to the sideshows.

A barker stood on a wooden platform yelling through a makeshift megaphone. "Step right up, folks . . . Step inside. Only twenty-five cents, a quarter of a dollar, to view all the wonders of the world!"

A huge tent billowed mysteriously behind him. Overhead flapped gaudy pictures of the hidden wonders: a two-headed baby grinned impishly from both its dimpled mouths; a bearded lady twirled her spiky, waxed mustache; and the India Rubber Man tied himself in knots beside an ugly dog-faced boy.

"Willa, Willa, give me my quarter!" I cried beseechingly.

"Don't be silly. It's a waste of money," she snapped.

"Aren't they real?" I asked, wanting desperately to believe.

"No. Only the midgets are real."

As if to prove her right, at that very moment a little tiny lady was being lifted to the stand by a great big man who leapt nimbly up beside her.

"Ladies and gentlemen, your attention please!" cried the barker, and the crowd quieted obediently. "You see before you the world's most unique mother and son. The son weighs in at two hundred pounds, the little mother at thirty-six and a half. At birth this young man was one quarter of his mother's weight. If you don't believe me, ask them for yourself."

"That's disgusting," sniffed a lady behind me.

"There's a family resemblance," said her companion.

"Hey there, fella, that really your mother?" asked a nervy red-nosed man.

"I swear by all that's holy," declared the two-hundred pounder, holding up a Bible. "If I'm lying, may God strike me dead!"

The crowd glanced furtively heavenward, but nothing happened.

"Do you believe him, Willa?" asked Arthur.

"Noooo," answered Willa uncertainly.

Well, I believed him. Who but a fool or a madman would tell a big fat lie with a Bible in his hand?

After covering every inch of the midway we headed, footsore and weary, to the lakefront. Dropping down on the littered, matted brown grass, we finished up our lunch. Above us the azure sky was gaily polka-dotted with escaping gas balloons. I was glad Willa hadn't let me buy one.

"See that long cloud up there shaped like a big cigar?" said Arthur, munching on a soggy sandwich.

"Don't talk while you're eating," Willa said.

"It looks like the R–100," Arthur said, ignoring her.

"What's an R–100?" I asked, leaning back on my elbows to watch gas balloons go drifting through the cloud.

"It's a dirigible. An airship. It sailed over Toronto a couple of years ago."

"How come I didn't see it?"

"It was real early in the morning."

"How come you saw it then?"

"Because I was going to the bathroom, stupid."

"Let's go," said Willa. "It's getting late."

"I have to put Sloane's Liniment on first," said Arthur, pulling the bottle of amber liquid out of his knickers pocket. "My growing pains are killing me."

Arthur never went to the Ex without his liniment. After giving his knees a treatment, he handed the bottle to me. "Peww!" said Willa, but she rubbed a little on her knees too. The stinging liniment felt good, soaking into our aching joints and easing the pain away.

Our second visit to the Pure Food Building was our last stop. Finally Willa relinquished our quarters. Then came the big decision. Back and forth we went from booth to booth trying to decide what to buy. Willa settled on a Neilson's bag and I followed suit. In it were six nickel chocolate bars, a pink blotter for school, a cardboard hat to wear home on the streetcar so everyone would know where we'd been, a sausage-shaped balloon and a miniature can of Neilson's cocoa. Arthur spent his quarter on a Rowntree's bag just to be different. But the contents were exactly the same except our hats were shaped like a crown and his had a peak on it.

"Mine's better," I said.

"Mine is!" he retorted.

"It's six of one and half a dozen of the other," remarked our sister dryly.

Dusk was falling. One by one the coloured lights blinked on as we made our weary way to the fountain. The gang gathered, a few at a time. We were too tired to talk, so we just gazed up at the pretty rainbows the fountain was spraying into the navy blue sky.

Sandy Beasley's truck was waiting for us at the gates. Scrambling over the wobbly sides, we huddled together on the splintery floor. The air seemed suddenly chilly as the truck lumbered away from the star-spangled world of the exhibition grounds.

Minnie Beasley started chanting, "*Ice cream, soda water, ginger ale and pop. Swansea, Swansea is always on the top!*" But nobody could be bothered joining in.

Limping through the backyard of our stuck-together house, we smelled the spicy, mouth-watering aroma of simmering chili sauce escaping from the open kitchen door. While the chili sauce was evaporating to just the right thickness, Mum was busy darning a sock stretched over a burnt-out light bulb. On the cutting board on the table, Dad was carving out a piece of rubber tire to fit the heel of his boot.

Proudly, each of us presented our mother with our miniature cans of cocoa. "Glory be!" she exclaimed appreciatively. "I'll be able to make a thumping big chocolate cake with all that lovely cocoa."

Dad put aside his work and blew up our balloons.

"Jakey can have mine," Willa said.

"Billy can have mine," Arthur said.

I kept mine and it didn't break for a week. Boy, was I glad I'd let Willa take charge of my quarter!

20
"Happy Birthday, Booky"

Aunt Milly invited us all up for supper on Billy's and my birthday. It was a rare treat to be asked to somebody's house for a meal during the Depression. It probably used up Aunt Milly's whole week's food voucher to feed the bunch of us. But that's the way she was, Aunt Milly. She always said the more you give away, the more that comes back to you.

Things weren't going too well at home. Mum and Dad were still fighting all the time; the rent was overdue again; there wasn't a speck of coal in the dugout; and the kitchen cabinet was nearly as bare as Mother Hubbard's cupboard. Then, like a ray of sunshine on a cloudy day, came the invitation.

Aunt Milly and Uncle Mort lived on Durie Street, just below Bloor. About four in the afternoon we started walking over. I walked ahead, pushing the baby in the old reed sulky. One of the wheels was bent, and it was hard to push. It went *thump, thump, thump* along the sidewalk, making Billy laugh. He had on a blue knitted outfit Mum had made from an unravelled sweater. The colour matched his eyes exactly. He was cute as a button when he wasn't crying. It was hard to believe he was the same pitiful baby born just a year ago that day.

Aunt Milly and Uncle Mort had three children. The youngest was a darling baby girl about Billy's age. She was named Bonny because she was so pretty. The middle child was a boy called Sunny because he was sunny-natured. The oldest was a girl called Dimples, and every time she smiled you could tell the reason why. Of course, these weren't their real names. They were just nicknames Aunt Milly had made up. I asked her once what nickname she would give me if I were her little girl. "Bunny," she answered promptly, "because you're quick as a rabbit and cute as a bunny." I liked that.

Aunt Milly's suppers were always something special. You never knew what to expect. So we could hardly wait to get there to find out what was in store for us.

"Halloo, dears!" came her gay greeting at the door. Uncle Mort hung our coats on the hallway hooks and we all trooped down the hall to the kitchen.

A coal fire crackled in the kitchen stove, making it warm and cosy. We hadn't had a fire in our stove yet, even though it was the beginning of November.

In her cute yellow housedress, with her auburn curls bouncing on her girlish shoulders, Aunt Milly flitted about the kitchen like a canary in a Hawthorne bush.

"What can I do for you, Milly?" Mum asked.

"You can sit yourself down, that's what," returned her younger sister. "Arthur and Willa will help me, won't you, kidlets?" She gave them a wink through thick mascara-darkened lashes.

She didn't have to ask twice. They both jumped up eagerly and ran to do her bidding.

Uncle Mort was as handsome as his wife was pretty. And he

was nice too. He offered Dad his tobacco pouch the minute they sat down, and told him to roll his own. Dad liked that.

Sunny and Dimples took Jakey down the cellar to play, and I squatted on the floor to amuse the babies. Bonny was walking already. Back and forth she toddled bringing toys to Billy. He sat on a pink blanket, his long legs spread-eagled to give him balance. He hadn't even stood up yet, let alone walked. So Bonny seemed awfully smart by comparison. Until she started to talk. That's when she had to take a back seat to our Billy. Her baby-chatter sounded like pure gibberish compared to his clear words and bright little sentences.

"I never heard anything like it, Franny," marvelled Aunt Milly. "It's uncanny, a baby talking before he can walk. Why, he's as sharp as a tack."

Mum and I exchanged proud glances.

It was lovely to see everybody happy and having a good time—Dad talking and smoking, instead of yelling; Mum smiling and relaxing, instead of nagging. It just did my heart good.

"Soup's on!" cried Aunt Milly, waving us to the table with her long red fingernails.

Uncle Mort held Bonny on his lap so Billy could use her high chair. Arthur and Willa sat on either side of Aunt Milly and I got squeezed on a kitchen stool between Mum and Dad. The three little ones sat like a row of midgets on the wash bench behind the table.

When dinner was served, it wasn't soup at all—it was fish and chips and ketchup! And instead of tea or cocoa or water to wash it down with, we each got a green glass bottle of Coca-Cola. One at every place!

"You shouldn't waste your money on soft drinks for us,

Milly," Mum said, taking a big slurp that started her hiccupping.

"It sure is fizzy stuff," Dad laughed. "It went right up my nose."

It tasted so good I could hardly believe it. Even better than Vernor's ginger ale at Eaton's. I wanted to sip it slowly the way Willa and Arthur had the sense to do, but a sudden craving came over me and I slopped the whole works down in five seconds flat.

"I've still got half mine left," teased Arthur.

"You should have made it last, Bea," chided Willa.

"Don't make a pig of yourself," scolded Dad.

My eyes brimmed with tears, but Mum stemmed the flood with her yearly warning. "If you cry on your birthday, Bea, it means you'll cry all the year round."

Then Aunt Milly came to my rescue. "Fiddle dee dee," she said, "there's more where that came from." She disappeared into the cellarway and came back with another whole carton. Boy, did Willa and Arthur empty their bottles in a hurry!

I made sure my second Coke lasted until all my fish and chips were gone. The mixture of those delicious flavours, all going down together, was just too wonderful to describe.

Mum jumped up to help clear the table.

"No you don't, Fran. You just sit back and relax. You look all fagged out."

"Thank you, Milly," sighed Mum, settling back gratefully.

Poor Mum. We hardly ever paid attention to how tired she was.

When the table was cleared, Aunt Milly disappeared again, this time into the pantry. Out she came carrying a lighted birthday cake, and everyone joined in singing "Happy Birthday" to Billy and me. Eleven pink candles encircled the round chocolate cake, with a blue one in the middle for Billy.

Uncle Mort switched off the kitchen light. I'll never forget that moment—that magical moment of flickering lights and glowing faces and shadows bouncing on the walls.

"Lights! Lights!" cried Billy, gleefully clapping his hands, the yellow flames dancing in his eyes.

I showed him how to make an "O" with his mouth and we huffed and puffed and blew the candles out together.

"Did you make a wish, Bea?" asked Willa.

"Oh, darn! I forgot!" I cried worriedly.

"It's too late now!" jeered Arthur.

"Indeed it's not," retorted Aunt Milly, handing me the bread knife. "You can wish while you're making the first cut, Bea. That works every time."

I made my usual wish, that I'd pass the following June, and hoped with all my might that Aunt Milly knew what she was talking about.

Uncle Mort began putting Dixie cups of ice cream and little wooden spoons in front of us.

"My stars, Milly," Mum exclaimed, her curiosity getting the better of her. "How in the world do you do it? How on earth can you afford all these treats? I haven't had ice cream and soft drinks in a month of Sundays."

"Fair trade's no robbery, Fran," asserted Aunt Milly, raising her plucked eyebrows. "I just ask the grocer for ice cream and Coke and he writes down peas and potatoes. What does he care? It's all the same as long as he gets paid."

"But—but—" spluttered Mum, "you're not allowed to get

confections on your relief voucher, Milly. You could get in trouble."

"That's why he puts down potatoes and peas. Try it, Fran. It's easy."

"I'd never get away with it," Mum said, a bit miffed. "I haven't got your way with people, Milly."

"We haven't even got a lump of coal, never mind ice cream and soft drinks," put in Dad sullenly.

"Coal?" chirped Aunt Milly mischievously. "You need coal? Run down the cellar and get Jim a bag of coal, Morty. Share and share alike, that's my motto."

Mum shook her head in disbelief. What would her outrageous little sister think of next?

When the dishes were done (I didn't have to help because it was my birthday) there were presents for the baby and me. I got brown ribbed stockings and flannelette bloomers, and a Big Little Book from Aunt Milly. Billy got Doctor Denton Sleepers and a rubber duck. It was a terrific birthday party, the best I'd ever had.

We started off home under a cold night sky. "Love you!" Aunt Milly called after us.

Mum pushed the sulky with the bag of coal hidden under Billy's covers. "Might as well keep it under wraps," her sister had said. "If you get asked no questions, you can tell no lies."

Dad carried Billy inside his khaki coat with only his head poking out. "Lights! Lights!" cried the baby, his head flung back, staring up at the starry sky.

We hurried home and rushed inside to get warm. But the kitchen was as cold as stone. Right away Dad stuffed the stove with torn paper and broken sticks and set a match to them. In seconds the fire roared up the chimney. Then, lump by lump, he added the precious fuel and put what was left in the coal shuttle.

Mum closed the door between the dining room and kitchen and soon it was warm and cosy. We undressed by the stove, being careful not to look at one another. Mum heated up the iron to make warm spots on our sheets.

"Happy Birthday, Booky," she said as she kissed my forehead and tucked the thin covers under my chin.

Booky. It was a nice nickname. I liked it even better than Bunny. And a lot better than Scatterbrain.

21
Turkey and mistletoe

The Christmas season started out a lot better than it had the year before. Dad got a few weeks' work shovelling snow, Aunt Aggie sent us a chicken again and two Swansea churches gave us food hampers. Mum hadn't decided which one to belong to yet, the Presbyterian or the Baptist, so we shilly-shallied back and forth between them, and that's how come we got two hampers. And besides that there were Star Boxes too!

Stuffing was piled high in the mixing bowl on the shelf of the kitchen cabinet. Christmas cake was aging in a tin on the sideboard, and plum pudding sat on a plate wrapped in cheesecloth ready for steaming. Mum had made them both way back in November.

On Christmas Eve Dad strung the red and green crepe paper streamers from corner to corner of the dining room. In the middle, where they came together, he hung the red paper fold-out bell. It was beautiful!

Then after supper he went out to get the tree. Jakey and I stationed ourselves at the front room window to wait for him. It wasn't long before we saw him humping down the street, his left shoulder riding up and down with his short left leg, a snowy spruce tree sweeping a wide path behind him.

He made a sturdy stand out of two pieces of crossed wood and nailed it to the bottom of the tree. Dragging it through the dining room, he set it up in the front room corner. It was the biggest tree we'd ever had. Its tip touched the ten-foot ceiling.

"Let's go to bed, Bea-Bea," begged Jakey, his brown eyes glistening.

"Okay," I agreed, even though it was only seven o'clock and I wasn't the least bit tired.

Snuggling under the covers with Dad's greatcoat piled on top, I began the ritual of the Christmas stories. The old beliefs came flooding back with the telling. I decided to give Santa one more chance.

The next morning our stockings were filled with the usual stuff—an apple, an orange and some candy cushions. But at the foot of the bed were two wonderful surprises—a bright red fire engine for Jakey and a green and red telephone for me. The very one I had asked for last year. Squealing with delight, we hightailed it down the hall to show our parents what Santa had brought.

All morning long Jakey shrilled his fire engine around the bare wood floor in front of the Christmas tree and I telephoned everybody under the sun. Arthur said the screeching siren and jangling bells would drive a man to drink. Then he took a long swig out of a gingerbeer bottle full of water. But he wasn't really mad, because he was too busy enjoying his new art pad and box of paints. Willa had put on her Sunday dress to show off her pink pearl beads. And Billy was chewing happily on the soft brown ear of his brand-new teddy bear.

Halfway through the morning, Dad stepped outside to put some garbage in the tin. Then he stepped back in again with a puzzled expression on his face. He had a bulky brown parcel in one hand and a sheaf of long white envelopes in the other.

"I found these on top of the garbage lid," he said, setting the brown parcel on the table.

A name was scrawled across each envelope—*Willa, Arthur, Beatrice, John* and *William*. Dad scratched his head and handed them around to us.

Eagerly we tore them open to find a beautiful Christmas card inside with a quarter taped to each. But no signature.

"Who could have done it?" wondered our bewildered Dad.

"I know! I know!" I screeched, renewed faith breaking over me. "Santa! To make up for last year!"

"He doesn't give money, dumb-bell!" scoffed Arthur. (But I noticed he didn't say there was no Santa Claus.)

"Oh, mercy, my fingers are all thumbs," Mum said struggling with the parcel. Then she gasped as she lifted a big fat fowl from the wrappings.

"That's a whopper of a chicken," Dad said.

"It's not a chicken, it's a turkey," Willa said.

"And it's all cleaned, ready for the oven," Mum marvelled, bending down to inspect the dark interior. A turkey! Imagine! With drumsticks as big as my fist!

Dad was studying the envelope the baby's card had come in. "The handwriting looks familiar," he mused.

Mum studied it too. Then she jumped up on the little stool that made her tall enough to reach the top of the kitchen cabinet and jumped down again with the "Neilson's Chocolates" receipt box in her hand. Rummaging through it, she found last month's rent receipt and held it out beside the envelope.

"'William' is written exactly the same as Billy Sundy's signature," Dad said.

"Didn't I tell you it was our lucky day when we moved into Billy and Maude's house?" Mum cried, tee-heeing and rubbing her hands in that excited way she had.

Dad just shook his head. He could hardly credit a landlord who gave his tenants food and gifts instead of sending the bailiff around to put them out.

"What'll we do with Aunt Aggie's chicken?" asked Arthur.

"It'll keep," Mum said. "I'll tie it in a potato sack and hang it out on the line. It'll freeze solid in no time and be fresh as a daisy for New Year's. Maybe we'll ask Charlie and Myrtle and little Sarah over to share it with us. Except Charlie spoils that baby so badly I can hardly bear the little imp."

In the afternoon I ran over to Grampa's. Joey was perched on the stool, nibbling. He fixed me with the evil eye.

"Where's Grampa?" I asked nervously.

"Who wants to know?" he growled.

Lucky for me I didn't have to answer because just then Grampa came up from the cellar. "Hello there, Be-a-trice." His mouth curved under his moustache. "Was Santa good to you this year?"

I showed him my toy telephone and told him all about what everybody got, and about the mysterious stuff on top of the garbage lid. While I talked, a mile a minute, he lifted a huge golden goose from the wood-stove oven. Mum had asked them over to our house, but Grampa had said no, she had enough mouths to feed.

He didn't have a Christmas box for me and I didn't expect

one. I knew he had too many grandchildren to buy presents for. But he had something for me just the same. With a quick twist of his wiry wrist, he snapped the drumstick off the golden goose and dropped it in a bag.

"Are you givin' *her* the leg of our goose, Pa?" cried Joey angrily.

His father didn't answer. Instead he ripped off the other leg, clean as a whistle, and dropped it in beside its greasy mate.

"Merry Christmas, Be-*a*-trice," he said, handing me the steaming hot bag.

I didn't dare look at Joey. I just took the aromatic present, kissed my Grampa under his moustache and high-tailed it home through the lane.

I steered clear of Grampa's for weeks after that. Finally he came over to see if I was sick.

"I got worried, Be-*a*-trice," he said.

"I'm sorry, Grampa," I said. "But I'm scared of Joey. He always gives me dirty looks, and he never smiles even when I smile first."

My words made his eyes cloud over. "You mustn't pay him any mind." There was a catch in his voice. "His bark is worse than his bite. You got to remember that he was younger than you when he lost his ma. I'm all he's got left."

That's when I understood how it was with Joey. And Evie too. I couldn't imagine what it would be like to have no mother. No Mum to iron my bed in winter; no Mum to take me downtown to Eaton's; no Mum to call me Booky. I'd be jealous too, if Dad was all I had left.

After that I managed to conquer my fear of my boy-uncle, and many's the laugh we had, when we grew up, about him sitting in the corner chewing seeds and spitting husks and growling like a bear to scare me off.

That Christmas night I went to bed contented, but I was so elated I couldn't fall asleep. Willa was sawing it off beside me and the boys had long since settled down. Even Billy. Come to think of it, he seemed to sleep a lot sounder now that his cot was in the boys' room.

The warm, happy day kept going through my mind like a talking-picture show. Mum and Dad hadn't had a crabby word between them. I had spent the whole peaceful day talking on my telephone and reading a book Willa had given me called *Anne of Green Gables*. I loved every word of it. Then and there I decided to be a writer when I grew up.

As I read, I gnawed away on one of my goose legs. The minute Arthur saw it he hollered, "Bits on you!" and Mum made me give him and Jakey the other leg to share. Lucky for me, Willa hated goose. "Eww!" she cried, wrinkling her nose. "I wouldn't touch the greasy thing with a ten-foot pole!" When the meat was gone I sucked the bone for hours. By the time I threw it in the garbage tin it was as clean and bare as a clothes pin.

Then came the turkey dinner. Instead of a drumstick, Dad gave me a slice of breast for a change. I'd never tasted anything like it, so succulent and tender. The rest of my plate overflowed with fluffy mashed potatoes, spicy bread dressing and lots of bright-coloured vegetables all glistening with golden brown gravy.

"Save room for plum pudding!" Mum cried. As if we needed reminding.

Then after the pudding came Christmas cake! "It would kill

a man twice to eat one slice of Mrs. Thomson's Christmas cake!" sang Mum gaily as she sliced up the delicious dark fruit loaf.

Thinking about all that lovely food made me hungry again. So I got up out of bed and tiptoed down the stairs. Only the kitchen light was on, so I saw them but they didn't see me.

Willa had tied a sprig of mistletoe to the light chain and Mum and Dad were kissing under it! My heart skipped a beat and thrills ran up my spine. What a way to finish Christmas!

I crept back up the stairs again and they never knew I was there.

22
Incredible news

My hollow tooth was acting up again. Every night Mum had to stuff it full of cotton soaked in oil of cloves. But that didn't help much. So one cold February day Dad took me downtown to the Dental College to have it pulled.

Boy, was that awful! The student dentist was young and smart-alecky, and he snickered at me the whole time he was doing it. Then, after he'd nearly killed me, Dad paid with a quarter and we left.

On the Dundas streetcar Dad handed me his clean hanky to hold against my mouth. Then he opened the window a crack so I wouldn't get sick. A nice lady across the aisle gave me a pitying look as the hanky slowly turned wet and crimson.

A warm sweet smell drifted in the open window.

"I smell hot cocoa, Dad," I mumbled through the soggy hanky.

"That would be Neilson's Chocolate Factory," Dad said. "You can smell it for miles around."

"Can we stop and ask for free bits, Dad?" (I had heard, through the grapevine, that Neilson's gave away free chocolate bits, the way Canada Bread sometimes gave away broken biscuits.)

"If we get off we'll have to walk the rest of the way," Dad said, looking at me anxiously. "Are you sure you're up to it?"

"I'm sure," I said, wiping the pink dribble off my chin and longing for the chocolate in spite of my sore mouth. "Please, Dad!"

The lady smiled encouragement. Dad smiled back and we jumped off the streetcar at the next stop. Neilson's was only a hop, skip and jump up Gladstone Avenue.

Just as we approached the factory, two men came staggering down the front steps carrying a stretcher. Over it was thrown a lumpy grey blanket with a pair of big black boots sticking out. The soles of the boots were covered with dark, thick chocolate.

Hastily Dad removed his cap and laid it flat against his chest. Respectfully I hung my head as the stretcher passed by and was loaded into a waiting ambulance.

It had no sooner pulled away from the curb than a man at the factory door said to Dad, "You looking for work, Mister?"

"Yes, sir!" answered Dad, clicking his heels like a soldier.

"Well, I just lost my maintenance man." The man jerked his head in the direction of the disappearing ambulance. "The job's yours if you can start first thing in the morning. Hours are eight to six, six days a week. Pay's twelve dollars. If you'll follow me, I'll sign you up and give you a week's advance."

My legs started to shake with excitement, so I sat down on a green bench in the entranceway while Dad went into the office. Was it really happening? Could it be true? When Dad came out, his face beaming, I knew it was.

"Would you like a bag of chocolate bits to take home with you, Missy?" asked Dad's new boss kindly.

"Yes, please," I whispered, my heart in my mouth.

We practically ran all the way home with our wonderful, glorious news.

It was Monday, so it was washday. The kitchen was draped from corner to corner with frozen flannelette sheets. They smelled clean and frosty, and they crackled when you brushed against them. It was like walking into an icy white maze. We couldn't tell who was in the kitchen.

"Don't lay a finger on my clean sheets!" Mum barked, tired and crabby, as usual, from scrubbing on the board all day. So we ducked under, and it was then she saw the smile on Dad's face.

"What are you grinning about?" she snapped crankily.

"I've got a job!" The words flew from his lips like a bird let loose from its cage. He could no more hold them back than I could still the wild beating of my heart.

"An odd job?" Mum asked, too quickly.

"No," Dad cried indignantly, "a full-time job. A steady, paying job! I've got work!"

"Steady—full-time—work!" repeated Mum dazedly.

The incredible news brought everybody out of hiding. Jakey popped up from under the table. Willa sidled through the sheets from the direction of the sink. Arthur appeared out of nowhere, and the baby started to cry for attention from the high chair. Dad scooped him up and tossed him in the air and the crying changed to gurgling, bubbling laughter. Nobody spoke. They just stood there gaping as if they daren't believe their ears. Then Dad told them the whole story.

"It was all Bea's doing," he said, smiling down at me and giving my head a pat. "If she hadn't persuaded me to stop, in spite of her sore jaw and against my better judgement, I never would have landed that job." Boy, was I proud of myself. And of my Dad, the maintenance man!

Willa and Arthur both gave me admiring glances. So I dumped my chocolate bits out on the table and told them to help themselves.

* * *

Dad was never out of work again. The humiliations of the pogey and the bread lines, the Star Boxes and the food hampers were all behind him now. He even allowed himself an occasional luxury, like a nickel packet of Sweet Caps or a package of "roll-your-owns."

And Mum finally got her washing-machine. A Thor, just like Aunt Hester's. She joined the Home Lover's Club at Eaton's and paid for it at two dollars a month, so it never had to go back to the store. And she kept her vow about the Annex too. It never saw her again for dust!

Visitors from Saskatoon

A Booky Story

Visitors from Saskatoon

On New Year's night of 1933 we all got a big surprise.

Jakey and Billy had been put to bed, and for once Billy had gone right off to sleep. Mum and Dad were sitting on either side of the stove. Mum was turning the collar of Arthur's Sunday shirt, and Dad was scraping the rust off a pocket-knife he'd found in the dump, while he was sifting ashes for coal. Mum and Dad weren't talking, this night, but they weren't fighting either.

Suddenly there was a knock at the front door.

Whenever there was an unexpected knock, especially at night, Mum's eyes would grow big and dark. It was a strange, almost haunted look.

"Maybe it's her," she'd whisper.

The words sent shivers up and down our spines.

"Her" was Mum's long-lost sister, Renee. We all knew Aunt Renee's story off by heart. When she was only fourteen, younger than our Willa, she ran away from home and was never seen or heard of again. Mum was sixteen at the time, and she had just bought herself a new spring suit from Eaton's. Well, when Aunt Renee took it into her head to run away, she did it in Mum's new suit. At first, Mum said, she thought she'd never forgive Renee. But as the years slipped by and her sister never returned she said the new suit didn't matter anymore. All that mattered was for Renee to come safely home again.

Us kids liked to imagine that Aunt Renee had run off to Hollywood and become a famous movie queen like Clara Bow or Norma Shearer or Renee Adoree. But Mum, who was a great fan of the silver screen, said no, none of them was Renee. She'd know her sister anywhere.

Dad went to answer the door, and we held our breath in hope. It wasn't our long-lost Auntie, but someone almost as exciting: Dave Atlas from Saskatoon, Saskatchewan, and his wife.

Dave was an old beau of Mum's, and he was tall, dark and handsome. He grabbed Mum right up off the floor and kissed her on the lips. Then he pumped Dad's hand and introduced Mary. He had such a jolly air that suddenly the whole house seemed to be sparkling with fun and laughter.

Mary Atlas took to Arthur right away. "Oh my, what a handsome boy you are!" she cooed, hugging him to her bosom. (Arthur always seemed to affect ladies that way). "How I wish you were mine." Looking up angelically through the ruffles of her bodice, Arthur favoured her with his most winning smile. Instantly the green-eyed monster jumped up inside of me. Arthur was downright pretty when he smiled like that, and I felt plainer than ever.

Dave Atlas was holding Willa by the shoulders at arm's length. "So this is the gold-medallist!" He beamed. "And such a fine-looking girl too. No wonder you're both so proud of her."

Mum and Dad were positively radiant, and I never saw Willa smile so big before. You could count every tooth in her head.

Suddenly it was my turn. Scooping me off the floor as if I was a feather, Dave sat me on the kitchen table. With twinkling eyes he looked me up and down, from the top of my straight fair hair to the tips of my scuffed-out toes. "Why, Fran," he exclaimed as I blushed to the roots of my buster cut, "this one is the image of you."

I was absolutely flabbergasted and so was Mum. Nobody had ever seen a resemblance between us before.

"Oh, no, Dave," Mum spluttered, "Bea is all Thomson. She's the dead-spit of Jim's sister Aggie in colouring, and she's got his mother's eyes."

"It's not colouring or eyes I'm talking about, Fran," insisted Dave, "it's expression. She's got the Cole expression all over her face."

Well, I was tickled pink and I think Mum was too. Not that I minded taking after Dad's side, or having his dead mother's eyes. But it meant something special to me to be told, for once, that I had inherited something from my vivacious mother. It was hard on me being the middle child, and a homely one to boot, so Dave's compliment thrilled me to pieces.

Oh, how I loved that man! His wife was nice, too, once you got to know her. But it was Dave who charmed us all. All except Dad, that is. He stayed in the background, saying very little.

Dave and Mary's visit lasted two whole days and nights. They went to the Kingston Road and brought back a giant bag of groceries: meat and can-goods and even a basket of fruit—fruit, and no-one was even sick! There were apples and bananas and tangerines and grapefruit. I could hardly wait to taste them.

Willa and I gladly gave up our room for the company. Willa slept on the davenport and I slept, or tried to, between two dining-room chairs shoved together. Two or three times each night they came apart and dumped me on the floor, but I didn't care. It was all the more fun.

The first night of their visit we played a parlour game. It was called, "Heavy, heavy hang over thy head."

Mum was the first one to be "It." She sat, blindfolded, on a chair in the middle of the front room. It seemed strange to see her sitting down playing a game for once, instead of rushing around trying to "get done." Dave stood behind her, waving Dad's best handkerchief over her head.

"Heavy, heavy hang over thy head," he intoned the magic words, winking at me.

"Fine or superfine?" asked Mum. She knew exactly what to say, so she must have played this game before, but us kids were puzzled. Mary explained: "Fine means the thing belongs to a boy or man. Superfine means it belongs to a girl or woman."

"Fine," Dave answered, grinning. "What shall he do to retrieve it?"

"That means, what penalty will he have to pay to get it back," whispered Mary.

Arthur and I could hardly keep from laughing.

"Now . . . let me see," said Mum, her dark-winged eyebrows rising over the blindfold. She must have heard our snickers and guessed the thing belonged to Arthur because she said, "To retrieve it, he must give Mary a great big kiss."

Off came the blindfold and our snickers changed to hoots of laughter at her expression as she recognized Dad's handkerchief. Then we squealed with glee to see our bashful Dad jump up, grinning from ear to ear, and plant a kiss right on the mouth of Mary Atlas.

Now it was Dad's turn in the chair. Over his wispy fair head Mary dangled her husband's gold pocket-watch.

"Heavy, heavy hang over thy head," she tittered, still blushing from Dad's big smacker.

"Fine or superfine?" answered Dad promptly.

"Fine. What shall he do to retrieve it?"

"Aha!" exclaimed Dad knowingly. "I think I hear a timepiece ticking overhead. So to retrieve it the owner must smoke a cigarette down to a stub in two minutes flat."

Taking a packet of Sweet Caps out of his shirt pocket, Dave offered one to Dad and lit them both with his lighter. He puffed like a steam-engine while Arthur and I jigged around him in crazy, squealing circles. His face turned red and the air turned blue and he nearly burnt his fingers, but he beat the deadline and got his watch back as we all gave him a rousing cheer. All but Dad. He was busy blowing smoke rings at the ceiling.

It was Dave's turn now. Over his head, Dad dangled Mum's only string of beads.

"Heavy, heavy hang over thy head," Dad chanted.

"Fine or superfine?" Dave returned.

"Superfine . . . what shall she do to retrieve it?"

"She must recite a poem that starts like this: *I asked my mother for fifty cents* . . . "

"Oh, Dave!" laughed Mum, reaching for her beads. "How in the world did you know they were mine?"

Whipping off the blindfold, he snatched the necklace out of her reach. "First the poem, Franny, just like you used to say it in my mother's back-kitchen."

"Oh, pshaw, Dave, I don't think I can remember it . . . let me see . . .

"I asked my mother for fifty cents,
To see the elephant jump the fence.
He jumped so high, he touched the sky
And didn't come back till the twelfth of July."

We all started to clap and cheer but Mum said, "Shhh, there's more . . . it's coming to me!

"I asked my mother for fifty more,
To see the elephant scrub the floor,
He scrubbed so fast he fell on his . . .
I asked my mother for fifty more!

"I haven't thought of that silly old ditty for thirty years." Mum laughed, then added quickly, "It's not very nice, is it?" But I thought it was hilarious.

Each of us had a turn at the game. What fun it was! Arthur had to run around the outside of the house three times to earn his bow tie back. Out he flew without his coat, with Mum shouting after him that he'd catch his death of cold. Willa had to say the alphabet backwards twice to win her imitation tortoise-shell barrette back. And to retrieve my best blue garters, I had to knock a dime off my nose with my tongue. I leaned my head back as far as it would go and Dave balanced the coin on the end of my knobby nose. I flicked out my tongue, like a frog catching flies, and sent the dime bouncing to the floor. Right away Arthur started jeering, "Snaky-tongue! Snaky-tongue!" But when Dave said I could keep the dime, Mum said that Arthur would have to laugh on the other side of his face.

We kids could have kept it up all night, but Dad said it was past our bedtime.

"Awww," moaned Arthur. And Dad said, "Give them an inch and they want a mile." So we went to bed before we spoiled everything.

The next night was almost as good. Mum and Dave started reminiscing about when they were young and growing up in Swansea. Dad sat back, quietly enjoying another cigarette. That made two cigarettes he had smoked in as many days. It was a wonder he didn't get sick. Mary cuddled Billy on her lap and Jakey sat on the short-legged stool with his head against her knee. We listened raptly to the sad and funny stories about brothers and sisters and friends.

"Remember Polly Vaughan with the long gold plait down her back? You were sweet on her, Dave. Remember?"

"Ah, yes." Dave grew misty-eyed. "But I only chased her to make you jealous, Franny. You were the only girl for me."

"Oh, pshaw, Dave. You say that to all the girls," Mum said, blushing. "Poor little Polly. She died of galloping consumption when she was only nineteen and she left a tiny baby behind. And her sister, Amy, the one with the red hair and freckles . . . she followed Polly home not six months later. Only she died in childbirth, poor little soul."

Willa and I exchanged a scared look. I vowed then and there never to have a baby when I grew up.

"Whatever became of Joel Harris, Fran, do you know?"

"Oh, sure. He married Veeny White and they moved up north to Huntsville. The last I heard they had eleven children. Isn't that a caution? And Myrtle Black . . . you remember the Blacks that lived in the tar-paper shack next to the schoolyard? Well, she went into nursing and stayed an old maid. Which wasn't such a bad idea, if you ask me. And her little brother, Morty, the one who walked like Charlie Chaplin? He married my little sister, Milly."

"What an Eaton Beauty doll Milly was," remembered Dave.

"Still is," put in Dad unexpectedly, "Even with three children."

"Ahhh," Mum sighed wistfully. "That old gang of mine."

Then Dave began to sing, softly. "Goodbye forever . . . dear fellas and gals . . ."

Mum joined in, "Goodbye forever . . . dear sweethearts and pals . . ." There wasn't a dry eye in the kitchen.

Then Dave swung into a rollicking chorus of an old World War I song. "Pack up your troubles in your old kit bag . . ."

Dad, always a soldier, joined in with "Smile, smile, smile." Then Dave and Dad made a duet of "It's a Long Way to Tipperary," only Dave changed the words to, "It's a long way to tickle Mary . . . " Mary gave him a playful smack and Arthur and I nearly died laughing.

It was the best possible way to begin the year. When Dave and Mary left the next morning, making us promise to come visit them in Saskatoon someday, the house suddenly seemed gloomy again. But I had seen a whole new side of my parents.

With Love From

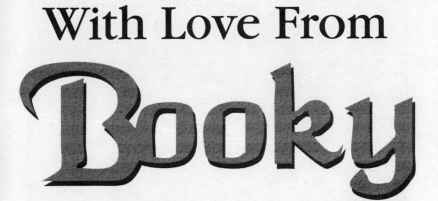

Booky

With love to my grandchildren,
Meredith, Lisa, Hunter and Franceline

With Love
From Booky

1
Cousins and 'lations

The summer I was sent away to Muskoka was the summer of my first big crush. I was madly in love with Georgie Dunn. He was one of the few kids in our gang who wasn't my cousin, so it was all right to be in love with him.

Almost everybody on Veeny Street was related in one way or another. For instance, my friend Gladie's father was my grandfather's brother. I thought this was sort of strange because Gladie and I were the same age. Ruthie's mother, who lived in the house next door, was my mother's first cousin. And Ada-May, who lived up the street, was Ruthie's second cousin on her mother's side and my third cousin on her father's side and I think she was Gladie's fourth cousin but I'm not sure what side.

Then there was Uncle Andy, who lived all by himself at the corner of Veeny and Mayberry in an old frame house with no electricity or bathroom. He was my great-uncle by marriage, but Great-Aunt Veeny, the one our street was named after, had got galloping consumption and gone home—that's what Mum called heaven—just three months after their wedding day.

All these cousins and 'lations—that's how Grampa Cole pronounced relations—were on Mum's side. Dad's family still lived in the log house his grandfather had built in Muskoka about a hundred years ago. Except for Uncle Charlie's family, who lived on Gerrard Street in Toronto. He had a barbershop in his front room instead of regular furniture, and he gave us free haircuts.

There were literally hundreds of us cousins and 'lations in Swansea, all descended from the very first settlers to emigrate from Swansea in Wales. That's how our little village on the western outskirts of Toronto got its name.

It was swell belonging to such a big, boisterous clan. But there was one drawback to being blood relations that all us kids had been warned about, and that was, when we grew up we could never marry each other or we'd all have crazy children like Roy-Roy the dumb boy.

Roy-Roy wore a flannelette bib around his neck and he slobbered and jabbered like a baby even though he was fourteen years old, the same age as Georgie and my brother Arthur. Roy-Roy and his mother, Raggie-Rachel, lived in a tarpaper shack down by Catfish Pond. Roy-Roy caught catfish with his bare hands—I even saw him do it once! Raggie-Rachel picked the dump for a living. We nicknamed her Raggie-Rachel because she always wore about five raggedy dresses piled on top of each other. Nobody knew who Roy-Roy's father was, but the grown-ups whispered behind their hands that he must have been Rachel's blood relation or how else could you account for Roy-Roy? Anyway, Mum said they were no kith or kin of ours.

So even though our gang was roughly made up of half boys and half girls, our friendships were mostly "plutonic." At least that's what my big sister Willa said, and she ought to know because she had just graduated into Fifth Form high school at the top of her class and she knew just about everything.

It was the end of June, 1935, and I had passed, by the skin of my teeth, into Senior Fourth. I was gleefully looking forward to hundreds of hot summer days, free as a bird, running all over Swansea, swimming in Lake Ontario, going to Sunnyside Amusement Park, playing street games and roasting swiped potatoes down in the woodsy hollows of the Camel's Back, when I suddenly took sick.

My chest went all wheezy and my face turned as grey as the sidewalk. At first Mum tried doctoring me herself; then, when that didn't work, she asked Maude Sundy to come over and take a look at me. Maude was our landlady but she was also a registered nurse, so everybody in Swansea called on her when they got sick. Well, Maude rubbed my chest with hot camphorated oil and dosed me with Friar's Balsam and purged me with Epsom salts and said I had to eat lots of eggs.

So Dad went right out and bought half a dozen eggs just for me, and Mum fixed me a lovely poached egg on toast every day. But when a week went by and I didn't show any signs of improvement, Maude said Mum had better take me to see a real doctor on Bloor Street.

Her name was Doctor Smelley—no kidding—and she was really nice so I decided I'd be a doctor when I grew up if doctors didn't have to be good in arithmetic. Well, Dr. Smelley said I had a bad case of bronchitis and it might turn into TB at any minute and what I needed in the worst way was fresh air and sunshine.

"You'll have to go to your Aunt Aggie's in Muskoka, Booky," Mum said, rubbing her hands together in that agitated way she had when she was worried. ("Boo-key" was the nickname she'd given me when I was a little kid.)

"But there's lots of fresh air and sunshine right here in Swansea, Mum!" I protested wheezily.

"Oh, pshaw, Bea." Mum's dark eyes were bright with fear. "What about all that black smoke belching out of the Bolt Works? And those awful fumes coming off the dump not a stone's throw from our front stoop? Why, it's enough to sicken a pig. No, Bea, I'm scared for you. You'll have to go to Muskoka."

Of course, I knew what she was scared of, that I'd get consumption and go galloping home in less than twenty-four hours, just like Great-Aunt Veeny did. I also knew that her decision was for my own good, but I could hardly stand the thought of being away for the whole summer and missing all the fun on Veeny Street.

And there was another reason why I didn't want to go. I hadn't breathed it to a living soul, not even to Gladie, who was my best friend. It was my crush on Georgie Dunn. I had planned on following him around all summer long until he noticed me. Now I wouldn't have the chance. So I argued and pleaded until I was blue in the face, but Mum wouldn't budge this time.

The very next Saturday some of Dad's relations, Cousin Harry and his big old wife Zelda, decided to make their annual one-day trek up to Muskoka. They said Dad and Arthur and I could ride for free in the rumble seat of their roadster. At least *that* sounded like fun. But it wasn't.

We had to leave at three in the morning to get there in time for breakfast. Well, it was so cold in the rumble seat that Arthur and I had to lie under a rug on the floor for the whole trip and Dad had to keep the rug from blowing off with his feet. It was the coldest I'd ever been in my life. It's a wonder we didn't get galloping pneumonia, if there is such a thing.

Arthur and I couldn't see a thing under the rug and we couldn't even talk for the noise of the wind and the tires. And the bumps on the road bounced us around and hurt something awful. All I could think about for the whole miserable journey was that my beautiful summer holidays would all be wasted and some other girl would be following after Georgie Dunn.

Aunt Aggie, who looked enough like me to be my mother, welcomed us with a whopping big breakfast. Even Grandpa Thomson, who Mum described as "an ugly man's dog if there ever was one," gave us a crooked smile and said he hoped I wouldn't eat him out of house and home.

Aunt Ida was there too. She was Dad's youngest sister and she had just recently separated from her husband, Uncle Wilbur. Well, in 1935 it was considered a pure disgrace to be separated so Aunt Ida had come up to her father's farm to try to live it down.

I didn't like her much. For one thing, she thought she was gorgeous. She had blonde, marcelled hair covered over with an invisible hairnet—which I could see as plain as day—and round blue eyes, and red bow-shaped lips. She wore floral, dimity frocks and high-heeled shoes and real silk stockings. And for another thing, she thought she was smart. She was forever showing off by reciting poetry: *Be good, sweet maid, and let who will be clever. Do noble things, not dream them all day long.* Every time she saw me she said those lines and I took it as a personal insult.

But I liked Aunt Aggie. She was a spinster and she stayed at home to help Grandpa work the farm. She was tall and lean and kind. Her straw-coloured hair was done up in a bun that looked like a cowflap and when she let it down at night it was long enough to sit on. Her face was lined and brown from the sun, and her bent-wire spectacles kept sliding down her shiny nose. She wore plain calico dresses, low-heeled house shoes and black cotton stockings that wrinkled around her ankles.

"Well, Bea, I like your new haircut," she said about my boyish bob. Mum had taken me down to Uncle Charlie's to have it cut that way so it would last all summer and start to grow out just in time for school. I liked it myself because it was easy to wash and comb and it made me feel like a boy.

Grandpa Thomson was old and stooped and grey. He had a wrinkled, leathery face and deep-set, piercing blue eyes. "You're getting to be a big girl, Beatrice," he said, and I took it as a compliment coming from him. It had been two years since I'd been up to Muskoka and he hadn't laid eyes on me in the meantime, so I guess I looked different to him. But as far as I could see I hadn't changed a bit. I was twelve-going-on-thirteen and I was still skinny as a rake and I hadn't even started to fill out where I was supposed to. Gladie had—and she was six months younger than me. That made me mad.

After we washed up the breakfast dishes we all trooped down to the barn to admire Bessie's brand-new calf. Grandpa let me name it and I called it Georgie even though it was a girl calf. Arthur called me a dumb-bell and I was afraid for a minute he'd guess about my crush on Georgie, but he didn't.

Then we all went to the back pasture to say hello to Major. He flung his head over the split-rail fence and nickered and nuzzled Arthur and me as if he remembered us. After that we followed Aunt Aggie to the hen house where she proudly counted out the laying hens. There were fourteen in all, sitting on their nests, chittering and blinking, their funny red eyelids going up instead of down. Clucking softly with her tongue, Aunt Aggie slipped a hand underneath each setting hen without disturbing it, and gathered some new-laid eggs to send back home to Mum.

Right after dinner, which was served at noon instead of supper time like at home, Cousin Harry jumped up and declared, "Well, we'd best be making tracks!" In spite of her broad backside wedged in the chair, Cousin Zelda was up like a shot and out the door leaving all the dirty dishes. (Cousin Zelda wasn't one of my favourite relations. She always said I was the deadspit of Aunt Aggie, then in the next breath she'd say Aunt Aggie had a face like a horse's rear end.)

Dad kissed me goodbye and gave me a nickel to spend in case we ever went into Huntsville—which was very unlikely since Grandpa only had a horse and buggy and it would take all day to get there. Arthur thumbed his nose at me in a friendly way as he hopped into the rumble seat.

I watched as the roadster pulled away, swirling up the Muskoka dust, with Dad and Arthur waving gaily from the back.

A lump the size of a peach stone rose into my throat, nearly choking me. I waved and waved until they disappeared around the red-dirt turning and into the tunnel of trees. The red dust settled and I could see the heat waves rising from the road. A stream of loneliness washed over me and I felt as if I was going to drown.

Then Aunt Aggie hugged me from behind. I wheeled around and pressed my face against her warm, flat chest.

2
My hero

The log house had a big kitchen, a long parlour and three bed-rooms upstairs. I slept in the smallest bedroom on a narrow cot with a straw mattress. There was a washstand beside the bed and a chamber pot underneath it, that's all.

"This was your dad's room when he was a boy," Aunt Aggie reminded me. "The same bed too, mattress 'n all."

"And that's my grandmother in the picture," I said, pointing to the likeness of a sad-faced woman who looked a lot like me and Aunt Aggie.

"Yes, that's Ma. She died long before you were ever thought of." Aunt Aggie kissed me on the forehead, blew out the can-dle and went downstairs. (Grandpa Thomson didn't hold with taking lamps upstairs just for getting into bed. Waste of kerosene, he said.) Anyway, I could see by the moonlight com-ing in the little square window and it made me feel less lonely sleeping in Dad's bed, with his mother gazing down at me from the oval frame above.

I curled up and began to rub the knob on the end of my nose. It was Cousin Zelda who had told me that if I massaged the knob every night it would gradually wear away. She said she knew a girl who had a nose just like mine and after five years of massaging it she'd won a beauty contest. Not that I expected to win a beauty contest, but I was tired of having to face everybody all the time so they wouldn't notice my awful profile. And I thought that maybe without the knob I'd be good-looking like Arthur. We looked a lot alike, since we both favoured Dad's side, but he had a nice neat nose.

With the tip of my finger I rubbed in a circular motion, thinking about home. Things were going much better now that Dad was working steady. His pay packet was only twelve dollars a week, but Mum was really proud of how far she could make a dollar stretch. They didn't fight like they used to when Dad wasn't working and we were on the pogey. But they still couldn't afford more than one quart of milk a day so there was never enough for drinking, only for porridge and tea and hot-water cocoa.

Aunt Aggie knew this so she made sure I got lots of fresh milk while I was on the farm. Every day, morning and night, I'd follow her down to the barn with my cup. She'd fill it to the brim with foamy, warm milk right from the cow, laughing as she squirted the creamy jet dead centre into my cup. She said I reminded her of a heifer being fattened up for the slaughter. She said funny things, Aunt Aggie.

Every night she dosed me with a tablespoon of goose grease.

"Please! No more, Aunt Aggie!" I begged, backing away from the vile grey stuff heaped up on the spoon. "I'm all better now, honest!"

"Open your mouth and close your eyes," chanted idiotic Aunt Ida, "and you'll get something to make you wise."

"Just hold your nose and you won't taste it," Aunt Aggie advised.

"No, please, Aunt Aggie!"

At that Grandpa yanked off his earphones (he always listened to his crystal set before turning in) and barked, "Would you like me to hold your nose for you?"

So I gagged the goose grease down and went to bed and rubbed my nose, longing to be home. Tears trickled between my fingers as I thought about all the things I was missing—city noises like clanging trolleys, cropping horses, tin lizzies blaring *Ahhh-ooogah!* I missed the corner store and Sunnyside and the nickel matinee at the Lyndhurst too.

And Glad had written to tell me I had missed the best Sunday School picnic ever. It had been held at Centre Island and on the way home a terrible thunderstorm struck and a huge wave nearly washed a little boy right off the upper deck of the *Trillium*. Everybody got seasick, including the captain. And I missed it!

I missed my family most of all. Even Arthur. I missed the gang on Veeny Street, especially Georgie Dunn. I wondered if he even noticed I was gone.

Finally I fell asleep on my wet pillow, still thinking about Georgie and gagging on the goose grease.

But I guess the greasy cure was worth it because a few days later I woke up feeling terrific. "Can I go to the post office with you today, Aunt Aggie?" I asked as I cheerfully dried the noonday dishes.

I was dying to get to the post office because I was expecting a parcel. During my convalescence I had written lots of letters home—to Mum and Willa and Gladie and Grampa Cole.

In my letter to Mum I had begged her to send me a pair of summer shorts I'd seen in Eaton's catalogue one day while I was sitting in the backhouse. The winter catalogue was used up already and we had started on the summer one. Aunt Aggie said not to use the shiny coloured pages because they weren't very absorbent, so I was just idly leafing through the pictures when I spotted the shorts. The ad read: *For the Modern Miss. Navy blue shorts with jaunty red stripes down sides. Only 59¢, delivered.*

I could just see myself in those shorts at the Heckley Annual Picnic. I was pretty sure, if I got them, that I'd be the only girl there sporting the newfangled style. I'd torn out the page, circled the picture and sent it off to my mum with a pleading letter.

Dearest *Mum,*

Today, in Eaton's catalogue, I found my heart's desire. Shorts! *I need them right away in time for the Heckley Annual Picnic. If you send them I'll never ask for another thing as long as I live (or at least not for ages and ages).*

Please excuse the shortness of this letter but Aunt Ida is going to the post office and she says she won't wait another minute. And you know Aunt Ida! But don't worry, I'll write again soon.

> *With love from*
> *Booky*

P.S.: Say hello to Dad for me, and kiss Billy, and maybe Jakey too, but not Willa and Arthur. Especially not Arthur! And don't forget my shorts!

> *Your devoted daughter,*
> *Bea (Me!)*

THE SPORTING THINGS
For Young Folk to Wear

72-720
Blouse
8 to 14 yrs.
59c

3-piece
Linene
Sport
Outfit

72-721
Shorts
8 to 14 yrs.
69c

72-722
Skirt
8 to 14 yrs.
59c

Back came Mum's postcard by return mail saying she'd get the shorts for me just as soon as she could scare up the fifty-nine cents. That was a week ago so I was sure they would have arrived by now.

Aunt Aggie hadn't answered my question about going to the post office yet and while she was thinking about it Aunt Ida butted in.

She had her head in the washbasin soaking her hair in lemon water to make it more blonde. Cocking her head to one side, she looked at me upside-down. "You're supposed to be here for your health, not to go gallivanting," she snapped.

Just then Grandpa came in carrying a bucket of well water in his gnarled old hand. When he saw the squeezed lemon halves lying on the washbench beside the basin he beetled his shaggy brows and growled, "That's a wicked waste of lemons."

Quick as a wink Aunt Ida thought up an excuse to justify herself. "I'm going to rub the pulp on my skin so it won't get all brown and freckled like Aggie's," she retorted.

Aunt Aggie's back stiffened and her eyes got a hurt look in them. "Some folks have to work for a livin'," she muttered. Then turning to me with a wry smile she said, "I have to help Pa hoe potatoes today, Bea, but I think you're old enough to go to the post office alone now, don't you?"

So away I ran down the road lickety-split, pleased as punch to be off by myself at last. Before I rounded the red-dirt turning I looked back to wave at Aunt Aggie, then headed into the tunnel of trees.

Heckley was the little hamlet nearest to Grandpa's farm. It was about a mile and a half down a wild and woodsy road. It had a pioneer stone church and a cemetery where Grandpa said most of his kinfolk were planted, an old log schoolhouse where Dad said he had learned the three Rs to "the tune of the hickory stick," ten houses and a post office.

The instant I walked into the post office Bertha Benchley, the postmistress (Aunt Ida said she was an evil old crone who read his Majesty's mail) hurried out from behind her wicket and handed me a parcel.

My heart leapt with joy. "Oh, boy! It's from my mother!" I cried ecstatically.

"Well, open it up and let's have a look-see," Bertha cackled as she obligingly cut the string. I tore off the paper and out onto the floor fell the strangest thing—a pair of old, faded, baby-boy rompers. My heart sank to the soles of my running shoes.

"Well, dearie, what did you git from yer mother?" Bertha's wicked, toothless grin puzzled me for a minute.

"My mother . . . ?" I knew my mother would never play such a mean trick on me. Curious, I picked up the paper and looked at the address. The writing was unfamiliar, the stamps old and brittle. And there was no postmark. Suddenly I knew!

"You did this, Bertha Benchley!" My disappointment turned to blinding rage. "Aunt Ida is right. You're a disgusting old Nosey Parker who reads the King's mail and you ought to be arrested!" With that I threw the horrid rompers right in her repulsive face and slammed out the door.

Back on the road, I broke into a run. I sped past the houses of friends I had intended to visit, tears streaming down my face, with Bertha's witchy laughter echoing after me.

It seemed to take forever to reach the red-dirt turning. When it finally came into sight I saw that my path was blocked by a whole herd of black-and-white cows. I stopped short, and as if

202

on signal they all turned their heads at once to glare at me.

I stood stock still, my heart banging against my ribs. The animals switched their tails, twitched their ears, chewed their cuds and swivelled their jaws. The one nearest me ran its long pink tongue right up its nose.

Oh, if only Aunt Aggie were here, I thought. She'd know what to do. I had seen her elbowing her way nonchalantly through a herd of cows lots of times. She had told me repeatedly not to be afraid of cows because they were too dumb to even know that I was a different species, but those huge brown eyes looked smart enough to me. So I waited and waited . . . and they stared and stared. Finally, after standing still as a statue for ages and getting eaten alive by mosquitoes, I decided that the only way I could outsmart them was to cross the creek. So I took off my running shoes and began tiptoeing through the icy, marshy water.

Suddenly a stinging pain shot through my leg. I looked down and there, stuck to my skin like long, slimy blobs of glue, were two transparent pink things with red-and-blue veins showing through. Bloodsuckers! Vampires! Draculas!

All the terrifying stories I'd ever heard about leeches tumbled through my mind: one leech can drain all the blood from your body in ten seconds flat; two of them can do it in five seconds and leave you dead as a doornail!

Screaming like a banshee, I bolted out of the creek and flew around the turning, great clouds of red dust pluming up behind me as I raced for the house.

"They got me! They got me!" I shrilled, streaking into the kitchen like lightning. I pointed to my leg, which seemed to be shrivelling up before my very eyes.

"Eeek!" screeched Aunt Ida, jumping onto a chair and pulling her flowered skirt tight around her legs. "Beatrice Myrtle Thomson! Get those filthy things out of here this minute! Do you hear me?"

In answer I let out a bloodcurdling scream that brought Aunt Aggie and Grandpa galloping in from the far corner of the potato field.

One glance told Aunt Aggie what to do. Grabbing the salt-cellar off the table she unscrewed the cap and doused my leg with salt. The greedy devils devouring me writhed and wiggled like frosty dew-worms, but they wouldn't let go. So my brave Aunt Aggie, completely ignoring the fact that she could be sucked to death in five seconds flat, pinched them off with dirt-stained fingers and flung them out the door.

"There, there, Bea." She gathered me to her chest. "You're all right now."

Then she looked up at her hoity-toity sister, still perched on the chair. "Get down from there, you silly jackass!"

For a second there was dead silence. Then Aunt Aggie and I burst out laughing, and even Grandpa couldn't help but join us.

Jumping down from her perch, Aunt Ida swept us with a furious glare. "Fools!" she shrieked. Then, with her nose in the air, she clickety-clicked up the stairs, banging the stairwell door behind her.

I never did get my shorts. Mum's letter came a few days later explaining that she couldn't afford them this year. Maybe next year, she said.

I never forgave Bertha Benchley, even though she insisted it was all in fun.

But ever after that hectic day, Aunt Aggie was my hero.

3
Home again

When it came time to go home I didn't know whether to be glad or sorry. I had renewed all my old friendships with the kids in Heckley, and Grandpa had even started letting me ride Major. Bareback! When he saw how gentle the horse was with me and how much we loved each other, he even said I could ride him to the post office. But that only happened once because on the way home a car came along and spooked Major and he jumped the barbed-wire fence beside the road. I managed to hang on to his flying mane and I landed right on his back again, so there was no harm done, but Grandpa got mad as a tethered bull and roared at me furiously, "He might of broke his leg, you thoughtless wretch!" So I wasn't allowed to ride him off the farm anymore.

I had a wonderful time at the Heckley Annual Picnic too. Aunt Aggie and I won the three-legged race (I thought she'd kill me, dragging me along) but the prize was worth it—a little china horse that looked a lot like Major. And Aunt Aggie let me keep it. Then Aunt Ida won the shoe-kicking contest (no wonder, since her high-heeled slippers only weighed about half as much as those heavy clodhoppers the farm women wore) and her prize was a green glass candy dish she kept herself.

And what a supper we had! It was out of this world. There were salads and sandwiches and puddings and cakes and pies galore, and the women churned homemade ice cream right before our very eyes. It tasted heavenly.

Then Grandpa (who had been in a mood and hadn't spoken to a living soul in weeks) suddenly got over it and played the fiddle to beat the band at the after-supper barn dance.

To top it off, while I was sitting on an upturned barrel digesting my supper and enviously watching the square dancers, Horace Huxtable, whose sister Daisy was my best Muskoka friend, snuck up behind me, kissed me on the cheek and told me that he loved me. I nearly fell off the barrel and for a minute there I almost forgot about Georgie Dunn.

Anyway, after nearly two months in Muskoka I was getting lonely. Especially for the baby. Billy was only two and I was afraid he would forget me. Also, I was anxious to get home in time for Kid's Day at the Ex.

So Aunt Aggie began asking around Heckley to see if she could cadge me a ride to Toronto. I was hoping she'd succeed because I knew if Grandpa had to take me all the way into Huntsville by horse and buggy and pay my fare on the train he'd be mad as hops.

He had a reputation for being stingy, Grandpa Thomson, and I could vouch for it. Why, he even called me a pig once just for asking for a second helping of blueberries. And I had spent the whole afternoon in the hot sun picking them all myself! ("Was Grandpa nicer when you and Dad were kids, Aunt Aggie?" I once asked her. I liked to think he was, and that he'd just got crabby with old age. But her nose screwed up and her specs slid down as she answered, "Does a leopard change its spots?")

Well, as it turned out, Horace Huxtable's Uncle Oscar had come up from Toronto one weekend and he said they could squeeze me in on the return trip. (Little did I know that they meant the word *squeeze* literally.) They were leaving Sunday afternoon so Aunt Aggie told me to go pack my grip.

That didn't take long because I didn't have much to pack. Besides my few clothes I had my china horse, some red chicken feathers to remind me of my pet rooster Reddy, and a shiny black bracelet I had braided myself out of Major's tail to remember him by.

That night I brought out my autograph book and asked my two aunts and my grandfather to each write a verse in it for me to remember them by. There were only a few empty pages left because everybody in Heckley had written in it. (Everybody except Bertha Benchley, that is. She offered to but I said no.)

Aunt Aggie's verse was cute and funny, like her:

Dear Bea,
Remember me when far away
And only half awake.
Remember me on your wedding day
And save me a piece of cake.

> *Lovingly,*
> *Aunt Agnes*

Aunt Ida's contribution was even worse than "Be good, sweet maid":

> *Beatrice,*
> *If you wish to partake*
> *Of heavenly joys,*
> *Think more of your prayers*
> *And less of the boys.*
>
> > *Sincerely,*
> > *Aunt Ida*

Grandpa surprised me with a pretty piece of poetry:

> *Dear Granddaughter,*
> *May your pathway through life*
> *Be as happy and free,*
> *As the dancing waves*
> *On the deep blue sea.*
>
> > *Fondly,*
> > *Your Grandfather*

Maybe he wasn't so bad after all.

I was to be picked up at three o'clock in the afternoon so first thing in the morning Aunt Aggie set a washtub full of rainwater out in the sun so it would warm up enough for me to take a bath right after dinner.

"I can't take my bath outside, Aunt Aggie!" I protested, horrified. "What if somebody sees me?"

"Who's going to look, the chickens?" she laughed.

She was right, of course. Nobody ever came that far along the road unless they were expected because there were no more farms beyond Grandpa's. And Grandpa was out in the field threshing and wouldn't be back until it was time to say goodbye.

The rainwater was soft and warm and deep and I was enjoying a good tubbing. I was washing myself with a flannel and the soap Aunt Aggie had made herself from her grandmother's recipe when I suddenly noticed that my chest was awfully tender and both sides were swollen.

"Aunt Aggie! Aunt Aggie!" I yelled in alarm. But Aunt Ida came instead.

"For mercy's sake, what is it now?" she asked irritably.

I had to tell her what I was yelling about but to my surprise her voice changed and became almost kind. "Oh, not to worry, Bea," she said with the pleasantest smile she'd ever bestowed on me. "It's just that you've begun to develop. You're turning into a woman, just like me."

Well, I was thrilled to be turning into a woman at last, but I hoped not just like her.

"Hurry up out of the tub and dry yourself off." She handed me a big piece of grey flannel. "I'll put a wave in your hair with my setting lotion."

That was the nicest thing Aunt Ida ever did for me, and it went a long way to making up for her natural nastiness.

My boyish haircut (I decided not to get it cut that way anymore, since I didn't want to be a boy after all) had grown out long enough for her to make a lovely deep wave. I sat out in the sun until it dried. Then she combed it out and fluffed it up and I couldn't get over myself. With my bright blue Thomson eyes and my deep suntan and my tawny wave dipping over my high forehead, I looked almost pretty in the mirror over the washbench. Even the knob on my nose seemed smaller. When I put on my clean dress and socks and shoes, Aunt Aggie said I looked cute as a bug's ear.

But the trip home was horrendous! I was squeezed into the back seat of an old tin lizzie with four other kids, all younger than me, and they carried on something awful. They threw up and wet themselves and cried and whined and pretty soon I was just as big a mess as they were. Then I'll be darned if we didn't pick up another passenger along the way, Norman Somebody-or-other, and he drank beer right out of a bottle and he kept pestering me for a kiss. So I shoved all the kids over beside him and stared out the window. I'd rather have been on the rumble-seat floor under a rug with Arthur any old day!

Well, after about a hundred stops to fix flat tires, go to the bathroom beside the road and have a hotdog, we finally arrived at Veeny Street about midnight. I was so tired I thought I'd die.

Horace's Uncle Oscar banged on our front door and woke the whole neighbourhood up as well as Mum and Dad.

"Who is it?" Mum called from the upstairs window. Her voice was music to my ears.

"It's me, Mum, Booky!" I cried.

Then Dad came down in his underwear to let me in. He gave me a hug and went straight back upstairs to bed. He said he had to get up for work in a few hours. Mum kissed me and squeezed me and said I stunk to high heaven.

"I looked nice when I left, Mum, honest. I was all bathed and

210

clean and Aunt Ida even waved my hair. But then those Huxtable kids got sick all over me and nearly made me sick too."

"Well, never mind. I'll make you some cocoa and then you can curl up on the davenport. Willa will never put up with the smell of you tonight. You can get cleaned up tomorrow."

Oh, it was nice sipping cocoa in my nightgown in our own kitchen with Mum.

"Your hair does look nice, Bea," Mum said. "Imagine old frosty-face fixing it for you."

The mention of Aunt Ida reminded me of what I wanted to tell my mum. "Guess what, Mum?"

"What, Bea?" She yawned sleepily.

"I've started to grow—right here." I patted my chest gingerly. "Aunt Ida says it's nothing to worry about. It's just that I'm becoming a woman. Isn't that swell, Mum? Aren't you glad?"

I drained my cup, then looked up, and to my amazement Mum's dark eyes were full of tears.

"What's the matter, Mum? Did I say something wrong?"

"No, no, Booky, it's nothing . . . " She dabbed at her eyes with her nightdress sleeve. Then she did the strangest thing. She drew me to her and gathered me onto her lap and held me close, whispering huskily, "My little girl . . . my baby . . . "

She hadn't called me a little girl in a month of Sundays, let alone a baby. And just when I was telling her about turning into a woman, too. Honestly, you never knew what to expect.

4
Grampa Cole

"Hi, Grampa! I'm home!" I poked my head inside Grampa Cole's kitchen door.

His back was to me, his tall, bony frame leaning over the stove. I smelled sausages and potato cakes sizzling in the black iron frying pan.

"Hello, Be-*a*-trice!" He turned around, holding the lifter in midair, his faded brown eyes lighting up. "How's my girl?"

That's what I'd come to hear. That I was still his girl.

"I'm fine, Grampa, I'm all better now. I gained five pounds in Muskoka. Can you tell?" I lifted my arms and spun around.

"Now that you mention it, you do look bigger—and taller too."

"Where's Joey?" I peered past him into the dim, dark-panelled dining room. Joey was my boy-uncle, the youngest of Grampa's thirteen children. (Mum was the oldest.) Joey was jealous of me and Grampa so he always bullied me and chased me home.

"He's gone off fishing—won't be back till nightfall. So you'll just have to make do with me."

"I like it when there's just you and me." I hopped up onto Joey's stool beside the stove to watch Grampa turn the sausages and flip over the pancakes.

"Aye, it's nice, just you and me," he agreed, a little smile ruffling his ragged moustache. He never smiled a big smile. Mum said it was because he had no teeth. "Get the plates down, Bea, and help me eat this here grub." He gave the pan a final shake.

His dishes were kept on open shelves over the big white porcelain sink. They were discoloured and cracked with age.

"Mmm, it smells good." I smacked my lips as he slid two golden sausages and two crispy potato cakes onto each plate.

"Want some ketchup?"

"Store-bought?"

"Yep. I got no homemade. Never turned my hand at preserving. When your Grandma was alive she used to make the spiciest ketchup you ever et."

"So does Mum. But I like store-bought." I doused the bright red sauce all over the steaming food.

He poured us both a cup of tea from a smoky graniteware pot and laced it well with cream and sugar. Then he tipped some into his saucer, blew ripples across it and sipped it from the edge. I followed suit. Willa would have had a fit if she could have seen us. She said it was the height of ignorance, drinking from your saucer. Once in a while Dad would do it and when he did Mum would get mad and Willa would leave the table in disgust. Then Dad would holler after her, "If you don't like it here you can always pack your grip and leave!"

"How're Mr. Thomson's crops this year, Bea?"

"Oh, pretty good, I guess. But Aunt Aggie says nothing grows well that far north. Every year Grandpa puts in corn and it never gets big enough to pick before the frost." I paused to wash my food down with a big slurp of sweet tea. "Boy, Grampa, my other grandfather isn't half as nice as you."

"Well, Bea, it don't pay to judge a man till you've walked a ways in his boots."

"I guess. You want to know what happened to me, Grampa?" I prattled on and on, telling him all the news. He listened attentively, sipping from the saucer, his unkempt moustache floating in his tea. Finally I said, "You need a trim, Grampa."

His coarse, iron-grey hair grew thick as a bush all over his head and down the back of his neck, straggling over the collar of his blue-checked flannel shirt.

"Well, that's your job," he drawled.

Ever since I was a little kid I liked trimming his hair. He must have liked it too because he always let me do it; then the next day he would go to the barbershop to get it neatened up.

I tied a grey dishtowel around his scrawny, sun-tanned neck and reached for the scissors hanging on a nail on the side of the cupboard. "Want to light your pipe first?"

"Don't mind if I do."

He got his corncob from the window sill, clamped it between his bare gums, struck a wooden match on the seat of his overalls and drew the flame, with a *putt-putt* sound, into the yellow bowl.

"Now hold still!" I commanded, and began my job. The wiry grey hair, tough as Major's tail, fell like bits of steel wool onto the towel.

"Tell me a story about when you were a boy, Grampa." His tales of the olden days always transported me back in time. "Tell me the one about Great-Aunt Gertrude."

"That one'll give you nightmares."

"I don't care. I like it." I shivered in anticipation.

"Well…" He closed his eyes, puffing his pipe, and the smoke wrapped softly around us. The mixture of smells that came from him—tobacco, wood smoke, sweat and axle grease—always lingered in my mind.

"It was this way," he began. "Great-Aunt Gertie was ninety-four years old and we had been expecting her to peg out for a long time. But when it finally happened it come as a shock, the way death always seems to do. Well, in those days there weren't no undertaker fellas. The womenfolk saw to the dead. So the neighbour ladies come to help my maither"—that's how Grampa said mother—"get the old lady ready. They laid her out in her Sunday best in a plain pine box in our parlour."

Putt-putt-putt went the pipe. *Crunch-crunch-crunch* went the scissors.

"Well, folks came from far and wide for the funeral, 'cause Great-Aunt Gertie was a Swansea pioneer and everybody knowed her for miles around. Pretty soon the parlour was overflowing and the menfolk had to stand up three deep along the back."

"Was it in this house, Grampa?" I leaned over backwards, peering through the creepy dining room into the gloomy parlour, half expecting to see the dark outline of a casket against the shuttered windows.

"No. I built this house for your Grandma and me when your maither was a baby. No, it was in my faither's house on the banks of the Grenadier. It's gone now. But in those days my faither's farm stretched all the way from High Park to Catfish Pond."

Putt-putt-putt. Snip-snip-crunch.

"Well, Reverend Ebenezer Stiles was preaching the service, and he just got to the part about what a fine upstanding Christian woman Great-Aunt Gertie was, when I thought I saw her fingers twitch—not much mind, just a mite. I darted a look at my maither and the rest of the family in the front row, but their eyes were all glued on the Reverend, so I guessed I was mistaken. He was a long-winded preacher, Reverend Stiles, and I was just a boy, so I begun to doze. Next thing I knew my maither was clutching my arm so hard I yelped. And ladies were fainting and the menfolk were gasping and Reverend Stiles was shouting, '*Praise the Lord, it's a miracle!*' And there, large as life and twice as ugly, sat Great-Aunt Gertie, bolt upright in her casket." He paused to tamp his pipe down and to strike another match. I was trimming the back of his neck and my hands were shaking so much I was afraid I'd pinch the loose skin between the blades.

"Go on, Grampa."

"Well, Great-Aunt Gertie stared straight ahead, looking neither to left nor to right, and cried out in a voice as clear as a bell, 'I want me tea!' Nobody moved. We was all transfixed. Then, before anybody had time to gather their wits and do her bidding, she fell back dead again."

A delicious shiver quivered up my spine. "Did she ever come alive again?" I whispered.

"Now you're gettin' ahead of me," he chided gently, then went on.

"Well, the Reverend cut his sermon short and shut the coffin lid with an unholy bang. And in the churchyard by the graveside, while he was saying 'ashes to ashes,' his eyes never strayed from that lid. It was as if he was expectin' it to pop

216

open any second. But the planting went off without a hitch and afterwards, back at the house, there was a fine feast and a good time was had by all."

"Could that happen today, Grampa?"

"No, Bea, nowadays doctors use a modern gadget to check for heartbeats, and those undertaker fellas drain out every drop of blood to make certain that you're cold."

"Now tell me the one about the boy who climbed out of his coffin in the middle of the night and went outside to fix his wagon and lived to be a hundred. Boy! Those sure were the good old days, Grampa."

"No, Bea, those were bad old days. Things are better now." He held out his pipe at arm's length while I trimmed the tea stains off his moustache. Then I undid the towel and shook it out the door.

"Well, that's all the storytellin' for now. I think I'll take a snooze. I cut a stack of wood this mornin' and I'm all done in."

"Okay, Grampa. Thanks for the story. I'm going to go home and write it down so I won't forget it."

"You'll have a hard time forgettin' that one. I think you know it better than I do." He lay down on the day bed under the dining-room window and I kissed him goodbye under his scratchy moustache.

Back home I rummaged through my school bag, found an empty workbook and wrote the story down as fast as my pencil would fly. Such eerie tales so sparked my imagination that I made up a gruesome one of my own about a man who had been buried alive. When he was dug up by grave robbers they found his hands full of hair because he had gone mad and torn himself bald. So the grave robbers learned their lesson and reformed and became just plain thieves.

When I was finished I ran out the front door to see if any of our gang was hanging around Veeny Street.

A bunch of little kids—my brother Jakey and Florrie and Skippy and Katie—were playing Kick-the-can, so I rounded them up and made them sit in a row along the curb. Then I saw Ada and Ruthie coming out of Hunter's Grocery Store on the corner. So I hollered, "Hurry up, you two, I'm going to read a story!" They both sat down, looking kind of skeptical. Then Arthur came out of our house and Gladie and her brother Buster came out of their house to see what was going on. I read them the stories, with lots of acting out and expression, and at the end Florrie and Skippy ran home screaming their heads off.

"I'm telling Mum on you, Bea!" Jakey's big brown eyes were glistening and his round face was as white as toilet paper.

"Those are dumb stories," declared Arthur, marching off.

"You're weird, Bea, you really are." Ruthie got up huffily, brushing the back of her skirt.

"They're not real stories," sniffed Ada, her bottom lip trembling. "They're not even printed. You just made them up."

"I did not! They're true as life. You can ask my grandfather," I shot back indignantly.

Even Gladie looked perturbed. "You're going to get in trouble, Bea," she whispered.

But her big brother, Buster, was exuberant. "Boy! Those are the best ghost stories I ever heard, Bea. Do you think you could memorize them for the corn roast down at the Camel's Back on Saturday night? It'll be too dark outside to read."

Just then Dad bellowed out the door, "Beatrice! You get yourself in here!"

Jakey had told on me, and Skippy's mother had come through the lane to our back door hopping mad, complaining that I had scared Skippy into hysterical fits. So Dad gave me a good tongue-lashing and sent me to bed without my supper. Then, about half an hour later, the door creaked open and Arthur shoved in a brown-sugar sandwich. Arthur, of all people! As Mum would say, wonders never cease.

I considered myself lucky to be let off without a razor-stropping, which was how Dad usually punished us for serious offences. So to take my mind off my stomach I recited the stories over and over while massaging the end of my nose, and by the time I went to sleep I knew them off by heart.

Then on Saturday night with the dancing orange flames of the bonfire casting ghostly shadows all around us, I acted out my scary stories in my creepiest voice and I was a huge success. Even Arthur and Willa joined in the applause and I was pleased as punch with myself because I'd never been the centre of attention before. And Georgie clapped and whistled and said my stories were the scariest of the whole night. Then to top it off he asked if he could walk me home; but just then Arthur interrupted and cranky old Willa insisted that I get home because it was past my bedtime. So Georgie went with Arthur and Buster and I walked home with Willa, my perfect evening ruined.

5
Senior Fourth

Mum let me wear my best dress for my first day in Senior Fourth. Now that Dad was working steady (touch wood—he'd been worried lately about layoffs at the factory) I had three dresses: a blue taffeta for Sundays, a blue cotton for school and a faded blue calico playdress. Blue was my favourite colour. Today I was wearing my taffeta.

The week before school started Willa had bought me a bottle of green Hollywood Waveset out of her own money. So I practiced setting my wave for a whole week and I finally got it perfect.

I walked across Veeny Street instead of running lickety-split, not wanting to disturb my wave. The brown sandy road had been freshly oiled to keep the dust down but the little kids had sprinkled a dirt path from one side to the other. I picked my way carefully across the zig zaggy path to Gladie's house so as not to track black oil onto the floors.

I was allowed to walk right into her house without knocking. Aunt Ellie, Gladie's pleasant mother, said that with so many chickens of her own in the nest, one more didn't make any difference.

As I came in the door she was straining her ears to hear Jim Hunter's news broadcast over CFRB while all the kids were scurrying around getting ready for school.

We didn't have a radio in our house. Dad said he didn't need a radio to tell him that times were bad, and he didn't want that blatherskite R.B. Bennett bellowing his lies in our front room. Dad blamed Prime Minister Bennett for the Depression, so I guess that's why he was a blatherskite. But if Mum had her way we'd have a radio—it was one of the wonders of the modern world, she said.

Sometimes I went over to Gladie's house to listen to the daytime serials. My favourite was *Our Gal Sunday*. Every day it started out with the same question: *Can a girl from a small mining town in the West find happiness as the wife of a wealthy and titled Englishman?* Boy, I thought, I bet *I* could if I had the chance. But day after day the question was left up in the air and we never did find out the answer.

"Bye, Mum!" Gladie called over the din.

"Bye, Aunt Ellie!" I echoed.

"Toodle-oo, you two, mind your p's and q's!"

Outside Gladie said, "You look swell, Bea. Sort of different and grown up."

"Gee, thanks, Glad." I decided to drop the "ie" from her name because it suddenly sounded babyish. "You look nice too." And she did. She had shiny black hair, sparkling brown eyes and even white teeth. Mum said Glad was a dyed-in-the-wool Cole.

"Senior Fourth is pretty nearly grown up, you know, Glad. That's as far as my mother ever went in school; then she got a job at Eaton's. But she says all us kids have to go to high school. She says if you want to get anywhere in this world you need an education. Oh, gosh, Gladie—Glad—how am I ever going to do Senior Fourth arithmetic?"

Arithmetic had been the bane of my existence ever since my first day in school. That day Mrs. Gumm, my Junior First teacher, had stood up in front of the class brandishing a big, thick ruler, and had announced to all us quivering kids that the first one to make a mistake would get the ruler over his knuckles. Then she looked straight at me and bellowed, "You! What's one plus one?"

Well, Willa had taught me one *and* one long ago, but I didn't know what 'plus' meant, so I burst out crying and crack came the ruler over my skinny little fingers. I had been terrified of arithmetic ever since.

"Oh, for Pete's sake, Bea, quit worrying. I'll help you," promised Gladie.

Her confidence cheered me up, for the time being anyway. Lucky for me she was good in arithmetic.

About a block from the school we heard the warning bell that meant it was five minutes to nine. We broke into a run, me cupping my hands protectively over my wave. In the schoolyard we joined the rest of the girls in our gang. They were all nervous and excited and talking a mile a minute.

Clang went the bell. Mr. Davidson, the school principal, held the big iron bell in one hand and hit the clapper inside of it with the other.

On the first clang we froze as if playing statues. The second sent us scurrying to our lines. Then he clanged the bell rhythmically: *clang,* march, *clang*, march, *clang*, march, right into our classrooms.

There were two Senior Fourths in Swansea School that year. Mr. Bewdley, who had a reputation for being a terrible tyrant, and Mr. Jackson were the teachers. Gladie and I were both lucky enough to be in Mr. Jackson's class.

He was leaning on his desk when we entered the room, one hand nonchalantly in the pocket of his blue serge suit. He was tall, dark and handsome—just like Ramon Novarro, the movie star whose framed picture Willa had on our bedroom wall.

All during Junior Fourth I had worshipped him from afar. And now, like a dream come true, he was going to be my teacher for a whole year. Maybe two, if my luck ran out.

"You may sit anywhere you like for the time being," he said, his rich baritone voice sending shivers up my spine. Glad and I made a mad scramble for the front seat right under Mr. Jackson's perfect nose.

He waited patiently for the shuffling and rustling to stop. Then, flashing a glittering smile, the like of which I'd never seen except in an Ipana toothpaste ad, he said, "Good morning, ladies and gentlemen."

"Good morning, sir!" we chorused in delight.

"The rest of the pupils in Swansea School are boys and girls," he continued. "Children. You might even call them kids if you're partial to baby goats." We rippled with appreciative laughter. "But everyone in *my* class is a young man or a young woman on the threshold of adulthood. *You* are Seniors!" He waved his hand dramatically across the room. "I intend to treat you like Seniors. And I expect you to act like Seniors."

This incredible news worked like a charm. We all sat up straighter, wiped the grins off our faces and tried our best to look like adults.

Going behind his desk he pulled open the top drawer, took out the dreaded strap and very deliberately dropped it with a *clunk* into the wastepaper basket. "Adults do not require spankings," he said. And that's the last we ever saw of the strap.

Now he sat down at his desk and rested his chin on his slender, folded hands. Gladie and I sighed blissfully in unison.

"I always like to start the new school year by getting acquainted," Mr. Jackson was saying. "I'm going to pass out foolscap and I want you to tell me all about yourselves." He went up and down the aisles passing out paper and talking as he went. "For instance, what are your future plans? Have you any hobbies? Or perhaps you'd like to tell me how you spent your summer. What did you do with those two glorious months of freedom? Tell me in your own words and in your own way. And we won't worry about spelling and neatness today. This is not an examination. No marks will be lost for errors."

While I waited for my paper I sucked the oil off my new pen nib and soaked it in the inkwell of the freshly varnished desk. There were a few things I liked about school—new pen nibs, full inkwells and blank foolscap just begging to be written on. I could hardly wait to get started. Everything that had happened to me in Muskoka that summer came tumbling into my mind: the leeches nearly sucking me to death, riding Major, Horace Huxtable actually stealing a kiss. I wrote small and fast, filling both sides of the page and even running up and down the margins.

"Yours is awful messy, Bea," whispered Gladie. Hers was neat enough to be entered in a penmanship contest. But her page was only half full.

"Well, he said neatness doesn't count this time," I reminded her. Then the person at the back of the row collected all the papers and gave them to Mr. Jackson.

After recess Mr. Jackson passed out more supplies. We sharpened our pencils and wrote our names on our workbooks. Gladie and I managed to get all our stuff packed into the one desk we shared. At twelve o'clock sharp the bell rang and we went home for dinner.

During dinner I asked Mum if she thought I could be a teacher if I really put my mind to it.

"Well, Bea, you'll have to work a lot harder than you've done in the past." She turned to Billy and wiped the honey off his cute face and untied the shoestrings of his little black boots.

"I will, Mum, I promise. Gee, I can hardly wait to get back to school this aft'."

"Well, by Jove, that's a good sign," she laughed.

"Bea-Bea!" Billy stretched out his long, skinny arms to me. "I want you!" He'd been saying that and clinging to me like flypaper ever since I'd come home from Muskoka.

"Fat chance of him ever forgetting you," Mum said.

"I'll take him up to bed, Mum," I volunteered, scooping him up and squashing him in my arms. He was nearly three years old and really too big for me to carry now, but I still liked to. I staggered up the stairs with his long, gangly legs hanging down past my knees. He was going to be tall and slim like Grampa Cole.

"You missed Bea-Bea, didn't you, Billy?" I kissed him all over his sweet face, then heaved him, with a loud grunt, over the railing of the old iron cot. "But I'm in a hurry today—so bye-bye!" I left him wailing indignantly, expecting me to jiggle his cot like I always did until he went off to sleep.

Seven-year-old Jakey, who was in Senior First this year, was standing by the door crying his eyes out because he didn't want summer to be over.

"You go with Bea, Jakey," Mum said, smoothing the dark curls off his forehead. "There's a good boy. I've got to get done while Billy's in bed." Poor Mum. She was always trying to get done.

"Do I *have* to take him this year, Mum?" I looked down without a twinge of pity at his round, tear-stained face. "He's big enough to go by himself now."

"I haven't got time to argue!" she snapped.

I decided I'd better take him. The school was only a hop, skip and a jump down the street and I'd be rid of him as soon as we got there because he had to go in on the boys' side.

"Bye, Mum!" I called through the screen door.

"Bye, Booky. Be good."

"Mum . . . "

"What is it now?"

"Don't call me Booky anymore, okay? It sounds too babyish and Mr. Jackson says we Seniors are on the threshold of adulthood."

"Oh, all right," she laughed, "but you'll always be Booky to me."

Up until then I'd always liked my special little nickname. Maybe I'd tell her it was okay as long as we were in the house.

The afternoon was as interesting as the morning. At recess Gladie and I were leaning back-to-back in the schoolyard, holding each other up and talking over our shoulders.

"Isn't Mr. Jackson terrific?" I said. "Doesn't he remind you of Ramon Novarro or Robert Taylor?"

"Yah!" Gladie agreed, the same note of rapture in her voice.

"Or maybe Gary Cooper. Did you see *Lives of a Bengal Lancer?*"

"I wonder if he's married?"

"Who? Gary Cooper?" I asked.

"No! Mr. Jackson."

"Oh, gosh, I hope not!" The thought really upset me. "Because I think I'm in love with him and it wouldn't be proper if he was married."

"Well, I'm in love with him too." Gladie stepped away all of a sudden and nearly let me fall on the ground.

"Not as much as I am though." I scrambled to regain my balance.

"Oh, Bea!" Gladie scoffed. Then the bell rang and saved us from having a fight.

The truth of the matter was, almost every girl in Senior Fourth had a crush on Mr. Jackson and the Georgie Dunns and Horace Huxtables of the world couldn't hold a candle to him.

After recess Mr. Jackson gave us back our marked compositions and I got ninety-two percent. I couldn't get over it!

"Your essays were of a very high calibre," he told the whole class, "and a few were so exceptional I'd like to hear them read out loud. We'll begin with Beatrice Thomson's."

I nearly sank through the floor. I felt a red flush spread up my face and creep under my stiff blonde wave.

Instantly my gallant teacher recognized my distress and came to my rescue. "Perhaps you'd like me to do the honours today, Beatrice, and you can favour us another time?"

So he did. He read my composition with such wonderful expression and enthusiasm that it sounded like a real story out of a book. The other kids all laughed at the funny parts and clapped their hands at the end.

Placing the foolscap back on my desk he said, "You have a fine flair for words, Beatrice. You show real potential. Keep up the good work."

I stared up at him in dumbfounded adoration. Never before in all my school life had a teacher complimented or encouraged me. It was one of the happiest days of my life. And it was a turning point. Never again did I feel quite so scatterbrained, or homely, or just plain dumb.

6
Our Arthur's birthday

On Arthur's birthday Mum said he could have a friend over for supper.

"When it's my birthday can I have somebody over too, Mum?"

"We'll see," she said, whipping the chocolate icing vigorously with a fork. "What with your birthday and Billy's landing on the same day it makes it kind of hard, but we'll see." Billy had been born on my tenth birthday so I always considered him my special birthday present.

My mouth began to water as Mum made chocolate swirls all over the top and sides of the double-layered cake. "Who's Arthur having for supper, Mum?"

She was poking blue candles in the peaks around the cake's circumference. "Oh, just Georgie Dunn," she said.

Just Georgie Dunn! The news made me forget all about asking to lick the icing bowl. Instead I bolted up the stairs, two at a time, to the bathroom. Jakey was standing on a little stool, splish-splashing in the sink the way little kids do.

"Beat it, Jakey!" I commanded. "I need the bathroom."

"Do you have to go bad?" he asked.

"Yes," I lied, shoving him out the door. Latching it behind

him I took a good look at myself in the mottled mirror hanging over the sink. I was a mess! My wave had fallen out, I had a ripe pimple on my chin and my neck was dirty.

I took the cake of carbolic soap from the wire dripcage suspended between the taps and gave myself a thorough sponging. Then I cleaned my teeth with baking soda. (There was no toothpaste, but now that Dad was working steady we each had a toothbrush. Mine was blue.) Next I squeezed the pimple and it came out clean as a whistle. Then, using the big white family comb, I set my corn-coloured hair with green Hollywood lotion. My boyish bob had grown out long enough, at last, to make a kiss-curl in front of each ear as well as a deep wave over my left eye.

On the shelf beside the baking soda sat a jar of Vaseline for cuts and scrapes. I smeared some on my finger and held it under my eyelashes. Then I fluttered my sparse, fair lashes up and down against my finger the way I'd seen Mum's sister, Auntie Gwen, do, and pretty soon they were all wet and shiny and glued together. Instantly my eyes looked bigger and bluer.

Next I went to Willa's and my bedroom and got my second-best dress out of the closet. It had a white pique collar and cuffs. (Mum had made it for me from a twenty-five-cent remnant she got on sale at Eaton's.) I found clean white socks in my drawer and put them on with my black patent-leather shoes.

Then I spotted Willa's lip rouge standing on the bureau beside her Pond's Vanishing Cream. Every night she slathered on the cream, hoping to make her freckles disappear, but they never did. The lip rouge was "Tangee Natural." I had often been tempted to use it but I had never had the nerve before. Pulling my lips taut against my front teeth, I smoothed it on and pressed my lips together. They weren't red enough so I did it again. Instantly my teeth looked whiter and the gaps between them didn't seem so wide.

Next I went to my parents' bedroom at the back of the house. Raising the window, I put the stick in place to hold it up and stuck my head out to let the setting sun dry my hair.

Ruthie Vaughan was in her backyard next door playing roundabout against their house with her India rubber ball. "Hi, Bea!" she called up to me. I said hi. She threw the ball against the imitation-brick siding, did a twirling roundabout that billowed out her red plaid kilt, and caught the ball on the rebound. "How come you're hanging out the window?" she asked.

"Oh, just for a breath of air," I answered.

"Well, c'mon out, why don'tcha?"

"Can't. I got to help my mother lay the table. It's our Arthur's birthday and he's having Georgie Dunn over for supper."

An expression of pure envy flitted across her face.

Quick as a wink she wiped it off, tossed her curly brown hair, cried "Well, whoop-dee-do!" and went back to playing roundabout.

I felt my wave to see if it was dry. Not quite, even though the sun was unusually warm for October. Dad said it was Indian summer. The leaves had begun to turn and I could see flecks of gold shimmering on top of Grampa Cole's soft maple. His yard backed onto ours, separated by a laneway. I hadn't been over to visit him lately and I missed him, seeing his tree.

I'll go over tomorrow, I promised myself. And I'll explain how busy I am in Senior Fourth. (I did my homework every night now—I'd do anything for Mr. Jackson.) I knew Grampa would understand because we were kindred spirits.

Just to the north of Grampa's place I could see the red and green leaves of Billy and Maude Sundy's big old oak tree. I'll visit Billy and Maude soon too, I thought. They must wonder what's become of me. Our landlord and landlady were my best grown-up friends. They were brother and sister and they'd never been married so they lived together. Imagine growing up and having to live with your brother! I'd rather eat dirt than live with Arthur.

Finally my wave was dry so I pulled my head back in, took out the stick and lowered the window.

Back in our bedroom I combed out my hair, put on some more Tangee and slipped my horsehair bracelet over my bony wrist. I didn't own any jewellery but the glossy black hairs from Major's tail matched my patent leather shoes exactly. Glancing in the mirror, I noticed that my dress was getting tight across my chest so I decided I'd have to hold my breath for the rest of the day. But generally speaking I was quite tickled with myself. Even my nose didn't look too bad. I went downstairs singing "You oughta be in pitchers . . ."

Mum had already set the round dining-room table with the white cloth and the good dishes. The table looked pretty with the chocolate cake in the middle. I counted the candles to make sure there were fifteen. Boy, Arthur was getting old!

"Help me put the chairs around, Bea," Willa said. Then she took a closer look at me and let out a big screech. "Bea! You rat! You've got my lip rouge on! How dare you touch my Tangee? You'll get germs all over it!"

"Oh, Willa, please . . ." If she made a scene in front of Georgie Dunn I'd die. "I won't do it again, honest, but *please*, please, don't be mad this time."

I could tell by the way her stern expression softened that she had guessed why I'd fixed myself up. "Oh, all right. I'll let you off this time. But don't you dare do it again. Tangee costs money, you know."

"I know. And I'll be eternally, perpetually grateful!" I promised fervently.

"Oh—you and your big words!" she scoffed, but not nastily. I used a lot of big words since Mr. Jackson had told me I had a flair.

Dad brought Billy's beat-up old high chair in from the kitchen, and when he saw me he frowned and said, "What's that warpaint doing on your face, Missy?" But I could tell he wasn't really mad by the little smile that played around his mouth.

Mum came in to see what all the fuss was about. She took one look at me and exclaimed, "My stars, Bea! Aren't you a bit young for that?"

"Oh, please, Mum, let me wear it just this once. Willa says it's all right." I knew what Willa said went a long way with Mum.

"Oh, well, what's the harm?" She laughed and pinched my nose shut. "It's a special occasion, and the colour suits you."

"Gee, thanks, Mum. Can I wear lipstick to Sunday School too if Willa lets me?"

"Mercy me, no! Give you an inch and you want a mile!"

Just then Arthur and Georgie came in the front door, laughing and poking each other.

"Sit yourselves down," Mum told them. "Bea, you and Willa can help me carry."

We had roast beef and gravy and peas and carrots and mashed potatoes, and it wasn't even Sunday. But of course it *was* Arthur's birthday.

I don't know whether it was just plain luck or what, but I

found myself sitting next to Georgie. I kept glancing at him out of the corner of my eye. (I had a bit of trouble doing this because the Vaseline stuck my lashes together and I had to open my eyes wide to unstick them.) Georgie was even handsomer than Arthur. He had sparkly blue eyes, curly black hair and a dimple in his chin.

"How's school, Bea? I hear you got Daddy Long-Legs this year."

"Oh, no!" His sudden question took me off guard and I got all flustered by his sparkly eyes. "I got Mr. Jackson and he's terrific!" Everybody laughed and my face went beet red as I realized that Mr. Jackson's nickname was Daddy Long-Legs.

"Well, how's Senior Fourth anyway?" continued Georgie, just as if I hadn't said a really dumb thing.

"It's great!" I tried to control the quaver in my voice. "And Mr. Jackson says I've got potential."

"Oh, for gosh sakes, Bea, why do you have to tell that to everybody?" said Arthur scornfully. "I must have heard it a million times already."

"You're just jealous," I taunted, spurred on by Georgie's attention.

"Jealous of *you*? Don't make me laugh!"

Mum glared at us and changed the subject before Dad had time to get riled. He had been in a bad mood lately and the long hours at the factory—ten hours a day, six days a week—were beginning to tell on him.

"Tell your mother to come over and have tea with me sometime, Georgie," Mum continued. Then Dad asked him how his father was making out with his new job at the Bolt Works.

When it came time for the cake Dad lit the candles with a wooden match and Willa turned the lights off. That was the

234

moment I loved, with the circle of faces all aglow in the candlelight.

"Make a wish, Arthur!" Mum's eyes rested lovingly on her eldest son's bright face and I felt a stab of jealousy. Sometimes I was sure that Arthur was Mum's favourite.

Billy and Jakey started to huff and puff impatiently and Dad said, "Settle down, you two." He had to relight two of the candles.

We all sang "Happy birthday, dear Arthur." Then he took a deep breath and blew out all the candles at once. Dad turned on the lights and Mum sliced the cake.

Throughout the meal I had been sneaking more looks at Georgie and the last time our eyes met he winked at me. I nearly keeled off the chair. It was the first time in my life I could only eat one piece of cake.

Afterwards Arthur opened his presents. I gave him an art pencil with an eraser on it because he was going to be an artist.

"Thanks, Bea. I can really use it," he said. That was the nicest thing he'd said to me since I could remember.

Willa gave him a drawing pad; Dad and Mum gave him oxfords; Jakey and Billy gave him a card they'd made themselves. Georgie gave him a pen-knife with all sorts of attachments. Arthur was thrilled with it.

When the table was cleared he suggested a game of euchre. Willa jumped up and got the cards out of the sideboard drawer. She loved cuchre.

When we cut the cards for partners I got Georgie and we won three games out of five. Willa and Arthur were fit to be tied.

Then Mum came in from the kitchen with the rest of the cake and some hot cocoa. While we were eating Georgie happened to notice my bracelet. "Where did you get it?" he asked.

"It's in memoriam of Major, my grandfather's horse," I explained. "I braided it myself out of his tail."

"Is he dead?" asked Georgie.

"Who, Grandpa?"

"No, the horse."

"No, why?" I was getting bewildered.

"Oh, Bea," chided Willa. "Don't show your ignorance."

"I thought you were supposed to be so smart with words," snorted Arthur. "Any dumb-bell knows that 'in memoriam' means in memory of somebody who's dead."

My face blazed with embarrassment and I couldn't speak for the lump that popped into my throat.

"Well, it's a unique bracelet anyway," said Georgie. I never dreamed a boy could be so nice.

At ten o'clock Georgie had to go home. "Thanks for the good time, Mrs. Thomson," he said politely while putting on his cap. "The supper was terrific. Especially the cake."

Mum just beamed. "Go out the front door, Georgie," she said. "My father always says the back door is only for tramps and peddlers."

I ran ahead of him to open the front door. On his way out he said, "Bye, Bea. Be seeing you."

Be seeing you! No boy had ever said that to me before!

"My, that Georgie Dunn turned out nice," Mum said as she tidied up the table. "And to think I used to call him a Peck's Bad Boy."

I went to bed in a daze with "Be seeing you" ringing in my ears. Boy, was I glad I'd been in Muskoka so I hadn't tried to follow Georgie around until he noticed me. It was like Mum always said: bad beginnings make good endings.

7
White Smock

My thirteenth birthday, and Billy's third, landed on a Saturday. We couldn't do any celebrating though, because both Billy and Jakey had the chicken pox. But I did get some wonderful presents.

Willa gave me my own Tangee. "So you can keep your germs to yourself," she said without cracking a smile.

Arthur gave me a pretty beaded comb. "So our comb won't be full of green jelly all the time," he joked.

And Mum gave me the best present of all—a permanent wave. "I've made an appointment for you at the Fair Lady Beauty Parlour on Bloor Street, Booky," she said, rubbing her palms together in that excited way she had. "Now what do you say to that?"

"Oh, Mum!" I flung my arms around her neck and gave her a big smacker. "Thanks profoundly!"

"Well, don't forget to thank your father profoundly too. He did without carfare all week to save the money for you."

"Gee, thanks, Dad." I kissed him too, but more shyly, because Dad wasn't much of a kisser.

"Well, thirteenth birthdays don't come a dime a dozen," he remarked drily.

Right after our noonday meal Mum gave me two dollars and fifteen cents. "On your way home I want you to stop at the butcher shop and get fifteen-cents worth of stewing beef for Sunday supper." She tied the money securely in my hanky. "Now don't lose it. There's no more where that came from."

I shoved the hanky deep into the pocket of my old winter coat and did up the top two buttons. Dad said it had turned cold overnight.

"That coat's way too short," Mum remarked, spinning me around for inspection. "My stars, Bea, ever since you got back from Muskoka you've been growing like a burdock."

At the corner of Veeny and Mayberry streets I saw Gladie coming out of Hunter's Grocery Store. "Hi, Bea. Where you going?"

"Oh, just to Bloor to get something for my mother." I was hoping against hope she wouldn't offer to come with me because I wanted my permanent wave to be a complete surprise. As far as I knew, no other girl in Senior Fourth had a permanent wave.

"Gee, I'd come with you but I have to go straight home and mind Florrie."

"That's too bad." I tried to sound disappointed. "See you later then."

I was so preoccupied, imagining how swell it was going to be not having to set my hair with green lotion anymore, that I bumped smack into Roy-Roy the dumb boy.

"S'cuse me!" I said, then, "Oh, hi, Roy-Roy!" I always tried to treat him like a normal kid because Mum had told me, what

238

with Raggie-Rachel for a mother and no brains to speak of, Roy-Roy had a hard row to hoe.

"Ha, ha, Bea-Bea!" His big hazy-blue eyes lit up and his wide mouth gaped open in a huge, wet grin. Rivers of slobber ran down his chin, soaking his flannelette bib.

We walked along together for a way, Roy-Roy hopping beside me with his peculiar, gangly gait, his long arms flailing the air in an effort to make me understand his gabbling.

I managed to catch something about a dog and a rabbit, and we were just starting to make some headway in the conversation when his mother's shrill voice shrieked at us out of nowhere. *"Roy-Roy! You git home this minute or I'll skin you alive!"*

Our heads jerked up simultaneously. There she sat on the upstairs window ledge of the Ashtons' house, cleaning the top window pane. Sometimes Raggie-Rachel did chores like that to earn a bit of money. *"Git! Git! Git!"* she screeched.

Each "git" was punctuated by a snap of the cleaning rag. Clouds of Dutch Cleanser billowed out around her tattered bottom. It was funny, I thought, that Roy-Roy was always dressed much better than his mother.

The poor boy was so terrified he shook like a leaf; the slobber flew in every direction.

"You leave my boy alone, girl, you hear!" Her face was livid and she shook her fist so hard I expected her to come tumbling out the window.

"I was only talking to him!" I dared to yell back at her because I knew she couldn't get at me from way up there.

"Well, he cain't talk, so don't you think you can fool Rachel Butterball!" (Her last name was really Butterbaugh, but everybody, including herself, pronounced it Butterball.) "I know all you smart-alecky kids make fun of my boy."

"Baa-baa, Bea-Bea!" Roy-Roy staggered frantically backwards, his wobbly legs going every which way.

"Bye-bye, Roy-Roy!" I ran backwards too and we kept on waving in spite of his mother shaking a Dutch Cleanser tempest all over the place.

I walked soberly the rest of the way, reflecting on how lucky I was. Sure, my family had been hard hit by the Depression. We'd gone hungry and cold lots of times. Once we'd even been put out of our house in the middle of the night. All the same, I felt rich beside Roy-Roy. Imagine having to live in a tar-paper shack down by Catfish Pond with a terrible mother like Raggie-Rachel. Poor Roy-Roy.

I was still half an hour early for my appointment when I got to Bloor Street so I decided to get Mum's meat first. The bell jangled overhead as I pushed open the heavy butcher-shop door. While I waited my turn I scraped up a pile of sawdust between my feet. It smelled nice and piney—like the woodshed behind the house in Muskoka.

"What can I do for you, Bea?" asked the butcher, wiping his bloody fingers on his white coat.

"Fifteen cents worth of stewing beef with some extra suet, please, Mr. Donnan." Immediately I began working the knot of my hanky undone. He waited patiently until I put the money in his hand. We ran a bill at Hunter's Grocery Store, but Mr. Donnan said he wouldn't give so much as a soup bone on tick. He said he'd been stung more times than a bear in a beehive.

I watched him slice up the meat on the big wooden chopping

block. One of the fingers on his left hand was missing and I tried not to think about it, but I couldn't help wondering who ate it.

I was still a little early when I got to the Fair Lady so I sat down on a wicker chair to wait. I put the package of meat on the window sill in the draft to keep it cool.

Strange smells drifted up from the back of the shop—sort of perfumey-mediciney smells all mixed together. Craning my neck around the archway I could see ladies' crossed legs sticking out.

Minutes passed and no one bothered with me, so I picked up a dog-eared *Silver Screen* from a messy, cigarette-burned table. Janet Gaynor and Charles Farrell were on the cover, his smooth dimpled cheek nestled into her curly brown hair. Could anybody be that beautiful? I wondered. Inside was a full-page picture of Tom Mix and his wonder horse, Tony. He was my favourite cowboy star but I hadn't seen his latest serial because I couldn't get a nickel for the Saturday matinee at the Lyndhurst.

I turned the page and was admiring a darling picture of Shirley Temple in her costume for *The Little Colonel* when a tall lady in a white smock appeared in the archway. She had peroxide-blonde hair and bright red lips that were bigger than her mouth.

"What do you want?" she snapped.

"My mum made me an appointment for a permanent wave." I held out the crumpled two-dollar bill. "I'm thirteen today." I couldn't resist telling her my wonderful news.

"Well, I couldn't care less!" she sneered, instantly shrivelling my soul.

Going to the desk, she glanced in a book, sniffed, took my money and slammed it into a drawer. After locking the drawer she dropped the key down the front of her smock. Then she herded me ahead of her, poking my back with her spiky fingernails.

We passed the ladies with the crossed legs. One was under a drying machine that looked like Mum's preserving kettle turned upside down, and one was getting a marcel wave from another hairdresser.

There were two chairs with sloped backs in front of two sinks on the back wall.

"Sit!" ordered White Smock.

I sat, and she wrapped a towel around my neck so tightly it choked me. When I gagged she gave me a dirty look. Forcing my head back on a tray, she hosed it down with freezing cold water, slopped on some liquid soap and began scrubbing to beat the band with her blood-red claws.

"The soap smells good," I ventured to say.

"It's not soap, it's shampoo!" she corrected, scratching like a wildcat as if to punish me for my stupidity.

I'd never had my hair washed with shampoo before. At home we always melted down Sunlight soap in hot water on the gas stove, then rinsed it out with soft water. Hard water just wouldn't do the job, so Mum kept a pail under the eavestrough spout to catch rainwater. In wintertime all we had to do was melt down some snow.

Next White Smock shoved me under a drying machine. Twirling the dial all the way around without looking, she left me there to boil.

Meanwhile she went to take care of her lady customer. I

242

couldn't help but notice how much better she treated her than she did me. And I was sure they were talking about me, even though I couldn't hear a thing because of the hot wind blowing in my ears. So I lowered my eyes and stared at the cracked linoleum floor. There were dead curls all around my feet—black and red and brown and blonde ones all mingled together. They gave me the creeps.

I didn't look up again until White Smock yanked me out from under the drying machine, cracking my head on the steel rim. I didn't dare complain.

This time she ordered me to sit on a big leather chair under a weird contraption with dozens of black wires dangling down.

"Do you want nice tight curls?" she demanded.

"I think so," I murmured.

"*What?*"

"I *think* so!"

"Just watch your tongue, Miss Smarty!"

Hurriedly, as if she could hardly wait to get it over with, she began yanking strands of my poker-straight hair through slits in small leather pads. When it was all sticking out, like porcupine quills, she took the scissors and began chopping it off in chunks. Next she rolled up what was left, mercilessly tight, onto small metal curlers.

When they were all in place, she lowered the strange contraption close to my head and snapped each curler into a viselike clamp attached to the dangling wires. Suddenly she moved aside and I saw myself in a mirror on the wall. Just as I realized that I was hopelessly trapped in an electric chair she threw the switch.

I started to shake and the more I shook the tighter the

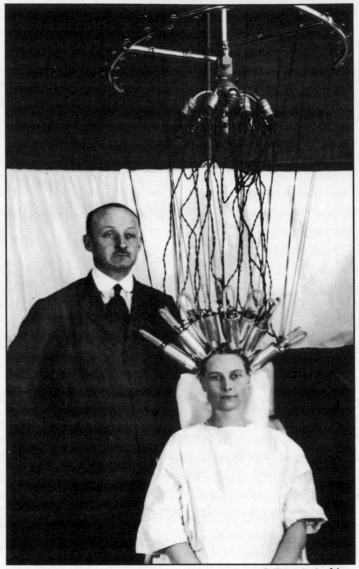

machine seemed to grip my head. So I used my best calm-me-down trick.

Closing my eyes, I imagined myself in the school-yard playing baseball with the gang. Buster was up to bat and Georgie was yelling from the pitcher's mound, "Okay, all you fielders—moooovvve back! Buster's up to bat!" We fanned out in all directions and Buster made a soaring hit, the like of which had never before been seen. But even with the sun in my eyes I reached up and plucked it out of the air as easy as pie. The roar of applause from my teammates suddenly turned into a loud hissing sound.

My eyes flew open and I couldn't see a thing for the cloud of steam swirling around my head.

"Help!" I yelled.

But nobody paid me the slightest mind. Both hairdressers were happily puffing on cigarettes, their backs to me, laughing and joking with their other customers. I knew I was sunk if I had to depend on them to save me. So I closed my eyes and began a fervent prayer. "Listen, God, I know I don't deserve your attention after playing hooky from Sunday School last week and spending my collection on a Sweet Marie, but I promise never to do it again if you'll just get me out of here."

Then I smelled smoke. My eyes flew open again and there it was, spiralling up from all the metal curlers.

"Help! Fire! Police!" I screamed.

White Smock came running, threw the switch and began ripping off the burning curlers, sucking her scorched fingers and swearing a blue streak. My hair was still smouldering when she plunged me, head first, into a sinkful of ice-cold water.

"Everything will be fine—you'll see!" She began rubbing my head in great agitation while the other ladies stood anxiously around us. "I'll give you my very best two-dollar finger wave and I won't charge you an extra cent. You'll be thrilled—you'll see. I've been hairdressing now for going on ten years and I've never had a dissatisfied customer. Isn't that right, ladies?"

They bobbed their heads, obediently, while giving each other furtive looks.

Well, she tried, I'll have to say that for her. But nothing she did could change the fact that my head looked like a ball of wool that a bunch of cats had been fighting over for a week.

"In a couple of months time it'll be beautiful. Just you wait and see. Mark my words." She gabbled worse than Roy-Roy as she herded me towards the door. "Here, let me help you on with your coat. What a lovely shade of blue. Teal, isn't it? And where's your hat, dear? You don't want to catch your death of cold, do you? Now run along home and tell your mother she's got a lovely daughter and that's the truth."

The old witch. As if her polite words could fool me. And I hadn't brought my toque because I hadn't wanted to mess up my brand-new permanent wave. *Ha!*

Yanking my coat collar up, I retracted my head like a turtle and made a beeline for home. Halfway there I realized I'd forgotten the dratted meat. Moaning aloud, I retraced my steps to the beauty salon, grabbed the package from the window sill, darted old White Smock a final, scathing glare and ran for home again.

I took all the unfamiliar side streets I could think of. But just as I turned onto Veeny Street Georgie rode by on his bike. "Hi, Bea!" he hollered. Normally I would have been thrilled to pieces, but this time I ducked my head down deeper and pretended not to hear.

Then Ada and Ruth called to me from across the street. I pretended not to see them. At last I made it to our back door.

Streaking through the kitchen I threw the meat on the table, ran past my startled mother and bolted lickety-split up the stairs to the trunk in the hallway. Flinging open the lid I rummaged wildly through it, found last year's woollen toque and jammed it onto my head until only my eyes were showing. Then I ran to the bedroom, slammed the door and cried my head off.

At supper time I crept downstairs and slid into my place at the table. *"I'm going to wear this toque for the rest of my life and I want to be buried in it!"* I shrieked.

Nobody laughed. Not even Arthur.

8

Dear Aunt Aggie

Dear Aunt Aggie,

How are you? How are Major and Grandpa? We are all fine down here except Willa has the pleurisy and Jakey's got pinworms and Dad's got a gumboil.

I received your most welcome letter some time ago but I haven't had a chance to answer it till now. First, I was busy with my examinations. (In case you have forgotten, I am in the entrance class this year.) I got 72%, which is the best I've ever done in my whole life. Mr. Jackson says he expects me to do even better at Easter. For his sake I'll try, but I don't think I can. (Our class gave him a Parker Fountain Pen for Xmas and he filled it at my *inkwell! He is so handsome, Aunt Aggie, you wouldn't believe it. Both Gladie and I are in love with him, but don't tell Grandpa I said that!) As usual, Willa got the highest marks in Fifth Form. She will be getting her Senior Matric this year. Can you imagine that? Arthur did well in Second Form and Jakey did good in Senior First. Did you have a Merry Christmas up there? We did down here, but for a while it looked as if we weren't going to. I'll tell you why. Two weeks before Christmas Dad got a notice in his pay packet saying his wages would be cut from twelve dollars a week to ten. Well, that started a terrible row between Mum and Dad that lasted until Christmas Eve. It was horrendous! (If you don't know what that big word means, Aunt Aggie, because you only went to the one-room schoolhouse in Heckley, then look it up in your dictionary. I use a lot of big words since Mr. Jackson told me I had a flair. I'll put quotations around them so you won't miss any.)*

Well, after Dad got the bad news about his pay packet he told Willa and Arthur and me not to expect any resents this year and that made me feel very "lamentable." But on Christmas morning we were in for a big surprise. First Dad made us all shut our eyes and not open them until he said so. Then we heard him grunting as he carried something heavy up the cellar stairs. You'll never guess what it was so I won't keep you in "suspension" any longer. It was a radio! Not a crystal set with earphones like Grandpa has in Muskoka, but a real mantle radio that you plug into the wall. It's shaped like a cathedral. Dad got it for only two dollars from one of his workmates who had been laid off.

So we didn't mind not getting presents after all because we listened "enraptured" to King George V's Christmas message and to carols all day long. The fires were so low in both the stoves that the house was freezing and the bunch of us were huddled together on the davenport listening to Scrooge's Christmas *when Mum said "Where's Arthur?" and Jakey said, very seriously, "He went outside* to get warm." Then we all screeched laughing. Isn't that a "hilarious" story, Aunt Aggie?

Have you seen Horace Huxtable lately? You said in your letter that you lanced his father's boil, but you didn't mention Horace. Does he ever ask about me? Be back in a jiffy. I have to wipe the dishes.

Jan. 5, 1936

Wasn't that a long jiffy? Please excuse the ink blots but Arthur threw the dishrag at me and it landed on my letter.

Well, let's see, where was I? Oh, yes—for New Year's day we went to Uncle Charlie's. Aunt Ida was there, too, as I guess you know. The first thing she said to me when I pulled off my toque and my hair sprang up like a bush (remember I told you about my hideous frizzy permanent?) was, "Don't you look a fright, Beatrice?" Well, I know I shouldn't say this because she is your sister and all, but she is an "intolerable" person and that's the truth and you know I am not a "prevaricator."

Our New Year's supper was great! The chicken was done to a turn and Uncle Charlie made four drumsticks out of the one bird and we can't figure out how he did it. For dessert we had plum pudding with money hidden in it. Jakey and Billy and I got a nickel and Willa and Arthur got a dime. Then Billy choked on his nickel and he had to be turned upside down and slapped. So Dad grabbed the money off both him and Jakey and caused a great hullabaloo. I was just going to complain about Willa and Arthur getting more money than me when Uncle Charlie pulled a quarter out of his pudding and stuck it in mine. Arthur turned green but Willa didn't bat an eye.

*Anyway, after supper while Willa and Mum were helping
Aunt Myrtle with the washing up—Aunt Ida had
"conveniently" disappeared, Uncle Charlie said—"Come into
the barbershop, Bea, and I'll see what can be done about
that mop." Well, he went to work on my hair with his
scissors and trimmed all the fuzz off and left me with a
headful of soft fair curls. Oh, Aunt Aggie, you wouldn't
believe the "transformation." It was almost like a miracle.
In fact I think it was a miracle because only the night
before I had "entreated" God to do something about my
hair. Wait till Georgie Dunn sees me now! He'll hardly
recognize me.*

*After the little kids had been put to bed we played
Forfeits—it's my favourite parlour game—and later I won
another ten cents for knocking a dime off my nose with my
tongue. So altogether I was forty cents richer. Wasn't I
lucky?*

*Well, Aunt Aggie, I must sign off now. Mum is after me
to get to bed again. She still worries about me getting lots
of rest because of my bronchitis which I don't have
anymore thanks to that awful goose grease you made me
take. (Gag! Gag!)*

*I hope you found this letter both interesting and
"informational." I tried not to use too many big words but
"simplification" is hard for me because of my "potential."*

> *Love and "salutations,"*
> *Your "affectionate" niece,*
> *Beatrice Myrtle Thomson*

P.S.: I had to tear open the envelope because I forgot to

tell you something "imperative." (Dad gave me heck for
wasting an envelope but when I told him I was writing to
his sister he gave me another one. I guess that's what
Mum means when she says that blood's thicker than
water.) Anyway, I forgot to tell you the trouble Arthur's in.
He and Georgie Dunn (he is sort of my boyfriend but he
doesn't know it yet) played hooky from high school and
went to the Uptown show at Yonge and Bloor to see Errol
Flynn in Captain Blood. Well, the next day they wrote each
other's notes and forged each other's mother's signatures.
Right away their form teacher, Mr. Grumble, got suspicious
because Georgie's writing is sort of peculiar. (When he was
little he was left-handed and he got slapped and was made
to stand in the cloakroom until he turned right-handed.)
Mr. Grumble marched them to the principal's office and
that night the principal phoned Mr. Dunn and Mr. Dunn
came straight over and told Dad. Well, Dad was all for
razor-stropping Arthur to within an inch of his life, but
Mum jumped between them and screeched, "Over my dead
body!" So Dad made Arthur stay in for a month after
school instead, and Georgie got the same punishment.
There . . . wasn't that "sensational" news?

> *Bye for sure this time,*
> *B.M.T.*

About a week later I got a letter back from Aunt Aggie that
was so full of big words I could hardly make head or tail of it.
I had to look up practically every word in Willa's dictionary.
That cured me of my big word habit. At least temporarily.

9
The unidentified hero

I'll never forget the day the king died because we had so much fun.

It was early on the morning of January 21, 1936, and Mum had just tuned the radio in to CFRB. Usually Jim Hunter's news broadcast came on with a blare of trumpets, like the start of a horse race, followed by his hearty greeting, "Good *Monday* morning, everybody!" (Or Tuesday or Wednesday or whatever day it happened to be.) But this particular day he began with a solemn declaration: *The King is dead. Long live the King!* We all gasped and stopped talking and listened to the grim details direct from Buckingham Palace. Then he said that all Canadian schools would be closed for a day of mourning.

Well, we got over the mourning quickly enough because King George V was old and we didn't know him personally anyway.

"Oh, the Saints preserve me!" Mum groaned when she realized the bunch of us would be home for the whole day.

"Yippee!" Jakey flung his primer up into the air. "That means me and Billy can play all day."

"Not until you've cleaned up the mess you made in the cellar yesterday." Mum believed in giving us all jobs to do, even Jakey and Billy, so we wouldn't grow up shiftless. So I had chores to do all morning.

In the afternoon Glad and Ruth and Ada-May and I each managed to cadge fifteen cents and two car tickets to go downtown to the picture show.

On the Bloor streetcar we argued about what to see.

"I want to see Shirley Temple in *Poor Little Rich Girl*," cooed Ruth. "She's so C.K." (C.K. was short for cute kid.)

"Let's go to the Uptown and see *Magnificent Obsession*," suggested Glad.

"Yah!" I agreed. "Robert Taylor is my magnificent obsession."

Ada raised her eyebrows about a foot at that. "I'd rather go to the Tivoli," she said. "George Raft and Ginger Rogers are in a dancing picture there." Ada was nearly fifteen so she was crazy about dancing. "I'll tell you what"—she rummaged through her purse and found a note pad and pencil—"we'll write our names on bits of paper and draw to decide. That seems fair."

We put our slips of paper into Ada's blue felt hat. Ruth squeezed her eyes shut, poked around in the hat and drew out Ada's name. So we headed for the Tivoli.

At Yonge and Bloor streets we stopped off on our transfers at my Aunt Susan's nut store. We saw her n the window heaving a big batch of shiny redskins out of the bubbling oil. "Well, what are you scally-wags doing running the roads?" Aunt Susan joked when we walked in.

She still treated us like children but we put up with it knowing she'd give us some nuts to munch in the show. She gave the other girls peanuts but she gave me cashews. I started nibbling right away. I just couldn't help myself. "Your mother must have been scared by a squirrel when she made you, Bea," Aunt Susan chuckled.

Just then a crowd of people jumped off the Yonge car and followed their noses into the Nuthouse. So we yelled our thank-you's over their heads and made our escape, clutching our hot, greasy bags.

The moving picture was called *In Person* and it was terrific. We discussed it all the way home. Actually we were all dying to learn to dance. Sometimes Arthur and I even tried a few steps when Shed Fields and his Rippling Rhythm came on the radio, but we generally ended up fighting because he always blamed me for getting out of step. He thought he was so perfect!

That night after supper, since we didn't have any homework, Glad and I went skating at the Grenny. That's what Swansea-ites affectionately called the Grenadier Pond.

I didn't own a pair of skates myself so Willa loaned me hers. She still had a touch of pleurisy and couldn't go out in the night air. Arthur couldn't go out either because he was still being punished.

It was an ideal night for skating—crisp and cold, with bright moonlight and a million stars. Right after New Year's there had been a January thaw and it hadn't snowed since, so the pond was as smooth and clear as a looking glass.

The ice was speckled with skaters, twirling, coasting, some gliding like dancers, arm in arm. (How I would have loved to link arms and skate like that with Georgie!)

Glad and I sat on a log frozen into the edge of the pond, to put on our skates. I had to wear two pairs of Dad's thick work socks with the toes folded over to fill out Willa's skates.

But Glad was even worse off. She had to wear her running shoes inside Buster's skates to make them fit.

Oh, but it was worth it! The sheer joy of sailing like seagulls, arms outstretched, the full length of the pond with the north wind pushing at our backs! But the return trip was another story. With such ill-fitting boots we couldn't really skate at all so we staggered and fell, our ankles twisting painfully as we fought against the wind.

"Let's go to Jasper's shack and get warmed up," I gasped, my words forming little clouds in the air.

"I haven't got any money." Glad was crying now, the tears freezing on her bright red cheeks. "And Jasper won't even let us in unless we buy something."

"I've got fourteen cents left over from New Year's so I'll treat. Ain't I magnanimous?"

"Ain't ain't in the dictionary," Glad managed to laugh as she chipped the tears away with icy mitts.

Jasper's shack, which he'd built himself with scraps of tin and boards and shingles, was a Grenny tradition. It had clung lopsidedly to the west bank of the pond for as long as I could remember. Its coal-oil lantern winked like a firefly through the bare, black trees. The shack was filled with a peculiar mixture of steamy, pungent odours: sweaty socks, hot cocoa, wood smoke and burning coal oil. Another lantern hanging from the ceiling bathed the room in a warm, orange glow.

"*Shut the dern door!*" bellowed Jasper as we squeezed ourselves inside. "*You want me to ketch pee-na-moneeya?*" He always said that.

Collapsing on the bench by the wall, Glad and I undid our

skates as fast as our frost-bitten fingers would allow. Each person could only stay ten minutes. That was Jasper's rule, because the shack only held twelve people, six on either side.

Wonderful heat radiated out from the makeshift box-stove in the middle. Two rows of bricks were lined up on its flat top and a blackened pot burbled at the back. With calloused fingers sticking out of raggedy gloves, Jasper dropped two hot bricks in front of us on the splintery floor. I paid him two cents each for them.

Gingerly we lowered our sock feet onto the roasting clay. Needles of fire pierced our frozen toes and it was all we could do not to scream out loud. But when the pain subsided, relief came in such a delicious, tingling flood that we *ooohhhed* and *aaahhhed* in ecstasy.

"Anything else, girls?" Jasper was a keen businessman.

"A Sweet Marie and two cups of cocoa, Jasper," I ordered.

Mum said that Jasper never washed the cups between customers and she forbade me to drink the filthy stuff, but I figured what my mother didn't know wouldn't hurt me.

So we each had a steaming mugful and shared the Sweet Marie. That was the end of my New Year's money.

Our ten minutes were up in no time and other skaters were clamoring to get in. "Don't get yer shirt in a knot out there!" Jasper hollered through the door. Then he gave Glad and me an extra two minutes on account of the trouble she had lacing up Buster's skates over her running shoes.

Out on the ice once more, warm and refreshed, we headed south again, riding the wind like eagles.

"What's that noise?" Glad yelled to me as she skimmed along on her boots.

A loud *crack*, like summer thunder, split the air. I darted a look over my shoulder and saw the ice breaking up behind us in great gaping wounds. "*Skate faster! Hurry! We gotta stay ahead of the crack!*"

Tilting our arms like banking birds, we veered towards the bulrushes.

No sooner had we scrambled up the bank to safety than the ice gave way with a piercing crash and someone sank, screaming, to his armpits.

"*Yi! Yi! Yi!*" came the terrified cry.

"*Help! Help! Help!*" shrieked Gladie and I.

We couldn't make out who it was. All we could see was a boy's white face bobbing eerily in the moonlight.

People came sailing off the ice from all directions. Inky black water flooded the cracks as far as the eye could see.

Soon a crowd had gathered on the bank. Everyone was panic-stricken, screaming and running and yelling for help, but nobody knew what to do.

Then out of the darkness strode a tall figure in a macintosh coat, his face wrapped up in a woollen muffler. Over his shoulder he carried a long wooden plank. The crowd quickly parted to let him pass.

Dropping the plank with a loud wet *slap* that sounded like a giant beaver's tail hitting the water, he fell to his knees and began crawling carefully forward. The ice cracked as he shoved the board ahead of him.

Now the people had become hushed and still. The only sound was the pitiful wailing of the boy as he clung to the jagged ice.

A minute seemed like an hour. At last, stretched out full-length, the stranger was just able to grasp the boy's hands. Then, inch by treacherous inch, he hauled him in to safety.

Now everyone sprang into action. One man took off his coat and threw it over the victim. Another unbuttoned his windbreaker and wrapped the boy inside. Then he hurried with him in the direction of Jasper's shack.

Meanwhile the man in the macintosh shouldered the plank again and disappeared up the wooded path to Ellis Avenue. Glad and I, our ankles twisting and turning on the slippery bank, scrambled after the man who was carrying the whimpering boy.

When the door to the shack opened and the lantern light fell on the ghostly white face, we instantly recognized him. Then the door shut and we turned slowly away.

Trembling with excitement, Glad and I shucked off our skates and found our frozen galoshes behind the log. The buckles were solid ice so we left them open and flapped our way home as fast as we could.

I kept my family spellbound as I told them the terrible tale. "And guess who it was that nearly drowned?" I had saved the best part to the last.

"Well, for pete's sake, who?" snapped Arthur.

"Guess," I tantalized.

"Oh, don't be ridiculous, Bea. Who?" demanded Willa.

In deference to her ill health, I told. "It was Roy-Roy the dumb boy!"

"Ah, the poor lamb," Mum murmured, shaking her head sadly. "Maybe it would have been for the best."

"*Don't say that, Mum!*" I was horrified.

"Well, Bea, you know he's not right. The poor thing's hardly got a thought in his head."

"There's lots of thoughts in Roy-Roy's head, Mum. He just can't get them out, that's all."

She gave me a long, searching look. "Maybe you're right, Booky. Who am I to judge?"

The next day the story was written up in all the papers. Mum had the *Tely* spread out on the kitchen table and we were poring over it together: *Unidentified Man Saves Dumb Boy From Certain Death In Icy Black Waters Of Bottomless Grenadier!*

"You know what, Mum?"

"What, Bea?"

"I think Grampa was the unidentified man."

"What makes you think so? It says here nobody saw his face."

"I know, but I saw the way he walked. You know—big long steps and sort of stooped over."

"Well . . . " Mum pondered the possibility. "It wouldn't be the first time that Puppa saved somebody from the Grenny."

I decided to go over and ask. I could see it now, tomorrow's headlines in letters two inches high: *William Arthur Cole, Beloved Grandfather Of Beatrice Myrtle Thomson, Admits To Being Unidentified Hero!*

Grampa was sitting by the stove puffing his corncob and reading the paper. There was a macintosh coat hanging on the cellar door.

"You got a new coat, Grampa?"

"About time, isn't it? First one in twenty years."

"Grampa . . . " I took my own coat off and sat on the stool

beside him. "It was you, wasn't it, who saved Roy-Roy?"

"What makes you say that, Be-*a*-trice?"

"Oh, you can't fool me. I recognized the way you walk—and that!" I pointed to the new coat.

"Then I reckon it was me. But I'd be obliged if you kept it to yourself."

"But why, Grampa?" My dreams of being a hero's granddaughter were vanishing like the smoke from his pipe. "You'd be famous. Why, the city might even give you a medal or a citation or something."

Tamping his pipe down with a tobacco-stained thumb he said, "I don't want no medals."

"But gee whiz, why?" I was really disappointed.

"Because the Book says, *Do your good deeds in secret*, that's why."

And *that* was my grampa.

10
A lesson learned

Mum was testing the oven to see if it was right for the popovers. Our new coal-and-gas range (second-hand but new to us) had a heat gauge on the oven door, but Mum said she could still judge better by just sticking her hand in.

While she was stirring the golden-brown gravy with bits of meat floating in it, I set the table.

"Mash the potatoes and turnips together, Willa," Mum said. "That'll be nice for a change."

"Eww, I'm not going to eat any then." Willa screwed up her nose as she started mashing. She hated turnips.

Dad wasn't home yet, so we all sat down without him round the old oilcloth-covered table. I had just poured some more gravy over my second popover when Dad came in the door.

As soon as we saw his hangdog expression we knew something was wrong, and in spite of the cold weather his face was as pale as a soda biscuit.

"I've been laid off!" He blurted out the terrible news as if to get it over with. All our spoons and forks stopped clinking at once. You could have heard a pin drop.

Then Mum's dark eyes began to smoulder. "There's not a

lump of coal in the bin," she muttered.

Dad went all quiet, like the air before a storm.

We finished eating in gloomy silence. Us kids exchanged furtive glances. Even Billy and Jakey, who usually squabbled through supper, were perfectly quiet as they toyed with their food. We all knew what was brewing. Our parents had trouble enough getting along at the best of times—they were so different in nature, like cat and dog, Aunt Ida said. But when they had money worries it seemed to set off fireworks inside them.

Willa washed the dishes and I wiped and Arthur put away without his daily protest that it was girls' work. ("You like to eat, don't you?" was Mum's tart retort to that argument.)

Jakey, who generally took refuge under the table when he felt a fight coming on, went into the front room instead and turned on the radio to hear Bobby Benson.

His favourite story had no sooner begun than Dad marched in and snapped it off in his face. "You little fool!" he yelled at Jakey. "Don't you know the radio wastes electricity? And electricity costs money? And I'm laid off! I'm out of work and there's no coal in the bin and you sit there listening to a foolish story. All you think about's your own self. Go to bed and get out of my sight!"

Well, it was only six-thirty and the poor little fellow wasn't used to Dad being mean to him, so he burst out crying and ran headlong up the stairs. After a while Billy, who didn't understand what was happening because he was only three, sidled up to me and whimpered, "I want you, Bea-Bea."

"Take him up to bed, Bea," Willa whispered. I handed the dishcloth to Arthur and he took it without complaint.

The minute the washing-up was done Willa and Arthur threw on their coats and beat it out the door. But I stayed, cowering on the chair by the stove, shaking the way I always do when I'm scared.

"Please don't fight with Dad tonight, Mum," I pleaded.

It was the wrong thing to say. Instead of stopping her, it seemed to set her off. "What am I supposed to do?" she began to rant unreasonably. "Just pretend everything's all right? How are we going to pay the rent? Easter's coming and you children haven't a stitch on your backs. I'm not a magician, you know. I can't make clothes out of the rag bag."

"You could keep your mouth shut!" Dad snarled as he came out of the cellarway. And that was the beginning of their worst fight in ages.

On and on it raged, for hours and hours, and just as I was certain it was going to come to blows—I tensed myself, ready to spring between them—Dad grabbed his greatcoat off the hook and went slamming out the door. The dishes rattled in the cabinet and I heaved a great sigh of relief.

After that they stopped talking to each other altogether. I didn't know which was worse, the lively battle or the deadly truce.

* * *

One day about a week later Glad and Ruth and Ada and I were standing around on Glad's front walk, talking about boys, when I suddenly caught sight of Dad coming from the direction of the dump. Clomping along behind him in her tattered sweaters and numerous skirts, with her old felt spats flapping around her ankles, was Raggie-Rachel. Both of them were toting bushel baskets full of coal with ash-sifters teetering on the top. They were covered in soot from head to toe. I could hardly make out their features under the powdery ash.

I thought I'd die. I wished the sidewalk would open up and swallow me whole. Turning quickly away, I said, "Can we go in your house, Glad, and listen to *Ma Perkins*?" Without a word the three girls lowered their heads and hurried up the walk. I followed, but before I went inside I glanced over my shoulder.

Rachel had gone. But Dad was still standing there staring straight at me. Even at that distance, and in spite of the soot rimming his eyes, I could see the hurt look on his face. I dropped my eyes and went into Glad's house and shut the door.

That night at supper I made up a question to ask, one I was sure would catch my father's interest. "Dad, when you were in France in 1917, did you and Uncle Charlie fight in the same battalion?"

Dad could always be depended upon to talk about the war, but this time there was no answer. His eyes never left his plate.

"Dad. . . " I tried again.

He raised his head slowly and gazed around, his red-rimmed eyes passing me by as if I was invisible.

"Who said that?"

"Bea said it!" Jakey piped up helpfully.

"Bea? Who's Bea? I don't know anybody by that name."

The rest of the family looked at him as if he'd lost his mind. Only I knew what he meant. And the shame I had felt on the street was nothing to the shame I felt at the table.

I moped around all evening, avoiding everybody, wondering what to do. Finally I went upstairs to get ready for bed. It was cold in our room so I undressed hurriedly in the corner behind the stovepipe and put my nightclothes on. Then I steeled myself and went down to the cellar.

Dad was still sifting ashes, carefully picking out the unburnt black coal with cracked, carbon-caked fingers. He had already salvaged two pails and a scuttle-full. Enough to keep both stoves going for a couple more days.

"Dad . . . "

This time he looked right at me and his eyes, behind the powdery lashes, were infinitely sad. "What is it?" he asked gruffly.

"I'm sorry, Dad." I could hardly speak for the lump in my throat.

"All right, Bea. But let this be a lesson to you, and don't ever turn up your nose at honest labour again."

"I won't, Dad."

He went back to his work and I dragged my heavy feet, in my worn-out slippers, up the two flights of stairs to bed.

11
Helping out

Well, things didn't turn out so badly after all. Mum and Dad started speaking again. Mum was too much of a talker to stay quiet for long. And Dad managed to get enough odd jobs to stay off the pogey. That was important to Dad, not having to accept charity. Because winter was nearly over, the stoves could soon be let out and Dad wouldn't have to pick coal from the dump much longer.

Arthur was able to help out some too. He had a paper route and on Saturdays he gave Mum every cent he earned. Then she gave him back twenty-five cents for spending money.

Willa got a job at Kresge's in corselettes. Her friend Minnie Beasley, who lived in the house stuck to ours on the north side, was working full-time at Kresge's in men's drawers, and when she heard about the part-time opening in corselettes she spoke up for Willa.

"If it interferes with your schoolwork you'll have to give it up. Your education comes first," Mum said. "Your father and I wouldn't be in this predicament, you know, if we'd had the chance to finish our schooling. But that's not going to happen to any of my children. You can bet your boots on that!"

"Oh, don't worry, Mum, I'll manage," Willa said. "Just so long as nobody finds out what department I'm in."

Arthur couldn't resist a snicker. "Everybody will see you there," he grinned.

"Well, you better not show your smart-alecky face at my counter," Willa warned.

Even though Arthur was bigger than Willa now, he was still a bit scared of her. Or maybe the fear had turned into respect. I don't know which.

Of the older kids, I was the only one who wasn't helping out and I felt awful about it.

"You can help by taking on some of Willa's jobs around the house," Mum suggested.

"It's not the same. Besides, I abhor housework. I wish I could help with money."

Then one day something happened that made my wish come true.

Aunt Ellie came running across the street and bustling in our door, wiping her doughy hands on her floury apron. "Franny, a woman wants you on the phone. She asked me if I knew where you were living now and I said right across the road, but she wouldn't even give her name."

"My stars, I wonder who it could be?" Mum dropped the broom in the corner and pulled on her sweater. "Bea, you keep an eye on Billy. I'll be back in two shakes."

Well, she was gone for ages and when she came back she was flushed with excitement. "You'll never guess who it was!" She rubbed her hands together gleefully. "My old school chum, Dorothea Moss. She's married to a druggist now and they're parked on Easy Street." Mum went straight to the sideboard

268

and got the photograph album out of the top drawer. "I think there's a snapshot of her and me in here somewhere." She flipped through the dog-eared pages. "Here it is! That picture was taken at a young people's picnic at Hanlan's Point. My, Dorothea was a handsome girl."

Mum looked at the picture for a long moment, memories flitting across her face and sparkling in her eyes. "Oh, my lands! I nearly forgot to tell you what the phone call was all about." Now she looked like the cat that had swallowed the canary.

"What, Mum, what?"

"She wanted to know if I could recommend a girl to help her with her new baby. A girl about thirteen years old."

"Did you say I'm thirteen, Mum? Did you? Did you?"

"Yas, Bea." That's the way she said yes when she was tickled about something. "And she said she's willing to pay two dollars a week for after school and Saturdays. They just moved to the Palisades—my, the homes are lovely over there—so you won't even need a streetcar ticket."

Mum's face went suddenly serious. "Mind you, I told her plump and plain that you couldn't do any hard jobs because you weren't too strong on account of your bronchitis."

"Oh, Mum, I'm strong as a horse. Watch." I flung my arms around her sturdy body and lifted her off the floor before she could stop me.

"Set me down this instant!" she ordered. I did, but I wasn't even breathless.

"Well, just the same, some of those well-to-do women like to take advantage of poor girls and work them to death for a pittance. But I'm sure Dorothea's not like that, and she assured me she only wants you to mind the baby. So I told her how good you've always been with Billy and she said you can start tomorrow."

Dorothea's baby was a beautiful, bright-eyed, bald-headed boy. I was hoping for a girl because, after two little brothers, I was sick of boys.

But he turned out to be a darling baby. His name was Goo-Goo. Of course, that was only a pet name, like Booky. His real name was Gugenheim. Gugenheim Higgenbottom, after his paternal grandfather.

"I would have named him Hubert, after my father," Dorothea confided to me, "but the Higgenbottoms have pots of money and I want him to be rich when he grows up."

Dorothea was very outspoken like that. I liked her a lot and she liked me. And we both loved Goo-Goo.

But I could hardly stand her husband. He was old and pinchy-nosed and stingy. Once I asked her why she married such an old crock—he must have been twice her age—and she answered with a sly wink, "It's better to be an old man's darling than a young man's slave." Boy, I wasn't so sure about that! Anyway, he watched like a hawk when she paid me, and once when she tried to give me an extra quarter he made me give it back.

Everything went along fine for about a month. At the end of each week I'd proudly hand over my money to Mum and she'd give me back twenty-five cents, just like she did Willa and Arthur. Then one Saturday night Dorothea asked me to stay late to mind Goo-Goo so she and Mr. Higgenbottom could go to the Runnymede to see *Broadway Melody of 1935*.

That night I found out just how stingy Mr. Higgenbottom really was because I stayed for supper. Dorothea had cooked three pork chops, with carrots and string beans. He took two chops and she had to share hers with me. Then he watched every bite I put in my mouth. Honestly, he was worse than Grandpa Thomson.

After they left I did the washing-up and put GooGoo to bed. He went right to sleep like the good baby he was, so I didn't know what to do next.

In a while I got bored so I decided to have some fun, and the first thing my eyes lit on was the phone. Beside it was a metal telephone directory with the letters of the alphabet sticking out on one side. I touched the *T* experimentally and the lid sprang open, making me jump. *Tom's Smoke Shop, Lyndhurst 6898* was the first number. I dialled the number and a man answered promptly, "Tom's Smoke Shop!"

I cleared my throat and in my best grown-up voice said, "Do you have Prince Albert in the tin?"

"Yes, ma'am, we do," he replied.

"Then let him out—he's suffocating!" I cried, slamming the receiver down and laughing uproariously.

Next I pressed the *L*. On the top of the page was written, *Liggett's Drugstore, Midway 9507*. This time I decided to disguise my voice by pulling my hanky tight over the mouthpiece. A woman answered my ring.

"Uumm—could you tell me if you're on the Bloor car line?" I asked innocently.

"Yes, ma'am, we are." (She fell for it hook, line and sinker.)

"Well, you'd better get off because a streetcar's coming!" This time I collapsed on the floor, rolling with laughter. Then I decided I'd better stop before the telephone company traced my calls and I landed myself in jail.

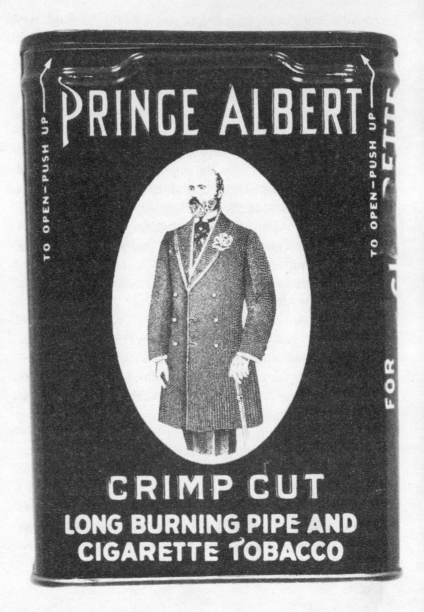

About nine o'clock I ended up in the kitchen. By that time I was starving from having had such a skimpy supper. I thought I'd just take a peek into their refrigerator. When I opened the door the light popped on, dazzling my eyes. There, spread before me, was a veritable feast: bowls of peaches and greengage plums, tiny pots of ketchup and mustard and relish on a silver tray that you could spin around, ham and milk and butter and syrup and apples, and a cold roast chicken sitting on a platter in clear pink jelly. Lifting it gingerly by the drumsticks, I stripped the dark meat off the back and crammed it into my mouth. Mmmm, it was good. I lowered it carefully back into the jelly so it would look as if it had never been touched.

Behind the chicken, way at the back, was a brown paper bag. Curious, I pulled it out and opened it up. Inside were at least a dozen huge, ripple-skinned California oranges. Giant oranges, the biggest I'd ever seen.

I hadn't tasted an orange since Christmas and my mouth watered at the wonderful sight. Grabbing one, I dug my fingernails deep into its shiny thick skin. Juice spurted out, hitting me in the eye and dripping off the end of my knobby nose. Curling my long tongue like a trough I caught the delicious stream and let it trickle down my throat.

"Ahhh!" I breathed ecstatically. But one orange only whetted my appetite. So I snatched another and another. Like a greedy vampire I tore them open and sucked and slurped and gobbled and demolished every one.

When I had finished, and was trying not to burp, I stared in dismay at what I had done. Heaped up on the table was a pile of pulp and seeds and orange skins. And at that very moment in walked Dorothea and Mr. Higgenbottom through the kitchen door.

I thought he was going to have apoplexy. His face puffed up and changed colours, from red to blue to purple. "*Why you—you—you gluttonous, conniving, thieving wretch!*" He sprayed saliva all over the place. "*It's plain to see where the likes of you sprang from!*"

Now he turned his wrath on Dorothea. "This is the thanks we get, showing pity on your poverty-stricken friends," he sneered.

Then back to me. "*Get out of my house! Get out of my sight before I lose my temper!*"

Shaking like a leaf, I tried to apologize. "I'm sorry, Mr. Higgenbottom—Dorothea—I'm sorry. I don't know what came over me." I started to cry uncontrollably.

Grabbing me by the shoulder, Dorothea shoved me towards the hall. "Get your coat on quick!" she hissed. Then she hurried me out the door and walked with me to Veeny Street because it was dark outside.

"You silly goose," she scolded. "Now see what you've done. I'm going to have to let you go. And I'll miss you too. And Goo-Goo does love you so. Oh, Bea!"

"Maybe Mr. Higgenbottom will forgive me?" I snivelled hopefully.

"Oh, sure—and maybe there'll be two moons in the sky tomorrow night. Honestly, Bea, you are the limit. But there's no use crying over spilt milk. Slip over and see me and Goo-Goo when old Higgy-Piggy's working. I'll look for you Friday afternoons. Now get home with you."

She wasn't the least bit mad. Just sorry. I could have kicked myself. If only I had been satisfied with the chicken!

When I came in Mum was just finishing up her ironing.

Her face sagged with fatigue and there were dark circles under her eyes.

"Where's Dad?" I whispered anxiously.

"He's gone to bed." She took one look at me and knew something was wrong. "What is it? What's the matter?"

So I told her the whole sordid story. She was mad as hops and gave me a terrible tongue-lashing. "Beatrice Myrtle Thomson. A girl your age. You ought to be ashamed of yourself, taking advantage of Dorothea like that. And what must she think of us? What kind of a home does a girl come from who would gorge herself on a dozen oranges?" My stomach heaved at the word "gorge."

"Why would you steal oranges? Were they at least small oranges?"

"No, huge," I admitted. "But I didn't steal them, Mum, I just ate them."

"I've a good mind to tell your father." Mum wasn't letting up on me any. "And you know what that would mean!"

"Oh, please, Mum!" I could hardly bear the thought of being razor-stropped at my age. "Don't tell him. Dorothea didn't give me any money this week, so that should pay for the oranges."

"That's true enough." Now Mum sounded thankful to find a legitimate excuse for me. "But what will I tell him? What if he runs into Mr. Higgenbottom on the street?"

"He won't because Mr. Higgenbottom drives everywhere in his new De Soto. And besides, he never comes near Veeny Street because of the dump. He says all our houses should be levelled to the ground."

"Oh, he does, does he? The old reprobate. I wish he'd say

that to me. I'd give him a piece of my mind. Well . . . we'll say Mr. Higgenbottom can't afford you any longer. That ought to make your father happy. He wasn't too pleased about you working for the old skinflint anyway."

"Thank you, Mum." I breathed a sigh of relief.

"Never mind the thank-you's. I'm not condoning what you did, mind. Now get to bed and we'll say no more about it."

I was so uncomfortable from my full stomach and wounded conscience I could hardly sleep all night. So I gave my nose an extra-long massage.

12
A visit to Birchcliff

After I lost my job at Dorothea's and couldn't help out any-more, I got all depressed.

Then, to make matters worse, Dad sold the radio right out from under our noses to get his two dollars back. Us kids all lined up in a mournful row and watched it being lugged out of the house. We felt like a friend had just died. The front room was as dead as a morgue without it. No more *Amos 'n Andy* or *Charlie McCarthy* or *Fibber McGee and Molly*. It was awful.

To add to my misery, instead of doing better on my Easter exams, I did worse. But Mr. Jackson said not to worry, I'd prob-ably pull up in the finals. The finals! Entrance exams! My heart sank at the thought. So instead of enjoying my Easter holidays I went moping around the house worrying and feel-ing sorry for myself.

Then Glad came over one day and changed all that. "You're wanted on the phone, Bea!" she said.

"Me? Are you sure?" Nobody ever phoned me.

"Well, they didn't ask for the cat," she joked. So I ran across the road with her, picked up the receiver off the chair where she'd dropped it and cried, "Hello!" into the conical mouth-piece on the wall.

"Hello yourself and see how you like it," came the crazy reply. "Know who this is?"

I said, no, I had no idea.

"It's me, Tootsie Reese. How are ya, Bea?"

I had to think for a minute. Then I remembered. Tootsie was one of the kids I used to know when we lived in Birchcliff. I'd never liked her much. Why would she be phoning me?

"Hi, Tootsie. It's, uh, swell hearing from you. I've missed you." I had, too. You don't have to like someone to miss them.

We talked for a while about old times, then she said, "The reason I'm calling is, my mother said I could have a friend stay over one night during the holidays, so I picked you. Wanna come?"

I had never had an overnight invitation outside the family before and I was thrilled. So I said I'd ask my mum and call her right back. A pencil stub hung on a string beside the phone. I wrote her number on the wallpaper among a hundred others, circled it three times so I could find it again and raced home.

"I guess you can go," Mum said, stirring batter in the big mixing bowl. "The change will probably do you good."

"And guess what, Mum!" I'd saved this news till the last. "Tootsie Reese's family have moved into our 'new' house on Cornflower Street."

"Well, I'll be dashed!" Mum declared as she spooned the frothy batter into the graniteware pan. "It'll be like old home week for you, going back there."

I could hardly wait to see the new house again. We still referred to it that way because it had been brand-new when we moved into it. We had hated to leave its sparkling newness after only six months, to come to live in the shabby row-house on Veeny Street.

Willa drew me a map so I wouldn't get lost going to Tootsie's, since it was the first time I'd ever travelled alone in the city. "It takes three streetcars, so don't lose your transfer," she warned. Mum reminded me not to talk to strangers.

"Don't worry, Mum. Gee whiz—I'm thirteen, you know."

It was a nice, sunny, slushy spring day. I loved the trip, gawking out the streetcar window. But by the time I got to Birchcliff two hours later I was glad to hop off the red wooden trolley and start walking down Cornflower Street—straight back into my childhood.

Stopping at the corner of Lilac Street, I looked at the ramshackle house where our Billy had been born. A huge lump welled up in my throat at the memory of that night. Then plain as day I saw myself, a skinny little ghost running lickety-split with my hoop and stick up the street to Audrey's. (Audrey Westover had been my best friend in Birchcliff. I had phoned her once—that's how Tootsie got Aunt Ellie's number—but when she moved to Oshawa we lost touch.) Heaving a big sigh over my lost childhood, I continued down Cornflower Street.

And there it was, the new house, with its wonderful upstairs veranda and its beautiful bay window. Inside, I could clearly picture the gleaming hardwood floors and the polished oaken banister with its round-topped newel post.

Just then the door flew open and out bounded Tootsie onto the downstairs veranda. "Hi, Bea!" I hardly recognized her. She must have grown five inches in the three years since I'd seen her, and her hair was red now instead of brown. Mrs.

Reese came to the door, blowsy and jolly as ever. "Welcome home, Bea," she smiled.

But the moment I stepped over the threshold all my glowing memories of the new house crumbled into dust.

A horrible smell wafted down the hallway. It was all I could do not to hold my nose. My feet stuck to the grime on the once spotless hardwood floors. Rungs were missing from the banister. The round top was broken right off the newel post. And the lovely bay window, which we had been so proud of, was streaked with dirt and covered by a ragged curtain hanging on a sagging string.

"Well, Bea, does it look the same?" asked Mrs. Reese.

"Nearly," I managed to lie.

That night for supper we had beans and bread. Willa would have died if she could have seen the dishes with egg yolk still smeared on them from the last meal.

After supper Tootsie and I went for a walk. As we strolled around Birchcliff, memories, some good and some bad, came flooding over me. I shuddered as we passed Birchcliff School where the teacher had called me a ninny every day for my zeroes in arithmetic. Mr. Jackson would never do that even if I did get zeroes, which I didn't anymore.

We sauntered past the white frame church on Kingston Road where I'd got saved every Sunday. The choir was practicing "He walks with me and He talks with me" and their voices, drifting out the window, made me feel saved all over again.

On our way home we passed Audrey's house and I half expected her to come running out the door. But instead a big, tough-looking boy came out, swung his leg over the porch railing and yelled, "Whatcha lookin' at, Stoopid?"

Tootsie hollered back, "Not much, Beanhead!" After a few more insults we sauntered on.

"Boy! You've got more nerve than a canal horse," I said.

"Nah! He's nuts about me," laughed Tootsie, tossing her new red hair. "You got a boyfriend, Bea?"

I thought about Georgie Dunn. But what if I told Tootsie that Georgie was my boyfriend and then she came to visit me in Swansea and I had to prove it?

"Nah!" I shrugged my bony shoulders carelessly. "I'm too busy to bother with boys. My teacher—you should see him, he looks just like Ramon Novarro—well, he says—"

"What's Arthur like now—cute?" she interrupted.

"You might think so," I answered shortly.

We got home just in time to hear the creaking door of *Inner Sanctum* coming on their radio. Then Tootsie's brothers came in from running the roads, as their father put it, and we all sat down at the sticky kitchen table for a game of cards. We had lots of fun. Then we had tea and toast with jam. Their lackadaisical mother didn't seem to care what time we went to bed, so it was nearly midnight before we hit the sack.

Once settled down in the rumpled bed, we talked for hours. Mostly about Tootsie's boyfriends.

It was very interesting. She told me things I wouldn't repeat to a living soul, not even Gladie. I didn't have anything to add, so for once I was the quiet one.

The last thing I remember before dozing off was the funny, sickly-sweet smell of the bedclothes. But the next thing I knew, I woke up with stinging needles of pain all over my body.

"Tootsie! Tootsie!" I shook her awake. "Something's happening!"

"Drat!" she cried, catapulting out of bed. "Get up quick, Bea, and don't touch the light switch!"

Grabbing my hand she yanked me down the dark hall to the smelly bathroom, shut the door and turned on the light. She took the cake of soap from the dish and lathered it up under the tap.

"What are you doing?"

"You'll see."

We crept back to the bedroom, the squishy soap in her hand.

"Now, you stand by the switch," she whispered, "but don't touch it until I say so. Okay?"

"Okay."

She tiptoed to the bed. "Okay!" she yelled.

I flipped the switch and she flung the covers back. Furiously she began dabbing all over the bedsheet with the mushy cake of soap. Frenzied bedbugs scurried in every direction in a vain attempt to escape her flying hand. When they had all disappeared she showed me the soap. It was covered with little brown creatures, their backs buried in lather, their legs wiggling frantically.

"Wow! I got a good batch tonight!" she gloated triumphantly as I followed her, goggle-eyed, back to the bathroom. Using the smooth side of the snaggletoothed family comb she scraped the sodden soap, bugs and all, into the toilet bowl. Then *swooooshhh*, away they went, still fighting for their lives, on their way to Lake Ontario.

"They won't bother us no more tonight," she assured me, and promptly fell asleep. They didn't, but I scratched the rest of the night anyway. And when morning finally came I couldn't for the life of me use that soap or comb, so I ran my fingers through my hair and let it go at that.

When I got home I told Mum all about it and she nearly had a conniption fit. She made me jump right into the bathtub and scrub myself from head to toe. Then she inspected me, inch by inch, and gave my hair a thorough fine-tooth combing. She soaked my clothes in Lysol and burned the Eaton's bag I'd carried my nightdress and slippers in.

"It's a sin and a shame," she declared, her tongue tut-tutting a mile a minute. "That lovely house falling into such filthy hands. Well, that puts the kibosh on Tootsie Reese. You can't go there anymore."

"Darn." I wished I hadn't told her. "And I had such a swell time too. Well, would it be okay if I invite Tootsie here? She's dying to see our Arthur again."

"*No!* Bedbugs travel! Can you imagine what your sister would do if she ever found a bug in her bed?"

I could imagine.

13
The invitation

Plop. A letter dropped through the slot in the front door and it wasn't the right time for the postman. Curious, I ran to the hallway and picked it up off the floor. The very neat handwriting on the envelope read *Arthur and Beatrice Thomson.*

Who would write to both of us? I wondered. It must be some kind of joke. I ripped open the envelope and unfolded a single sheet of notepaper. *You are cordially invited to a surprise party for Ada-May Hubbard on the occasion of her fifteenth birthday at 8 p.m. on Saturday, May 9, 1936, at 24 Veeny Street.* That was only a week away.

"*Arthur!*" He was down the cellar helping Dad.

"*What?*"

"Come see what we got!"

He came up with an inquisitive expression on his face. I handed him the note. After reading it he asked, "Are you going?"

"Sure. Are you?"

"Not if you are."

"Well, I couldn't care less!" I had borrowed that terrific phrase from old White Smock. Then I added, for good measure, "So put that in your pipe and smoke it!"

I had never been to a mixed party before, much less one at night, and I was both worried and excited about it. First of all I was worried because I didn't have any money for a present for Ada. Neither did Arthur, who had decided to go after all. (I knew he would.)

Mum suggested giving Ada things we'd made in school.

"Like what?" asked Arthur skeptically.

"Like that lovely wooden jewellery box you made in Senior Fourth," Mum said. She hopped up on the little stool that made her tall enough to reach the top of the kitchen cabinet and got the box from way at the back. Stepping down, she blew the dust off. "This bluebird you painted on it is real as life." She traced the picture with her finger. "I'm sure Ada would appreciate it."

"But the manual training teacher only gave me forty-six out of a hundred on that," objected Arthur.

"Well, you're an artist, not a carpenter!" retorted Mum.

That pleased Arthur so much he went ahead and polished up the jewellery box with Hawe's Floor Wax and wrapped it in some coloured paper Willa gave him.

"What'll I do for a present, Mum?" I asked anx-iously.

"Why don't you give Ada that nice set of hankies you made in domestic science last year?" she suggested.

"But, Mum, Miss Boyle said my sewing was the worst mess she'd ever seen, and that I'd never make a needlewoman." (That was good news to me, because the last thing I wanted to be was a needlewoman.)

"Oh, for mercy's sake, bring them here." Mum was getting irritated. "I'll fix them up if I have time."

Mum made time. She even embroidered Ada's initials on each handkerchief and they turned out lovely. Then Willa arranged them, like four little fans, in a flat box with *A.M.H* showing in each corner.

Willa hadn't been invited to the party, but she didn't care because she had a boyfriend now, Wesley Armstrong. He had auburn hair and eyes to match. He had taken her out twice already, once to supper and once to Shea's Theatre to see *Annie Oakley*. Gee, it must be swell to be eighteen.

* * *

The night of the party both Arthur and I were in a tizzy getting ready. Arthur had slicked back his hair with brilliantine and Mum was having a fit about it.

"It makes your nice blond waves all straight and brown-looking," she lamented.

"That's what it's supposed to do," Arthur said.

"Can I use your pink nail polish, Willa, to match my new dress?"

"You can if you promise two things," Willa bargained.

"I'll promise anything. Just tell me what."

"First, stop biting your fingernails. They look a sight. And second, stop massaging the end of your nose. Especially in bed. It keeps me awake."

"I promise," I answered without giving a serious thought to how hard it would be to give up my favourite bad habits. Then she lent me her nail file to smooth the ragged edges and showed me how to apply the nail polish, leaving the moons bare.

When we were all ready Mum walked behind us to the front door, straightening Arthur's collar and fussing with the back of my skirt. "Now keep in mind about Mr. Hubbard and don't go getting rambunctious," she warned.

Mr. Hubbard was an invalid who had been bedridden with sleeping sickness for twenty years. Everyone said Mrs. Hubbard was a saint for waiting on him hand and foot all those years, instead of packing him off to the Home for Incurables like lots of women would have done.

The only part of Ada's father I had ever actually seen was his feet. Once I had gone upstairs with her to the bathroom and I got a glimpse of his feet through the open bedroom door. It was a hot day so he had no covers on. I remember thinking that his feet looked like a collection of bleached bones on the desert.

"Ada says it doesn't matter how much noise we make, Mum," I assured her, "because her father can't hear a thing."

"Just the same," Mum insisted, "I expect you to behave yourselves and not carry on like you do at home."

We both promised, then started walking up the street together, staying as far apart as possible.

"What are you eating, Arthur?"

"None of your beeswax, Bea."

"Oh, you're a card! A real card!"

He laughed and poked out his tongue. On it was stuck a tiny black square. "It's Sen-Sen," he explained. "For halitosis."

"What's halitosis?" It sounded like a swell new word.

"Bad breath."

"Have you got bad breath?" I took a quick step backwards.

"No! It's so you won't get it, dopey. Here." He gave me one.

I put it in my mouth and spat it right out again. "Ugh! Vile! I'd rather have bad breath."

Just then Glad ran across the road to join us. He gave her a Sen-Sen and she sucked it happily.

Ruth was invited to the party too, but she had conspired with Ada's mother to take Ada to Bloor Street on a mock errand and to bring her back after all the guests had arrived.

When Mrs. Hubbard let us in I knew instantly why Arthur was so anxious about halitosis. Lined up in a row on the couch were three gorgeous girls who looked like they'd just stepped out of Eaton's Spring and Summer Catalogue. "These are some of Ada-May's high school chums," Mrs. Hubbard said as she introduced us.

Cora was a bleached blonde (I could tell by her black roots), Nadine was what Mum would call a raven-haired beauty and Fanny was a flashy redhead. I was green with envy.

"Oh, we already know Arthur Thomson!" gushed the gorgeous Coral. "Come sit with us, Arthur." She patted the seat beside her and they all wriggled over to make room. Then that silly brother of mine grinned and blushed and went and squeezed himself in between them.

Two high school boys were there too. Alvin Wetmore (Wetmore!) was fat and short and pimplyfaced. And Harry Greenwood was tall, dark and handsome.

"Bea, I'd like you and Glad to keep a sharp lookout at the window," Mrs. Hubbard said. "The minute Ada-May and Ruth come in sight, off go the lights."

Glad and I stationed ourselves behind the curtains, thankful to have somewhere to look. Just then Buster and Georgie and Elmer Finney came up the walk.

I could hardly wait for Georgie to see me. For once I was pretty sure I looked nice. I had rinsed my hair with lemon juice and put it up in pin curls. Then Willa had brushed it out for me and the way she fluffed it up around my face made my nose look almost normal. The pink lipstick and nail polish matched my new dress exactly. Mum had made it with just a remnant she picked up at an Eaton's Opportunity Day sale. Glad said it was absolutely dreamy. And even Arthur had remarked that I didn't look half bad, which was a fantastic compliment coming from him.

When the three boys came in I stepped out from behind the curtain.

"Hi, Bea. You look swell!" said Elmer Finney.

"Yah!" agreed my cousin Buster.

But Georgie didn't even seem to notice me. His sparkly eyes and dimpled smile were riveted, positively riveted, on those three Eaton's Beauty dolls lined up on the couch. Glad and I exchanged knowing looks and shrank in our homemade Sunday School dresses.

Darn that Georgie! I decided then and there that I never wanted a boyfriend. And I was never, ever, going to get married as long as I lived.

"Here they come!" Luckily Glad had remembered her job at the window.

"Lights out!" called Mrs. Hubbard.

The room was plunged into darkness. And in the sudden quiet I could hear Elmer Finney whistling through his buckteeth. He had halitosis, too!

The Hubbards' front door opened directly into their front room, so the minute Ada and Ruth stepped inside Mrs. Hubbard flicked the switch and we all yelled "*Surprise!*"

"Oh, my gosh!" Ada grabbed off her hat and fluffed up her

nut-brown hair. "Oh, Mother, how could you? If I'da known I'da changed my dress. Ohhh, for pete's sake!" She went on like that for about five minutes while we all laughed and clapped and jumped around her.

"Are you surprised, Ada?" her mother kept asking. "Are you really surprised? C'mon now, tell the truth."

"Oh, Mother, how can you even ask? Look at me! I'm red as a beet and shakin' like a leaf."

Finally, Mrs. Hubbard was convinced and the party got underway.

"Let's start the kissing games!" crowed rabbit-faced Elmer Finney.

"Yah!" agreed Buster, "Where's the milk bottle?"

Mrs. Hubbard obliged with a milk bottle, then she laughingly retired to the kitchen.

I had heard all about kissing games, but I had never actually participated before. In fact, I had never really been kissed by a boy except when Horace Huxtable pecked me on the cheek. Sometimes, for practice, I'd kiss the bureau mirror. (Once I forgot to wipe the Tangee lips off the glass and Willa got mad as a wet hen.)

We formed a circle—boy, girl, boy, girl—then Buster gave the bottle a fast spin in the centre of the linoleum carpet. I was scared skinny and thrilled to death, both at the same time. The bottle blurred, like a whirling top, then gradually slowed to a breathless stop. Hoots of laughter broke out when one end pointed at me and the other end at Arthur.

"Oh, no, puke!" cried my horrible brother, pulling a face like he'd just sucked on a lemon.

"Ewww!" squealed flashy Fanny. "I'll trade places with you,

Bea. A boy can't kiss his own sister."

We traded, and I never saw Arthur act so excited before. He went red to the roots of his brilliantined hair. Then he jumped up, bounded over and gave Fanny such a long kiss that I'd swear, if I didn't know better, he'd had some practice.

Changing places with Fanny had put me right opposite Georgie Dunn. By this time he had smiled and winked at me twice, so I didn't feel so badly. But for some reason the bottle never stopped its spin to point at us. After about an hour the game ended and we were the only ones who hadn't been kissed. Nobody else seemed to notice, but I sure had.

"Now let's play post office," giggled Coral.

"My favourite!" cried Nadine.

"Mine too!" agreed goofy old Elmer. He was sitting right beside me now and I happened to glance up under the shelf of his big yellow teeth. Ugh! I thought, shifting over. A person could get rabies.

"You go first, Ada; it's your party!" Ruth pushed the reluctant birthday-girl towards the closet under the stairs. "I'll be the postman."

After whispering her message to Ruth, Ada disappeared behind the closet door.

"I've got a letter here—" announced Ruth, staring fixedly at her empty palm, "addressed to Harry Greenwood."

Harry sprang up, and ducking his head, vanished into the cubbyhole. The rest of us held our breath until we heard a loud *smack*. Then we squealed with laughter as Ada emerged, her face flaming, leaving Harry behind.

"What's it like?" I whispered, trying not to sound envious.

"Oh, boy!" she whispered back, whatever that meant.

One by one the boys and girls got letters, but my name still hadn't been called.

Just then Elmer was called to the closet. Before he left he leaned down, his teeth making me want to run away, and said in a stage whisper, "You're next, Bea!"

Oh, no! I couldn't get my first kiss from ugly old Elmer! I had to think fast. I jumped up and ran to the kitchen where Mrs. Hubbard was preparing things to eat. On the table was a plateful of buttered raisin bread that looked so much like Tootsie's soap it made me gag. Averting my eyes I said, "Can I help you, Mrs. Hubbard?"

"Why, that's nice of you, dear. Maybe you'd like to stir the punch." So I stirred the pink punch that smelled like raspberry jelly until I was sure Elmer's turn would be over. Then I sidled back into the front room and sat down quietly on the first empty chair, which happened to be beside Alvin Wetmore. "I'm gonna getcha, Bea!" he chortled, and bounded for the closet.

I had to escape again. "Ada!" I whispered frantically, "I have to go to the toilet!"

"Well, for Pete's sake, go!" She gave me a disgusted look.

I hurried up the stairs. Mr. Hubbard's door was closed this time so I didn't see his feet. I stayed in the bathroom as long as I possibly could.

I had no sooner got settled down again than Nadine declared, "I've got a letter here for Beatrice Thomson."

Well, by now I was so confused that I didn't know who was in the closet. "Who's in there, Glad?" I whispered.

"That's for us to know and you to find out!" she giggled.

Then all the kids pushed and pulled and shoved me into the closet. Just before someone slammed the door behind me I realized with a shock that I was face to face with Georgie. Then we were in the pitch dark. The closet smelled of wet mops and dust rags and lemon oil. My heart was hammering so hard I was afraid he'd hear it.

"Hi, Bea."

"Hi, Georgie."

Our noses were only inches apart. I was glad he couldn't see the knob on mine. His breath smelled sweet and fresh. I wished I had sucked a Sen-Sen.

I felt Georgie's arms go around my waist. Then he kissed me, right on the lips. It was a soft, tender kiss with no smacking sound. I knew I would remember it for the rest of my life.

14
High school!

Willa graduated from high school at the top of her class. Her principal, Mr. Bruce, was determined she should go to university. He even came to our house one night to have a conference about it with Mum and Dad.

The little kids were in bed already, so Mum herded us big kids into the kitchen and shut the door so the grown-ups could have privacy in the front room.

The three of us held our breath and eavesdropped. Willa had her ear glued to the keyhole and Arthur and I knelt down to listen at the crack below the door. We heard the whole conversation as plain as day.

"Willa is my star pupil," Mr. Bruce was saying, "and I feel it's essential that students of her calibre receive higher education."

"What's 'essential' mean, Willa?" I couldn't resist collecting a new word for my vocabulary.

"Shhh! It means important," she whispered.

"I always knew she'd make us proud," Mum's voice was fairly glowing. "She took top honours in her entrance exams and won the gold medal, you know."

"Good grief," sighed Willa.

"Yes, I know, Mrs. Thomson," Mr. Bruce said gently. "And now to the problem at hand. Is there any way you could manage the yearly tuition fee, Mr. Thomson? It's a hundred and fifteen dollars."

"I'd work day and night if I could," Dad said earnestly, "but I've been laid off at Neilson's and I only have odd jobs to depend on. It's all I can do to meet the rent and—"

"The money he brings in wouldn't keep body and soul together," Mum interrupted.

"Ye gods!" muttered Arthur.

"Well . . . I'm willing to contribute fifty dollars out of my own pocket," declared Mr. Bruce. Willa gasped.

"My word," Mum said, "that is generous of you, Mr. Bruce. But the other sixty-five dollars might as well be a thousand to us."

"There's just one chance . . . " Dad began.

"What's that?" Mum and Mr. Bruce asked simultaneously.

"The Veterans' Emergency Fund." A trace of pride filtered back into Dad's voice. "It was set up to help families of overseas veterans. I served three years in France, so I ought to qualify."

"Fine! Fine!" We heard Mr. Bruce scrape back his chair and move towards the door. "Well, good night to you both. Be sure to let me know when you hear something."

The very next day Dad high-tailed it down to the Department of Veterans' Affairs. We could hardly wait for him to come home with the good news.

"What are you going to be, Willa?" I was awestruck at my sister's glittering future.

"I'll decide later," she hedged, starting to set the supper table.

"She's going to be a doctor." Mum let go of the potato masher long enough to rub her hands at the exciting prospect.

Jakey was following Willa around the kitchen, his brown eyes sparkling. "If you be a doctor, Willa, I'll let you take my tonsils out on the kitchen table."

"Me too!" agreed Billy happily. They both loved the gory story about Willa and Arthur suffering through that terrible ordeal on the kitchen table.

"They don't take tonsils out at home anymore," Willa explained, filling the teakettle at the sink. "You have to go to the hospital now."

Just then Dad came in the door. We knew as soon as we saw his long face that the news was bad.

"What did they say?" demanded Mum, her eyes already shooting sparks.

"They said they might have considered it if she was a boy," Dad spat the words out angrily, "but they wouldn't lay that kind of money out on a girl. They said girls don't warrant a university education."

"And what did you say to that?" Mum was fuming.

"I said, 'Then how is it my girl got the highest marks in Fifth Form?' Then I lost my temper and shook my fist in the sergeant's face and he had me put out on the street. It took two privates to do it too," he added defiantly.

Bright red spots flamed on Mum's high cheekbones and her dark eyes flashed furiously. "If I had the money I'd sue!" she raved. "I'd take it to the highest court in the land!"

"Never mind," Willa put in suddenly. "I'll go back and take a business course next year. I'm pretty sure I can do the three-year commercial program in one. I don't want to be a doctor anyway. I hate the sight of blood."

"The commercial course should qualify you for a good job," Dad said, sounding relieved.

"A good job is not a profession." Tears of frustration were running down Mum's face.

"What about Normal School, Willa?" Arthur suggested helpfully.

Willa shook her head. "I don't want to be a teacher. If I can't be a doctor, maybe I can work in a doctor's office."

Mum and Dad were somewhat mollified, but utterly deflated. They didn't argue about it anymore though.

Willa sighed thankfully; she hated fighting. But late that night I thought I heard her crying herself to sleep.

* * *

Well, after all that excitement over Willa my last regular day in Senior Fourth didn't seem very significant. Of course, with the finals looming ahead maybe it wouldn't be my last day after all.

Glad and I both came out our front doors at the same time. It was a hot day for the middle of June, and dusty Veeny Street hadn't been oiled for summer yet. The Canada Bread wagon raised the dust as it trundled by, leaving steaming horse-buns in its wake. Mum always made Arthur scoop up the fresh horse-buns in the dustpan for her flower bed. He hated that job and Willa flatly refused to do it.

"Watch your step, Jakey!" I called as he and Florrie and Skippy went yelling and tripping down the road after the wagon to try to hitch a ride on the step at the back.

Canada Bread is full of lead!
The more you eat, the quicker you're dead!

I had to laugh to hear them singing that same old ditty that we used to sing when we were kids. I guess they were all excited because the summer holidays were coming.

Shortly after the second recess Mr. Jackson got up from his desk and said, "Put all your books away, class. No one will be staying in after three-thirty today."

Glad and I were still sharing the same seat at the front of the room under Mr. Jackson's perfect nose. I liked it there because we faced him most of the time, so he hardly ever saw my profile. It had been the happiest school year of my life, thanks to my wonderful teacher, but I still couldn't shake the awful foreboding that my lifelong nightmare was about to come true and I was going to fail.

I gazed at Mr. Jackson, my heart thumping, as he waited patiently for the class to come to order. I noticed a few silver threads in his jet-black hair, and some spidery lines crisscrossing his blue-shadowed cheeks. A melancholy wave washed over me at the very thought that he might someday grow old.

"Ladies and gentlemen," he began, "today I have some good news and some bad news." Sighs and shuffles and nervous giggles rippled across the room. "So I'll start with the good news. I'm very pleased to announce that eighteen of you have passed without trying. And by the same token, I'm sorry to say that twenty-two of you must write final examinations."

My heart sank. In spite of the fact that I had done fairly well all year long, even in arithmetic, I was convinced that I could never pass the finals. I just knew I'd go all to pieces and I wouldn't remember a thing I'd learned.

Mr. Jackson was holding up his hand for silence. Then he

began reading the eighteen lucky names in alphabetical order. "Morris Albert Adams—good for you Morris. Margaret Jane Becker—congratulations, Margaret. Gladys Pearl Cole—you did very well, Gladys . . . " He had a kind word for each new graduate.

"Oh, gosh, Glad," I whispered, sick with envy, "you're so lucky."

"You will be too." She grinned at me.

"Don't be so dumb!" I felt like smacking the self-satisfied grin right off her face.

After that everything went strange. I felt light-headed and there was a peculiar ringing in my ears. Mr. Jackson's voice seemed to float away and the room started revolving around me.

"Beatrice Myrtle Thomson!"

"Yes, sir?" I jumped to my feet and the class snorted and snickered at my obvious confusion.

"You've passed without trying, Beatrice. Now be sure to work hard in high school in order to reach your potential."

My legs started wobbling as I collapsed on the seat beside Glad. Mr. Jackson was smiling down at me, his dark eyes sparkling.

I didn't hear a thing after that. When class was dismissed Glad had to lead me by the hand out the door.

Halfway across the schoolyard I stopped in my tracks. "I forgot to tell Mr. Jackson thank you, Glad!"

"No, you didn't, dummy." She was grinning from ear to ear and now I thought her smile was gorgeous. "You must have thanked him a hundred times. And he asked us both to come back and visit him next year. Don't you remember?"

"Are you sure?"

"Sure I'm sure."

"Okay, let's go home. I can hardly wait to tell Mum." We broke into a run and made a mad dash for our houses.

Bursting in the kitchen door, I slammed it so hard the pie on the window sill did a little dance. *"Mum! Mum!"*

"What is it? What's the matter?" Mum came racing up the cellar stairs, clutching a water-wizened hand over her heart. "For mercy's sake, what's wrong?"

"Nothing's wrong, Mum, but guess what?"

"What, for pity's sake!" Breathlessly she leaned against the doorjamb.

"I passed without trying, Mum! I'm in high school now." As I said the words I could hardly believe them. Imagine—high school.

At first Mom just looked shocked. And then she cried, "Oh, Booky!" and rubbed her bleached white hands together. "Why, that almost makes up for Willa not being able to go to university."

"Oh, Mum!" I grabbed her and kissed her and danced her around the room. "That's the nicest thing you've ever said to me."

She stopped short, panting. Then reaching up, for I was taller than her now, she placed a cool, damp hand on both my cheeks.

"Well, I've got something nicer to say, Bea. I'm proud as punch of you today . . . and I might not tell you often enough, but I love you to pieces!"

Tears glistened in her eyes as she flung her arms around me and gave me a big bone-cracker.

"Oh, Mum. I love you too!"

Talk about happy! I could hardly wait to tell Grampa.

15
Good omens

Ruth and Glad and Ada and I spent most of our time down at Sunnyside Beach that summer, cooling off in good old Lake Ontario. The water was exceptionally warm that year because of the heat wave.

And what a heat wave! Torontonians dropped like flies as the temperature soared to a hundred and five degrees. Eggs were fried on the steps of City Hall to prove how hot it was. Black tar boiled up in the cracks of the sidewalks. And Belle Ewart Ice Company dumped thousands of pounds of ice into Sunnyside Bathing Tank to make it cool enough to swim in. (But was Willa ever lucky. Her boyfriend took her to Loew's Theatre to see *San Francisco*. It was air-conditioned and she said it was so cold it made her teeth chatter!)

The nights were the worst. The temperature didn't seem to cool off even after sunset. Every day Mum would draw the green paper shades down to keep the heat out, then at night she'd throw the windows wide open in hopes of capturing a cool lake breeze. There were two windows in the boys' room at the front of the house and we'd all kneel down on the floor with our noses denting the mosquito net-

Heat Leaves 550 Ontarians Dead, 225 in Toronto

80-Degree Maximum Forecast for Toronto Today, But Some Days Must Elapse Before Rain

CROPS ARE RUINED

O NTARIO'S worst heat wave in more than a century, and the most destructive in its history, was on the move southward today after holding the more than 3,000,000 inhabitants of the Province in its torrid grip for a week.

Toll of Nearly 550 Dead.

It left in its wake a toll of nearly 550 dead—approximately half of them in Toronto—and thousands of acres of parched and burning crops and farmlands, some irreparably ruined.

But if relief, temporary at least, from the burning heat of the seven-day period was at hand, long-sought rains had yet to come. Weather officials have withdrawn from their forecasts the possibility of rain. There was not enough moisture in the air, they said, and although it would probably follow the cooler weather, it would not be for some days.

As temperatures dropped in all sections of the Province before a cooling breeze yesterday afternoon, the death toll lessened correspondingly.

Hospitals Get Respite.

Victims of terrific heat were still being recorded, but not in such alarming numbers. Hospital staffs, overworked for a week as prostration cases

Not So Bad

104—	—Windsor
102—	—Chatham
	—Wallaceburg
100—	—Brantford
	—Galt
98—	—Simcoe
97—	—London
96—	—Sarnia
95—	—Hamilton
89—	—Goderich

poured in. enjoyed a respite that came just in time.

At Hamilton yesterday. Dr. Miles Brown. Assistant Superintendent of Hamilton City Hospital. declared if cooler weather did not come soon it would come too late to benefit either patients or nurses.

Toronto today awaited its coolest day since July 7. The temperature, weather forecasters prophesied. would be about 80 degrees, but after the 90's and 100's registered during the past week. that reading would be welcomed. Water in storage for city use had dropped from a normal average of 83.000.000 gallons to less than 53.-000.000. a decrease of 30,000,000 gallons in the one-week period.

Ice Prices to Rise.

Ice dealers' at Hamilton Beach warned that prices would be likely to advance as much as 50 per cent. today. Rise in price of fruit and vegetables was freely discussed also as from the parched fruit belt of the Niagara Peninsula came stories of fruit baking on the trees.

Essex County arose to the position of prime producer of Ontario's peas, as the crop escaped serious injury and canning factories were working overtime to keep up production. Elsewhere the crop was said to be an almost hopeless failure.

ting, trying to catch a breath of air.

On such hot summer nights the smell from the Swansea Village dump would knock you flat.

"I can't stand it another minute," Willa snapped one night as she got up from the window sill. "That stench is enough to cause malaria."

"You can only get malaria in tropical countries," said Arthur.

"Well, what do you call this, the Arctic?"

As Willa left the room, Arthur said, "Listen to the crickets. There must be a million of them."

"That dump is a regular breeding ground for the filthy vermin. I've got to go down and spread the cricket powder." Mum got up, rubbing her knees, the sweat dripping off her nose like tears. "I don't know which stinks worse, the powder or the crickets."

The strange city crickets were a real problem for those of us who lived near the dump. They were big, smelly, brown creatures, not at all like regular crickets. They came up by droves at night and invaded the nearby houses.

Once in the middle of the night, not being able to get any water from the upstairs tap because of low pressure, I went downstairs for a drink. I didn't turn on the light because I could see plain as day by the moonlight streaming through the open doors and windows. As I padded barefoot across the dining-room floor I heard a strange *crunch, crunch, crunch* underfoot and felt a sensation like walking on walnut shells. Switching on the light I saw that the floor was carpeted with a layer of ugly brown crickets. The sudden brightness brought them leaping and bounding to life. I let out a bloodcurdling scream that woke the whole family and brought them on the run. The bunch of us nearly went crazy trying to murder the horrible creatures before they found the stairs.

The heat wave was finally broken by a huge thunderstorm. All the kids on Veeny Street ran outside in their bathing suits and revelled in the cloud-burst. Even Willa was tempted, but she decided against it on account of her old-fashioned bathing suit. (It was the same as mine, faded blue cotton with a button on one shoulder and a red stripe around the bottom of the knee-length skirt.) But the rest of our gang—Arthur and Buster and Elmer and Georgie and Glad and Ruthie and Ada and I, and even Roy-Roy—joined all the little kids, splashing and cavorting in the soft, warm rain, glorying in our last lovely fling of childhood bliss.

Lots of other interesting things happened that summer too. Willa's friend Minnie Beasley was a runner-up in the Miss Toronto Pageant. And our Arthur won the Harry Home's Contest with his painting of a green parrot perched on the rim of a Sun-Dried Coffee tin. Underneath it he had printed in neat gold letters the Harry Horne radio jingle: *We all love Sun-Dried Coffee. . . C–O–double F–double E!* His prize was a huge tin of Campfire marshmallows and his prizewinning picture was mounted in a gilt frame, ready to hang.

Mum was just bursting with pride as she climbed on a chair to hang it on the front-room wall in place of Grandpa Thomson's grim portrait.

"Here, Bea." She handed me Grandpa's picture. "Put this in the back of the hall closet and if the old tyrant ever comes to visit we'll switch them around in a hurry."

"I think it's a good omen, Mum," I said, coming back from the closet. "Arthur's winning the contest."

"What do you mean, Bea?" Mum stood admiring the picture. Now she was absolutely convinced that Arthur was destined to be a great artist some day.

"I think it means our luck has changed, and next Billy will win the Canada's Loveliest Child contest." Willa had taken an adorable snapshot of Billy with her Brownie camera and it had come out crystal clear, so she sent it in.

"Oh, pshaw, Bea, there'll be hundreds of entries. He won't have a ghost of a chance."

She was right, of course. The winner was a little girl who looked like Shirley Temple. Since Doctor Allan Roy Dafoe, the Dionne quintuplets' doctor, was one of the judges, I had to accept his expert opinion. But it took me days to get over it.

The very best thing that happened that summer was Dad getting called back to work.

"I guess you were right about good omens, Bea," Mum said when Dad told us the news.

"And I never once had to beg for pogey," Dad said triumphantly. The odd jobs he had managed to get, plus the help from Arthur and Willa (and me until I got fired), had been enough to tide us over and we didn't owe a single cent to a living soul. Dad was really proud of that.

With his first pay packet he did the most extravagant thing. He bought another radio. This time it was a floor model just like Tootsie Reese's. It wasn't new and it had a few scratches here and there, but Mum said a good rub with lemon-oil would make them disappear like magic.

It was wonderful, almost like a family reunion, to welcome all those familiar voices back into our parlour. Having a radio in the front room, especially a "DeForest Crosley," made it seem more like a parlour. We could hardly wait for Monday night to hear Cecil B. DeMille intone the magic words, *This is Lux Radio Theatre . . . coming to you from Hollllyyywooood.* And on Sunday nights when Eddie Cantor sang "I love to spend this hour with you" Mum actually had tears in her eyes.

Boy, I thought, life is just a bowl of cherries!

16
My first date

"Mum . . . I've got something to ask. Don't say no 'til I'm finished, okay?"

"Well, that depends." Mum dipped the collar of Arthur's Sunday shirt in boiling starch, then squeezed the excess into a pot with two red fingers. "I can't promise anything until I know what you want."

I took a deep breath and blurted out, "Georgie asked me to go to the show on Saturday."

"Oh, Bea . . . " Now she was starching the cuffs of Willa's white blouse. "You're only thirteen, and that Georgie has turned into a regular young rip. I've never trusted him since he got our Arthur into trouble playing hooky from school."

"Georgie's not really bad, Mum. Mrs. Sundy says he's just mischievous. And she says he's exceedingly good to his mother. And she says any boy who is exceedingly good to his mother can't be all bad."

"Well, I don't know about that." Mum rolled the starched clothes up in a towel and left them to dampen. "He's always getting into exceedingly bad mischief if you ask me. Why, only last week he stole—stole, mind you—two tires off the ragbone man's wagon. Then not ten minutes later he sold them back to the poor old gaffer for fifteen cents each."

"That wasn't Georgie, Mum. It was Elmer who did that."

"Are you sure? Mrs. Hubbard told me—"

"I'm absolutely, positively sure. Mrs. Sundy says—"

"Mrs. Sundy is *Miss* Sundy, Bea. You ought to know that." Mum picked socks out of the laundry basket and began folding them inside out. "Oh, I guess you can go if you come straight home after."

* * *

On Friday night I did my hair up in pin curls and decided to massage my nose for an extra half-hour.

"Stop rubbing your nose, Bea! You're jiggling the whole bed!" Willa gave me a hard poke in the ribs.

"Well, Zelda said—"

"Oh, Zelda's nuts. She doesn't know what she's talking about."

I'd never heard Willa use such terrible slang before, so I knew she was really mad. And she was probably right too. Zelda was the kind of person who could make you believe anything, just the way she said it. And the plain truth was that I had been massaging my nose faithfully for over a year and the knob hadn't gotten any smaller. Still, I was afraid to stop now just in case this was the crucial time and it would suddenly begin to work.

"Just five more minutes," I said, circling my finger round and round my nearly numb nose.

"Bea! You promised!" Willa screeched. "And if you don't stop by the time I count three I'm going to push you out and make you sleep on the floor. One . . . two . . . "

I stopped. The fact was, I really *had* forgotten my promise.

And besides, I always lost our bed fights because Willa was a lot stronger than me.

* * *

The show went in at one-thirty Saturday afternoon, so Georgie and I started walking up Veeny Street about half-past-twelve. We had never been alone before and we suddenly discovered we were both shy. Then, to make matters worse, Jakey and Florrie came running after us hollering "Georgie lo-oves Bea-Bea! Georgie lo-oves Bea-Bea!" I could have wrung their scrawny little necks. But luckily they had to turn back at Hunter's Store because they weren't allowed to go past the corner.

Finally I asked, "What show are we going to, Georgie?"

"To the Runnymede!" he answered, proud as a peacock.

"Oh, boy!" I had never been to the Runnymede Theatre before but Willa said it was fabulous. It had a blue-domed ceiling that looked just like the sky, with clouds and airplanes floating by. When the lights went out, the whole thing was covered with twinkling stars. She said just to look at the ceiling was worth the price of admission.

"What's on?" I asked, to keep the conversation going.

"*A Message to Garcia* starring John Boles," he said.

"Oh, boy!" I repeated. Willa said John Boles was as handsome as anything and could sing like a nightingale.

As we walked along Bloor Street Georgie unexpectedly took my hand. I was thrilled. But when we got to the theatre, instead of stopping at the ticket booth he led me right past it, around the corner and down the side street to the back alley.

"What are we doing here?" I asked apprehensively.

"You'll see!" he answered impishly, and I couldn't help but wonder if Mum was right about him after all.

At the back of the theatre was a big metal door with no handle. Georgie glanced furtively up and down the alleyway. There was no one in sight. So he picked up a stone and knocked on the door, a sharp, metallic *rat-a-tat-tat*. Nothing happened. So he repeated the signal. This time the door creaked open a tiny crack.

"Georgie?" I whispered uneasily.

"*Shhh!*" He pressed his finger to his lips. Just then, through the crack, we heard the roar of applause and the stomping of feet and the wild whistling that meant the lights had gone out and the show had begun.

"*Hang on, Bea!*"

I hung on for dear life as we burst through the door and went sailing up the aisle. My feet never touched the ground. Suddenly, Georgie yanked me down beside him into the first two empty seats.

The flood of daylight from the exit door had brought two uniformed ushers bolting down the aisle.

"Watch the screen," hissed Georgie.

We stared, transfixed, at the newsreel, *The Eyes and Ears of the World*. My heart was in my mouth.

But the trick didn't work. Seizing us both by the scruffs of our necks, the ushers dragged us to our feet.

"Hey!" Georgie cried indignantly, "What's the matter with you guys? We didn't do anything."

"Yah? Tell it to the manager, bud!" growled the biggest usher as he shoved Georgie, stumbling, up the aisle ahead of him. As for me, my legs were wobbling so badly that the other usher had to literally carry me by the collar.

Hundreds of curious eyes followed our disgraceful exit. Everybody hissed and booed and whistled as we were dragged up the aisle, through the lobby and into the inner sanctum of the manager's office. Standing in front of the great man himself, Georgie still tried to brazen it out. "We were in our seats for fifteen minutes," he lied.

"Tell us another one, bud!" sneered the burly usher.

I was shaking so violently I thought for sure I'd collapse.

The manager, a mean-looking man with no hair and beady eyes, glared first at Georgie, then at me.

"Well, miss," he spoke in a raspy, nasal voice, "what have you got to say for yourself?"

Trembling and stammering I said I had nothing to say for myself.

"*Nothing! Nothing is it?*" his voice rose to a squeal. "Well, we'll just see about that! You!"—he jabbed a commanding finger at the usher still holding me up by the collar—"Go outside and fetch Officer Bently in here."

Georgie drew in a sharp breath. I darted him a quick look and when I saw fear shining in his dark eyes I broke down and sobbed. And the harder I tried not to, the harder I cried.

He put his arm around my shoulder. "It's all right, Bea," he said. Then, in a voice as steady as a rock, he made his confession. "I'm guilty, mister. It was all my fault. She didn't even know what I was up to. If you'll let her go you can do what you like with me."

I gazed at him adoringly through a blur of tears. Never in my whole life had I known such bravery. And for me! I couldn't get over it.

"Very well!" The manager seemed pleased as punch with himself as he waved me towards the door. The usher shoved me through it and the next thing I knew I was out on the street. I leaned on the glass case outside the show, with John Boles' face looking over my shoulder, until my legs stopped shaking. Then I began crossing and recrossing the four corners of Runnymede and Bloor, never letting the theatre doors out of my sight, except once when a helmeted policeman rode leisurely by on his bicycle. Guiltily I turned away and stared into a shop window.

At last the show let out and I searched every laughing face. But no Georgie. There was only one answer I could think of. They must have taken him to jail through the exit door where all our troubles began. I didn't know what to do so I went home.

"Don't set foot on my clean floor!" Mum yelled the second I showed my nose at the screen door. So I teetered on the doorstep waiting for her to tell me I could come in. Back and forth across the already shiny floor she swung the long-handled polisher, like a giant toothbrush, until I could see my reflection in the sheen. "Wait until I get the papers down," she added breathlessly. She always covered the freshly waxed floor with old newspapers to keep it spotless for Sunday. When the last paper was spread I stepped in gingerly.

"How was the picture show, Bea?" Mum sat down, fanning herself with one hand and holding her heart with the other.

"Oh, swell, Mum. John Boles is my favourite movie star."

"That's funny. I thought Robert Taylor was," she said, leaning down to read something interesting under her feet.

"Not anymore," I called over my shoulder as I made a beeline for the stairs, pretending I was in a hurry to go to the bathroom. Actually I wanted to change my dress before she noticed the torn collar.

That night after supper Arthur signalled me with his eyes to

312

follow him down the cellar. "George said to tell you everything is okay, so you can stop worrying. He got expelled from the Runnymede for a whole year but the manager finally let him go home and get the money to pay for the tickets."

"But we didn't get a chance to see the movie or the ceiling or anything!" I protested.

"Well, stupid, it's better than going to jail, isn't it?"

I had to agree with him there.

"George said they gave him the third degree about who unlocked the door from the inside too, but he swore up and down that it was unlocked all the time and they finally believed him."

"Who *did* unlock it?" I hadn't even thought of that.

"What you don't know won't hurt me." He grinned, just as impishly as Georgie had. Then he mounted the ladder-like cellar stairs whistling *Send me a letter. . . send it by mail . . . send it in care of . . . the Birmingham jail!*

Boy, that Arthur! If Mum and Dad ever found out, neither one of us would be allowed to see Georgie again.

I was still awake at about ten-thirty when Willa came to bed. "Well, Bea," she said in that friendly voice she used when she was talking to someone she considered her equal. "How was your first date?"

Not only her tone of voice but her question took me by surprise. My first date. . . sneaking into the show by the exit door. . . getting caught red-handed . . . being dragged in disgrace to the manager's office . . . Georgie, his arm protectively around me, bravely taking all the blame.

"Memorable!" I sighed romantically. "Absolutely, positively memorable!"

314

17
No answer

"Mum," I said as I came into the kitchen one sunny August morning wearing my pink dotted-swiss dress, "I'm sick of Sunday School. It's boring."

"Well, you either have to go to Sunday School or church. Take your pick."

Glad's mother had given her the same ultimatum, so we both picked church and went together. This particular Sunday was communion, which meant it would be an extra-long service.

By the time the elements were being passed around Glad and I were really bored. So we bent down, heads locked, and whispered behind our hands. "Remember when we were little kids and we thought the bread cubes were angel food cake?" I snickered.

"Yah," she giggled. "And remember how disappointed we were when we discovered the wine was only grape juice?"

"*Shhh*!" Willa poked me hard between the shoulder blades with her hymnal. "Act your age, for heaven's sake!"

Her choice of words sent us into silent hysterics. By the time the benediction had been given our sides were splitting with pent-up, lunatic laughter. But once outside on the sun-baked lawn we became perfectly sane again.

People were milling around under the shady old trees, chatting and fanning themselves with their church calendars. Glad started talking to a girl I didn't particularly like, so I sauntered over to where Maude and Billy Sundy were standing.

"Faith and begorra, Bea, where have you been hiding yourself?" Maude's Irish blue eyes twinkled over her rimless spectacles. "You've been as scarce as a leprechaun lately." Maude and Billy were my best grown-up friends. I used to visit them regularly when I was a little kid.

"Oh, I've been awful busy, Mrs. Sundy." I *knew* she was Miss Sundy, but childhood habits die hard.

"Have you been to see your Grampa lately, Beatrice?" Billy's usual pixie smile was replaced by a reproving frown. "I talked to him over the fence last week and he says he misses you."

My heart thumped with guilt. "I'll go over the minute I get home," I promised.

So I hurried home, changed my dress, gulped my sandwich and was on my way out the door when Willa said, "It's your turn to do the dishes, don't forget."

"I'll do them later. I have to go see Grampa now," I called back through the screen.

"You've always got some excuse!" she yelled after me.

She was right too. I was notorious for sneaking out of the dishes. And when I got back from wherever I'd been Willa almost always had them done.

I started to run lickety-split down the yard and through the lane when I remembered I wasn't supposed to do that anymore. Willa said that since I would be going into high school in September I had to learn to act more dignified. Well, Willa

was the most dignified person I knew, so I tried to emulate her. (Emulate was my newest word.)

Mum said I couldn't have picked a finer example to emulate. She was exceedingly proud of her first-born. Sometimes I wondered if Willa was her favourite. Then other times I thought it was Arthur, or Jakey, or Billy—or even me. But one thing for sure, I *knew* I was Grampa Cole's favourite. We were kindred spirits, he and I.

Suddenly I was bubbling over with all the things I'd been up to—things he'd be dying to hear. He was the world's best listener and I figured I could even tell him about my date with Georgie. So putting my dignity aside I ran lickety-split the rest of the way.

Hoping Joey wasn't home, I pushed open the door. It was never locked. Nobody in Swansea bothered to lock their doors, even at night. Mum said that's because most of us were cousins and 'lations and it would be an insult to lock out your own kith and kin.

"Grampa?"

No answer.

I stepped inside the kitchen. There was a plate on the table with dried egg on it, and a grey scum floated on the tea in the saucer.

"Grampa?" I stepped up the one high step into the dining room. The house was so quiet I could hear his pocket watch ticking on top of the Victrola.

He was lying on the day bed under the window. His corncob pipe lay on the floor near his hand. I went over, knelt down and picked it up. It was cold, like the tea. Still on my knees, I looked to see if I'd wakened him.

His mouth hung slack, and under the tea-stained moustache I caught a glimpse of his shrunken gums. His eyes were only half closed and the brown irises seemed oddly hazy. And his usually suntanned, weather-beaten skin was strangely smooth and parchment yellow.

I watched him for quite a while, the seconds ticking by, before I realized that his shallow chest, under the checkered shirt, was absolutely still.

"*Grampa!*" Dropping the pipe, I grabbed his hand. It was cold too.

"*What do you want?*"

I leapt to my feet and whirled around, my heart nearly jumping out of my mouth.

There stood Joey, glowering at me from the doorway.

"It's Grampa," I whispered.

He brushed past me and stared down at the still form on the couch. Then with an anguished cry he dropped to his knees and began shaking his father. "*Pa! Pa! Pa!*"

I let out a scream and ran from the house, sobs tearing at my throat, tears coursing down my face.

* * *

The day of the funeral I went over to Grampa's in the morning by myself.

Joey sat on the porch steps, the picture of dejection. He didn't look up or speak; he just moved over to let me pass.

Inside, the air was thick with the smell of flowers. The kitchen was all cleaned up. In the dining room and parlour the normal furniture had all been moved and folding chairs were lined up in neat rows, like in a theatre.

Under the parlour window, surrounded by baskets of bright

blossoms, the dark, wooden coffin rested on a long bench. The lid was open and I could just glimpse my grandfather's angular profile showing over the white-ruffled edge. My legs began to shake so I clung to the archway between the two rooms for support. Then I took a deep breath and walked straight up to the casket.

Grampa looked really nice in his new black suit. I'd never seen him dressed up like that before. His wiry hair and moustache were neatly trimmed and his gnarled old hands were folded stiffly across his still, still breast.

"You look handsome, Grampa," I said.

I stood for a long time, memorizing his face. Then I said, "Don't forget your promise, Grampa." He had once told me he'd wait for me outside St. Peter's gate, and not go in without me. Holding my breath, I half expected him to answer. But not a whisper escaped the sealed, waxen lips.

It was then that I realized he was truly gone. Once when I was young he had said to me, about death, "The body is just an old overcoat, Be-a-trice. When it's wore out and you've got no more use for it, you shuck it off and leave it behind."

That's what I was looking at now, his shucked-off overcoat. But it was still *his* overcoat. So my fingers touched the coarse grey hair and my lips brushed the cold cement brow and I said goodbye to Grampa.

On my way out I saw his corncob pipe on the kitchen window sill. I picked it up and slipped it into my pocket.

I passed my boy-uncle on the steps. "Be seeing you, Joey."

"Be seeing you, Bea."

I wasn't afraid of him anymore.

I don't remember much about the funeral, except for one

incident. Just before the service was about to begin—every chair was filled and the men were standing all along the walls—who should arrive but Raggie-Rachel.

She came in through the kitchen door and the men sucked in their stomachs to let her pass. The undertakers were just about to close the lid when they saw her coming towards them and stepped back hastily. A hush fell over the assembly. She was wearing her usual summer rig and she looked for all the world like a bundle of rags. But out of respect she had pulled on a frayed black sweater, the buttons done up all askew, over her raggy dresses.

Mum and my aunts stirred nervously, not knowing what to expect. I was in the second row so I got up, squeezed past Willa and went and stood beside Rachel.

"Hello, Rachel." I didn't know what else to say.

She didn't answer me directly. But her voice, when she spoke, was calm and natural. "He was a good man, Mr. Cole. He saved my boy. We'll never see his like again." She reached into the coffin and patted his parchment hands. Then she turned and let herself out the front way. The grey wreath on the door rustled softly as she closed it behind her.

I only wished he could have heard her words. He would have liked them a lot better than what the preacher said.

18
Come!

After the funeral I went all melancholy. Mum didn't know what to do with me.

"If only I had gone over last week, Mum," I reproached myself bitterly, remembering Mr. Sundy's words. "Maybe he felt sick and nobody knew."

"I don't think so, Bea. He was over here borrowing flour for potato cakes on Wednesday and he seemed fit as a fiddle then."

"Did he ask for me?"

"Yes, and I said you were down at Sunnyside swimming with your friends. And he said—"

"What, Mum, what?"

"Well . . ." She set the iron on end, wet her finger on her tongue and tested the iron to see if it was hot enough. "He said he missed you, but he was glad you were having a good summer. Not like last year when you were so sickly."

"I hate myself!" I exploded vehemently.

"Ah, you mustn't fret yourself like that, Booky. Everybody has regrets. I sure had plenty when Mumma went home." She shook her head sadly at the memory, folded the smooth dish-towel and spread out a wrinkled one on the board. "You've got nothing to flay yourself for. You were good to Puppa. Many's the time I heard him say he wouldn't have known what to do without you." That made me feel even worse.

A week went by and I still couldn't shake the sadness. Willa bought me a new lipstick to cheer me up since mine was nearly gone and I had to dig it out with a hairpin. Arthur even offered to take me to see *Rin Tin Tin*.

"Want me to read you a story, Bea?" asked Jakey. He was a good reader now, and knew his First Book off by heart.

"Maybe after, Jakey," I replied listlessly.

"Bea-Bea." Billy's big blue eyes searched my face anxiously. "Don't you love me no more?"

"Sure I do, Billy." I hauled him up on my lap and gave him a big bear-hug. He had grown so much that his toes were touching the floor. "What makes you say such a silly thing?"

"You don't play with me no more," he said plaintively.

"I'm sorry, Billy," I sighed, blowing a furrow through his fine, fair hair. It seemed as if I'd been neglecting everybody I loved that summer. "I'll play with you soon, I promise."

"Run along and leave Bea alone, Billy," Mum said. Then she took the ironing board down from between the two chairs and hid it behind the dining room door. "Maybe tomorrow we'll take a run down to Eaton's and get you some new shoes for high school, Bea. What do you say to that?"

Ordinarily the prospect would have tickled me pink. But today I just said okay because I knew that's what she wanted to hear. Then the next day I worked myself up to a bilious attack and I stayed in bed all day.

On the following Saturday Mum came home all played out from helping her sisters tidy up Grampa's things. Handing me a musty old shoebox she said, "Here's a job for you, Bea. Sort through that box and see what on earth's in it. You might find something you'd like to keep."

It was mostly rubbish in the box. Old receipts and yellowed newspaper clippings and broken spectacles and bits of stale tobacco. Then I found a tea-stained envelope with my own handwriting on it. It was the letter I had sent Grampa from Muskoka the summer before.

"He didn't answer it, Mum."

"No. Puppa wasn't much of a writer. But he sure was pleased as punch to get it. He told me every word you said." She reached out and stayed my hand as I was about to open it. "Don't read it now, Bea. Put it away with your keepsakes."

I had just about given up finding anything else worthwhile when, at the bottom of the box under all the junk, wrapped carefully in layers and layers of tissue paper, I found a perfectly preserved tintype of a woman and a boy.

The woman in the photograph sat in a wicker chair. She wore a long black dress with a high, ruffled collar. Her dark hair was parted in the middle and drawn back severely into a tight bun, but on either side a few strands had come loose and curled towards her large dark eyes. Mum's hair did that sometimes when she tried to tuck it up under her dustcap. One or two curls always managed to pop out onto her temples.

The boy stood beside her, his hands crossed dutifully on her lap. He wore an old-fashioned velvet suit and a big bow tie. He had thick black hair and solemn dark eyes. I recognized those eyes instantly.

Mum was looking over my shoulder. "It's Grampa, isn't it, Mum?"

"Yas." She took the picture gently into her hands. "My, he was a handsome lad. And that's his mother, my Grandma Cole. Only she was an Arthur before she married Matthew Cole. That's where our Arthur gets his name." She studied the picture a moment longer. "I don't remember either one of my grandparents, more's the pity, but Puppa said he lifted me up to see both of them in their coffins."

"Oh, Mum, that's awful!"

"Yes. I think so too. That's why I didn't take Jakey or Billy over. But that's what folks did in those days. Everyone was obliged to pay their last respects regardless of their age."

She handed me back the picture. I looked long and hard at Grampa—a little boy, just like Jakey. A pain throbbed in my throat. Then I switched my gaze to his mother. She was dark like Grampa and Mum and Jakey, but . . .

"*Mum!* Do you know what? Your grandmother's got my nose!"

Mum came over and scrutinized the picture again. "Well, by Jove, you're right, Bea. Doesn't that beat all! Only it's the other way around: you've got her nose. So I guess that proves you do belong to me after all. And here I always thought you were one hundred percent Thomson." She laughed and gave my new-found nose a pinch that made it stick together. She was always *doing* that!

"I wish I'd got her eyes instead of her nose," I grumbled, wriggling that offensive part of me, like a rabbit, to make it come unstuck.

"Well, I wouldn't complain if I were you." She sounded a bit miffed. "I'll have you know my grandmother was considered something of a beauty in her day."

"Really?" I jumped up to peer in the mirror hanging over the sink, in hopes that a minor miracle had taken place in the last few seconds. Turning sideways, I swivelled my eyes around to get a view of my profile. "It still looks too big to me," I said glumly.

"Well, that's because you haven't quite grown into it yet. But mark my words, Bea, you're getting better-looking every day."

At last I allowed myself to be convinced. "Then maybe I won't need to rub it anymore." I sighed with relief at the thought of being rid of that tiresome nightly ritual.

"Well, thank goodness for small blessings," remarked Willa drily as she swept the floor with the cornbroom.

Carefully I rewrapped the tintype and took it and my letter upstairs to store among my keepsakes in an old chocolate box. My keepsakes were a strange assortment: the little china horse, Reddy's bronze feathers (all that was left of my poor little chicken), my horsehair bracelet that I didn't wear anymore but kept in memory of Major (who was still alive, thank goodness), the corncob pipe, a dried rose from the family wreath and the ribbon with *Puppa* written on it. (There was no *Grampa* ribbon or I would have saved it too.) Putting my letter and the tintype flat on the bottom of the box under the other stuff, I replaced the lid. On the lid I had pasted a white piece of paper over Laura Secord's picture, and on it I had printed in big letters: *MEMORIALS OF MY CHILDHOOD. THIS BOX BELONGS TO BEATRICE MYRTLE THOMSON. ALL OTHER INDIVIDUALS KEEP OUT!*

After shoving the box to the back of my bureau drawer I went straggling downstairs again. The pungent odour of the pipe and the sweet fragrance of the rose had brought back, in full force, my melancholy mood.

Mum was stirring a big pot of hamburger stew on the stove. Normally that lovely smell would have made me ravenous, but today it just made me feel queasy.

"Mum."

"Yes, Booky."

"When I was a child, Grampa promised me once that instead of going straight into heaven he'd wait outside the gate for me. Do you believe that?"

Her back was to me and she stood stock still for a moment. Her hands became busy dropping soft blobs of dough into the bubbling brown liquid. Then she covered the pot with an inverted plate. When she turned around her eyes were dark pools of tears. "Well," she answered huskily, "Puppa had a reputation for always being as good as his word."

That night at supper I couldn't swallow my stew.

"Eat up," Dad said automatically.

"I can't." I pushed my plate away.

"What's that old saying carved on our bread-board?" he asked meaningfully.

I'd cut up so much bread on that board I knew the words off by heart. But Jakey beat me to it. "It says 'Waste Not, Want Not'!" he piped up proudly.

"That's right," agreed Dad. "Now eat up, Bea."

"I'm sorry, Dad, but I've got a sick headache." I started rubbing my brow to prove it.

"Bea"—Dad broke into a fluffy dumpling and the steam escaped with a little puff—"why don't you drop your Aunt Aggie a line?"

What a nice thing to hear when I was expecting a lecture! "Gee, thanks, Dad. I think I will." Then, trying to please him, I ate a snowy white dumpling even though it did upset my stomach.

After supper Willa wordlessly took my place at the sink. Dad brought me the bottle of ink and a writing tablet. Mum got the pen out of the sideboard drawer. "Oh, pshaw, the nib's broken," she said. "Half the point's missing."

"I know where there's a new one." Arthur ran upstairs and got it, licked the oil off, pulled out the broken piece and inserted the new one ready to use.

Everybody was so nice to me I couldn't get over it. And I felt a little better just writing Aunt Aggie's name at the top of my letter.

Dear Aunt Aggie,

I guess you know by now that my Grampa Cole is dead. Dad says that you and Grandpa Thomson are alone on the farm this year because Uncle Wilbur asked Aunt Ida to come back and live with him. (Aunt Ida says he begged her to come home. I find that hard to swallow.) Anyway, what I'm writing for is to ask you if I can come up and spend the rest of the summer with you. I really need to talk to you, Aunt Aggie. Tell Grandpa Thomson that I won't be any trouble this year because I am all grown up now. I am not a child anymore.

> *Please answer immediately,*
> *Your loving niece,*
> *Beatrice*

Three days later Aunt Aggie's reply slipped through the slot in our front door. The envelope was so thin I thought she had forgotten to put her letter in. Usually her letters were just bursting at the seams with all the Muskoka news.

Anxiously I tore it open. Out onto the dining room table dropped a single sheet of paper with one huge word scrawled on it in letters two inches high: *COME!* And pinned to the corner of the page was a round-trip train ticket to Huntsville. All bought and paid for. Imagine!

* * *

The night before I left the whole gang came over to say goodbye. It was almost like a going-away party except nobody had been invited. Even Roy-Roy had come over earlier in the day— I don't know how he got wind of my trip—and brought me a catfish he'd caught by hand. I promised him I'd have it for my last supper. Of course, the minute his back was turned Mum wrapped it up in a pile of newspapers and threw it straight into the garbage. Willa said we'd be lucky if we ever got the smell out of the house. But Mum said it was the thought that counted.

Glad gave me a Sweet Marie to eat on the train. "Try to cheer up, Bea," she whispered worriedly. I said I'd try. Ruth gave me a brand-new *Silver Screen* with Myrna Loy and William Powell on the cover. And Ada loaned me her latest Elsie Dinsmore book. Arthur gave me a nickel and Willa gave me a dime and Dad had already given me a shinplaster to spend in Huntsville.

Georgie was the last to leave. When we were alone in the hallway he reached inside his shirt and pulled out a flat package wrapped in white paper and tied with a pink ribbon. All this time it had been next to his skin so it was kind of sweaty because it was a hot night. But I didn't mind.

"Promise you won't open it until you're on your way?" he said. I promised. He bent down—he was a lot taller than me now—and kissed me right on the mouth. Then he high-tailed it out the door before either one of us had a chance to be embarrassed.

Mum went with me the next morning to Union Station. I was wearing a new blue dress with a white bolero. It wasn't that the pink dotted-swiss was worn out or anything—I had actually outgrown it! Even when Mum let the seams out it didn't fit me properly, so there was nothing to do but make me a new one.

Union Station was right across Front Street from the Royal York Hotel. "The Royal York looks something like a castle, doesn't it, Mum?"

"And so it should," Mum said, "because that's where the Prince of Wales stayed on his visit to Toronto." I stared up at all the hundreds of windows, trying to figure out which one the royal eyes had actually looked out of.

I had never been inside Union Station before so I was absolutely enthralled by its cathedral ceiling and stone archways and marvellous marble floors. We sat on a hardwood bench under the clock, waiting for our train to be announced. I got a crick in my neck gazing up at the high, curved dome and reading all the names of the provinces carved around the edge.

"Now, here's your lunch." Mum sounded kind of agitated. "All your favourite foods are in it. Bologna sandwiches on white bread with store-bought mustard, and a little jar of your Aunt Ellie's rhubarb preserves. I've put a kitchen spoon in to eat it with, so don't lose it or I'll be one short. Your Aunt Susan sent you this box of nuts. And here's two big oranges from Dorothea. Now I want you to eat up every crumb because you've been looking awful pasty-faced since Puppa went home."

I winced and she hurried on. "Oh, mercy, I'm sorry for reminding you, Bea. But that's life, isn't it?" Then she gave me a big, long bone-cracker as if to try to make amends for life.

At last we heard the echoing voice of the train announcer floating through the vast hall, telling us where the train was leaving from.

Mum persuaded the trainman to let her go with me to the tracks by telling him that I'd never travelled alone before and that I was only thirteen years old. "Thirteen and a half— geeez!" I muttered indignantly. He smiled and let us both go down the stairway.

The train was half empty so I found a window seat easily and stuffed my grip under it. Then I looked for Mum out the streaky glass. I saw her before she saw me. She was searching all the windows, her forehead furrowed in a frown. Suddenly, from this strange perspective, she looked different to me— smaller and sadder and just a little bit old. The sight of her pierced my heart. "Don't die, Mum!" I cried instinctively. I don't know whether I spoke out loud or not.

The train began to move and she hadn't seen me yet. I banged on the window, frantically, and our eyes met. Then her whole countenance changed and she burst into a radiant smile. We waved and waved until we lost each other from sight.

I settled back on the seat and gazed out the window.

The train wended its way through the city, tooting at crossings and spewing black smoke in its wake. Women in their backyards, their mouths full of clothes pins, stopped just long enough to give the sooty monster dirty looks.

Then came the countryside, meadows and barns and horses and cows and red-winged blackbirds on fenceposts. And I was on my way.

That's when I remembered Georgie's present.

My fingers trembled as I undid the bow and tore off the sweat-stained paper. Inside was the most beautiful box of stationery I had ever seen. It was pale blue with a tiny forget-me-not in the corner of each page. A folded sheet of ordinary paper lay on top. I opened it and read:

From your most ardent admirer.
Guess who! Give up? I'll give you a hint.
His initials are G.D.
Write soon. XXXOOO

It was my very first love note. I planned to answer it the minute I arrived.

Sighing blissfully, I gazed dreamily out the window. The train began steaming up a hill. Out of the morning mist it rose, into the dazzling sunlight.

And with it rose my spirits.

As Ever,

Booky

To Lloyd, with love

As Ever, Booky

1
Guess what!

"Guess what, Mum?"

"What, Bea?" Mum always looked startled when I began a conversation that way.

"Nothing to worry about, Mum—just the opposite. Remember me telling you I made a new friend on the first day of school?" I was in second form at Runnymede Collegiate.

"Yes. Gloria Somebody-or-other," Mum recalled as she expertly pinched the edge of a piecrust.

"Gloria Carlyle. Isn't that a glorious name? It sounds like a screen star's name, doesn't it? Like Carole Lombard or Jean Harlow. I wish I had a romantic name like that. Anyway, Gloria's father owns a whole chain of hardware stores and her mother has a housemaid and plays tennis every day. And guess who lives right next door to them?"

"For mercy sakes, how should I know? I can't stand around playing guessing games when it's nigh on suppertime." Nudging me aside with her round hip, she opened the oven door and turned the gas on full blast. Then she struck a wooden match on the sandpaper strip along the side of the Eddy box and poked the flame into the hole in the oven floor. It lit with a bang. But she turned it down too quickly and it went out. "Drat!" she declared and repeated the whole process.

Closing the oven door, she turned her attention back to me. Her face was red from scurrying. Damp, dark curls, threaded with grey, clung to her high forehead. "Well, Bea, are you ever going to tell me who lives next door to glorious Gloria?"

"Aw, Mum, don't make fun of her. She's really nice for a rich person." I let a few seconds drift dramatically by, but then I saw that Mum was getting irritated, so I exclaimed rapturously, "L.M. Montgomery!"

"No!" Her stunned reaction was all I could have hoped for. "Not the woman who wrote *Anne of Green Gables?*"

"Yes! But that's not all!"

"What do you mean, not all?" Her dark eyes were flashing with interest now.

"Well, Gloria told Mrs. Macdonald about me—that's her married name. Her real name is Lucy Maud Montgomery, but her husband is the Reverend Ewan Macdonald. And she's got children too, Mum. Imagine having L.M. Montgomery for a mother!" I saw a hurt look flit across her flushed face, so I added quickly, "But I still think you're the most perfect mother in the world, Mum."

"Oh, pshaw, Booky"—that's what Mum used to call me when I was a kid, *Boo*-key, and every now and then it still slipped out—"I'm a far cry from perfect. But it's nice you think so." She reached up (I was taller than she was) and pinched my cheek with floury fingers. "Are you ever going to tell me what this is all about?"

"Oh, sorry, Mum. Well, Gloria told L.M.—I mean Mrs.

Macdonald—all about me. You know, how I'm always writing stories and that she's my favourite author—stuff like that. And do you know what she said?"

"Bea, stop asking me questions I can't answer and lend me a hand here. Either that or get out of my road." She bustled past me to the kitchen cabinet, pulled the flour bin out on its hinges and scooped up another cupful of flour.

So I blurted out the rest. "She said Gloria could bring me over to her house for tea!"

"Sakes alive!" Mum whirled around, rubbing her hands together in that excited way she had, sending mists of flour floating through the air. "When?"

"Saturday afternoon. *This* Saturday afternoon."

"Oh, my stars, what will you wear?" Mum popped the pie into the oven. "You'll just have to get busy and let down your navy skirt. You'll need to look your best to meet such a grand lady." Her voice was positively reverent. She had almost a holy respect for people of letters, and she liked L.M. Montgomery's books nearly as much as I did. "If you get the chance," she added diffidently, "tell her your mother greatly admires Judy Plum in *Pat of Silver Bush*."

"Tell who?" My brother Arthur came in just in time to catch the tail end of the conversation.

"Bea's been invited to meet L.M. Montgomery!" Mum announced proudly. The way she said it you'd think I'd been invited to Buckingham Palace.

"Who's that?" asked Arthur, piling his school books on a kitchen chair. He was in fourth form and he had tons of home-work.

"Oh, good grief, don't show your ignorance." I gave Arthur

a disgusted look. "She's just the most famous author in Canada, that's all."

"You're nuts!" he scoffed. "Ralph Connor is."

"He is not!"

"He is so!"

"Who is so?" Nine-year-old Jakey had come hightailing it up from the cellar to see what all the fuss was about.

"Oh, you're too young to understand, Jakey." I brushed him aside impatiently.

"I am not!" he cried, his dark eyes blazing.

"You are so!" Five-year-old Billy's squeaky voice came up from under the table where he was playing cars.

"Stop it, all of you!" Mum yelled, scattering cutlery onto the oilcloth-covered table. "Arthur, get at your homework. Bea, finish laying this table. Jakey and Billy, scoot down to the cellar out of my sight before I skin you alive. Your father and sister will be home any minute and I haven't even got the stew thickened yet, let alone the dumplings made."

Dad had been working steady as a maintenance man at Neilson's Chocolate Factory for over three years now. At the beginning of the new year, 1937, he had had his wages raised from fourteen to sixteen dollars a week because he was such a good worker. After weathering all those grim Depression years, a steady job with good pay was something my parents didn't take for granted. Dad said he hoped he'd never have to stand in a food line again as long as he lived.

When we were on the pogey he had to walk all the way downtown with our food voucher. Then he had to carry a potato sack full of tinned goods over his shoulder all the way home again. It was ten miles from our house to the food station, but the pogey didn't allow for streetcar tickets.

My sister Willa had a job now too. She had finished fifth form with top honours. Then, when she knew there was no hope of affording university, she went back to high school and took the three-year commercial course in one year. Now she was a receptionist in a doctor's office—as close as she would ever come to her dream of being a doctor. She earned twelve dollars a week, with Saturday afternoons off. Every Saturday night, like clockwork, she handed Mum six dollars board money. Mum was tickled pink.

The first time Willa paid her, she looked around the spotless kitchen, her eyes bright with longing. "Maybe someday we'll have enough money to buy this place from Billy Sundy," she said. Billy Sundy was our landlord.

"We'd need two hundred dollars to put down," Dad said hopelessly. "It might just as well be two thousand." There went Mum's fondest dream up in smoke again.

"I'll buy it for you when I get big, Mum," Billy promised solemnly.

"That's nice, Billy-bo-bingo," she'd said, squeezing his cheeks so his lips opened up like a fish's.

The second my sister set foot in the door I said, "Who's the most famous Canadian author, Willa?"

Without hesitation she answered, "L.M. Montgomery."

"See, Arthur!" I hooted triumphantly. He let out a loud moan and banged his head on the dining room table where he was doing his homework.

I told Willa my news and she was really impressed, which made up for Arthur's stupidity. Even Dad, who didn't know much about books and authors, had heard about L.M.

Montgomery, so he gave me some advice. "Now, Bea, you're inclined to be a chatterbox"—I groaned inwardly but didn't interrupt—"so try to hold your tong." That was his old fashioned way of saying tongue, and no amount of criticism would make him change it. "If you listen to the lady, she might be able to help you with your writing. And be sure to ask for her autograph. It might be worth something someday."

It was only Monday. I thought the week would never end.

2
Tea and advice

At exactly one o'clock on Saturday I met Gloria on the corner of Jane and Bloor. She looked gorgeous in her new tunic with the razor-sharp pleats and her red velvet jacket. Her stylish outfit made me acutely aware of my old navy pleatless skirt and blue sweater, neatly darned at the elbows. But Mum had painstakingly turned the collar and cuffs of my white blouse, so it looked almost as good as new.

The night before I had done up my fine hair in pin curls and it had combed out kind of frizzy, but not too bad. I had wet my eyelashes with Vaseline, which made them look thicker and longer, and put on two layers of lip rouge. (Willa said not to use too much or I might look cheap.) I couldn't do a thing about the shape of my nose, but on the whole I was quite pleased with myself.

Under my arm I carried a grammar-school workbook with my latest story penned carefully inside. The title was "Victoria, the Girl Who Never Told a Lie in Her Life." I was sure it was the best thing I'd ever written.

Veering left off Bloor Street we walked along a tree-lined avenue, called Riverside Drive, on the banks of the Humber. It was a beautiful, winding road with rolling lawns and weeping willows, and no sidewalks. The houses were big and far apart. Glittering stone driveways curved up to wide, two-car garages.

On Veeny Street in Swansea, the little village on the western outskirts of Toronto where I lived, we didn't have garages. Our houses were so tightly packed together there was barely enough room for alleyways between. But it didn't matter because nobody on Veeny Street owned a car anyway.

Gloria stopped in front of a magnificent mansion where a man was busy raking up a pile of red and gold leaves. "That's my house," she said, a bit smugly I thought.

"Is that your father?" I asked innocently.

"No! That's Willy, the gardener."

Willy the gardener tipped his cap to Gloria, then stared me up and down as if I was an oddity on Riverside Drive.

Gloria pointed to the house next door. "That's where the Macdonalds live," she said matter-of-factly.

I gazed, speechless, at a white stone house with gabled windows, all hemmed in by shrubs and trees and flowers. A rustic sign nailed to a fence post read *Journey's End.*

At that moment the dark wooden door swung open and out stepped a regal lady who looked for all the world like Queen Mary, the king's mother, even to the long string of pearls looped twice around her neck. She smiled and beckoned to us and my heart did somersaults.

"She looks like a genius!" I whispered.

"She is!" my friend agreed knowingly.

Gloria introduced us. "Mrs. Macdonald, this is my friend Bee-triss." (She had wonderful manners, but terrible pronunciation. The way she said my name made it sound like a vegetable!)

"I'm pleased to meet you, Beatrice." It sounded entirely different coming from *her.* She reached out and took my hand, and my legs turned to jelly.

Completely forgetting Dad's well-meant advice, I started to babble. "Oh, Miss Montgomery, I love all your books and I've read every one at least twice, some of them three times, and I especially love *Emily Climbs* and *Anne of Avonlea.* My mother loves *Pat of Silver Bush* best and she told me to tell you if I got the chance that she greatly admires Judy Plum. But I personally adore *The Story Girl* and *Kilmeny of the Orchard* and *The Blue Castle*—oh, Barney was so romantic— and I hope you have time to write a hundred more books because I think you're the greatest writer the world has ever known."

Luckily, I ran out of breath.

"That's very kind of you, Beatrice, and do thank your mother for her compliment about Judy Plum." She spoke just as if I'd said something perfectly sensible. "Gloria tells me that you're a story girl too. Come into the garden and we'll talk about it."

We followed her down a white gravel path that led to a backyard filled with daisies and chrysanthemums and evergreens. At the foot of one big pine tree was a smooth granite rock with the word Lucky painted on it.

"That stone was shipped up to me from my home in Prince Edward Island," the author explained softly, "and under it my dear little pussycat lies sleeping. He was my inseparable companion for fourteen years and I miss him sorely."

Suddenly I was consumed with jealousy over the bones of that old dead cat.

As we sat down on red cedar chairs, I felt a splinter snag my silk stocking—or I should say Willa's. I had no silk stockings, just lisle, and I had borrowed Willa's best pair. Only she didn't know it yet.

I was trying desperately to think of something intelligent to say when the back door was pushed open by a woman's behind. Out she came with a loaded tray and set the table with china dishes, silver spoons and a fancy teapot with little legs on it. Then she set two glass plates within easy reach. One held sandwiches and the other teacakes.

"Thank you, Marny," Mrs. Macdonald said, then to me, "Cream and sugar, Beatrice?"

"Yes, please." We never had real cream at home, just milk.

She put the cream and sugar in the cup first, then poured the tea. Mum never did that.

"Help yourselves, girls," she said. Then she leaned back, casually sipping her tea as if she had nothing better to do than entertain two schoolgirls, when all the time I knew there was another great novel churning around in her head just dying to get out.

I watched Gloria surreptitiously and copied everything she did. She spread a linen napkin on her lap, so I did too. She took two sandwiches, so I did too—a three-cornered egg-salad with the crusts cut off and a green-cheese pinwheel. Green cheese! Imagine!

I had never tasted anything so delectable. We ate six sandwiches. When Mrs. Macdonald offered us more Gloria politely refused. So I did too, even though I could easily have eaten the whole works in two minutes flat. Then we each had another cup of tea and a teacake. The pink icing cracked when you bit into it. Inside, it was soft and white as a marshmallow.

Finally Marny came and cleared it all away.

"May I see your work, Beatrice?" asked Mrs. Macdonald suddenly. My work? At first I didn't know what she meant. Then I followed her eyes to my notebook. My hand shook as I passed it to her.

The pages rustled as she turned them. Sunlight filtered through the leaves and glinted on her silver hair. Gloria and I slanted glances at each other, but we didn't say a word. A bluebird flashed by almost close enough to touch.

Presently Mrs. Macdonald closed the book and removed her gold-rimmed glasses. "Your story is lovely, Beatrice." Her voice was gentle and kind, but I didn't like the word "lovely." I had hoped to hear "brilliant" or "witty" or just plain "excellent."

"My dear"—now her tone had become very serious— "allow me to give you some advice from my own experience. *Do* keep writing. You have a lively imagination and your characters ring true. But do not, I repeat, *do not* expect to publish at your tender age. The inevitable rejections would surely defeat you. Instead, channel your energies into your studies."

My heart sank. "But—but—it's more fun to write stories than do homework!" The stupid words were out before I could stop them.

"True. But your first priority must be your schoolwork, because no one needs higher education more than a journalist. Will you remember that, Beatrice?"

"Yes, Miss Montgomery," I said, but I was already defeated.

The thought of all that higher education struck terror in my heart. And besides, I was dying to be done with school so I could go out to work and make money to buy nice clothes like Gloria's.

We said goodbye, promising to come back soon. But I never did go back. And I'd even forgotten to get her autograph.

"Well, you dumb-bell, you wasted your whole Saturday afternoon," jeered Arthur. For once I agreed with him.

"Don't fret, Bea," Mum consoled me. "When you write Miss Montgomery your bread-and-butter note you can ask for her signature then."

So that's what I did. About three days later back came her reply in her own handwriting, which was so hard to read that I had to ask Willa to decipher it for me. In it she repeated her solemn advice and her compliment about my "lovely" story. The letter was signed *Sincerely, L.M. Montgomery Macdonald.*

I put it and my story far back on the closet shelf and didn't look at them again for years.

3
Mixed company

I went all melancholy for weeks after that. Then one day Mum snapped me out of it with a swell idea.

"How would you like a real grown-up party for your fifteenth birthday, Bea?" she asked.

"Really? Girls *and* boys?" I had never had an honest-to-goodness party before. Since Billy and I shared the same birthday, our celebrations were usually family affairs, with Aunt Milly or Aunt Maggie and their families for company.

"If Bea has a party, can I have one too?" begged Billy.

"Oh, I suppose so. But not on the same day. That would be too much of a good thing. You can have five friends for supper, Billy, since you'll be five years old. You're growing up at last, Billy-bo-bingo," she said, pinching his button nose shut so he had to wriggle it like a rabbit to get it unstuck. "I wouldn't trade you for all the tea in China, but I sure hope there's no more where you came from."

"Where did I come from, Mum?" Billy's blue Thomson eyes lit up with curiosity.

"Oh, oh, little pitchers have big ears!"

Mum was stymied by the unexpected question, so I jumped

in and saved the day. "How many friends can I have, Mum, fifteen?"

"Mercy, no! This house is way too small for such a crowd. You'll have to make ten your limit, Bea."

Ten kids! It was more than I'd dared hope for.

That night I sat down at the dining room table and cut out neat squares of paper and began writing invitations in fancy script. Jakey was sitting across from me doing his homework.

Soon Billy came out from under the table and leaned his chin on my elbow curiously. "Whatcha doing, Bea-Bea?"

"Making invitations for my party, Bingo."

"Who's coming?"

"Oh, a bunch of my friends."

"Are you going to ask Roy-Roy the dumb-boy?"

"Billy, don't say Roy-Roy the dumb-boy. His name is Roy Butterbaugh."

Jakey looked up, glad of the interruption. "You call him that, Bea. Everybody does, because he don't know nothing."

"I used to call him that when I was young and silly," I admitted. "But you're wrong about him not knowing anything, Jakey. Roy-Roy knows more than he gets credit for."

Roy-Roy and his mother, Raggie-Rachel (that's what all the kids called her because she wore four or five raggedy dresses piled on top of each other—she wasn't smelly or dirty, just raggedy), lived up Veeny Street in a tumbledown cottage that belonged to the village. They used to live in a shack down by Catfish Pond and Rachel picked the dump for a living. Now she took in washing. Her backyard was always flapping with other people's bed sheets. She scrubbed by hand over a washboard, outside in summer, inside in winter. Mum said poor Rachel had a hard row to hoe.

No one seemed to know exactly what was wrong with Roy-Roy, only that he'd always been peculiar. His body jerked constantly and he slobbered and gabbled when he tried to talk. But I had found out years ago that if you listened really carefully he usually made perfect sense.

"Are you going to invite him?" Billy persisted.

"No, Billy, not this time."

"Why not? You always say he's your friend."

"Well, he is. But his mother wouldn't let him come anyway. She never lets him out of her sight anymore. And besides, he'd be embarrassed."

"Awww, he ain't smart enough to be embarrassed." Jakey was still unconvinced.

"Yes he is, Jakey. And if *you're* so darn smart, how come you keep saying dumb things like 'ain't' and 'don't know nothing'?"

Jakey stuck out his tongue and went back to his books, and Billy got bored and went away. So I finally got my invitations done.

Most of them were going to our gang on Veeny Street, but a few were addressed to new friends I'd made in high school. Gloria Carlyle was one, of course. And Lorne Huntley.

Lorne was the handsomest, most popular boy in Runnymede Collegiate (a "dreamboat," to quote Gloria), and to top it off, he was a football hero.

He had spoken to me only once, when he accidentally bumped into me on the staircase and knocked my books all over the place. He gathered them up and handed them back to me with a gorgeous grin and a "Sorry, kiddo!" Then he ran to catch up to his classmates. It was the nicest apology I'd ever had. But other than that we hadn't exchanged a word. So how I had the colossal gall to ask him to my party I'll never know.

Anyway, the next day I handed out the folded invitations between periods.

"What's this?" asked Lorne, flashing his incredible smile and running his long fingers carelessly through his curly brown hair.

"It's an invitation to my fifteenth birthday party." I faced him squarely so he wouldn't notice my bumpy nose, which all my life had been the bane of my existence. My heart beating like a triphammer, I added, "You don't have to come if you don't want to."

Darn! I was always saying dumb things like that.

"I'll be there with bells on," he promised. Then he went loping down the hall, leaving me gaping after him.

At first Gloria said she wasn't sure she could make it. Our friendship had cooled quite a bit since she realized that I would probably never be rich and famous like her neighbour. I was awfully disappointed in her, but Mum wasn't surprised. She said you couldn't mix oil and water. Anyway, when I told Gloria that Lorne was coming she quickly changed her mind and said she thought she could make it after all.

The Huntleys lived in a ritzy district known as Baby Point, where two big stone pillars stood like guardian angels at either side of the entranceway. So Gloria had decided that Lorne was her type.

Walking home from school that day with Gladie Cole, my cousin and best friend, I told her I had invited Lorne to my party.

"Geez, Bea," she marvelled, looking at me as if I'd just had an audience with the king, "I wouldn't have the nerve to ask him in a million years. Just seeing him in the halls makes me nervous as a cat."

"Well, maybe you'd better not come then," I teased.

"Wild horses wouldn't keep me away!" she hooted as we crossed Bloor Street and headed for Woolworth's, where a sign in the window read: *SPECIAL . . . Spanish peanuts, ten cents a pound!* Glad's mother had given her a nickel for a bottle of milk at lunchtime, so she bought half a pound.

"Are Ruth and Ada coming?"

"Sure." Ruth Vaughan, Ada-May Hubbard, Glad and I had been a foursome for years. Our houses were within a stone's throw of each other on dead-end Veeny Street, and we were all related in one way or another. But we had drifted apart since high school because Ruth and Ada were a year older than Glad and me, and they were in third form.

Even Arthur seemed interested in my party (that puzzled me a bit), and Willa helped Mum make about a hundred sandwiches. That's the kind of sister Willa was. We were five years apart, so we didn't have much in common, but she was always doing things for me. Mum said she took after no stranger. "She's like Mumma," she said, meaning her mother. "Still waters run deep."

Dad was swell too. He worked his head off Saturday afternoon when he got home from the candy factory, steel-woolling and waxing the old oak floors. Then he shone them up with the long-handled lead polisher that always put me in mind of a giant's toothbrush. I couldn't get over all the fuss that was being made for my fifteenth birthday.

"I don't remember getting all this special attention on my birthday," remarked Arthur. "How come she rates?"

"'Cause Bea's nicer nor you!" piped up Billy.

"She is not!" argued Jakey. Honestly, those two were always bickering about something. They made Arthur and me seem like friends. And they nearly drove Mum crazy.

I spent hours getting myself ready. I washed my hair with real shampoo. Willa bought real shampoo now that she was working steady. She said no amount of rainwater would rinse out Sunlight soap.

"Don't use more than one capful!" she called through the bathroom door.

"I won't!" I promised as I measured out the second capful.

After I rubbed my hair dry, Willa offered to curl it for me with her new curling tongs. She felt a strand between her fingers. "It's too damp," she said. "Go stick your head in the oven."

"That's a terrific idea!" grinned Arthur.

"Arthur"—Mum was up to her elbows in suds in the kitchen sink—"unless you want to be put to work, you'd better make yourself scarce."

"Boy, am I ever glad I'm naturally good-looking," he crowed as he went out the door laughing.

I didn't think his joke was particularly funny because it was true. We looked a lot alike, but by some quirky trick of fate Arthur had turned out smoother than me.

Willa had the curling tongs heating in the blue flame of the gas jet. I pulled my head out of the oven for a breather and saw them turning orangey-red.

"Oh, ye gods, Willa. Don't burn me!"

"Be quiet!" she ordered. Then she took a folded page of

newspaper, clamped it between the tongs and held it tight until it smoked. Releasing her grip, she examined the scorched, curled paper. "Too hot," she decided. She blew on the tongs for a few seconds until the glow began to fade, then tested them again. "That's better," she said. "Now hold still."

I closed my eyes and didn't move a muscle. Just then Dad came in with a handful of table knives. He'd cleaned the rust off them by running the blades in and out of the earth, and now he handed them to Mum to wash.

Sniffing suspiciously, he said, "Something's burning!" Dad had a terrible fear of fire ever since he saw a house burned to the ground when he was a boy. We all knew the gruesome story of how Hannibal Hobbs had come screaming out of the inferno, a flaming torch, and thrown himself into a snowbank. For the rest of his life he wore a perfect line down the middle of his body, from head to toe. One half of him was scarred beyond recognition; the other half was handsome as the day is long.

"It's only Bea's hair," Willa explained, and Dad sighed with relief.

The whole curling operation took about half an hour. "Go look at yourself," Willa said when she'd finished. She was a person of few words.

I looked in the mottled mirror hanging over the kitchen sink and was thrilled to death. My hair was parted in the middle and curled under all the way around in the very latest style.

"Oh, gee, thanks, Willa."

"Well, don't say I never did anything for you." She couldn't help smiling at her own handiwork.

4
The party's over!

By seven o'clock I was ready. I thought I looked pretty good. I was wearing a red crepe de Chine dress, my birthday present from Mum and Dad. It was the first dress I ever owned that Mum hadn't made out of a remnant. Willa had given me a red lipstick to match. It was the reddest I'd ever dared to use and Dad said it looked as if I'd cut my mouth. But he didn't make me wash it off.

Glad and Ruth and Ada arrived together. They looked swell too. Then a bunch of boys arrived, including Georgie Dunn. I still liked Georgie—who wouldn't, with those sparkly eyes and that mischievous grin—but I didn't consider him my boyfriend anymore, mainly because he was always hanging around a girl in third form named Wanda Backhouse. She was really cute and she had a nice neat nose, so I was extra glad that she had such a terrible name. She pronounced it "Backus" but it didn't fool anybody.

The last guests to arrive were Gloria Carlyle and Lorne Huntley.

"Lorne walked me all the way here and he's promised to walk me home," Gloria told me as I took her upstairs to leave her coat on the bed.

Mum had worked extra hard making new curtains and a matching bedspread especially for this occasion, so when I saw Gloria's eyes taking everything in I was expecting a compliment. But it didn't come. Instead she said, "Whose room is this?"

"My sister's and mine."

"Where do all your brothers sleep?" The way she said it, you'd think there were ten of them.

"In the big front room," I answered defensively.

"My brother and sister and I each have our own room," she said. Then she laid her grey fur coat on our new spread and sidled out the door.

Suddenly our house seemed shabby. I noticed worn brown spots on the hall runner, water marks in the corner of the high ceiling and broken edges along the rubber stair treads. I wished I hadn't asked Gloria.

Arthur already had the radio tuned in to a staticky station. He and Ada started dancing, then Georgie asked me. I wasn't a very good dancer, but since it was my birthday all the boys were obliged to ask me, so at least I wouldn't be a wallflower.

Mum and Dad stayed in the kitchen with the door ajar. I was hoping that being stuck together like that wouldn't start getting on their nerves, because if it did, a fight was sure to erupt. Aunt Ida, Dad's prissy sister, always said with a sniff that Mum and Dad were about as compatible as a cat and dog. She should talk. She and Uncle Wilbur were always disgracing the family by getting separated. Anyway, tonight the kitchen remained peaceful.

Willa had gone to the show with Wesley Armstrong, her steady beau, to see Rose Marie. At least he thought he was her steady beau. Willa said nobody was. She was very independent.

A soft pink light shone from under the rose-coloured fringe of the lamp shade. It was only a 40-watt bulb, so it was very romantic. And when the band played "This Can't Be Love," Lorne asked me to dance!

An hour or so later Mum suddenly opened the door and switched on the ceiling light. All the dancers, who had been snuggling cheek to cheek, jumped apart as if stung by bees.

"Refreshments!" Mum announced cheerily.

After the sandwiches and tarts, Dad brought the lighted cake in and Mum carried the steaming teapot. I made an impossible wish (about Lorne Huntley), then managed to blow all the candles out at once. Everyone cheered and began singing "Happy Birthday." After they'd finished, I opened the presents.

Glad and Ruth and Ada had gone together and bought me a real leather-bound diary with a lock and key and my name embossed in gold on the cover. I was thrilled to pieces. I also got hankies and gloves and two pairs of real silk stockings. Willa hadn't noticed the snag in her best pair yet, so now I could replace them and get away scot-free! Lorne Huntley asked Ruth to relay his present, a box of chocolate-covered cherries, my favourite. I couldn't get over his shyness because at school he acted like he was cock of the walk.

Gloria had saved her gift until last, when she was sure everybody was watching. Then she handed me a beautifully wrapped oblong package. It felt like a book. It was—an autographed first edition of L.M. Montgomery's latest novel, *Jane of Lantern Hill*. A few weeks before I would have given my right arm for that book, but now it just reminded me of my impossible dream and I couldn't keep the pained look off my face. I didn't even trust myself to speak.

"Well," she snapped impatiently, "don't you like it?"

"Oh, sure," was all I could manage to say.

"Well, that's gratitude for you!" Turning on her heel, her full skirt swirling, she flounced into the front room.

Someone turned off the overhead light again and Mum went back to the kitchen. I heard Dad say he was going down to the cellar to half-sole Jakey's leaky shoes. Good, I thought, that'll keep him busy so they won't fight.

The band began to play a real oldie, one I'd often heard Mum sing: "When Frances dances with me . . . holy gee!" Mum got a kick out of that song because her name was Frances. I was just beginning to enjoy myself with a boy named Victor Barnes, who made dancing seem easy, when a loud commotion started in the front room.

Mum ran in and switched on the light just in time to see Lorne Huntley punch Georgie Dunn right in the mouth. Georgie went sprawling across Dad's slippery floor, knocking over the floor lamp and smashing it to pieces.

In the rumpus that followed, a dish of blue grapes got knocked off the table with a resounding crash.

The fruit flew all over, squashing and splattering everywhere. Arthur, who came charging to help Georgie, slid on them and bowled Ada right off her feet. Sitting among the grapes, her new white dress splotched with purple juice, she started to cry.

"What's going on here?" The racket had brought Dad running up from the cellar.

"He started it, Mr. Thomson." Everybody, including myself,

pointed accusingly at Lorne Huntley. When the chips were down, our gang on Veeny Street stuck together.

"I'm sorry, Mr. Thomson," simpered Gloria, reaching out and clutching Dad's arm. "I'm afraid it's all my fault. The boys were fighting over whose turn it was to dance with me. I *told* them they'd both get a chance but they wouldn't listen."

Even Dad, who had a volatile temper, simmered down under her spell. "No harm done," he muttered gruffly.

But Mum was livid. "No harm, my foot!" she screeched, glaring at Gloria with flashing black eyes. "Maybe *your* mother doesn't have to worry about where to get another floor lamp, but I do!" In a frenzy she started grabbing up the broken pieces. "Get your coats on, all of you. The party's over."

In five minutes flat everybody had cleared out except Glad and Ruth. Poor Ada had gone home to soak her new white dress in vinegar and water.

"We'll stay and help clean up, Cousin Fran," said Ruth nervously. She and Glad started picking up grapes.

I thought I'd never forgive Mum for embarrassing me like that. How could I ever face my friends again? Especially Lorne Huntley. What would he and Gloria be saying on their way back to their classy neighbourhoods?

Complaining bitterly, Mum swept the mess up into the dustpan. Dad began grimly wiping grape stains and bloodstains off the floor he'd worked so hard on. We girls stood around not knowing what to do next. Mum and Dad stopped grumbling, but the air was tense. Sometimes upsets like that were all it took to start a full-blown fight between them.

I was expecting that to happen any second when a ghostly voice drifted down from above. "What's going on down there?" We all looked up to see Billy's impish face framed in the stovepipe hole. The sight made everybody laugh and the tension was broken.

Then Willa yelled up at him, "You get out of my room, Billy!" She and Wesley had come in the kitchen door unnoticed. Quick as a wink Billy's face disappeared and we heard him padding barefoot down the hall.

"What happened?" asked Willa, staring at the shattered lamp.

"The less said the better," muttered Mum. So Willa told Wesley he'd better go, which was a perfect excuse not to have to kiss him goodnight in the hallway. Poor Wesley. I felt sorry for him.

"I guess we'd better go too," said Glad uneasily.

"Thank you, girls," said Mum breathlessly, her hand over her heart. Then she added, "There's no friends like old friends."

Ignoring that remark, I gathered up my presents and stomped upstairs. Throwing Gloria's gift on the closet shelf, I stuffed the other things into my drawer and opened my new diary.

Inside, in a slot, was a gold pencil. I wrote:

Nov. 9, 1937
Dear Diary,
Today I am fifteen years old and my life lies in ruins at my feet.
B.M.T.

I locked the diary with the miniature key and looked for a

place to hide it. I noticed a knothole in the thick wood base-board. The key fit neatly in the hole and when the knot was replaced no one would ever know it was there.

5
Three Smart Girls

Between the loss of my "calling" and the loss of a potential boyfriend, I was about ready to take Arthur's advice and stick my head in the oven. Then along came a new idol who changed all that.

Ever since I'd seen my first silent moving picture at the Kingswood in Birchcliff years ago, I'd been mad about movies. So when Glad and Ruth and I went downtown to see a Christmas special called *Three Smart Girls* we could hardly wait to get there. The newspaper ad read: *Scintillating young Canadian soprano, Deanna Durbin, sings her way right into your heart!*

Well, did she ever. She was just fifteen, the perfect age for an idol. And what a fascinating name—Deanna Durbin! It made Gloria Carlyle sound like Zazu Pitts!

As usual, we stopped off on our transfers at Yonge and Bloor to visit the Uptown Nuthouse, my Aunt Susan's store. Poor Aunt Susan, she had so many relatives who just happened to stop by to say hello on their way downtown that she must have given away a hundred pounds of nuts every year.

When we came out of the show two hours later, we blinked in amazement at the bright winter sun.

"I forgot it was still daylight," I said, narrowing my eyes against the sudden brilliance. "I felt as if I was in another world, didn't you?"

"I was living in the picture," said Glad dreamily. "I felt as if I was one of the three sisters."

"Wasn't it exciting how they rescued their beloved father from that wretched gold digger?" exclaimed Ruth.

"And the family reunion—the father and mother and three daughters together again. Oh, it was magnificent!" As a story-teller, I loved the dramatic, happy ending.

"And the music was simply divine!" added Ruth, who was a born musician herself.

We drifted onto the Yonge streetcar to the tune of "Waltzing in the Clouds" and settled on the round wooden seat at the back.

"I've got a swell idea," said Ruth mysteriously.

"What? Tell us!"

"Let's form an exclusive club called the *Three Smart Girls Club*."

"Terrific!" I agreed.

"What will Ada say?" worried Glad. Ada had a Saturday job now and hadn't been able to come.

"Well, we can't have four smart girls," reasoned Ruth.

"I want to be Deanna Durbin," I said.

"You can't be. Your hair's too fair," said Ruth.

"Then I will!" Glad flashed a smile.

"You can't either. Your hair's too dark," said Ruth, fluffing up her own nut-brown curls.

We argued all the way home, then Glad and I had to admit that Ruth, with her Deanna Durbin hairdo (completely accidental) and her round, nice-featured face, actually was the best choice. That left the other two movie sisters to choose from, which was easy because Nan Grey was a blue-eyed blonde, like me, and Barbara Read was a brown-eyed brunette, like Glad.

That night we had our first meeting in Glad's kitchen and drew up the club rules.

The Three Smart Girls Club. Ruth printed the title neatly at the top of a page of foolscap.

Rule 1. Only the three of us can belong because that's what makes it exclusive. That was Ruth's contribution.

Rule 2. We must see every Deanna Durbin movie together if humanly possible. That was mine.

Rule 3. We will buy all Deanna Durbin records and all movie magazines featuring her pictures, and the club will own them collectively. That was Glad's idea, but how we were going to do it I couldn't imagine because we hardly ever had any money.

Rule 4. We will begin a giant scrapbook devoted to our idol's life and fabulous career.

"Anything else?" Ruth tapped the pencil on her front teeth thoughtfully.

"Well, if there are any more rules or regulations they'll have to wait," interposed Aunt Ellie, "because I need the table now."

"Okay. We'll meet here every Saturday night after supper. Is that all right, Mumma?"

"That's just dandy," Aunt Ellie agreed. Then, with Florrie's play dress draped over her arm, she shook her ragbag onto the table and began searching for a patch.

This is one of Deanna's early pictures, from Three Smart Girls. *With her are Nan Grey (left) and Barbara Read. Deanna surely is growing quickly.*

The Three Smart Girls Club

After that we lived from one Deanna Durbin show to the next. Night after night I dreamed that every time I opened my mouth her glorious voice would come soaring out in radiant high Cs.

One Saturday during an afternoon meeting of the club Glad's mother interrupted with some exciting news. "Just hearken to this," she said, spreading the weekend newspaper out in front of us on the table. "It says here there's going to be a Deanna Durbin look-alike contest. Maybe Ruth could win it."

The green-eyed monster leaped up in me. It was bad enough that Ruth was the chosen one in our club, but if she actually won a look-alike contest I'd have a bilious attack and die.

"Don't worry," Glad consoled me as we crossed the street Monday morning, watching our step. (The Silverwood's Dairy wagon had just passed by, leaving steaming horse-buns in its wake.) "Ruth probably won't be able to afford film for the camera. And Cousin Aimie probably won't let her use it anyway."

But Glad was wrong. Cousin Aimie did better than that. She was so intrigued with the idea of her daughter winning a famous screen-star contest that she marched Ruth straight down to Paramount Studios on Yonge Street where they had a special on, four poses for a quarter. One of the pictures turned out to be a remarkable likeness.

Although it nearly killed me, I managed to wish Ruth luck. But the results weren't going to be announced until early in the new year. It was going to be a long winter.

6
Cousin Winn

A week before Christmas something happened that distracted me from the contest. Cousin Winnifred came to board with us.

Actually Winn's mother had been our mother's second cousin, so we weren't very closely related, but Mum had a special soft spot for Winn because her mother, Cousin Addie, had died when Winn was only a tyke, three years old. The saddest thing I ever heard Winn say was, "I never knew my mother, but I've missed her all my life." Those sober words, coming from the lighthearted Winn, chilled me to the bone.

Winn had landed herself a swell job in the west end of Toronto in a big food store called Loblaw's Groceteria. Before that she had been a housemaid for a rich family in Birchcliff, in the east end. Her pay there was twenty dollars a month and they only gave her one night off a week. Mum said it was a sin and shame how rich people took advantage of poor girls. But when Winn got hired by Loblaw's she had the last laugh. She left her stingy employers high and dry without any notice so they didn't have a "char" to do their dirty work.

At Loblaw's Groceteria you carried a wicker basket and helped yourself from the shelves. Then you took your purchases up to the cashier. That's who Winn was, the cashier. But Mum still preferred to deal at Hunter's corner store. She liked the friendliness and convenience. If you ran short of anything, even on a Sunday, all you had to do was knock on their back door and they'd cheerfully get you what you wanted. And besides, you could run up a weekly bill at Hunter's. At Loblaw's you had to have cash.

Every Saturday night after the store closed, at eleven, Winn would come home dog-tired and hand Mum six dollars for board, exactly the same as Willa. Mum said we'd soon be on Easy Street. She even told me she was thinking of opening a bank account—imagine!—in hopes of saving enough money to buy the house on Veeny Street. But she swore me to secrecy.

* * *

We had a swell Christmas that year. The best ever. Jakey got a Big Ben pocket watch and all day long he went around asking, "Does anybody want to know what time it is?" Santa had brought Billy a wind-up train that kept him spellbound the entire day. And Dad even bought Mum a present—a two-slice Waverley toaster. She was pleased as punch. I don't remember him ever buying her a present before.

Willa and Winn went together and bought me a powder blue blouse. Mum and Dad gave me a pleated flannel skirt. "Now all I need is saddle shoes," I said. Gloria had saddle shoes.

"You can't expect to get everything at once," Mum pointed out.

Later in the day, to my astonishment, Lorne Huntley came to the door with a box of chocolates (cherry centres again), and because it was Christmas Day Dad let him step inside the hall. So that made my day perfect.

Wesley Armstrong gave Willa a tapered blue bottle of Evening in Paris perfume. "Boy, oh boy," teased Winn, "he's sure a-courtin' you, Willa." Willa never let on she heard, but her cheeks turned pink.

"I'll trade you my cherry centres for your perfume, Willa," I said, tempting her with a sample. If she agreed I could pretend that Lorne had given me the perfume, which was much more romantic than cherry centres. But she just said, "You've got hopes," popped the sample into her mouth and went away laughing.

We had a beautiful big turkey for Christmas dinner. Usually Aunt Aggie, Dad's sister in Muskoka, sent us a chicken through the mail. Sure enough, it arrived right on time, so Mum saved it for New Year's. She tied it in a potato sack and hung it on the clothesline. Then Dad propped up the line with a pole. The chicken froze solid and was perfectly preserved a week later.

Having Winnifred for Christmas made a real difference. For one thing Mum and Dad tried not to fight in front of her. Also, Winn was more fun than a barrel of monkeys. She always had a joke or a trick to play on somebody.

"I stuck up for you last night, Arthur," she said in a serious voice as she helped herself to more dressing.

"You did?" Arthur fell for it hook, line and sinker.

"Sure did!" Winn's blue eyes were twinkling. "Do you know a girl named Marjorie Tabbs?"

"Yeah." Arthur coloured up. He had a crush on Marjorie Tabbs, who was in fifth form and wouldn't give him the time of day. "What about it?"

"Well. . ." Winn paused so long, twirling her fork in the air, that we all stopped eating to listen. "Marjorie said that you weren't fit to eat with pigs . . . and I said you were!"

For a split second there was dead silence. Then we all roared with laughter.

"I owe you one, Winn!" grinned red-faced Arthur. One thing I'll say for my brother, he could take a joke on himself.

"Oh, Winn"—Mum was wiping the tears from her cheeks—"you're your mother all over again. Addie was always the life of the party." Then she began to laugh and cry at once, remembering her long-dead friend. I laughed so hard myself I had to leave the table to go to the bathroom.

"Bea," Billy said with a puzzled frown when I came back and sat down beside him, "will you understand it for me?"

His funny little question set us all off again. "I'll try, Billy, but Winn's jokes are kind of hard to explain."

"I understand it," said smart-aleck Jakey. "I'll explain it to you later, Bill." (Bill!) He took his watch out of his pocket and studied it importantly. "I'll explain it to you at seven o'clock," he promised. That started us laughing all over again. I can't remember when we were all so happy at the dinner table.

That night I wrote in my diary:

Dear Diary,

Christmas was fun this year! I hope Winn stays forever, even though I hate sleeping three in a bed. She and Willa make me sleep in the middle and sometimes I wake up actually gasping for air. And they think it's funny! Also they say I talk in my sleep and answer all their questions, so now they know all my secrets. I could kill them for that! But I still hope Winn stays. I think she's going to bring us

good luck in the new year. 1938, imagine! Time sure flies.
Mum says if time begins to fly it means you're getting old.
Well, I'm in my sixteenth year so, as Aunt Aggie would
say, I'm "no spring chicken anymore!"
   B.M.T.

Locking the diary, I hid the key in the knothole. Then I tried
to get to sleep before Winn and Willa came to bed and smothered me again.

7
My first job

Both Glad and Ruth had been lucky enough to get Deanna Durbin dresses for Christmas. But no matter how hard I pleaded Mum said she simply couldn't afford a new dress for me right now and I'd have to earn it myself.

I had been trying for months to get a job after school, without success. Then one day Ada-May said she was quitting her baby-minding job because she'd finally been taken on steady at Stedman's Department Store. She recommended me for her old job—and I got it.

New Year's Eve was my first night. "Be here sharp at seven o'clock," said Mrs. Bosley over the telephone.

"Yes, Mrs. Bosley," I answered politely. Ada called her Mrs. Bossy—because she was!—but she warned me never to let it slip out of my mouth.

I got there on the dot of seven to find a sinkful of dirty dishes and the twins running around still dressed in their Little Lord Fauntleroy suits.

"Now do the dishes first"—Mrs. Bosley started right in giving me orders—"and be extra careful how you handle my precious stemware." Stemware? "It was a wedding present from my Great-Aunt Emma in England and is practically priceless." That's how she talked, to show off. "Mind you keep a sharp eye on the boys while you're doing the washing up. And be sure you put all the tableware in the right cupboards. The good dishes go in the sideboard and the glassware goes in the china cabinet." The glassware must be the stemware, I thought.

"After that you may bathe the twins together in the same tub, but be sure you wash Gaylord's hair and not Gaston's. He's got the sniffles. In case you can't tell them apart—the darlings even fool me sometimes—Gaylord is the one with flecks of brown in the blue of his left eye. It's an inherited trait from his father's side. All my family have pure blue eyes.

"When you get them into their sleepers—Gaylord's are yellow and Gaston's are blue, I've already laid them out on their beds to save you trouble—they may stay up for exactly half an hour, not a minute longer, to listen to our Philco. I shall depend on your integrity to choose a fitting program for their young ears. I don't want them to hear any slang or indelicate words.

"After you put them to bed and hear their prayers you may listen to the radio yourself for an hour as a special New Year's Eve treat. You should enjoy that because I'm sure you don't have a radio in your house. Now, are there any questions, Beatrice?"

"No, Mrs. Bossy," I answered without thinking. "But we do have a radio—a DeForest Cro—"

"*What did you call me?*"

Good grief, it had slipped out. "Oh, I'm sorry. I meant to say *Bosley*. You see, I have this slight impediment in my speech. The doctor says it's nothing to worry about. It's just that I was born with too short a tongue." Actually I had an extra long tongue that I could dart out like an anteater and touch the end of my nose with. But at least she seemed to accept my excuse.

The minute their parents went out the door those two little "darlings" changed into devilish imps. I knew I'd never be able to handle them and the stemware together, so I decided to get rid of them first.

I dragged them, kicking and screaming, up the stairs and threw them into the bathtub together.

"Which one of you is Gaylord?" I demanded, peering into their identical faces, trying to find the brown specks in one blue eye.

"Me! Me!" they squealed in unison.

"All right, I'll give you one more chance." I used a really mad voice. "Which one is Gaston?"

"I am! I am!" they said gleefully. So without another word I shoved both their curly heads under water. Up they came, spluttering and shrieking and calling me terrible names.

At last I got the twins into their sleepers and sat them down side by side on the chesterfield. In the time it took me to tune in the radio they had started a real cat-and-dog fight. I squeezed myself between them and pinned their arms to their sides so they couldn't move a muscle.

A ghost story was just beginning on CFCA. It scared the daylights out of them and when it was over they ran up to bed, covered their heads and wouldn't even come out to say their prayers. I never heard another peep all night.

At last I got around to tackling the mountain of dishes. By the time I was done I was worn to a frazzle. It was almost midnight when I turned the radio on again. I just managed to catch the tail end of Guy Lombardo's band playing "Auld Lang Syne" before I fell fast asleep on the soft velour chesterfield.

The radio was still crackling when the Bosleys arrived home at two. Mr. Bosley was in a good mood, singing loudly, "It's shree o'clock in the morning . . . we've danched the whole night shroo . . ." But Mrs. Bosley was fit to be tied. "How dare you fall asleep!" How dare I? I was so tired after all that work that I couldn't stay awake. And I hadn't broken a single piece of stemware either. "My precious babies could have been murdered in their beds!" Who'd want to murder them? I wondered. Except me. "And the radio still blaring, wasting electricity when the station has long been off the air."

She clicked off the radio (which was crackling, not blaring), snapped open her purse (evening bag, she called it) and slapped a quarter and a dime into my hand.

"I had fully intended giving you fifty cents, since it's New Year's Eve, but considering your negligence there'll be no gratuities for you, my girl!" (Her girl, my foot!)

By the time I got my coat and galoshes on, Mr. Bosley had his off. His nose was red and he yawned hugely as he chucked me under the chin. "Happy New Year's, wushyername," he slurred, then went stumbling up the stairs.

"Now you go straight home," ordered Mrs. Bosley as she shoved me out the door.

"Where else would I go?" I muttered into my scarf. There was no place I'd rather be than safe and warm in bed beside my sister.

The night was pitch-black, freezing cold and eerily quiet. Mayberry Hill seemed like a mountain as I trudged up it to Windermere Avenue. From the top of the hill I could look down the street and see Grampa Cole's old cement-block house. I stopped for a second, wishing I had the nerve to take the shortcut through his yard and across the lane to ours. If he'd still been alive I might have. It was more than a year now since he'd "gone home," as Mum put it. "Oh, Grampa," I mourned, missing him for the thousandth time. But I knew the back lane would be as dark as a graveyard, and at least there were a few lights on the street.

Just at that moment I saw the figure of a man come creeping out of Grampa's laneway. As soon as he spotted me under the lamppost he started running toward me. Terrified, I flew along Mayberry and down Veeny Street, my screams piercing the air like flying icicles.

I could hear loud yelling and pounding feet closing in behind me.

Our house was in total darkness. That meant the front door was locked and I'd have to go through the black alleyway between the houses. He'd catch me for sure in the alleyway. He'd kill me in the alleyway! A picture of my frozen, blood-stained body flashed through my mind. Who would make the grisly discovery in the morning? I wondered.

Suddenly, across the road, Aunt Ellie's light flashed on. She must have heard my screams, because the door flew open just as I came stumbling through it.

"A man! A man!" I shrieked hysterically. Shoving me inside, she stepped fearlessly out the door in her kimono. And there was the man, panting like a runaway horse, his greatcoat flying in the wind. My dad! My very own dad!

"Jim!" cried Aunt Ellie. "It's yourself! For mercy sakes, you nearly scared Bea half to death."

"You foolish girl!" Dad yelled, pulling me roughly into his arms. "Didn't you hear me calling you?"

"Oh, Dad!" It had been a long time since I'd felt the comfort of his old khaki coat. "Am I ever glad it's you!"

"I'm sorry I gave you such a fright, Ellie," he apologized over my shoulder. "What in thunder are you doing up at this hour?"

"I came down to boil an onion," explained Aunt Ellie. "Our Florrie's got the earache again. Well, all's well that ends well, Jim. See you tomorrow."

"Much obliged, Ellie. I hope Florrie gets relief."

Aunt Ellie nodded her head wearily as she latched the door behind us.

Mum was sitting in the kitchen with her feet up on the oven door, an open book on her lap. It was *Anne's House of Dreams.* Funny how you notice things like that in a crisis.

"It's a good thing you sent me after her," Dad said. "She was let walk home all alone."

"You mean to say"—Mum sprang to her feet and the book flopped on the floor—"that Mr. Bosley allowed you to walk all the way home alone at this ungodly hour?"

"I think he intended to walk me home, Mum." I had a feeling this whole affair was going to end up to my disadvantage. Besides, I kind of liked *Mr.* Bosley. "But he was a bit drunk. His nose was all red and he sort of staggered up the stairs."

"Well, he can just stagger right down again." Sparks of outrage flew from Mum's dark eyes. Going straight to the phone on the dining room wall, she dialled Bosleys' number furiously. It must have rung at least a dozen times.

"Let me speak to Mr. Bosley," Mum demanded. Then she

said, "Well, wake him up if you don't want the police at your door."

The threat worked and presently Mr. Bosley came on the line. "This is Beatrice Thomson's mother." Mum's voice quivered with anger. He must have said he'd never heard tell of me because all of a sudden my mother—my God-fearing, church-going mother—started swearing a blue streak. Then, when she got that out of her system, she said, "My girl could have been attacked coming home alone tonight. And if anything had happened to her I'd have gone for you myself!" With that she slammed the receiver down, with a fierce jangle, in his ear.

Needless to say, I never minded Gaylord and Gaston again. I never got my Deanna Durbin dress either. What's more, when the school nurse weighed me on the first day in the new year she found I had lost five pounds. So I guess that's what's known as being scared skinny—literally!

8

We, the undersigned

At long last the big day came when the winner of the look-alike contest was to be announced. Glad and Ruth and I congregated anxiously at Ruth's front-room window waiting for the paperboy.

"Here he comes!" I spotted him about ten houses up the street on the other side.

"I'll run to meet him!" cried Glad.

"You'll catch your death without your sweatercoat!" called Cousin Aimie after her. But Glad flew recklessly out the door, leaving it wide open. The wind nearly blew it off its hinges. Cousin Aimie yelled, "For mercy sakes!" and jumped up to shut it. Ruth stood still as a statue, her face ghostly white.

Back came Glad, bursting through the door, the cold air rushing in behind her. "For mercy sakes!" cried Cousin Aimie, jumping up to shut it again.

Tingling with suspense, we scattered the paper all over the floor. We found the picture—but it wasn't Ruth. It was a girl who looked so much like Deanna Durbin that she could have been the famous soprano's twin sister.

Big tears gathered in Ruth's eyes and spilled onto the

The real
Deanna Durbin . . .

. . . and her double.

picture, spreading in damp grey blots. Suddenly I was glad I hadn't had a chance in the contest. At least I was spared the agony of losing.

"Never mind, Ruthie." Even as I consoled her I felt a surge of relief inside me. "You're prettier than her anyway." It was a lie, of course, but at least it was a white lie.

"Yeah!" agreed Glad. "And I'll bet anything she can't play the piano half as well as you can." Ruth had perfect pitch. She could play absolutely anything by ear. She had heard Deanna sing "I Love to Whistle" only once, in the movie *Mad about Music*, and she could play it perfectly right straight through.

But Ruth was inconsolable.

"I think it's time you girls forgot about moving picture stars and got at your homework," said her mother, trying vainly to hide her own disappointment.

Glad and I didn't see Ruth for weeks after that. Then one day she met us after school and told us some very disturbing news. It seemed that Deanna Durbin's Canadian look-alike had sent an autographed copy of her prize-winning photograph to the famous actress and it hadn't even been acknowledged, let alone answered in kind.

Immediately we called an emergency meeting of the Three Smart Girls Club.

"What shall we do about it?" asked Ruth.

"Well, it's an insult to all Canadians," I said in righteous indignation. "After all, she is a Canadian."

"Was," corrected Glad. "I read she's an American now."

"Just the same," said Ruth, "I think it's our duty as members of her fan club to write her a letter of protest."

The suggestion was passed unanimously. Glad contributed

the pen, paper and four-cent stamp. Ruth wrote the letter because her penmanship was the neatest (and also, she was the injured party) and I dictated the words because I was the best at composition.

16, 17, 18 Veeny Street,
Swansea, Ontario, Canada,
March 17, 1938

Dear Deanna,

Let us begin by stating that we, the undersigned, are probably your most avid fans on the face of this earth. In fact we have formed an exclusive club appropriately named the Three Smart Girls Club in honour of your grand and glorious pictures. It is our considered opinion that you are the finest soprano in the world today. Together we have assembled a giant scrapbook filled with photos and articles about your life and sparkling career.

Therefore it grieves us deeply to have to find fault with you in any way. However, it has come to our attention that the winner of your Canadian look-alike contest (who, by the way, is a complete stranger to us) sent her prize-winning, autographed photograph to you and it was completely ignored.

However, we the undersigned feel that this can only be an oversight on your part because your obvious sweet nature (which is apparent in all your films), as well as the fact that you are a Canadian by birth, would never allow you to be so thoughtless and cruel.

Therefore we beg of you, on behalf of Toronto's look-alike, to rectify this error as soon as possible.

*We, the undersigned, will remain forever your faithful
and devoted fans.*

> *Ruth Aimie Vaughan,*
> *Gladys Pearl Cole,*
> *and Beatrice Myrtle Thomson.*

We addressed the envelope c/o Universal Studios, Hollywood, California, United States of America, and dropped it in the mailbox on our way to school the next morning.

Time passed and the letter was forced to the back of our minds by the awful throes of Easter examinations. Then a few weeks later the three of us were sauntering down Veeny Street sharing a bag of humbugs when we saw Ruth's mother standing on their front stoop waving something high in the air. She looked really excited, so we broke into a run.

In her hand she held a flat parcel about ten inches square. "Look at the postmark!" she cried when we reached her.

"Oh, my gosh!" Ruth squealed. "It's from Hollywood!"

Screaming like magpies, we tore open the package. Inside was an absolutely gorgeous coloured photograph of our idol. A typewritten letter was enclosed explaining that the exact same portrait had been sent to Canada's look-alike with profound apologies.

A bit of brown wrapping paper still clung to the bottom of the picture frame. Ruth ripped it off and there in the lower right-hand corner, in the star's own handwriting, were the words *To Ruth Aimie Vaughan and Gladys Pearl Cole, with all my very best wishes, Deanna Durbin.*

My name was conspicuously absent. Frantically we turned the picture over. But it wasn't on the back either. My heart fluttered and seemed to stop and I thought I was going to drop dead. Bursting into tears, I bolted out the back door, leaped across the alleyway that separated our houses and went crashing into our kitchen, scaring the wits out of Mum.

"Booky!" She always reverted to my nickname when she was frightened. "What in the name of heaven is the matter?"

I sobbed out the whole awful story.

"Oh, pshaw, Bea." Mum sounded relieved. "Nobody ever died of envy, you know." That made me cry all the harder. Then, when she realized the depths of my despair, she added quickly, "Why don't you sit yourself down and write Deanna a nice letter explaining the oversight? I'm sure it's all a big mistake."

Her advice gave me a glimmer of hope. Immediately I composed another letter and mailed it secretly. I didn't want the other two "smart girls" to know until I had the autographed photograph right in my hands.

For months and months I waited, sometimes going up the street to meet the mailman, until at last I had to accept the fact that I was never going to hear a word from Deanna Durbin.

Oddly, I didn't blame *her*. Willa had told me that sometimes famous movie queens had jealous secretaries who threw away fan letters if they were too thrillingly complimentary (which mine was), and the star herself never knew a thing about it.

I was convinced that this was what had happened. So my loyalty to my idol remained untarnished, but I never told Glad or Ruth about it. And I never really got over it.

9
The Pally

By the time spring came and the weather turned warm and balmy I was sick to death of my Christmas outfit. Every other night I had to wash and iron my blue blouse and Mum sponged and pressed my grey flannel skirt.

"If only you weren't so skinny, Bea," Mum complained, "you could grow into Winn's and Willa's things."

One morning as I was getting my clean blouse out of the closet I noticed Willa's new one hanging there invitingly. It was peach-coloured with long, full sleeves and a ruffled neckline. It was absolutely irresistible.

"She'll kill you when she finds out, Bea," Glad said, shifting her load of books from one hip to the other as we trekked up Jane Street.

"No, she won't, because I get home before her and I'll be sure to hang it in the same place at the end of the closet."

"Which end—left or right?"

"Right. I think. Darn you, Glad, now you've got me worried."

The blouse was a mile too big, so I got Glad to pin it at the back in the school washroom. Also the shoulder seams hung too low, so I had to thrust my shoulders back, which did wonders for my skinny figure. Across my forehead and in front of my ears I had set sugar-water kiss curls. The curls combed out a bit crispy, but not too bad. The peach-coloured georgette blouse seemed to brighten up my complexion (I was sallow when I wasn't suntanned), and even my eyes looked bluer. For once I was halfways satisfied with myself.

At lunch time in the basement cafeteria I was carefully eating my meatloaf sandwich so as not to let the homemade mustard drip onto Willa's blouse, when all of a sudden Glad got up and vanished. Lorne Huntley took her place. He straddled the bench, drinking from a big bottle of Kik Cola.

"How's tricks?" he asked, as friendly as anything, just as if he hadn't been ignoring me for months. Everybody knew that he and Gloria Carlyle were keeping company. "Want a sip?" He bent the soggy paper straw towards me.

"No thanks." I was going around with Georgie again, so even though my heart was racing a mile a minute, I decided to act choosy.

"I'll get a new straw," he said, and before I could stop him he went leapfrogging over the rows of tables and brought back a fresh straw. So I took a sip.

"You busy Friday night?" he asked.

"Maybe," I hedged, facing him squarely so he wouldn't notice my knobby nose. Was I glad I'd had the nerve to wear Willa's blouse! "Georgie Dunn usually comes over."

"How's about going dancing with me at the Pally?"

The Pally! That was short for the Palais Royale and going there was beyond my wildest hopes. Besides, I was a terrible dancer. Sometimes Arthur and I tried out a few steps, but

Arthur always said he might as well be dancing with the floor mop. Outside of that and my disastrous birthday party I hadn't had much practice.

"I'll have to ask my mum," I said, knowing I sounded like a ninny, but needing time to think.

"Okey-doke. I'll call you Thursday." He winked one beautiful eye and went bounding away.

Instantly "bunch" (that's what we girls who hung around together had dubbed ourselves—not "the bunch" or "our bunch," just bunch) popped up from all directions.

"What did Lorne want?" Glad asked, her gleaming eyes following his tall figure as he went loping, two steps at a time, up the cement staircase.

"He invited me to the Pally on Friday night," I said, trying to sound casual.

"Oh, wow!" exclaimed Wanda Backhouse.

"Talk about luck!" Jane LaRose stared at me as if I had a four-leaf clover stuck to my forehead.

"What did you say?" persisted Glad.

"I said I'd let him know Thursday."

"You're kidding!" cried Glad.

"Oh, wow!" crowed Wanda again. She was definitely the dumbest member of "bunch." No wonder Georgie had gotten bored with her.

Speaking of dumb, I didn't learn a thing that afternoon. Math gave me enough trouble without having Lorne on my mind. But I did manage to remember, when I got home, to hang Willa's blouse up exactly where I'd found it.

Thursday night the phone rang. Winn and Willa and I all jumped for it at once, but Willa grabbed it first. Then she handed it to me. "You're always on the phone," she grumbled. That was true. Mum said I had phone-itis. I'd no sooner say goodbye to Glad at the front than I'd go straight in and phone her. I couldn't get over the thrill of having a phone of our own at last. But this time I didn't talk long. What can you say to a boy when there are four big ears listening in?

When Lorne picked me up on Friday he was dressed fit to kill in a blue serge suit with a felt fedora to match. He was the only boy I knew who owned a fedora.

I was wearing my birthday dress, which Mum had let out to fit. Willa had done my hair with the tongs again, and Winn said I could borrow her new string of beads as a finishing touch. Mum insisted that I wear my threadbare spring coat because it was bound to be chilly down by the lake.

She and Dad weren't too happy about my date. "I'll never forget that boy's performance at your party," Mum said skeptically.

Arthur looked up from his artwork and said, "Aw, it wasn't any more his fault than mine and Georgie's."

That seemed to mollify Mum and Dad. "Thanks, Arthur," I said.

"You're welcome, Bea." He grinned. We were getting positively civil to each other.

Lorne and I walked along the boardwalk holding hands, but not talking much. Lake Ontario glittered like gold in the setting sun. Soft waves lapped on the sand of Sunnyside Beach. The amusement park was open and we could hear wild screams coming from atop the roller coaster. I don't remember ever feeling so thrilled and happy before.

Sweet music floated out of the open Pally doors. The electric sign above read: *Bert Niosi, Canada's King of Swing!* A notice tacked to the door said: *Ten cents a dance.* Lorne jingled a pocketful of dimes.

The dance floor was crowded already and the band was playing "Love in Bloom." Lorne slipped his arm around my waist, under my coat, and swung me around the huge ballroom. A fresh lake breeze blew in the open doors at the back, ruffling our hair. I was in seventh heaven!

A little while later, as we danced by the bandstand, Lorne called out to the dapper man with the baton, "Hey, Bert, how about 'Smoke Gets in Your Eyes'?"

The band leader winked and nodded without missing a beat. Sure enough, the next piece he played was "Smoke Gets in Your Eyes."

"Do you actually *know* Bert Niosi?" I asked, flabbergasted.

Lorne shrugged nonchalantly. "He's a friend of the family."

"Oh, wow!" I cried, sounding just like Wanda. Wait till I tell bunch about this! I thought.

It was a wonderful evening. We danced to "Always" and "Carolina Moon," and every time I tripped over Lorne's feet he apologized and said it was all his fault. Afterwards we went to the amusement park and had a terrifying ride on the roller coaster. Then we shared a paper conc of vinegar and chips. Finally we headed up Ellis Avenue, our arms around each other under a star-spangled sky. Fireflies blinked their lights all over Grenadier Pond. It was a magical sight.

Home again, we sat on my front stoop and kissed four times. Everything would have been fine if I'd said goodnight right then and gone in. But Lorne pulled a five-cent packet of Turrets out of his shirt pocket, and scratching a match alight with his thumbnail, very romantically lit two cigarettes at once.

It was my first cigarette and I didn't know how to hold it. "Pinch it between your thumb and finger and take a big drag and swallow it. Then let it out real slow, like this." He demonstrated, drawing in deeply. Then he formed his lips into a circle and blew a halo right over my head. It dissolved in the soft night air.

Laughing, I tried to copy him and instantly went into an uncontrollable coughing fit. The awful racket I made, choking and gagging, brought my dad running to the door. He took one look and erupted like a volcano. In two quick motions he smacked the cigarette out of my mouth and kicked Lorne down the steps. Lorne landed on his feet, like a cat, the cigarette still clamped between his handsome lips.

"You," Dad snarled at me, his pale eyes smouldering, "get yourself inside! And you, boy, get out of my sight before I take my belt to you!"

"Help, Mum!" I screamed. I was really scared of Dad when his eyes changed from blue to grey. Mum came flying from the kitchen. At first she put her arm protectively around me. But when she heard the story she angrily ordered me to bed.

Embarrassed by Dad and feeling betrayed by Mum, I burst into sobs and went racing up the stairs.

Winn was away visiting one of her brothers, so Willa and I had the bed to ourselves. I thought she was asleep, so I stifled my sobs and crept miserably in beside her. Then she did the most extraordinary thing. Willa, who never touched anybody if she could help it, actually patted my back. "Never mind, Bea," she comforted me. "I know exactly how you feel. Only it was even worse for me when I was your age because I was the oldest and they always expected me to be perfect."

"I guess it's worse for Arthur too, then," I sniffled, "since he's two years older than me." I hoped it was, because misery loves company.

"No," Willa dashed my hopes. "He's a boy. Boys get away with murder." She gave my back a final pat, more like a slap, and added sternly, "But don't you dare start smoking or I'll make you sleep on the floor. You reek!"

With that she turned over and got as far away from me as possible, and that was the end of our discussion. It wasn't much, but it was the first time my sister and I had had a heart-to-heart talk. So, as Aunt Milly would say, "Things are never so bad they couldn't be worse"—or one of those old sayings.

The next day I wrote the whole episode up in my diary, and when I read it over it sounded for all the world like a page out of *True Romances*.

10
Aunt Milly

On Sunday Willa got her peach blouse out of the closet to wear to church. Instantly she spotted the soiled collar. "You dirty rat!" she screeched. That was the worst thing Willa ever called anybody, a rat, but I'd never heard her use the adjective before. She chose another blouse and glared at me all through church.

That afternoon she washed the blouse in the kitchen basin and hung it out to dry. Later, when she went to iron it, she was so busy bawling me out that she forgot to wet her finger to test the iron so she scorched the blouse. She was so mad she flung the filmy thing right in my face. "Here, take it," she yelled. "It's ruined now anyway!" Then she grabbed her coat and went slamming out the door.

Standing with the blouse draped over my head, I felt awful. But I thought I might as well make the best of it, so I went upstairs and put it away in my drawer.

Hidden at the back of the drawer, underneath my underwear, was a printed rejection slip from *Love Story* magazine. Secretly I had written a fabulous story about a handsome hero named

Lance who had hung himself in his bedroom closet when he was jilted by his lady-love. But the hook broke and he ended up with only a sore neck. When Angela, his paramour, found out what he had done she was so remorseful that she married him. But they didn't live happily ever after because they found out that they didn't really like each other, never mind love, so they got a divorce.

Seeing that rejection slip was the last straw. I decided I had to see my Aunt Milly. All my life when I had serious problems I took them to Aunt Milly. Mum said her little sister attracted troubles like honey draws flies.

Aunt Milly was fifteen years younger than Mum and fifteen years older than me. So she was still young enough to remember what it was like to be fifteen. And she still looked like a girl. She had long auburn ringlets, bright sparrow's eyes and blood-red fingernails. She wore spike heels and short skirts and she still had a girlish figure in spite of the fact that she'd had three children one right after the other. Lots of people criticized Aunt Milly and said she should grow up and act her age. But Mum said jealousy would get them nowhere.

Aunt Milly and Uncle Mort lived in a house just like ours on Durie Street. So on Monday I stopped in after school.

"Halloo, Bea!" The door swung open as wide as her smile. "You're just in time to share a Coca Cola."

A bucket of soapy water with a string mop sticking out of it was sitting in a puddle on the kitchen floor. "Oh, I'm sorry if I'm interrupting your spring cleaning, Aunt Milly," I apologized. Mum had our house turned upside down with spring cleaning, and I knew she wouldn't thank anybody for dropping in unannounced.

"Oh, bother spring cleaning," snorted my carefree auntie. "I don't go by seasons. If it's dirty I clean it, whether it needs it or not."

We laughed and joked as she put sweater-coats on Bonny and Dimples, her two little girls, and chased them out to play. Then she gave Sunny, her boy, a quarter and sent him up to the Cut-rate Meat-market on Bloor Street for a pound of sausages for supper.

When we were alone, she tiptoed across the clean half of the floor in her spike heels (she never wore house shoes, even when she was cleaning) and lifted the top of the icebox. "I just got fifty pounds of ice an hour ago, so this pop should be good and cold. But if Morty forgets to empty the ice pan one more time I'm going to order up a Frigidaire."

"You sound just like Mum," I laughed as she snapped the cap off the frosty green bottle and handed it to me for the first sip. "Every night at bedtime she says, 'Did you empty the ice pan, Jim?' and Dad answers, 'Always do.' Then Mum grumbles, 'Well, you always don't because there was a puddle on my clean waxed linoleum this morning.'"

Aunt Milly chuckled, then she said seriously, "Fran works too hard. It'll be the death of her." Sitting down at the table, she kicked off her shoes, put her feet up on a chair and said, "A penny for your thoughts, Bea?" She could always tell.

So I began to pour my heart out. I told her all about how Mum and Dad were still mad at me for smoking, and how Lorne had gone back to Gloria Carlyle after Dad pushed him down our porch steps, and how Willa had discover the dirt on her peach blouse and wasn't speaking to me, and how I couldn't find a job to save my life, and how *Love Story* magazine had rejected my romance. "Now Georgie Dunn is all crazy about dopey Wanda Backhouse again, so I haven't got a boyfriend, and I haven't got any decent clothes, and I know I'll never be a writer. And besides, I don't think I'm going to pass this year."

Aunt Milly took another sip of Coke and shoved the bottle across the table to me. "I've got an idea about a job at least," she said, her dark eyes twinkling conspiratorially. "I'm going to be working at your Aunt Susan's store for the summer. How would you like to work there with me?"

"Oh, Aunt Milly, do you think I could? I've never used a cash register and I might cheat somebody."

"Just so long as it's not your Aunt Susan!" she laughed. "Anyhoo . . . keep it under your hat until I get a chance to talk to Susan. She generally likes her helpers to be older than you because she says the young ones eat up all her profits. But I think I can get around her in your case."

I knew if anybody could get around her, Aunt Milly could. She had a reputation for being able to wrap all sorts of people around her little finger. And she was Aunt Susan's favourite sister. Everybody knew that.

"Now for your part of the bargain, Bea. You'll have to set your mind to passing your exams so you'll be free for the summer. And stop worrying about boys. Boys are like streetcars— there's always another one coming along. Just you remember, young lady, you've got a little bit of 'it' and you got it from your Aunt Milly." I loved to hear her say that. It made my heart feel five pounds lighter.

"And about that story of yours," continued my optimistic aunt, "well, you probably sent it to the wrong magazine. Love stories are supposed to have happy endings. It sounds more like a *True Story* to me." Of course! Why hadn't I thought of that?

Just then Sunny came back with the sausages and Aunt Milly sent him out to the backyard to amuse Bonny and Dimples while she finished up the floor.

"I have to run, Aunt Milly," I said, startled to see that it was five o'clock by the clock on top of the kitchen cabinet. "Mum's gone downtown and I have to make supper."

My hand was on the front doorknob when Aunt Milly said, "Just a tick." She dashed upstairs and down again with a pink sweater in her hand. "Try this on for size," she said with that wonderful twinkle in her eye.

"Oh, Aunt Milly, it looks brand new!" I pulled it on and did up the pearl buttons. It fit like a glove.

"Like it?"

"Do I!"

"Then it's yours."

"But—but—it's your new sweater."

"Well, fiddle-de-dee! When you give something away you always get back double."

That was her philosophy. Mum said her little sister was the living end. She'd give you the shirt right off her back—literally.

"Toodle-oo! Love you!" she called from her front stoop. I turned on the run and blew her a kiss.

That very night I practically begged Arthur to help me with my homework. He looked at me skeptically, but grudgingly agreed, and from then on he helped me every night, with some prodding from Mum and Dad. They were both pleased as punch with my sudden interest in school, so they weren't mad at me anymore. And I passed my exams.

Sure as her word, Aunt Milly wrapped Aunt Susan around her little finger and got me my first summer job, at the Uptown Nuthouse.

11
The Nuthouse

I was tickled pink, as well as dressed in pink, as I hurried up the street on the first day of my new job. Lost in thought, daydreaming about the new clothes I would buy—real silk stockings, step-ins instead of bloomers, and maybe even spectator pumps—I hardly noticed Roy-Roy sitting on the porch in his rocking chair, his head lolling down on his chest.

Usually I stopped to talk to him no matter what. But on this particular day I would have just passed by if he hadn't called out "Ba-Ba! Ba-Ba!" I knew that meant "Bea-Bea! Bea-Bea!"

I crossed the road and hurried up the walk. "Hi, Roy-Roy," I said. "I'm sorry I can't stop to visit with you today. I'm on my way to work and I haven't got time."

Poor Roy-Roy, he tried so hard to communicate. He rolled his head and flailed his arms and slobber flew in big drops from his gaping mouth. I reached out and touched his bony shoulder—he had gotten so thin lately. "I'm sorry, Roy-Roy. I'll come back another time, okay? Bye for now."

"Ba-ba-ba!" he cried pitifully after me. I turned around to wave to him, but his head was already slumped down on his chest again.

It was an hour's ride on the Bloor streetcar from Durie Street to Yonge and I'd been given strict orders to be there at ten o'clock sharp. I managed to dash breathlessly in the door at ten minutes after ten.

"Well, Lady Jane!" Aunt Susan came scurrying from the back of the store with a load of raw cashew butts. "Better late than never, I always say."

"I'm sorry, Aunt Susan. I missed a streetcar because I stopped to talk to Roy-Roy."

"Never you mind, Bea"—she gave me a welcoming smile—"I'm just pulling your leg. Where's your funnybone?"

Relieved, I went behind the counter, took off my new sweater, folded it carefully and put it on a high shelf where it wouldn't get dirty.

"Where's Aunt Milly?" I asked anxiously.

"She'll be here any minute. She phoned to say she'd be late because Gertie Witherspoon, that good-for-nothing layabout who minds her children, hadn't got there yet. Milly pays her fifty cents a day too. It's highway robbery if you ask me."

"What should I do?" I asked hesitantly. I'd heard that Aunt Susan was a tartar to work for, so I was nervous as a cat being alone with her.

"Just make boxes until the noon-hour rush." She handed me a pile of flat, odd-shaped pieces of cardboard. I tried every which way to bend and twist those darn things into boxes, but all I succeeded in doing was tearing the end flaps off.

"Good gravy, Bea, if you keep that up you'll owe me money before the day's out. Here now, pay attention."

Deftly, with practiced fingers, she creased and shaped those boxes, tucking the end flaps in and snapping the lids shut so you could see the picture of the squirrel on the top with the acorn in its paws. Under him, in red letters, were the words *The Uptown Nuthouse*, and along the sides it read *Nuts to you!*

But even after being shown, I had trouble. It reminded me of the time I tried to teach Billy how to tie his shoestrings. It looked so easy when you knew how.

Just then Aunt Milly came breezing in the door with a cheery "Halloo!" and my heart sang at the sight of her. In seconds she taught me the trick of folding the boxes, and in minutes I was an expert boxmaker.

At noon the store quickly filled with customers. It was a nice day and the door stood wide open. The lovely smell of roasting cashews went drifting down the street, tempting everybody within half a mile,

Aunt Milly taught me how to weigh the nuts and figure out the price on a little pad.

"I'm not good at arithmetic," I apologized nervously.

"By the end of the day you will be." She gave me a good-natured poke in the ribs. "But don't expect to learn everything at once. Just leave the money on the till and I'll ring it in. Now, it's up to us to wait on customers while Susan does the cooking, so look alackey!" Mum often said that and I knew it meant "Look alive!" So I did.

The gas cooker was in the front window of the shop where it could be seen from the street. All day long people pressed their noses against the steamy glass to watch Aunt Susan stir the nuts in the big iron cauldron. And all day long they streamed through the open door, with a string of crazy, nutsy jokes about how things were in the "Nuthouse." It was more fun than a picnic.

Aunt Milly knew practically everybody by name. "And how's my Ernie today?" she inquired of the shoeshine boy as she gave him ten cents worth of peanuts for a nickel. "What's your pleasure, Curley?" she asked the Eaton's driver who had parked beside a no-parking sign to dash into the store. "How's the old ticker, Meggie?" She showed genuine concern for the pale-faced woman who tottered in on shaky legs.

That first day I met almost all the regular customers, from the blind man who ran the newspaper stall at the corner of Yonge and Bloor to John David Eaton himself.

"Here comes Mr. Eaton!" Aunt Susan announced, all a-twitter as she wiped her greasy hands on her greasy apron. "I'll look after him myself."

I couldn't help but stare at the man who owned the giant department store where all Toronto did its shopping. He looked right at me and smiled, so I smiled back, just as if he was an ordinary man. I couldn't get over it.

"Wait'll I tell Mum!" I whispered to Aunt Milly. She was nibbling hazelnuts behind the cash register. I followed suit and popped a handful into my mouth.

When the great man had left, Aunt Susan declared, "He's a fine, well-to-do gentleman, is Mr. Eaton." She was proud as a peacock of her most illustrious customer. "He took two five-pound boxes of my best mixture," she boasted.

"Well, he might be fine and he might be as rich as Rockefeller," snapped Aunt Milly, punching the cash register keys noisily, "but he's not one wit better than the rest of us mortals. The cat can look at the queen, you know!" I wasn't sure what the connection was, but I got the message anyway.

That was a big day for celebrities. About an hour later, who should come in but Mister Gordon Sinclair, the *Star's* famous newspaperman. I recognized him from his picture and my eyes nearly popped out of my head. Aunt Susan and Mr. Sinclair had a running joke going about which one of them was going to become a millionaire first. Aunt Susan got a great kick out of that.

Later still, when business had slowed down (actually, there was hardly ever a minute when the store was empty) a tired-looking young woman came in. Her coat was shabby and threadbare and she was carrying a baby in a faded blue blanket. Two little hollow-cheeked girls clung to her skirts.

"Five cents worth of redskins, please," she said in a quiet voice. She held out a nickel in her chapped red hand.

As I began to scoop the hot, fresh nuts onto the scales, I glanced quickly at Aunt Susan. Her back was to me and she was humming "The Old Grey Mare" as she cooked in the window. I could hear Aunt Milly rattling tins in the storeroom. Nobody else was in sight. So, quicker than you could say "Jack Robinson" I loaded up a five-pound bag and handed it over the counter. I took the nickel, my heart thudding.

The young mother's eyes filled with tears. Stuffing the oily brown sack under the baby's frayed blanket, she turned and scurried out the door without a backward glance, the little girls scampering after her.

"What a mess that one was!" Aunt Susan glanced up with the dripping wooden spoon in her hand. "Did she buy anything?"

"Sure!" I sighed with relief. "A nickel's worth of peanuts."

"Well, last of the big-time spenders!" snorted Aunt Susan. If she knew the truth she'd fire me on the spot.

After a long day during which we had no time to eat anything except nuts, Aunt Milly and I climbed wearily onto a westbound Bloor streetcar. I was carrying a big box of mixed nuts home to Mum (the second best mixture) but I wasn't the least bit tempted to dip into them. For once in my life I'd had my fill.

"How much did Susan pay you, Bea?" asked Aunt Milly.

"Two dollars," I said, "and carfare."

"Well, she must think you're the cat's meow because that's exactly what she pays me." She didn't say it jealously, she said it joyously. "See? Didn't I tell you every cloud has a silver lining?"

"Speaking of silver, Aunt Milly—" I knew I had to confess to somebody and she was the ideal person, so I told her about the woman with the three children that I'd given a huge bag of redskins to for a nickel. "She looked so poor and hungry," I explained.

Well, you could have knocked me over with a feather when my loving, generous aunt frowned and said, "It's all right this time, Bea. But don't let it happen again. I know why you did it. The same reason I gave the shoeshine boy a little extra. Poor little nipper—his old man drinks up every cent he brings home. But you have to be careful not to get taken in. Some people dress like ragbags to fool the likes of you and me. And half the time they could buy and sell the both of us. And make no mistake, Bea, your Aunt Susan deserves every cent she gets. She's worked her fingers to the bone building up her business, right through the Depression, with no help from anybody. Don't you forget that."

I promised I wouldn't. I was really surprised to learn that

there actually were people in the world who would pull a mean trick like that. But I was absolutely sure the young mother, who had been too choked up to say thank you, wasn't one of them. So I didn't really feel guilty. Just glad I didn't get caught.

That night I recorded everything that had happened in my diary. When I read it over, I thought to myself, "This would make a swell story . . . if only I could be a writer."

12
Long time no see!

Summer was nearly over when I got a letter from Aunt Aggie. She was Dad's sister who lived in Muskoka, in the log house she was born in. Long ago the little house had been crowded with people—parents and grandparents and children—but now Aunt Aggie was all alone.

Heckley, Muskoka,
August 21, 1938

Dear Niece,
   Long time no see! (Where did Aunt Aggie learn those modern slang sayings, I wondered, isolated up there in the wilderness?) *Lovely sunshiny day today. Not too hot. For some reason you've been on my mind all day, so I decided it was high time I sent you a line. I haven't heard a peep out of you since your Grandpa Thomson passed on. It's lonely here in the log house without him, even if he was an old curmudgeon. Ouch! I bit my tongue on a bit of sprucegum. Serves me right for speaking ill of the dead.*
   Got a letter from your father last Saturday. He says you are a working girl now making big money in your

aunt's nut shop. Just thinking about those scrumptious nuts makes my mouth water. She gave me a pound once and I doled them out to myself and made them last two months. Haven't tasted the likes of them since.

I don't suppose you'd have time to slide up for a visit before school starts? I've sure missed you these past few summers. Every time I cross the creek coming home from the post office I remember the bloodsuckers stuck to your leg and I can't help laughing. Imagine you thinking you'd be sucked to death. Poor little thing.

Yesterday I stopped in on Lily Huxtable. She gave me tea. Horace and Daisy both asked for you. (Horace and Daisy Huxtable were my best friends in Heckley.) I had to say I hadn't heard from you in a dog's age. How about dropping your old aunt a line? And tell that brother of mine if he'll send you up by train I'll see you get back. You can hitch a ride in from Huntsville with Jimmy Hobbs—he's Hannibal's baby brother, in case you forgot. Jimmy meets the train from the Big Smoke (that's what Aunt Aggie called Toronto) every afternoon. He's our mailman now. Good steady job for a young fella. He'll make a good catch for some lucky girl in a few years' time.

I cut oats this morning, then gathered a honey pail of big, juicy huckleberries this afternoon. Got lots of cream— you could eat your fill! One of my chickens got killed last night and the pig ate it. Don't that beat all? Well, if you come up we'll eat the pig just for spite. Ha, ha!

Have to turn in now. Must clean this lamp chimney
tomorrow. I can hardly see what I'm writing, so excuse
the hen scratches. It's eleven p.m. Write soon.

Lovingly,
your Aunt Aggie.

I showed the letter to Mum. She stopped ironing to read it. "I think it's a good idea for you to visit your Aunt Aggie, Bea." She folded the dishtowels on the board stretched between two chair backs. Mum was an incurable ironer. She even ironed dust rags!

"I'd love to go, Mum, but what would Aunt Susan say? I don't want to lose my job. It's the best job I ever had."

"I know, Booky, but you're getting peaked looking. And I think you've lost some weight. You know what they say—a change is as good as a rest. Besides, you'll have to give it up when school starts, so one week won't make much difference."

"Will you ask Aunt Susan for me then?"

"I'll get Milly to ask her."

So once again Aunt Milly wrapped Aunt Susan around her little finger and off I went to Muskoka.

Sure enough, Jimmy Hobbs was there to meet me in Huntsville. He was kind of cute and we took a shine to each other right off the bat. We flirted all the way to Heckley in the mail truck. After dropping off the mail sack, he drove me right to the log-house door.

Aunt Aggie was outside looking expectantly up the road. I jumped out and we squealed and hugged each other. Holding me at arm's length, she declared, "You're a sight for sore eyes, Bea!"

"So are you!" I cried.

She hadn't changed a bit. Her straw-coloured hair was still piled up like a cowflap on top of her head, her skin was brown and lined from the sun, and her wire spectacles were perched on the end of her nose. And, if I wasn't mistaken, she was still wearing the same calico housedress and low-heeled house shoes, and the black cotton stockings that wrinkled around her ankles.

But she couldn't get over the change in me. "Why, you're all grown up, Bea. Your grandpa—may he rest in peace—would hardly know you. Where on earth did that little scatterbrain go who used to take her bath in a tub of rainwater beside the house?"

"The same place as the kid who used to braid bracelets out of Major's tail." I laughed excitedly. "By the way, how is Major?"

"Oh, he'll do for an old fella."

"I'll go see him after supper," I said.

"Well, come in and stay awhile. You must be starved." Suddenly we both remembered Jimmy Hobbs. He was swinging on the truck door, grinning awkwardly. "Would you care to join us for a bite, Jimmy?" invited Aunt Aggie.

"No, thanks just as much, Miss Thomson." Aunt Aggie and I were both Miss Thomsons since she'd never married. "I'll be going now. But if you've no objection, I'll drop around tomorrow."

He tried not to look at me as he said this, but we both managed to slide our eyes towards each other without moving our heads. Aunt Aggie didn't miss a thing.

"Sure, Jimmy, anytime. You're always welcome."

He drove off with a wave and we went inside the log house.

It seemed like ages since I'd been there. When Grandpa Thomson died, just Dad and Aunt Ida and Uncle Charlie had come up for the funeral. Dad and Uncle Charlie had dug their father's grave themselves.

A fire crackled in the wood stove, but it was a cool day so the room wasn't too warm.

Gradually my eyes adjusted to the house's dim interior. Great-Grandpa Thomson, one of the first settlers in Heckley, had built the log house in 1848—you could still read the date carved over the low doorway. Two narrow kitchen windows were on either side of the big black range. A yellow fly-sticker hung over the wood box. Dozens of flies were stuck on it, some still alive, buzzing frantically. Mum never used fly-stickers because she said they were too unsightly. Instead she set poison pads in saucers of water on the window sills. The unsuspecting flies would come for a drink, take one sip and drop dead.

As if reading my mind, Aunt Aggie said, "It's time I put up a new one of them eyesores." Taking the loaded sticker down, she dropped it into the hot stove. It flared and sizzled and cremated all the flies. Then she unrolled a nice new one and thumbtacked it to the same ceiling beam. In seconds two flies were trapped, their feet stuck fast, their wings fluttering in a wild frenzy.

"Muskoka is a fierce place for flies and skeeters," remarked Aunt Aggie. "It's all the lakes and ponds that breed the filthy vermin. Ah, well," she shrugged resignedly, "I guess we need the little beggars to remind us we're alive."

I laughed at her homey joke as I gazed around the old famil-iar room, at the homemade wooden furniture on the bare

413

plank floors, and the old-fashioned pictures on the rough pine walls. The only thing that was different was the 1938 calendar tacked to the back of the door leading to the woodshed. On it was a picture of the Dionne quintuplets looking like five little pink dolls. I noticed the day of my arrival was circled in red and Aunt Aggie had written inside the circle, *Bea's coming!* That sure made me feel good.

Aunt Aggie already had the table laid with Great-Grandma Thomson's china tea set, brought all the way from Nottingham in 1847. Two bowls of big, sugar-frosted huckleberries sat on the hand-embroidered tablecloth. She wrapped a flannel cloth around her right hand and lifted a pan of steaming baking-powder biscuits out of the hot oven. Then we sat down cosily together.

13
Story time

Over the table Grandpa Thomson frowned down on us from his homemade criss-crossed frame. There used to be a baby's picture in that frame, I remembered. I think it was Dad's little brother, who died of the ague. But I guess Aunt Aggie had replaced it with her father's picture so she wouldn't be so lonely. His eyes seemed to be watching every bite we ate. He sure would have been upset at all the butter we were slathering on our biscuits.

Aunt Aggie read my mind. "What he don't know can't hurt us now, Bea. He was a stingy old codger and there's no denying it. But I miss him just the same and I hope he's resting easy beside Ma." Her plain face clouded over. She rubbed her eyes underneath her glasses. "They had a hard row to hoe here in the wilderness. You come from hardy stock, Bea, and that's a fact."

It was the first time I'd given much thought to my roots. On both sides of my family I sprang from pioneers. And in a sense Aunt Aggie was still a pioneer. She hauled her water from the spring, cut her own firewood and stacked it up for winter, filled her pantry with wild preserves and buried her vegetables in the root cellar. She cleaned oil lamps and milked the cow and churned the butter and went deer hunting in season. She was a good shot too.

"Last winter I bagged a buck that was so big he fed every soul in Heckley for two months," she bragged.

"How come it didn't spoil without an ice box?"

"Hung it out in the woodshed." She inclined her head towards the woodshed door. "It's cold as charity out there in wintertime. Go look in the parlour and you'll see his head. Antlers six feet wide. Stuffed him myself, I did."

I poked my head into the musty, unused parlour. Sure enough, a huge head stared at me from gaping, empty sockets. "Where's his eyes?" I shut the door with a shudder.

"Oh, I never got around to ordering glass ones from Elwood Peebles, the taxidermist in Huntsville. You can't leave the real eyes in, you know. They'd go all maggoty."

"Oh, Aunt Aggie!" Suddenly her existence seemed primitive, almost barbaric. "Why don't you sell this old place and come to live with us or Uncle Charlie?"

"Live in the city?" You'd think I'd suggested she go live in a jungle. "Well, if it ever comes to that you'd better order me up a plot in the nearest graveyard because I'd be dead in a month. All that noise and confusion, folks rushing every which way like ants on a sandhill, smoke and fumes from motor cars, and so many electric lights you can't even find the Big Dipper at night. And what in tarnation would I do to keep body and soul together? I got no skills to speak of. Up here I get along just dandy. I can barter and trade with my neighbours for anything I need. I bake bread for Lily and she knits stockings for me.

Barney Usher does my ploughing in spring and I help with his haying in summer. Around these parts we're like kinfolk. We look out for each other."

She filled both our cups with strong tea and put a dollop of cream on my third dish of huckleberries. "There's more to life in the country than meets the eye, Bea," she continued thoughtfully. "Why, only last week I was putting a bunch of daisies on Ma's grave—it was her birthday. It's twenty-two years since she passed away and I still miss her . . ."

"I know what you mean," I nodded wisely. "Grampa Cole has been gone for almost two years now, but it seems like only yesterday. I still say, 'Hi, Grampa!' when I pass his house, and I can almost hear him answering, 'Hello, there, Be-*a*-trice, how's my girl?'"

"Then you understand how I feel. You'd have liked your grandma, Bea. We're alike as three peas in a pod, you and her and me. Well, as I was saying, I was setting a jar of yellow daisies out when I heard the sound of snapping twigs behind me. I scrunched around, expecting company, when lo and behold, I found myself staring eyeball to eyeball with a big black bear."

"Oh, Aunt Aggie! What did you do?"

"I just sat still on my haunches and stared him out. I could tell he wasn't crazed because he was calm and he wasn't frothing. In a few minutes he ambled off into the bush and went about his business. Now where on earth would you see a sight like that in the city, I ask you?"

I had to admit you'd never see a bear in Toronto, except in Riverdale Zoo. And then he'd be in a cage.

She told me a lot more hair-raising stories and exciting

adventures. Then she asked about my job at the Nuthouse.

"Oh, that reminds me," I cried. "I brought you a present." I undid the clasp of my old leather grip and instantly the lovely aroma of fresh nuts escaped into the room. Aunt Aggie sniffed and wiggled her nose.

Handing her the big box with the squirrel on top, I announced proudly, "It's five pounds of our best mixture. And Aunt Susan sends her warmest regards too."

"That's mighty generous of her. Tell her I said thanks a bunch." She picked out a big cashew and placed it on her tongue. "Will you have one, Bea?" she offered.

"No, thanks. I'm sick of nuts. But I love working at the Nuthouse." Then I told her all about it. "Everybody comes there, Aunt Aggie. And some of the people are rich and famous. Aunt Milly said she even filled an order for the governor of New York State once. Imagine!"

"It sounds like a grand job," said Aunt Aggie, still savouring the same nut.

"It is. And Aunt Susan says I can work there for the Christmas rush if I stop acting the fool with Red Macpherson. Red is a boy who comes in after school to help clean up. He's loads of fun. He swears like a trooper and throws peanuts in the shell at me to get my attention. Aunt Susan gets hopping mad and says she's going to take every peanut out of our pay. But she never does."

Chuckling with delight, Aunt Aggie piled the dishes in the graniteware dishpan, covered them with rainwater and set the pan on the stove to warm up. Then she sat down again. "Tell me more," she urged. "I haven't had such a good chinwag in a month of Sundays."

418

So I told her about the excitement we'd had a few days before I left home. "You should have been there," I announced. "Aunt Milly had just rung up a big sale when a man yelled, 'Gimme all your money.' "

"Mercy," said Aunt Aggie. "What did she do?"

"She gave him all that was in the till, but Aunt Susan had just cleaned it out, so he didn't get much. Then he yelled at everybody to get out of his way and nobody would get hurt, so they all squeezed up and made a path for him and he escaped. *Then* guess what Aunt Susan did?"

"Heaven only knows!"

"She took after him with the wooden paddle she stirs the nuts with, hollering 'Stop! Thief! Police!' "

"Did he get away?"

"No, because Big Bill Brown, the Yonge Street policeman, was going by and stuck out his foot just in time to trip him and send him sprawling. When Aunt Susan got there she started beating the thief with her paddle. She got all her money back too—twenty-five dollars."

"Your Aunt Susan's mighty foolhardy. Did the man have a gun?"

"Yeah, only it was carved out of soap and covered with shoe black."

"You may have a grand job, Bea," said Aunt Aggie, "but it sounds like a dangerous one."

"Not for me," I pointed out. "Aunt Milly's the cashier. You should have heard Aunt Susan bawling her out for giving away her hard-earned money. Aunt Milly got mad and started to leave, but Aunt Susan apologized and everything got back to normal."

I went on talking all the time the water heated and Aunt Aggie did up the dishes. She wouldn't let me help. By then the big lamp was lit and the old log house was filled with mysterious shadows. Finally she said, "I could listen all night, but you must be plumb tuckered from your trip and I have to get up with the chickens."

So she lit us each a candle and blew out the oil lamp. Then she unlatched the stairwell door and led the way up the ancient, creaky stairs.

I thought I'd be bored stiff in Muskoka for a whole week. But the time whizzed by so fast it made my head spin. Aunt Aggie was swell company. And one night Jimmy Hobbs took me to a picture show at the Town Hall in nearby Elmsdale. We went in the mail truck. He said it was against government regulations but he didn't care. It was a silent picture starring Laurel and Hardy, which reminded me of my childhood. All the pictures in Toronto were talkies now.

Afterwards we went to a soda fountain and Jimmy ordered a whole brick of ice cream cut in half and served on two glass plates. Then he ordered a bottle of Whistle and two straws and we shared it with our heads together.

Another time Daisy and Horace Huxtable and Jimmy and I went to a church social in Heckley. That was the first time two boys ever fought to sit beside me. It was thrilling except that it hurt Daisy's feelings and I didn't like that. After supper there was square-dancing and I was surprised at how fast I learned the steps. Of course, Jimmy was a good teacher.

I was sorry when it was time to go home. Jimmy drove me to the train and kissed me goodbye—twice. We promised faithfully to write to each other.

Relaxing in the soft red seat on the way home I had time to think. I realized now that Aunt Aggie's life in the wilderness was full to overflowing with zest and excitement and wealth—not money, but another kind of wealth, the kind money can't buy.

And Mum had been right about a change being as good as a rest. I felt marvellous!

Aunt Milly had been right too. Boys were just like streetcars—there was always another one coming along.

14
Sad news

I was surprised to see Dad waiting for me at the West Toronto station. I hadn't expected anyone to meet me. He must have just finished his ten-hour work shift because he was carrying his lunch pail. I noticed he looked tired and a bit old. It was funny, I thought, how people seemed to change when you didn't see them for a while. Even as short a time as a week.

As soon as we were settled on the streetcar I started telling him what a good time I'd had and how much I admired his sister. He nodded, looking away from me out the window. It was then I realized that something was wrong. I felt a swift stab of fear. "What's the matter, Dad?" Suddenly I remembered Mum going around holding her heart. "Is it Mum? Is she sick?"

"No, Bea. No." He gave my hand a reassuring pat. "It's not family. But your mother thought I'd better tell you on the way home before you hear it on the street, since you were so fond of him."

"Who?"

"Well—it's young Roy-Roy."

"What about Roy-Roy?"

"He passed away yesterday, Bea."

I was so shocked I couldn't speak. I felt numb all over.

Passed away. That's what Aunt Aggie had said about Grandma and Grandpa. They'd passed away. What a strange word to use for dying. You "pass" people on the street. You "pass" an exam at school. You "pass" in a card game. But where on earth do you "pass away" to? I wondered.

"You mean he died," I said bluntly.

"Yes. He died."

Walking silently down Veeny Street, we "passed" Roy-Roy's house. There was the rocking chair he had been sitting on the day I was in too much of a hurry to visit. He had spent the last year of his life in that rickety old rocker, swaying to and fro, thinking things nobody knew. Suddenly I noticed something strange. "There's no wreath on the door," I said.

"No. He's at the Undertaking Parlour. Rachel's too broke up to have him at home."

"Won't that cost a lot of money?" I had heard that it cost as much as two hundred dollars. That's why everybody we knew got buried from home.

"It seems like Rachel's got more money than anybody surmised," Dad said. "I hear tell she's paid cash for the funeral, and the young lad's laid out in a solid oak coffin."

That brought to mind what Aunt Milly had said. "Some people dress like ragbags to fool the likes of you and me, and they could buy and sell the both of us." It's amazing how she knew things like that.

The funeral was to be held the next day. Our gang on Veeny Street had gone together and sent a huge basket of flowers. I was glad when Mum told me they had remembered to put my name on the card.

We decided to go in a group to the funeral, so we met in Aunt Ellie's kitchen. Six of the boys—Georgie, Arthur, Buster, Charlie, Alvin and Elmer—had been asked to be pallbearers.

The minute we entered the Undertaking Parlour my legs turned to jelly. Glad grabbed my elbow. She always knew when I was in danger of keeling over. I had never set foot in a funeral parlour before in my whole life. It seemed sinister and mysterious, filled with hushed voices and muffled music and the heavy scent of flowers.

A man in a black suit and dough-coloured skin met us in the front foyer. "Whom do you wish to view?" he asked in a funereal tone. View! Cold fingers traced up my spine.

"Roy-Roy the dumb . . ." Georgie stopped, embarrassed.

"Roy Butterbaugh," explained Arthur, unconsciously copying the man's weird monotone.

The undertaker pointed a pale finger. "Mr. Butterbaugh is resting in the chapel straight ahead," he said.

Mister! Resting! Roy-Roy!

We crept in a cluster down the long corridor, the sound of our footsteps smothered in the thick maroon carpet. Plush furniture and gloomy pictures lined the dark-papered walls.

The sign over the chapel archway read: *Mr. Randolph Roy Butterbaugh*. We exchanged incredulous glances.

"Randolph! What a beautiful name," whispered Ada in a soft, surprised voice.

The miniature church was overflowing with blossoms. The fragrance was almost overpowering. "I think I'm going to be sick!" gasped Ruth, pressing her hanky to her mouth.

424

Slowly we made our way down the aisle between the polished pews. Then we all gathered around the shiny wooden casket.

Roy-Roy looked incredibly handsome. He was all dressed up in a dark suit with a blue tie and white shirt. Now he didn't need a bib to catch the slobber from his lips. Now his fine-boned hands didn't flail uselessly in the air. His usually tousled brown hair was combed in neat waves back from his white brow. His features were smooth, no longer twisted with the terrible effort to speak.

"I didn't realize how handsome he was," Ruth whispered.

We all murmured in agreement.

"He was the most beautiful baby the Lord ever made." Rachel came out from a curtained-off alcove and stood beside us. She wore a plain black dress (just one), and her normally dishevelled hair was pulled back in a smooth brown bun. She barely resembled the Raggie-Rachel we all knew.

We stepped back respectfully as she approached the coffin. Leaning down towards her son, she whispered, "Sweet dreams, little one," the way a mother would whisper to her sleeping baby.

Then she sat in the front pew and patted the space beside her. "Sit here, Be-*a*-trice," she said. I was surprised. Only one other person had ever pronounced my name that way, my Grampa Cole. She motioned to the rest of our gang. "All of you sit around me. You were Roy's family," she told us. "You were his brothers and sisters."

The chapel was full when the service began.

During the eulogy Rachel's eyes never left Roy-Roy's sweet face. She had insisted that the coffin be left open, as if to keep him with her as long as possible.

"*Auf Wiedersehen*, my dear," I heard her murmur.

I thought I'd choke to death on the lump in my throat. Everyone was crying all over the chapel. I wept openly, full of regret and sorrow, wishing with all my heart that I had given my sick "brother" more of my time. Why, oh, why hadn't I stopped longer that day on the way to work?

After the service our whole gang rode with Rachel in the long black limousine to Park Lawn Cemetery. Only a stone's throw away was Grampa Cole's grave. I couldn't even look in that direction.

A canvas canopy fluttered over the open grave site. As the clergyman said "Ashes to ashes . . ." the oak casket was slowly lowered into the ground. The last thing I saw, through a blur of tears, was Rachel's huge spray of flowers tied with a wide blue ribbon. On the ribbon, in gold letters, were the words *My Beloved Son*. The pain in my throat was excruciating.

Afterwards, instead of going back to the deceased person's house, which was the custom, Rachel did the most extraordinary thing—eccentric, the grown-ups called it. Totally ignoring them, she gathered our gang around her and invited us all to Hunt's Bakery on Bloor Street. And we rode there in the long black limousine!

At the back of the bakery, entirely separate from the bake shop, was an ice-cream parlour. "Sit yourselves down." She waved us to the white enamelled tables. "I've ordered treats all round."

"I won't be able to swallow a mouthful," I whispered to Glad.

"Me neither," she answered huskily.

But when the chocolate eclairs and ice-cream sodas were set

before us our appetites miraculously returned. Rachel sat alone at a table by the wall drinking cup after cup of black tea. She watched us with a sad smile through dark-circled, glistening eyes.

The very next day she moved away and didn't take a thing with her. Neighbours said she just walked up the street and was gone. Weeks passed, and when she didn't return, workmen were sent in to clean out her cottage. "They had to use shovels," Mum said, clucking her tongue. "There wasn't a blessed thing worth salvaging."

One nice autumn evening a few weeks later Glad and I took a shortcut home from Sunnyside over the hill called the Camel's Back. As we passed the village dump, which was within sight (and smell) of our houses, we saw something red fluttering in the garbage heap. Holding our noses, we edged closer. The red thing was the remains of one of Rachel's raggedy dresses. And only a few feet away, almost buried under the trash, were the broken pieces of Roy-Roy's old rocking chair.

We broke into a run, the tears coursing down our cheeks.

15
The bravest man I know

After Roy-Roy died, life sank into the doldrums.

Then one day when Winn was reading the pink *Tely* she said, "Here's something right up your alley, Bea."

"What? Let me see!" I made a grab for the paper but missed.

"Just keep your shirt on," she teased. "I might be interested myself."

I made another grab and managed to snatch it out of her hand. Scanning the first page, all I could see was bad news about the war clouds gathering over Europe. Mum and Dad argued almost continually about that subject. Mum was sure another war was brewing, but Dad stubbornly insisted that the Great War, the one he'd fought in, had been the war to end all wars. "Besides," he declared to support his argument, "Mr. Chamberlain and Adolf Hitler have just signed a peace pact."

"Hmph!" Mum snorted. "It's probably not worth the paper it's written on." Sometimes they would wrangle like that for hours.

"For pete's sake, Bea, open your peepers." Winn jabbed a broken fingernail at a paragraph near the bottom of the page that read:

Do you know a real live hero? Do you have a true story of valour to relate? If so, send it to our Story Editor in care of the Toronto Telegram, *Bay and Melinda Streets. Your essay must not exceed two thousand words and must begin with the sentence: "The bravest man I know . . ." The rest is up to you. First prize is a genuine 14-karat gold Bulova* (Bulova!) *wristwatch, men's or ladies', valued by the T. Eaton Co. at $40.00 retail. Second prize is a crisp new ten-dollar bill, and five one-dollar bills will be awarded as consolation prizes. The decision of the judges is final. Good luck!*

"Gee, thanks, Winn. I might have missed my chance."

I got the writing tablet and a pencil stub from a sideboard drawer and asked Dad to sharpen it with his penknife. I had decided to compose my story in pencil and recopy it in ink.

"Don't start that until the dishes are done," Mum said to me.

"I'll do them later," I promised. "Unless someone else will do them for me," I suggested hopefully.

Willa turned on me, disgusted. "Why don't you grow up? You've been saying that since you were ten years old. You're almost sixteen now and you're just as irresponsible as ever."

"She is not," objected Billy. He was always on my side.

"She is so," piped up Jakey. He always took the side opposite to Billy.

"You go ahead, Bea," Winn said obligingly. "I'll take your turn at the sink tonight since it was all my idea."

"She gets away with murder!" muttered a disgruntled Arthur.

"You should talk," I snapped back. "Stupid boys never do anything."

"Oh, ya? Who do you think invented the telephone?"

"Not you, that's for sure."

"Probably *Mrs*. Bell," Willa said dryly.

"The next one that says a word goes to bed," growled Dad.

Winn leaned in from the kitchen and made a zipping motion on her lips with soapy fingers. We all grinned. Then Dad went into the front room and snapped on the radio. He'd been awfully surly lately, so we all shut up and went about our business.

Sitting across the dining room table from Arthur, I was soon lost in thought. "The bravest man I know . . ." Grampa Cole was the first person to come to mind. He had saved countless lives from the Grenadier Pond without a thought for his own skin. But he was dead now, and the beginning sentence was definitely present tense.

I knew Dad had been a brave soldier during the Great War. He had a medal to prove it. But he hadn't done anything exactly heroic. Then there was Andy Beasley, the fireman who lived next door. He risked his life regularly and didn't even get paid for it because the Swansea Fire Department was manned by volunteers. Whenever the fire siren wailed at the top of Veeny Street we would hear Andy, through the thin wall that separated our houses, pounding down the stairs and out the door. It was very exciting and in summertime we'd all chase after him to see the fire. But still Andy wasn't my idea of a hero.

Suddenly, like a bolt out of the blue, I got an inspiration. My pencil began to fly across the page. Back and forth it went as if it travelled of its own accord.

When I was finished I copied the essay in ink, over and over again until I was convinced it was a flawless masterpiece of neatness and brilliance. I read it one last time and sighed with satisfaction.

Arthur glanced up. "Let's see it," he said.

"No!" I folded it quickly. "Read it in the paper."

"Fat chance!"

Ignoring his insult, I cut open a brown paper bag and made a big flat envelope. Slipping my precious manuscript inside, I glued it shut before anybody else could ask to see it. I addressed it in big block letters and Winn gave me stamps.

"Dad?" He had turned off the radio and was scowling at page one of the newspaper. I think he was afraid Mum might be right about the war. "What is it?" he asked.

"Will you post this on your way to work tomorrow?"

"Leave it under the sugar bowl," he said. Then he headed upstairs, saying he was all in.

That night, propped up on my pillow between Winn and Willa so I could breathe, I touched Winn's shoulder to see if she was still awake. If she wasn't, nothing short of a good wallop would disturb her. "Winn!" I whispered.

"Hmmm," came her drowsy reply.

"When I win the Bulova watch will you buy it off me for twenty dollars?"

"Don't you mean *if*?" put in Willa. I thought she was asleep.

"No, I mean when." I had never been so sure of anything in my whole life.

"It's a deal, kiddo," agreed Winn sleepily. Then she reached over her shoulder and gave me a limp handshake to seal the bargain.

The reason I needed the money more than the watch was because I'd already spent every cent I'd earned at Aunt Susan's store. I'd bought all my textbooks for third form, two new blouses, flesh-coloured celanese step-ins, a garter belt and three pairs of real silk stockings. Mum had bought me the saddle shoes I wanted, but I still needed a new fall coat.

With a self-satisfied sigh I finally fell asleep sitting up.

16
The winner!

Waiting for the day the winner would be announced seemed like an eternity. Then the miracle happened. There it was—my story!—on the second page of the pink *Tely*. Above it, a paragraph read:

> *Gold Watch Winner . . . The first prize of a genuine 14-karat gold Bulova watch, valued by the T. Eaton Company at $40.00, will be awarded to Miss Beatrice Myrtle Thomson of Swansea. Miss Thomson won for her unique and heartwarming story entitled: "The Bravest Man I Know Is a Woman." Congratulations, Miss Thomson, and best wishes for a successful writing career.*

The story took up half the page. I was flushed and speechless (for once) with victory. Dad was flabbergasted that I had chosen his sister, Aunt Aggie, as my hero. Mum was proud as punch of me. "I hope L.M. Montgomery sees it," she cried, rubbing her hands together gleefully.

Mum had to go with me to the *Telegram* office to claim my prize because I was under-age. I was the youngest contestant, they said. Mum couldn't get over that.

When we were outside on the street again, with the gold Bulova gleaming on my wrist, she said, "Let's celebrate, Booky. Just you and me."

So she took me to Loew's Theatre to see Nelson Eddy and Jeanette MacDonald in *Sweethearts*, and that was the end of Deanna Durbin. Oh, I still liked her a lot, but she wasn't my idol anymore. Now I had two idols, and the way they sang love songs to each other would tear your heart out by the roots.

Winn let me keep the watch for a while so I could show it off at school. Willa didn't say a word.

At school my popularity soared. Georgie and Lorne, who were both in fifth form now, started hanging around me as if I were a celebrity.

Sitting on the cafeteria bench eating lunch, Glad said, "Now you don't need to feel bad about your name not being on our Deanna Durbin picture. Winning a story contest is a lot more important anyway."

"I know," I agreed loftily. "Let's disband the Three Smart Girls Club. It seems so juvenile now."

"You're right, Bea," Ruth agreed. "At this stage in life we have more important things to do." Ruth had been extra busy lately practicing for her piano recital at the Conservatory of Music.

At the far end of the table Gloria was sitting alone eating her fresh fruit salad. That's the kind of stuff she brought in her lunch every day. Imagine! "What's it like to be famous, Bea?" she called out, sort of sarcastically. She hadn't spoken to me for months.

"Marvellous! Simply marvellous!" I gloated.

"Oh, wow!" exclaimed Wanda. For once I thought her favourite word was suitable.

Mr. Ransom, our English teacher, read the story aloud to the class. He pointed out only two errors, which was pretty good for him.

For a whole week I basked in the warmth of my glory. I couldn't talk about anything else. Every time whoever I was with changed the subject I promptly changed it back again. Pretty soon I noticed that I was alone a lot. Glad was about the only friend I had left.

"I've decided to lengthen my story into a book and rename it 'Woman of the Wilderness,' " I confided to her one frosty fall day when the air was filled with the smell of burning leaves.

"Well, when you do, don't tell me about it," she snapped. "I can't stand any more of your bragging."

"Jealousy will get you nowhere," I snapped back as we parted and went in opposite directions.

But even Glad's turning traitor didn't dampen my spirits for long. Now that I was a person of letters, I decided I needed some new duds to spruce myself up. So that night I sold my watch to Winn for the twenty dollars she'd promised me.

On Saturday I went downtown by myself, since nobody would go with me, and bought the new fall coat I had my heart set on. It was pure wool, royal blue, with a wide leather belt. It cost $16.95. I had $3.05 left over, so I bought a hat to match, with a turned up brim. The saleslady put my old coat in the Eaton's box and I wore the new one home. I felt like a million in it.

Sauntering down Durie Street, I hoped I'd run into somebody I knew. I stopped at Aunt Milly's but she wasn't home.

Disappointed, I looked around for someone, anyone, to show off to. Only the Canada Bread man came in sight. "Hi, Pete!" I waved at him gaily. When I was a little kid I used to holler at him every day, "Canada Bread is full of lead! The more you eat, the quicker you're dead!" But I'd outgrown that childishness long ago.

"You're looking mighty spiffy, Bea!" he called back above the clatter of old Barney's hooves.

As the bread wagon passed by I saw two little boys riding on the back step. Suddenly the kid in me jumped out and I yelled at the top of my lungs, "Hookey on behind!" The bread man didn't hear me but the boys did and they stuck their tongues out about a mile. That made me laugh all the way home. But I didn't meet another living soul. What a letdown.

When I stepped into the kitchen Mum stopped stirring the huge kettle of delicious-smelling chili sauce she had simmering on the stove. Looking me up and down, she asked suspiciously, "Where did you get those glad rags?"

The tone of her voice took the wind out of my sails. "I sold my watch to Winn for twenty dollars," I said.

"Well, that's scandalous!" Mum banged the pot lid down with a puff of steam. "It's plain highway robbery. That Bulova was worth twice that much, and what's more, Winn knows it. Wait till I see that girl. I'll give her a piece of my mind." She did too, but Winn and I stuck to our bargain.

Dad had sent several copies of the newspaper up to Aunt Aggie. Her letter of congratulations almost made me cry.

You've made me the proudest woman in Muskoka County, she wrote glowingly. *And just think, when you're a little old lady and I'm long since pushing up daisies, you'll look at that beautiful Bulova and remember your Aunt Aggie. I wish your grandpa could have read your story. The old curmudgeon used to say I was only good for digging potatoes. I guess he was disappointed in me for not getting married and having children. But if I had, I couldn't have become the "bravest man you know," now could I?*

But Aunt Aggie was alone in her admiration of me. Ruthie Vaughan told everybody I was absolutely obnoxious. Ada-May called me insufferable. Even Glad had finally deserted me for a new friend. But worst of all, I heard through the grapevine that Lorne Huntley said I was an agonizing bore. And Georgie Dunn, the stupid drip, was going around with goofy old Wanda again.

Then Sylvia Lamont, a new girl in third form who hadn't had time to get sick of me yet, told me something that nearly made me die of envy. "I heard that Gloria Carlyle and Lorne Huntley went to the Silver Slipper last Saturday night," she said.

The Silver Slipper was a dance hall built on the side of the South Kingsway hill. It was shaped like a lady's high-heeled shoe. At night its unique shape was outlined with electric lights that glittered through the trees.

"I don't believe it," I snorted. "Who said?"

"Gloria."

"She'd say anything for attention," I muttered.

But I believed it, all right, because Lorne had passed me on the school staircase between periods and had purposely looked the other way. With a heavy heart I remembered that he had half promised, that soft spring night at the Pally, that he would take me to the Slipper someday.

There was nothing left for me to do but throw myself into my work and show them all. So I began to write feverishly, sending stories off pell-mell in all directions. Back came the rejections thick and fast. Only one editor had the decency to write me a letter. It was from Liberty magazine.

Dear Miss Thomson,

I have read your stories with considerable interest. They are very good for one so young. (I had casually mentioned my age, hoping the editor would think I was a teenage genius like Deanna Durbin.) *However, I regret that your contributions do not meet the high standards of* Liberty.

May I suggest, Miss Thomson, that you further your education before attempting to write professionally? Also, I urge you to acquire a typewriter (a typewriter!) *since handwritten material is seldom read by editors. I hope this advice will be helpful to you and I wish to thank you for sending us your lovely essays. Keep writing and good luck!*

Sincerely,

Joan M. Smith, Editor

With a huge sigh I abandoned my writing career forever.

17
Ostracized

Gloria was having a Hallowe'en party on her sixteenth birthday and she didn't invite me.

"Isn't that just like a witch to be born on Hallowe'en?" I snorted to Glad, who was grudgingly speaking to me again.

If I thought she'd laugh at my joke I had another think coming. She didn't react at all. Right away I got suspicious. "Are you going?" I asked.

"Well—I've been invited," she hedged, not looking me in the eye.

"Yeah, but are you going?"

"I think so," she admitted hesitantly.

"Well!" I huffed indignantly. "With friends like you, who needs enemies!" Then I wheeled around and darted across Jane Street, nearly getting run over by a horse. But actually my sarcasm was just a smoke screen. Inside, my heart was as heavy as lead.

Gradually I found out that not only was "bunch" going, but all our gang from Veeny Street too! Even Arthur.

"I thought you didn't like Gloria," I said reproachfully.

"I don't particularly, but Marjorie Tabbs will be there."

"What about Georgie? Is he going?"

"Of course, stupid. He's taking Wanda."

I nearly choked on the next question. "How about Lorne?"

"Well, what do you think? Gloria's his girlfriend."

I went upstairs, my nose and eyes dripping, and spilled it all out in my diary. I called everybody filthy names and used as many swear words as I could think of. Then I locked it up and hid the key in the knothole in the baseboard.

A couple of days before Hallowe'en I happened to hear Winn and Willa discussing a come-as-you-are party.

"We'd better ask Mum before we make any plans," Willa said. She knew Mum better than Winn did. Mum didn't like unexpected company.

But this time she was surprisingly easy to persuade. "Well, glory be, that sounds like fun," she said. "I don't mind as long as you two are willing to foot the bill."

"Oh, that's no problem, Cousin Fran," Winn assured her. "The boys bring the fruit and pop and the girls make the sandwiches, so it's no hardship for anybody."

Mum thought that was a wonderful arrangement. "I'll bake some banana cupcakes," she volunteered.

Willa sat right down at the dining room table and made out a list. Then Winn phoned everybody and told them what to bring and that it was a "come as you are" party.

"There's fifteen coming altogether, Cousin Fran. Is that okey-doke?"

"Land sakes, that'll be a houseful. But I guess we can manage," Mum agreed.

All this time I'd been sitting on the leather rocking chair in the front room pretending to read *Jane of Lantern Hill*. I had read it four times already so it didn't take much concentration.

I glanced up. Winn and Willa had their heads together going over the list.

"How many boys are coming?" I asked casually.

"Eight. But they're not boys, kiddo, they're men. Archie Bones is the youngest and he's nineteen."

"How many girls?" I tried to sound indifferent.

"Seven, counting Willa and me. Why?"

"Well . . . if I stayed it would make it even."

"I thought you'd be with your own gang, or bunch, or whatever you call them," Willa said.

The sudden lump that came up in my throat made it hard for me to answer. "They're all going to Gloria Carlyle's birthday party and I wasn't invited," I confessed.

"It serves you right!" Arthur was always butting in where he had no business. "The way you've been boasting since you won that darn contest would make a person puke."

Willa shot him a withering glance for using such a disgusting word. Then she said to me, "You have been particularly obnoxious lately, Bea. It's no wonder you've been ostracized by your friends."

"I know," I agreed ruefully. "Even Glad is still mad. She's going to Gloria's party too."

Suddenly Winn loomed over me, hands on hips, and peered at me through narrowed eyes. "Do you think it would be humanly possible for you to go through one whole night without mentioning that contest even once?"

"Oh, Winn, I promise. I intend never to mention it again as long as I live."

I knew I'd won when Willa said, "Well, you'd better ask Mum first."

Mum was crying because she was chopping onions for green tomato pickles. "They're too old a crowd for you, Bea." She sniffed and wiped her eyes on her apron. "You should stick to friends your own age."

"You'll make a fool of yourself," predicted Arthur with a smirk. "You're just a kid."

"I won't—I'm not—oh, please, Mum, say it's okay."

"Well, if you'll help me tidy the house without complaints I'll think about it," she said, scraping the onion off the board into the big preserving kettle.

I knew that was as good as yes and I was ecstatic. This would be a real adult party. One that would make Gloria's seem like kid stuff.

The day of the party I worked like a trojan. My jobs were to wash the kitchen and bathroom floors. But no sooner had I finished than Mum got down on her hands and knees and did them all over again to make sure they were spotless. Then she went around holding her heart.

"It's your own fault if your heart hurts, Mum. Nothing ever suits you," I said crabbily.

"I know." She sat down heavily, fanning herself by flapping her apron up and down.

I felt bad and told her I was sorry.

Next I helped Billy get dressed for shellying-out. It was his first experience, since he'd been sick the two years before, so he was beside himself with excitement. I made him into the cutest pirate with a black eyepatch and charcoal moustache. Jakey wore an old sheet with eyeholes cut in it, so he could scare the daylights out of his little girl friends.

By seven-thirty everything was ready.

Winn came downstairs all gussied up, looking like she'd just stepped out of a band-box. She had tons of rouge and lipstick on.

"I thought this was a 'come as you are' party," I said. "You had on your old housedress and Mum's dust cap when you were phoning."

"Soooo, who's going to know if you don't squeal?"

I raced upstairs, painted my face and put on Willa's peach blouse with my grey flannel skirt. If only I had spectator pumps, I thought, I'd look five years older. Willa frowned when she saw me. "I hope you don't mind, Willa." I crossed my arms to hide the scorched sleeve.

"Oh, I guess not. It's yours now anyway. But if I ever catch you sneaking my clothes again I'll wring your skinny neck."

At last the guests started to arrive. Everybody must have been wearing their Sunday best when Winn phoned because that's what they were all decked out in.

On went the radio and down went the lights. Luigi Romanelli's band was playing "Oh, Johnny!" and everybody began to dance. I felt a bit shy at first, so I sat in the corner by the Quebec heater. Suddenly a boy (a man—he looked at least twenty-one) took my hand and pulled me to my feet. "Hi, Doll, my name's Bucky White. Wanna dance?"

Bucky White was the spitting image of Tyrone Power. My knees wobbled as he put his arm around my waist. But he was such a smooth dancer that I fell right into step. When the music stopped, he kept his arm around me as if he didn't want to change partners.

"Is that your real name—Bucky?" I asked as we began swaying to the tune of "Now's the Time to Fall in Love."

"Nah. My old lady nicknamed me that when I was a kid and it stuck." He grinned down at me engagingly. "Rupert's my real name. How's that for a monicker?"

"Rupert's a gorgeous name," I said. "My name's Beatrice but my mother calls me Booky. How's that for a monicker?"

"Hey, I think I like that. Booky and Bucky. We should make a great team."

Oh, wow! I thought to myself.

I was having the time of my life. All the men asked me to dance, and halfway through nearly every dance Bucky cut in and took me back again.

Before we knew it a couple of hours had rolled romantically by. We were all stepping lively to a brand new song called "A-Tisket A-Tasket" when Jakey and Billy came bursting into the front door with their loaded Eaton's bags. They dumped their loot on the dining room table, which had been shoved into a corner to make room for dancing. Then, before Mum could stop them, they ran straight out again.

"Greedy little monsters," laughed Winn, popping a jelly baby into her mouth. We all followed suit, helping ourselves as we danced by the table. Pretty soon what had been a big pile was reduced to a few miserable scraps.

It was about nine-thirty when Jakey and Billy straggled in with their second bagful. It wasn't nearly as full as their first. When they saw what had happened to their precious hoard they both flew into a furious rage.

"Grey-eyed greedy guts!" screamed Jakey, his black eyes flashing.

"Greedy guts!" echoed tired little Billy, the tears streaming down his face and washing off his moustache.

Mum came in from the kitchen to see what the fuss was about, and when she saw what we'd done she swept us all with a scathing look, her eyes flashing just like Jakey's.

"Never you mind," she began, wiping their tears with her apron. "I'll fix the lot of them. I'll save the best of the party food for you two, and you can share it in the morning. Now off you go to bed. You look like little lost urchins!"

Then she got her biggest cake tin and filled it to the brim with our most delectable food. But there was plenty left, and we still had a wonderful time. We danced and drank pop and stuffed ourselves right up until midnight. And I never missed a single dance!

As always, Winn was the life of the party, but Willa was the belle of the ball. Wesley Armstrong had brought a friend by the name of Clifford Best and he and Willa hit it right off. Poor Wesley, he was absolutely desolate. He slipped away early and Willa didn't even notice.

When Arthur came home from Gloria's party we were having our last dance. "Did you have fun?" I called over Bucky's broad shoulder.

"Drop dead!" Arthur snarled and he headed straight upstairs.

Later, when Glad and I made up again, she told me Marjorie Tabbs had snubbed Arthur all night and he'd had to settle for Ada.

The next night, right after supper, Billy hopped down from the table, grabbed his grubby Eaton's bag off the chair and headed for the door.

"Whoa there, young fella!" Dad caught him by the tail of his sweater. "Where are you off to?"

"Shellying-out, o'course," Billy said with a grin.

"Dummy!" sneered Jakey, twirling his finger above his head to show how dizzy Billy was. "Hallowe'en's over, stoopid! Don't you know nothing?"

Poor Billy was crestfallen and embarrassed. Tears spurting from his eyes, he high-tailed it down to the cellar to hide in the coal bin, our laughter echoing after him.

* * *

The holiday season that year was both happy and sad. Christmas was a madhouse at the Nuthouse, but it was worth it because I could afford to buy everybody a swell present. I bought Dad a set of Westinghouse tubes for the radio, and Mum a picture of a rose-covered cottage in a gold frame. Superimposed on it was her favourite poem: "It takes a heap of livin' to make a house a home." They were both thrilled.

New Year's Day was nice too. We were all invited to Uncle Charlie's and Aunt Myrtle's for a chicken dinner. Then a week later came the sad part.

Winn had to move away. She'd been promoted to head cashier in a new Loblaw's Groceteria in Birchcliff. Birchcliff was at the opposite end of the city from Swansea, so she had to find another place to live.

She had tears in her eyes when she told us. "My grandma used to say, 'Be careful what you wish for, for you might get it.' Now I know what she meant," she lamented, carefully packing her things.

"I'm sorry you have to go, Winn," I said sincerely. I didn't tell her I'd be happy to get my half of the bed back. It would be heavenly to be able to roll over again.

We all loved Winn. Jakey even got into a fist fight with one of his chums because the boy said Winn wasn't really his sister and Jakey swore she was. He was really proud of the black eye he got to prove it too.

Billy cried when she kissed him goodbye, so she gave him a nickel to make him stop. He had found out recently what money was for.

Dolefully we stood together at the front room window watching Winn trudging up the street with her grip. She turned and waved and we all waved back, banging on the window. Then she bent her head against the cold north wind, and hanging onto her hat with her free hand, disappeared up Veeny Street in a swirl of snow.

It was strange, I thought as I wandered around the house after she left, how one person's leaving could make a place seem so empty.

18
Caught in the act

One bleak winter evening I was feeling especially lonely for
Winn. I had found that sometimes when I was upset about
something it helped to tell it to my diary. It had become like a
true friend. It was even more trustworthy than Glad, since it
couldn't talk and tell my secrets. The little book was already
crammed full and I'd had to add a sheaf of pages at the end.

I went upstairs and felt for the key in the knothole. It wasn't
there! Panic-stricken, I dashed downstairs. "Hey!" I yelled.
"Who stole the key to my diary?"

"Hay's for horses," grunted Arthur.

"Who'd want to steal it, for pity's sake?" muttered Willa.
She'd been kind of crabby ever since Winn left.

"Hold your tong!" Dad barked. "We're trying to listen to a
good play about the war of 1812."

"You probably mislaid it, Bea." Mum didn't look up from the
sock she was darning, stretched over a light bulb.

"I didn't mislay it! I always keep it in—In a special place. It's
full of my private thoughts and whoever stole it is a criminal.
There's a law against invasion of privacy, you know!"

"Get upstairs and look for it. You'll find it right where you left it." Dad gave me a fierce glare. If looks could kill I'd be dead I thought as I stomped back up the stairs.

At the top of the staircase I happened to notice the sound of exaggerated snoring coming from the boys' room. Jakey had been sent to bed early without his supper for breaking a window in the school basement with his slingshot.

When I heard the phony snore I said to myself, "Aha!" Creeping into the room, I stood as still as a statue beside Jakey's bed. Billy was asleep beside him, his head under the bedclothes. Jakey's eyes were squeezed shut and he let out another loud snore. Then he gradually opened one eye a crack. When he saw me standing there he nearly jumped out of his skin. I snarled viciously, "Jakey! You brat! Where's my key?"

His dark eyes were wide open now, shining brazenly in the light from the hallway. He didn't answer, so I grabbed him by the nightshirt and yanked him to a sitting position. "If you don't fess up"—my lips were just inches from his nose—"I'll pinch you black and blue."

He felt under his flat pillow and came up with the little gold key. I snatched it out of his hand. "How dare you invade my privacy? Don't you know you could go to jail for that?"

I could tell by the impudent look on his face that he didn't believe a word of it. Now that he was a husky ten-year-old he wasn't too easily scared. He wasn't even afraid of Dad anymore. Only yesterday Dad had chased him, hell bent for leather, down the yard waving a gad in his hand. Jakey had leaped like a jackrabbit to the top of the board fence and from there to the woodshed roof. Dancing around the flat roof like a whirling dervish, he had looked so comical that even Dad had to laugh, so he got away scot-free.

"How much of my diary did you read?" I demanded ferociously, tightening my grip on the neck of his nightshirt until he started to gag. "Tell me or I'll go downstairs this minute and call the police."

"I read it all!" he choked, still defiant, but looking a bit scared now. "And if you let go my nightshirt, Bea, I'll tell you something good."

"Good! What could a sneak thief say that's good?"

"Your diary was just like reading a real book, Bea."

That was the last thing I expected to hear, and it took the wind right out of my sails. So Jakey rushed on. "I liked it even better than *The Western Boy* by Horatio Alger and you know how famous he is."

Such a huge compliment made me suspicious again. "What were you doing in our room anyway?" I asked, still using a menacing voice, but loosening my hold on his nightshirt.

"I was just hollering out the window at Wally. He wanted to know why I couldn't come out and play dibs. Then the knothole popped out all by itself, so I got curious and stuck my finger in just for fun. Then I found the key so I thought I might as well hunt up your diary. But I didn't intend to read it all, Bea, honest. Only once I started I couldn't stop. It's a swell story, Bea. I bet you could make it into a book."

By this time I was completely disarmed. I let go his nightshirt and he fell back onto the pillow. "I'm sorry, Bea," he said.

I'd never heard Jakey apologize before. At least not to me. And his big brown eyes shone with sincerity.

"You mean it, Jakey?"

"About being sorry?"

"No. About my diary being more interesting than *The Western Boy*."

"Sure. The part about Aunt Susan chasing the thief down Yonge Street made me laugh my head off."

This tickled me pink and I had to smile. "Okay, I believe you. But Jakey, I want you to promise me something."

"What?"

"That you won't tell any of your friends about it, okay? They're my private thoughts and I don't want them spread all over Swansea."

"Okay, I promise." Jakey crossed his heart. Then he slid his hand under his pillow again and pulled out my diary!

"Jakey! You brat! You've got more nerve than a canal horse."

He laughed and said, "Night, Bea!"

"Night, Jakey." I gave him a pretend punch on the chin.

"Don't let the bedbugs bite!" chirped a squeaky voice from under the covers.

"Billy! How long have you been awake?" I demanded.

"You just woke me up now," he answered plaintively.

"Go to sleep, both of you," I said and shut the door.

When I was ready for bed, I opened my diary. But instead of writing in it, I started to read it from page one, November 9, 1937.

Jakey was right! It was a swell story. It made me laugh and it made me cry. I decided then and there I *was* going to be a writer, no matter what.

19
Easter

Easter Sunday fell on April 9 that year. The day was as warm as toast, so right after church Glad and Ruth and Ada and I went down to the boardwalk to show off our new spectator pumps. When I got home a few hours later a heavenly aroma was filling the kitchen.

"Mmmm. What's for supper, Mum?" Jakey came into the kitchen at the same time I did.

"Roast pork, butter fries and tapioca pudding. How does that suit Your Majesty?" Turning towards him, she let out a shriek. "In heaven's name, child, what have you done to yourself?"

Jakey's saucy face was littered with red-dotted bits of toilet paper. "I needed a shave," he said solemnly.

"Have you taken leave of your senses?" Mum scolded. "You're only ten years old. Arthur only shaves once a week and he's eighteen."

"Is that why the girls call you 'Peaches,' Arthur?" I snickered.

"Get lost, Bea," he snapped.

"Did you use your father's straight razor?" demanded Mum,

wetting the flannel and wiping the blood none too gently off Jakey's face.

"Sure," he admitted, not even flinching as she dabbed each cut with stinging peroxide. "And I sharpened it on his strop too. I'd better tell him to be careful."

"You'd better keep your mouth shut if you know what's good for you," warned Arthur.

I could tell by the weird look on his face he was remembering the worst beating he ever got with the razor-strop. It was the day he had set the toilet paper on fire. Mum had gone to the dentist's to get a gumboil lanced and the dentist had just injected the novocaine when Mum got a "flash" of disaster. Leaping out of the chair, she ran all the way home with the white bib still around her neck and raced upstairs just in time to douse the flaming bathroom curtains. Dad had stropped Arthur so hard he cried all night and had to sit on a pillow for a week. Mum and Dad had had a terrible row about that. And Dad never hit Arthur again.

"Aww," Jakey answered, smart-alecky, "Dad don't strop Billy nor me."

That was true. Mum said he was getting soft in his old age, but personally I think he'd learned his lesson.

Just then Billy came up from the cellar sniffing the air. "You're the best cooker in the whole world, Mum," he said.

"Oh, pshaw, I bet you say that to all the girls," teased Mum, pinching his nose.

Then she called Willa to lay the table in the dining room, because Easter was a special day. Her good mood was contagious and there was a happy feeling in the house. "Too bad Winn isn't here," she said to no one in particular.

454

Just then Dad came in the back door. He'd been across the road talking to Gladie's father when we came home. Ignoring everybody, including Jakey, he went right into the front room and switched on the radio. When the tubes warmed up we could hear the faint chiming of a clock.

"That's Big Ben from London," Dad said loud enough for all of us to hear. He recognized the sound because he had stood under the famous clock to have his picture taken during the Great War.

We all paused to listen, sort of reverently. Then Big Ben stopped bonging and some faraway voices started chanting, "Stop Hitler! Stop Hitler! Stop Hitler!" Then another station floated in and drowned out the fearful chant with the lilting tune, "In your Easter bonnet . . ."

Mum stood in the doorway between the kitchen and the dining room bunching up her apron in nervous fingers. "I knew it!" she cried. "There's another war coming. Oh, how I wish you were younger, Arthur."

Arthur acted as if he didn't even hear her. "If England goes to war with Germany, Dad, will Canada go too?" he asked eagerly.

This time Dad didn't even try to deny the likelihood of another war. "There's no doubt about it." He nodded gravely. "If it comes to that it'll be our bounden duty to fight for king and country. And that's the long and short of it, Arthur."

"I don't want to hear another word!" Mum went back to the stove and started banging pots and pans.

"If men had the sense of fishing worms," she ranted, "there wouldn't be any wars."

Suddenly the Easter spirit had been snuffed out like a candle. Then, just as suddenly, the front door flew open.

"Hello the house!" came a cheerful greeting. It was Winn, looking fresh as a daisy in her new Easter rig-out.

"Winn! Winn!" we all cried in unison. We hadn't seen hide nor hair of her since New Year's. And her timely visit was like the sun breaking through on a cloudy day.

"Well, for land's sake, speak of the devil!" Mum wiped her hands on her apron and gave our favourite cousin a big bear-hug. "We've got lots to eat, Winn, so why don't you take off your hat and stay a while?"

"Why don't you stay all night, Winn? I'll lend you my side of the bed," I volunteered happily.

"Yeah, Winn, stay! Stay! Stay!" begged Billy and Jakey.

Winn looked herself up and down. "Well, by cracky"—she always knew all the latest slang—"I don't know what I've got . . . but whatever it is I should bottle it and make a fortune."

Laughing, she took off her hat and coat and hung them on the hall tree. Then she handed Billy and Jakey each a purple box with a yellow chicken pictured on it. Inside, nested in a bed of green shredded cellophane, was a huge Laura Secord Easter egg, the kind with the creamy filling and the yellow yolk in the middle.

They squealed their thanks and Mum cried, "Now don't you two eat a bite before supper. I haven't been slaving all day over a hot stove just to have you turn your noses up."

"Oh, don't worry, Mum," Jakey said, testing the heft of the egg in his hand. "I'm so hungry I could eat a horse."

"Me too!" echoed Billy. For once they agreed on something.

Willa hadn't been able to get a word in edgewise, but she had a smile on her face as she set another place at the table.

Winn and Willa were best friends, as well as cousins, just like Glad and me.

Billy begged to sit beside Winn at the table, so just for fun (trust Winn to play a joke on somebody) she switched his china dinner plate for a glass one. We all knew why. Billy had a bad habit of hiding his crusts under the rim of his plate, and try as she might, Mum hadn't been able to break him of it.

He was so chirpy with excitement, perched on the telephone book beside Winn, that he didn't even notice the transparent plate until the bread crusts tucked around the edge showed right through. Realizing he'd been tricked, he threw a tantrum right at the table. Dad didn't even bat an eye. He sure had changed! Either that or his mind was far away—somewhere in France, maybe, about twenty-two years ago.

"Oh, for pity's sake, child, stop your caterwauling. You're enough to try the patience of a saint." Mum jumped up and whisked the plate, crusts and all, off the table and replaced it with an ordinary one.

When Billy settled down again Winn said, "I was just pulling your leg, Billy-bo-bingo. Give us a kiss to make up."

Billy was pouting, trying to stay mad, but in spite of himself he started to giggle. Then he puckered his lips and lifted his face for her kiss. His childish laughter was infectious and pretty soon we all joined in.

And the war clouds that had seeped into our house through the airwaves were blown away by Easter joy.

20
Dear Diary

Dear Diary,

So much happened in Toronto today that I thought I'd better record it for posterity. (I wonder if anybody will read these words after I'm dead? Mum says when she has a creepy feeling like that it's as if someone just walked over her grave.) Anyway, the biggest event of the day was the visit of King George and Queen Elizabeth to our fair city. The only disappointment was that they didn't bring the little princesses with them.

Glad and Ada and I went down to the Exhibition Grounds to see them. Ruth couldn't come because her little brother, Wally, has scarlet fever and they've got a red quarantine sign tacked on their front door. Mum says they won't be allowed to poke their noses out for at least three weeks. I sure hope we don't get it!

The three of us managed to find a spot that wasn't too crowded, and we sat on our coats and waited for ages. Mum would have had a fit if she'd seen me sitting on my new spring coat. But it was worth it.

KING ABDICATES, YORK SUCCEEDS
All British Dominions Give Assent

BRITISH EMPIRE'S NEW SOVEREIGNS

EDWARD, ABDICATING SAYS 'CAN NO LONGER DISCHARGE HEAVY TASK'

'I AM GOING TO MARRY MRS. SIMPSON, I AM PREPARED TO GO' H. R. IS QUOTED

HOME AND SPORT EDITION

'EVERYTHING INDICATES MARRIAGE IS THE IDEA' SAYS CANNES' FRIEND

SAY KING WILL BE PLAIN MR. WINDSOR

AIR OF MYSTERY

AWESOME HUSH FILLS HOUSE AS KING RENOUNCES THRONE

NEW KING'S TITLE TO BE 'ALBERT I'

SCENE IS DRAMATIC

DOCTOR, WRITERS WOUNDED AS REBELS CRASH 'PLANE

YOUNG BOB FELLER STAYS AT CLEVELAND

CANADA TO ACCEPT KING'S ABDICATION

TO CELEBRATE BIRTHDAY AS NEW KING OF ENGLAND

'PLANE LIKE EDWARD'S LEAVES FROM HENDON

DONATIONS TO STAR SANTA CLAUS FUND

TELL OF ATTACK

SACRIFICES COVETED HAT FOR SISTER IN HOSPITAL

EMPIRE STANDS UNSHAKEN SIR WILLIAM MULOCK SAYS

INDICATES EDWARD WILL LEAVE SOON

FIFTY INTERESTED IN ELECTRIC TRAIN

THE WEATHER

CONTRIBUTE TODAY

DEATH NOTICES

'COLDER TO-NIGHT' SAYS WEATHERMAN

First came the Mounties in their red uniforms, sitting straight as arrows on the backs of their black horses. Those beautiful animals are so well trained that even a couple of stray dogs nipping at their heels didn't make them miss a step.

At last came the moment we had been waiting for — Their Imperial Majesties gliding by in an open limousine. The shiny black Rolls Royce was only travelling about two miles an hour so everybody got a good look. I wonder what it's like to be on display like that? It is hard to believe that they are merely flesh-and-blood human beings like the rest of us, who eat and clean their teeth and go to the bathroom. Arthur says they don't even dress themselves or comb their own hair. But I imagine they get to go to the bathroom privately.

Anyway, the limousine was moving along so slowly that before the Mounties could do anything about it a man broke from the crowd, jumped on the running board, stuck out his hand and shouted, "Hi, King!" This upset the Mounties no end, but His Majesty didn't seem to mind a bit. He just smiled and shook the man's hand and answered politely, "I'm fine. How are you?"

I was so close I actually heard him speak. He has a gorgeous English accent and his voice sounds much nicer than it does on the radio in his Christmas message to the Empire. Also, he is much handsomer than his pictures. He has a nice suntan (it must be warmer in England than it is here) and marvellous white teeth. (Arthur says no wonder, he has his own private dentist. I don't know where he gets all his information from.)

I couldn't see the Queen too well because she was waving and bobbing her blue hat to the people on the other side. But the King happened to wave and smile directly at us and for a fleeting second his deep blue eyes met mine. It was a thrilling moment but Glad spoiled it by insisting he had been looking straight at her. Then Ada said we were both wrong, the King's attention had been riveted right on her. Honestly, dear diary, I am continually amazed at how unobservant the average person is. I guess that's because I'm gifted with an eye for detail. Born writers are noted for that.

When it was over we caught the streetcar at the Dufferin gates. It was packed solid with people all buzzing with excitement over the great event. One woman cried ecstatically, "Imagine. We have just witnessed history!" and her friend replied, also ecstatically, "Now I can die happy!"

Nearby two men started to argue. "They didn't come all the way over here for nothing," growled the tall one.

"What d'ya mean by that?" the other man, who was short and stocky and mean looking, growled right back.

Just then the streetcar gave a big lurch and the short man bumped smack into the tall one's stomach, knocking the wind out of him. Glowering down at the smaller man, he said, "I mean they come here to drum up patriotism, that's what. Next thing you know us Canucks'll be singing 'Pack Up Your Troubles in Your Old Kit Bag' again."

Then the short one stuck out his chest and declared belligerently, "Well, I for one would be proud to fight for king and country."

The tall one sneered, "Would you, now? Well, I say let

461

them damn limeys fight their own battles. I lost a brother in the last war and I ain't about to lose a son in the next one."

When the little man dared to mutter "coward" under his breath, all heck broke loose. All the men on the streetcar started yelling and punching each other, but the crowd was so thick nobody had room to fall down. Glad and Ada and I were lucky to be sitting on the circular seat at the back out of harm's way.

Suddenly the streetcar jolted to a stop and the motorman jumped out and hailed a policeman. As luck would have it, a Black Maria was parked right beside the curb. So the crowd shoved the two men who had started the ruckus out the doors and the policemen hustled them into the back of the Black Maria, jabbing them with their billies.

I've never seen anything like that happen in Toronto before. I guess that's why our city is nicknamed "Toronto the Good." Anyway, the three of us could hardly wait to get home to tell about it.

But the minute we turned down Veeny Street we knew something was wrong. Mum was running up one side of the street and Aunt Ellie was running down the other. They were both shouting at the top of their lungs, "Billy! Billy! Billy!"

Well, dear diary, my blood ran cold. Terrible visions of my little brother drowned or killed or kidnapped flashed through my mind. "What's wrong? What's happened?" the three of us yelled.

Mum screamed hysterically, "Billy's lost! He's been gone for hours. Oh, the good Lord have mercy! If only I hadn't spanked him yesterday for stealing buns off the baker's wagon. Maybe that's why he's run off."

"Call the police! Call the police!" I screeched. Then Arthur announced they already had. His face was the colour of a soda biscuit.

Aunt Ellie had to practically carry Mum over to her house to try to calm her down. Mum kept crying, "Oh, my baby! My little Billy-bo-bingo. If the dear Lord brings you back to me I'll never lay a hand on you again."

Arthur and I sat on our front stoop, panic-stricken. There was nothing we could do but pray, so I said right out loud, "God, if you bring Billy home safe and sound I'll never miss church again," and Arthur added, "Amen!"

Jakey came up the walk and sat on the bottom step. His eyes were bright with fear. "I'm not going to punch Billy anymore," he promised solemnly.

We lapsed into silence. Then about five minutes later a police car came cruising down the street and stopped in front of our house. And who should hop out, all smiles, his face smeared with chocolate, but Billy-bo-bingo.

Mum and Aunt Ellie came high-tailing it across the road and Mum swooped Billy up in her arms. First she hugged him, then she hit him, then she hugged him, then she hit him. The poor little guy was completely bewildered. "Ow, Mum! Ow, Mum! Whatcha doin' that for?" he cried.

At last Mum got hold of herself, and setting Billy down, she grabbed his chin in a tight squeeze and made him look at her. His blue eyes were as big as saucers. "Where have you been, young man?" she demanded. "I've nearly been out of my mind. Just wait till your father comes home! Where have you been? Answer me."

"Gee whiz, Mum"—Billy rubbed his bottom and stared in

confusion at the crowd gathering around him—"I just went to see the King like everybody else."

The policeman filled in the story. Billy had walked along Bloor Street all the way to Lansdowne Avenue (about eight miles from home) looking for the King. There a woman found him crying and took him to the police station.

"Why didn't you tell the police your name and address?" Arthur asked. Nobody else had even thought of that.

"'Cause if I told, I'd get found too fast and I wanted more ice cream," explained Billy. When Mum heard that it was all she could do not to smack him again.

Well, all's well that ends well, as Grampa used to say. I've got to go to sleep now. I'm dog tired. What a day!

B.M.T.

May 18, 1939

In today's pink Tely there was a full-page report of Their Majesties' visit and a beautiful picture of the Queen with the Dionne quintuplets. Apparently the Queen had especially asked to see them. In the photograph she's leaning over and smiling down at the five little angels just as proudly as if they were her own. Which they practically are since they've been made wards of the Crown.

On the next page there was a long column about the big fight on the Dufferin streetcar and the arrest of the two culprits.

Of course there wasn't a word about a little boy who was lost for hours searching for the King. If I was a reporter that's the story I would have written.

B.M.T.

21
The end of school

June came, and wonder of wonders, I passed again. Now that I had my commercial diploma I decided to hunt for a permanent job.

"I'm proud as punch of you, Bea," Mum said as she scanned my final report card, "but I still wish you had a little more education." She wanted so much for all of her children to be well educated. It had haunted her all her life that she'd never gone to high school.

"Well, Mum"—it was nearly supper time, so I got the plates down from the kitchen cabinet and slid them around the oil-cloth as if I was dealing cards—"don't forget I'll be seventeen in November. You were only fourteen when you started work at Eaton's." I set a glass full of spoons in the middle of the table. "Besides, I want some new clothes and a permanent wave. I think I'll go downtown tomorrow and fill out an application at Eaton's."

Mum's brow furrowed as she poked the carrots with a fork. "Well, if you must go to work, Eaton's is the best firm to work for." She was a dyed-in-the-wool Eatonian.

So the next day I applied for a job at Eaton's. Then, afterwards, since it was a nice warm day, I decided to go window shopping up Yonge Street. I stopped in front of Loew's Theatre to look at scenes from the picture playing there, *Lucky Night*, starring Myrna Loy and Robert Taylor.

Suddenly, from behind me, a voice that was so close it seemed to come out of my hair whispered, "Wanna buy a duck?" It was a perfect imitation of Joe Penner, the comedian. I only knew one person who could do that. I spun around and sure enough it was Lorne Huntley. "What are you doing downtown all by your lonesome?" he asked, looking as handsome as Robert Taylor himself.

"I just applied for a job at Eaton's," I answered proudly.

"How would you like to go to the pictures?" he asked, inclining his head toward the ticket box.

"No thanks, I've already seen it." The second the words left my mouth I could have bitten my tongue off. Imagine missing a chance to go to the pictures with Robert Taylor . . . I mean Lorne Huntley.

But he surprised me by saying, "Okay, how about George Brent and Bette Davis? They're at the Tivoli in *Dark Victory*."

So off we went, hand in hand, around the corner to the Tivoli. The show was marvellous, but the newsreel—*The Eyes and Ears of the World*—was really scary. It showed Adolf Hitler reviewing his troops, children in England being taught how to use gas masks, fighting on the borders of Albania (wherever that is), and dead soldiers lying on the ground.

"I hope we get into the war soon," whispered Lorne. Our heads were almost touching because he had his arm across the back of my seat. "I'm going to be an air gunner." An air gunner! The very words sent shivers up my spine.

But once outside in the sunlight again I soon forgot the bad news because Lorne asked me to have supper with him at a fancy restaurant called Muirhead's. I was so unused to restaurants that I didn't know what to do. So Lorne ordered for both of us. "Cordon Bleu for two," he told the waitress. I'd never even heard of it before.

We didn't talk much, but whenever I glanced up, Lorne was watching me. His grey eyes were twinkling, and the way his long dimples creased his cheeks made him look the spittin' image of Gary Cooper. I couldn't for the life of me figure out what a homely girl like me was doing downtown in a fancy restaurant having supper with a boy who looked exactly like a motion picture star.

The next surprise came when he led me right past the street-car stop and around the corner to a parking lot. Swaggering over to a shiny blue car, he patted its hood lovingly.

"Whose car is it?" I asked nervously. What if the owner came along and caught us touching his car?

"It's mine . . . who else's?" he answered with a big self-satisfied grin. "It's a 1932 Chevy roadster in perfect condition," he explained as we circled around it. "It's got everything—celluloid side curtains that snap on in winter, a roof that folds back in summer and a rumble seat that's hardly ever been used."

He yanked open the rumble seat and sure enough the brown leather shone like new.

"The salesman told me it used to belong to a little old lady who only drove it on Sundays," he said proudly. Then he swooped his hand like Sir Galahad and invited me to hop in.

The inside was as perfect as the outside. "Did your dad buy it for you?" I asked naively.

"You must be joking." He scowled, and I wished I hadn't asked. "My old man wouldn't give me an apple for an orchard. I had to work for it, in his factory. I've been so busy lately I haven't had time to call anybody. Not even you."

What a perfect excuse! "It sure is a beauty. What's this for?" I touched a knob on the front panel. Without answering he turned the knob and in a minute the radio warmed up and started playing "My Blue Heaven." The song seemed to suit our mood to a T as we took off up Yonge Street.

"Are you cold?" he asked.

I wasn't, but something told me to say I was. So he flipped a switch and on came the heater full blast.

"Didn't I tell you Demetrius had everything?" he bragged.

"Demetrius?"

"Yeah. That's her name."

Imagine a car with a name! It sounded like a masculine name to me but I didn't mention it.

Lorne drove like an expert, shifting gears and manoeuvring in and out of the streetcar tracks. "Have you got a driving licence?" I asked.

"No. I'll probably get it next week," he answered confidently. That was good enough for me. I was proud as punch sitting beside him, the radio blaring and the streetcar behind us ding-ding-dinging its bell. The heater was burning my knees and the wind was tangling my hair, but I thought blissfully, "Boy! I wouldn't call the king my uncle!"

As we passed High Park and got closer to Swansea I leaned out the window in hopes of seeing somebody I knew to shout at. But I didn't, so I asked Lorne to go down Durie Street and stop at Aunt Milly's. She and Uncle Mort were sitting out on their front stoop. They both jumped up and came to admire Lorne's car. I could tell Aunt Milly took to Lorne instantly by the way she batted her eyelashes and squeezed my arm. Uncle Mort said the car was a jim-dandy, which pleased Lorne no end.

By the time we got parked in front of my house it was quite dark. The radio was playing "My Blue Heaven" again.

We looked at each other in the pale light of the street lamp. "That must be our song," Lorne said, and my heart skipped a beat. Then he suddenly grabbed my hand and blurted out, "Bea . . . have you got a boyfriend?"

Georgie Dunn was the first name I thought of. We'd been "going around" off and on ever since we were kids. But he was

Arthur's best friend, so he seemed more like a brother than a boyfriend. Besides, he only owned a bicycle! Then Jimmy Hobbs came to mind, but he hadn't even answered my last letter and that was weeks ago. And there was Bucky White. I'd been to the pictures with him a few times. He had a car too, but it was only an old flivver that had to be cranked. Anyway, he'd met a girl about nineteen or twenty who looked like Ann Southern, and had dropped me like a hot potato. Only my pride was hurt, because I didn't like Bucky much. He was always making jokes about how dumb girls are. I told him if he thought he was so smart he ought to try matching wits with Winn or Willa.

"Well?" Lorne interrupted my thoughts. "Have you?"

"Not right now," I said.

"Bea . . ." His voice became suddenly shy like Jimmy Stewart's.

"What?" Mine went all husky like Jean Arthur's.

"Will you be my girl?"

"Yes," I said before he had a chance to think it over.

Then he tried to kiss me and we bumped noses. We both laughed self-consciously and tried again. This time we succeeded. I had never been kissed like that before. It was like the first sip from a glass of honeydew.

I stood on the sidewalk as he started the engine, put the car in gear and spun away. "Goodnight, sweetheart!" he yelled out the window.

Sweetheart! What a gorgeous word!

When the car had disappeared in a cloud of Veeny Street dust, I hurried into the house and up the stairs two at a time. Getting my diary from my drawer, I took it to the bathroom

470

and latched the door. Then I sat on the toilet lid and wrote shakily:

June 15, 1939

Dear Diary,
I think I'm in love!

22
War clouds

On September 10, 1939, Canada declared war on Germany. And on the very next day I started my first full-time job at Eaton's. I was dying to tell somebody about the happenings of my first day at work, but the war news made everything else seem trivial.

At the corner of Yonge and Queen streets a newsboy yelled out the awful headlines: "Canada declares war! Young men flock to volunteer. Read all about it!"

In the few minutes it took for the streetcar to come he sold all his papers. A hush fell over the crowd as they anxiously scanned the front page. You could feel the tension in the air.

"I only hope it's over before Arthur is twenty-one," Mum was saying as I came in the door.

"Do you think the war will last until I'm big enough to go, Mum?" asked Jakey hopefully.

"Don't talk nonsense," she snapped. "It's not you I'm worried about."

"How about me, Mum?" piped up Billy.

"No, son. It won't affect you boys. It's our Arthur I'm fretting about."

Folding the newspaper inside out, as if to make the dreaded truth disappear, she began to mash the potatoes viciously. "Oh, pshaw, they're burnt!" she declared as a few black specks appeared. "Willa won't touch them now."

"Add some pepper, Mum, and she might not notice," I suggested.

She sprinkled a pinch of coarse black pepper on.

"Mum," I said.

"What is it, Bea?" She poured too much milk into the potatoes and made them mushy. "Drat!" she exclaimed. "Willa loathes wet potatoes."

"Mum," I repeated.

"What is it, Bea?" She was beginning to sound impatient.

"Can I tell you about my job now?"

"I'm listening."

"Well, I thought I was going to be a salesgirl in the store, but I'm not. I'm a stuffer in the D.A. office."

"For mercy sakes, what's a stuffer?"

"A stuffer stuffs bills into ledgers," I explained. "And I had to pass a typing test too."

"What's typing got to do with stuffing?" At last I'd caught Mum's interest.

"Well, the forelady said it might come in handy if I ever start to climb the ladder."

"What ladder?" asked Jakey. He was sprawled on the worn linoleum floor colouring a map of the world.

"The ladder of success," I told him importantly. "It means that I might get promoted to operator some day."

"I wish you had more schooling," Mum lamented.

"I don't need it, Mum. Miss Barlow—that's my forelady—says I'm well qualified for the job."

Just then Arthur came in the door. He had obtained his senior matriculation in June and had been out job hunting ever since. Usually he came home down at the mouth, but today he was elated. "Mum!" he announced excitedly, "I'm going to join the navy!"

"Over my dead body!" she barked.

"But all the fellas are volunteering, Mum. Don't you know there's a war on?"

"I can read," she returned bitterly. "But you're only nineteen so you'll need my permission and I won't give it. Do you hear?"

Dad and Willa came in. "Dad"—Arthur turned away from Mum—"I'm thinking of joining the navy."

"Well, I don't know much about sailoring, Arthur, but a soldier's life is no bed of roses, I can tell you that firsthand." Dad opened his dinner pail and broke a leftover gingersnap in half for Billy and Jakey. Then he put his thermos to soak in salt water at the tin sink. "Still, if it comes to fighting for king and country you'll be obliged to serve, same as me."

"Not if I have anything to say about it," snapped Mum.

Dad and Arthur exchanged a secret glance. Then Jakey jumped up to show Dad his map and they dropped the gritty subject. "See all them pink countries, Dad?" Jakey pointed them out. "They all belong to England."

"That's right." Dad nodded. "The sun never sets on the British Empire."

Supper was ready so we all sat down glumly at the table.

Sure enough, Willa wouldn't touch the potatoes. I was dying to talk about my job, but I knew it would have to wait until another time.

23

A small brown envelope

The D.A. office (that's what everybody called Eaton's
Deposit Accounts office) was on the fifth floor, a huge room
with a high ceiling held up by big cement posts. It was
jammed full of girls clacking typewriters and men giving
orders. A glassed-in corner of the room was the office of the
boss, Mr. Bentley. Mr. Bentley was a white-haired, cross-
looking man with stooped shoulders and a permanent
frown. Every fifteen minutes, like clockwork, he came out of
his sanctuary and pussyfooted between the rows of book-
keeping machines, spying from around the posts at the nervous operators.

We stuffers sat sideways on swivel chairs beside the operators, stuffing as fast as our fingers would fly. Mine wouldn't
fly fast enough. "You won't last long here if you don't get a
move on," warned my operator. So I tried to go faster, but my
fingers were all thumbs.

Every time Mr. Bentley popped out from behind a post I nearly jumped out of my skin. "The more hurry the less speed,
Miss Thomson," he remarked coldly. He prided himself on
knowing all the workers by name no matter how new or

insignificant they were.

After he slunk back into his cubicle, Miss Barlow leaned over my shoulder and whispered kindly, "Don't pay him too much mind, Beatrice. His bark is worse than his bite."

I calmed down after that and pretty soon I picked up speed and began popping the bills between the yellow pages as quick as you could say "Jack Robinson."

A few days later I met a girl named Anne Davidson, another stuffer. She had red-gold hair, green eyes, golden lashes and a nice neat nose. In other words, she was beautiful. But she was also nice, which saved me from being too jealous. That and the fact that she said she'd trade her red hair and green eyes for my blonde hair and blue eyes any day of the week. She didn't mention my nose.

"I wish our job didn't have such a stupid name," complained Anne as we sat together in the crowded lunchroom. "It sounds as if we stuff feathers into pillows."

"Or breadcrumbs into turkeys," I laughed, munching on a black-flecked mashed-potato sandwich.

That very afternoon, as if wishing had made it so, Mr. Bentley came out of his glass office, clapped for attention and pompously announced that from that day forward we stuffers would be known as filing clerks.

The title had such a superior ring to it that I could hardly wait to tell somebody. So on my way home I stopped off at Aunt Milly's. Sunny came out the front door with his hoop and stick. "Hi, Bea," he said. "Ma's in the kitchen." Then he rolled the hoop down the stick and ran lickety-split after it.

So I went right in and down the hall to the kitchen. Aunt Milly was sitting with her feet crossed on a chair, balancing one high-heeled slipper on the tip of her big toe and sipping from her favourite green bottle.

"Halloo, there, love!" She slipped her shoe back on and jumped up to fetch me a frosty Coke from the ice box. "Here, sit yourself down and take a load off your feet. Morty's gone for fish and chips, so why don't you stay and have a bite with us?"

"I'd like to, Aunt Milly, but I'm in a hurry to get home."

"Well, what's up? You look like the cat that swallowed the canary."

So I told her all about my life as a filing clerk. Her dark eyes sparkled as she listened to my exaggerated tales. Then she tilted her head back and drained the bottle with a long, satisfied "Ahhhh!"

Suddenly she became quite serious. "I'm tickled pink you like your job, Bea," she said, as she slid the vinegar bottle and salt-cellar onto the chipped enamelled table top. "It'll be good experience for you working downtown in the big city. But don't lose sight of your dreams, Bea. Hitch your wagon to a star. Remember what I've always told you—you're special. You've got a little bit of 'it' and you got it from your Aunt Milly!" She always said that.

That Saturday at quarter to six Miss Barlow came around carrying a green metal tray filled with small brown envelopes. They were lined up in alphabetical order, so it took a long time to get to the T's. My heart skipped a beat when she finally handed me the one with my name on it. With shaky fingers I tore off the top and withdrew my first week's wages— two five-dollar bills and two ones. A thrill ran through me at the thought that I'd get a pay packet like this every single Saturday—as long as I kept a move on.

The streetcars were crowded with tired people all glad to be going home on Saturday night. I had to stand all the way and by the time I got to my stop my arm was killing me from hanging onto the bar above my head. On my way out the middle doors I bought a whole dollar's worth of streetcar tickets from the conductor. It was the most I'd ever bought at one time, enough to last me all the next week if I didn't go anywhere but work.

Hurrying down Veeny Street, I buttoned up my sweater. A cool breeze sent coloured leaves sailing through the air. "Falling leaves . . ." I sang the popular song softly to myself, "Tumbling down . . . fading out . . . on the ground . . ."

I stepped into the kitchen just as Mum was lifting a pan of crispy bread pudding from the oven. Her face was flushed, as usual, from hurrying. I must remember, I thought worriedly not to rush through life like Mum. For once I was glad I took after Dad. He was more of a plodder.

"Hi, Mum."

"Hello, Bea. Supper will be ready soon."

Snapping open the clasp of my worn leather purse (an inheritance from Winn) I took out a five-dollar bill and a one.

Mum was busily laying the table. I noticed the oilcloth was threadbare at the corners. "Will you cut up the bread, Bea, like a good scout?" she asked.

"Sure, Mum, but first stop for a second."

The rubber heel of her house shoe made a squeaky sound as she pivoted around to face me. I held out the six dollars. "What's this for?" she asked, without taking it.

"It's my board, Mum," I answered proudly.

"Oh, pshaw, Bea. You don't need to give me all that out of

your first week's wages. Your father just got a raise to twenty dollars a week, so we're fine and dandy now."

"Well, I want to." I pressed the bills into her hand.

She stood dumbly for a minute. Then she began rolling the money between her palms in that excited way she had, as if she was making a roll-your-own cigarette. Suddenly her face lit up and her dark eyes gleamed. "I know what I'm going to do with the extra money," she said. "I'm going to put it in the bank towards a down payment on this house." She looked around the old-fashioned kitchen.

"If this place was mine," she whispered, even though we were alone in the room, "I'd make short work of that ugly tin sink and those unsightly sewer pipes from the bathroom." As if to prove her point, someone flushed the toilet and the water rushed down the pipe with a great gurgling sound. She turned away, disgusted, and glanced into the dining room. I could tell she was stripping the layers of wallpaper off in her mind's eye.

"Billy and Maude Sundy said they'd take two hundred dollars down and the rest we could pay like rent. Then 18 Veeny Street would be ours. And, by Jove, I mean to have it!"

Now she began smoothing the rolled-up bills in the palm of her hand. "You remember I was going to start a bank account when Winn was here, Bea? Well, I never did because by the time I made the payments to Eaton's Home Lover's Club for my new sewing machine there was never anything left." She paused, as if meditating. "I guess I could have done without my Singer. My mother's old treadle works as good as ever and it's a regular dust collector sitting upstairs in the hallway. Still, I get my sewing done a lot faster on the Singer. And anybody

480

who does as much mending and sewing as I do deserves an electric machine, wouldn't you say so?"

"I sure would, Mum," I agreed.

"But now, Bea, with this extra money I can see my way clear to salt some away. I'll go straight to the bank on Monday morning and open up a house account. But we better keep it to ourselves, just in case. It'll be a secret twixt me and thee." She laughed as she used her grandmother's old-fashioned phrase.

"Yeah, Mum, twixt me and thee." I was thrilled to pieces. Imagine my board money actually helping to buy Mum her dream. I couldn't get over that.

Jumping up on the little stool that made her tall enough to reach the top of the kitchen cabinet, Mum pulled forward the metal box from the back. Lifting the lid, she carefully hid the six dollars under the rent receipts and returned the box to its place.

Stepping down, she turned to me with a strange light in her eyes. Suddenly she reached up and took my face between her work-roughened hands. "My stars, Booky," she declared in a surprised voice, "it's just this minute dawned on me. You're not a girl anymore. You're an independent woman now."

Then she threw her arms around me and gave me a tight, bone-cracking hug.

Epilogue

The war lasted six long years and one by one all the boys in our gang went off to fight for freedom. Mum's greatest fear came true when Arthur joined the navy and sailed happily away.

Suddenly the Great Depression was over. Jobs popped up like toadstools. As the boys joined the armed forces, the girls took their places at the workbench. All except Ruthie Vaughan. She joined the women's air force and had the time of her life.

There was big money to be made in war work, but I stayed on at Eaton's and worked my way up the ladder to the grand sum of twenty-one dollars a week.

To help with the war effort, butter and sugar were rationed, so along came margarine and saccharin. You couldn't buy soap for love nor money, so detergent was invented. No more silk came from Japan, so nylon stockings were born. I'll never forget my first pair of nylons, because the thread was so strong they lasted a whole year.

At last, in 1945, the war ended and the boys came back. But not all of them. Jimmy Hobbs never returned to his mail truck. Charlie and Alvin were lost at sea. Victor Barnes came home wounded, with only one leg. And Bucky White, who was an

R.A.F. pilot, had bailed out of his flaming Spitfire and spent three years as a prisoner of war in Germany. When he came home, thin and haggard, he refused to talk about it.

My sailor brother and Georgie Dunn and Lorne Huntley, who both served in the R.C.A.F., all came back unharmed.

Lorne and I married and had two little girls. Glad married Harry Greenwood and did the same thing. Willa married Clifford Best and Wesley never got over it. Winn married an air force officer. We all quit our jobs to raise our families. That's the way it was then.

Jakey and Billy missed the war altogether because they were too young, thank goodness. They both became successful businessmen. And fathers.

Dad lived to be eighty, still insisting that World War I should have been the war to end all wars.

And Mum? What about my loving, high-strung, vivacious, black-eyed mother? Well, one day when she was hurry-hurry-hurrying, her tired heart gave up and stopped. She never did live to realize her dream of a home of her own.

Sadly, the money she had painstakingly saved in her house account went towards her funeral. And ironically, about six months after she died Dad did manage to scrape up enough money to put a down payment on 18 Veeny Street.

And I, that scatterbrain Booky? I *did* become a writer, against all odds and predictions. So, as Aunt Milly would say if only she were here, "Every cloud has a silver lining."

About the Author

Like her character Booky, Bernice Thurman Hunter was a storyteller from an early age. When her own children were small, she wrote stories for them, but it was not until they were grown up that she began to get her work published. Now she is one of Canada's favourite writers of historical fiction, with a dozen books to her credit, including the Margaret trilogy, *Lamplighter, The Railroader, The Firefighter, Amy's Promise, Janey's Choice*, and *Hawk and Stretch*—a book that tells the story of Booky's little brother Billy.

Many of Bernice's books—particularly the Booky series—are based on her own childhood. One of her greatest strengths as a writer is her ability to bring those childhood memories to vivid life for readers of all ages.

She has received many awards, including the Vicky Metcalf award for her contribution to Canadian children's literature. *That Scatterbrain Booky* was the winner of the 1981 IODE Award, and *Hawk and Stretch* and *The Firefighter* received a Toronto Historical Board Commendation.

Bernice lives in Toronto, Ontario.

Books by Bernice Thurman Hunter:

Booky: A Trilogy
    That Scatterbrain Booky
    With Love from Booky
    As Ever, Booky

Hawk and Stretch

A Place for Margaret
Margaret in the Middle
Margaret on her Way

Lamplighter

The Railroader

The Firefighter

Amy's Promise

Janey's Choice